PRAISE FOR
LOVE SONGS FOR SKEPTICS

"Do you ever feel like an author reached into your brain and pulled out the exact book you wanted, at the exact right time? This is what it felt like from the very first page of *Love Songs for Skeptics*. Voicy, heartfelt, hilarious, propulsive—this book is brilliant. With the ache of second chances, the chaos of family, and in the iconic backdrop of London, *Love Song for Skeptics* strikes the perfect notes of romance, snark, and yes, even sweetness (hold the schmaltz)."

—Christina Lauren, *New York Times* and
USA Today bestselling author

"I'm blown away that this was a debut. Christina's writing is polished, engaging, and witty; I was invested in Zoë's life straight away, and I loved, loved, loved Zoë's personal growth. *Love Songs for Skeptics* hooked me from the first page, made me smile all the way through, and immediately cemented itself as one of my all-time favorite contemporary love stories."

—Sarah Hogle, author of *You Deserve Each Other*

"I loved it. It's an absolute joy… I finished the book with a huge smile on my face."

—Beth O'Leary, bestselling author of *The Flatshare*

"Funny, sweet, and full of surprises, *Love Songs for Skeptics* is the perfect rom-com for music nerds."

—Kerry Winfrey, author of *Waiting for Tom Hanks* and *Not Like the Movies*

Love Songs for Skeptics

CHRISTINA PISHIRIS

sourcebooks
landmark

Published by Sourcebooks Landmark, an imprint of Sourcebooks
P.O. Box 4410, Naperville, Illinois 60567-4410
(630) 961-3900
sourcebooks.com

Originally published as *Love Songs for Sceptics* in 2020 in Great Britain by
Simon & Schuster UK Ltd. This edition issued based on the paperback edition
published in 2020 in Great Britain by Simon & Schuster UK Ltd.

Library of Congress Cataloging-in-Publication Data

Names: Pishiris, Christina, author.
Title: Love songs for skeptics / Christina Pishiris.
Description: Naperville, IL : Sourcebooks Landmark, [2021] | Originally
    published as Love Songs for Sceptics in 2020 in Great Britain by Simon &
    Schuster UK Ltd. This edition issued based on the paperback edition
    published in 2020 in Great Britain by Simon & Schuster UK Ltd.
Identifiers: LCCN 2020000076 | (trade paperback)
Subjects: GSAFD: Love stories.
Classification: LCC PR6116.I77 L68 2021 | DDC 823/.92--dc23
LC record available at https://lccn.loc.gov/2020000076

Printed and bound in the United States of America.
VP 10 9 8 7 6 5 4 3 2 1

For my parents

1
THE FIRST CUT IS THE DEEPEST

I'M NOT SAYING I DON'T believe in love, but my last relationship ended after twelve days.

We might have managed a full fortnight if I hadn't come back early from a weekend away and found him with his hand down a barmaid's shirt.

Shame, really. It was my local, and they do 2-for-1 mojitos on Sunday nights.

If anybody asks, I tell them my one true love is music. I can honestly say it's what gets me through long days and lonely nights. I can listen to almost anything, but the one thing I *can't* stand is a schmaltzy love song.

My brother's getting married in a few weeks and has asked for help picking a song for his first dance. I suggested Kiss's "Love's a Slap in the Face."

It didn't go down well. He's still trying to find the perfect song.

But all songs are imperfect. That's what makes us keep listening. Who wants perfection? I suggested he write his own song, but I think he decided it was too much work.

I've got a bit of a track record for making stuff up. Before I became a music journalist and got paid to interview real-life musicians—I *still* have to pinch myself sometimes—I invented my own personal rock star. That's how I came to be president of the Zak Scaramouche Fan Club, which, at last count, had exactly two members: me and Simon Baxter.

Simon and I made up Zak Scaramouche when we were twelve, using the initials of our names: "Z" for Zoë and "S" for Simon. We imagined him as a kind of rock star secret agent—James Bond with eyeliner, if you will.

Simon was the one who wanted him to be a secret agent. *GoldenEye* had come out and he was obsessed with Pierce Brosnan. Zak combined the two roles effortlessly, strumming a Les Paul while a loaded Walther PPK sat discreetly in his shoulder holster. In my head he always looked like Jim Morrison or Marc Bolan: tousled dark hair and piercing eyes ringed with kohl. What better cover for a spy than a glam rocker partial to makeup? And who'd suspect that under his unbuttoned shirt and snakeskin trousers, he'd be packing a license to kill?

Zak always timed his concerts to coincide with missions, and the fan club was how he communicated with his sources.

When one of us went on holiday, we'd send the other a postcard from Zak. The first one Simon sent me featured a donkey wearing a sun hat under the moniker: *Greetings from Lanzarote!* On the back, his neat handwriting swallowed all the white space.

Dear Member,

I'm in sunny Lanzarote for an open-air concert at the Playa Blanca. Rehearsals are going great, but damn, that sand gets everywhere!

I've been super busy. Since releasing my tenth album and divorcing my fourth wife, I've taken up the classic card game Baccarat—I'm a natural!

In unrelated news, international arms dealer the Crook has been spotted at Lanzarote's Royale Casino, a short drive from Playa Blanca.

That's all for now, fans.

Keep doing the Fandango!

Zak x

Those postcards meant the world to me. I was young and hopeful then. I still believed that bad guys always got their comeuppance and that love was all hearts and flowers. But as I got older and the postcards petered out, I seemed to lose my faith in romance. And after Simon got married, the postcards stopped altogether. I blamed the internet. Who sent anything by post anymore? The internet ruined love too. Dating apps encouraged you to make split-second judgments about people. What happened to getting to know someone slowly? Life moved too fast for that.

But about a year ago I was invited to join the Zak Scaramouche Fan Club page on Facebook, so our secret childhood club was reborn. Nothing had changed. We were still the only two members, and Zak was still trotting the globe wowing fans in between catching bad guys.

As for Simon and me, we kept doing the Fandango, shuffling around our feelings for each other via an imaginary rock star, never quite getting the steps right.

2

YOU'RE SO VAIN

I WAS FACE-TO-FACE WITH THE man that a million schoolgirls had their first crush on.

I could sort of see why—his genetics alone qualified him to be in a boy band: he was pretty, with wide-set blue eyes, and non-threatening, with smooth cheeks that didn't need to be scraped every morning with a razor. His floppy hair was long enough to look rebellious, but short enough to keep middle-class parents happy. That's the thing about teenage crushes: it's fun imagining the under-the-cover fumblings, but the real fantasy is to marry them.

Right now, Jonny Delaney—aka "The Cute One" from Hands Down—didn't fit the image of fantasy lover; he looked constipated. His waxed eyebrows were scrunched together in concentration as he recited all the reasons why the review we'd given him was "total arse bollocks." I tried to act like I was listening, sipping my champagne and nodding, but I was scanning the room for someone else: Patrick Armstrong, the man we were here to celebrate.

It was dark in the bar so I couldn't make out faces. The walls and ceiling were draped in black velour and the only illumination came from Perspex candelabra blinking on mirrored tables. It was like being in Ozzy Osbourne's boudoir with one of Sharon's yapping dogs for company.

The only thing I could clearly discern were Delaney's teeth. They were blue-white and as symmetrical as tabs of chewing gum. They had to be capped—no one in London had a set like those by the grace of God. He grabbed a bottle of beer from a passing waiter and slung back his head to take a gulp. A flash of gray gave me hope. Was that an amalgam filling? If he'd only open his mouth a bit wider…

"Are you even listening, Zadie?"

Zadie? Was that even a name?

I corrected my gaze to meet his eyes. "Of course I'm listening."

"It's the best album we've ever made. You need to review it again."

"That's not how it works."

"Make it work—you're the editor."

Being the editor didn't mean I had everything my way. I still had to fight my publisher to convince him that a boy band like Hands Down had no business in our magazine. I'd lobbied hard against including the review that was causing Jonny all this excess spittle. Except the piece had prompted so much discussion on our website that the extra traffic had almost vaporized our servers. Even the print edition had benefited: after twenty-three months of declining sales, circulation had gone up.

But neither our core readers nor the new readers were happy; my inbox was overflowing with disgruntled subscribers, while my Twitter feed had been scorched by teenage girls venting their outrage in block caps.

Everyone hated me this week, except for my publisher. Above the din of the party, I tuned back into Delaney, whose drunken yammering was now up to eleven. I caught a whiff of his breath—it smelled of rotting garlic. The most snoggable man on the planet—according to the tabloids, at least—had an unfortunate case of halitosis.

"I bet you didn't even listen to it, you stupid bitch."

Wow. He thought calling me names would help his case?

Maybe I shouldn't have been surprised. This was someone whose highest form of self-expression were the emojis on his liner notes.

He was right about one thing though: I hadn't listened to it. I hadn't even written the review. But I wasn't going to tell him that; I was going to have a little fun.

"I didn't need to," I said. "A boy band's third album is the 'grown up' record. You co-write the songs yourselves so every track is about sex, the cover showcases your newly acquired tattoos and the one song that isn't about sex is about the price of fame. This time next year, one of you will have a baby, one of you will come out as gay, and one of you will have found Jesus. None of you will ever make a record again."

Delaney's mouth dropped open, and rather than wait for another blast of hot air and bad breath, I made my escape.

I was breathing hard, and it was only after I'd put several bodies between me and my dime-store Prince Charming that I could relax. I smoothed down my chiffon dress and unclenched the hand that was coiled around my champagne glass.

It wasn't my most professional hour, but I didn't care. I wasn't going to let that idiot derail what I was here for: toasting the retirement of Patrick Armstrong, one of the biggest managers in the business, who also happened to be my mentor and friend.

Years ago, when Patrick first set up Armstrong Associates, he used to rent the office above my parents' restaurant in Acton and would pop in for his daily fix of *keftedes* and tzatziki. I used to work lunchtimes during the school holidays and usually hated those afternoons behind the bar because my mum never trusted me to do the fun things, like use the wall-mounted optics to measure out spirits, or make Irish Coffee—even though I'd secretly perfected pouring the cream over the back of a spoon to get a perfect swirl. No, all I got for my efforts was a face blasted by dishwasher steam and ears assaulted by the seventies Greek pop that my parents insisted on playing and my mum insisted on singing along to, always half a tone off-key.

But Pat's visits were a high spot, and we got talking. I was fascinated by what he did, and later, when I'd finished university, he introduced me to a couple of music journalists who invited me to write some reviews. I owed Patrick my career. He knew everyone and was famous for always wearing a bow tie and never being without a tumbler of Gordon's in his hand. Twenty years on, and countless neat gins later, two hundred of us were crammed into a private club in Fitzrovia to give him a proper send-off.

His company had moved from a couple of rooms on Acton High Street to a three-floor office off Old Compton Street, but now he'd sold it to Pinnacle Artists, a conglomerate whose head office in London inspired the wrath of Prince Charles for its spiky steel façade.

As I moved around the bar, I kept a lookout for any other moon-faced boy-banders in case their radars had beeped to tell them one of their own had been disrespected.

I found Patrick among a group at a nearby table. I caught his eye as a waitress in a pencil skirt leaned closer to whisper in his ear and slip something into his jacket pocket. Anyone else might think contraband was being exchanged, but I recognized this for what it was: an enterprising musician getting her demo into the hands of a very influential man. Patrick nodded, the waitress left with a flirty smile, and he came over.

"It's never the pretty young men that whisper in my ear," he said.

"I'm not sure there are any here tonight. But if I see one, I'll send him your way."

He clinked my champagne glass with his gin and we both took a sip. Mine was depressingly warm, thanks to Delaney.

"I almost didn't recognize you," he said. "You're wearing a dress."

"All in honor of you, Pat."

"And you look very good in it too. I saw how that Hands Down chap was looking at you."

"That was fury, not lust," I said. "What's he doing here anyway?"

"Pinnacle look after the band. I've seen the sales figures. You wouldn't believe the units they shift," he said, shaking his head. "My goddaughter asked me to get her tickets to Hands Down for her tenth birthday."

I wrinkled my nose. "Ten seems a bit young. Have you heard their lyrics? They wail about bumping and grinding, without any attempt at a metaphor, and they're marketed at pre-teen girls. It's not right."

"Aren't they just love songs?"

I rolled my eyes. "Those boys wouldn't know love if it bit them on their waxed arses."

He smiled a refreshingly nicotine-stained smile. "Maybe I'll buy her a subscription to *Re:Sound* instead."

"Much better idea." I gave his hand a squeeze. "I'm going to miss you, Pat. Are you sure you want to retire?"

"Hardest decision I've ever made."

"You're sixty-five, Pat. You deserve some time off for good behavior. A chance to let that suspiciously full head of hair down."

He ran a hand through hair that seemed to get thicker every time I saw him. "I don't know what you're implying. Elton might have given me the name of a specialist, but that's all I'll say…"

"You should have been a diplomat," I said. Then, rather *un*diplomatically, I added: "I don't suppose you've heard anything from Marcie?"

He shook his head and my stomach lurched. Marcie Tyler was a notorious recluse, and I'd staked everything on an interview with her for the magazine. She'd sold 150 million albums, was rumored to have been the inspiration for David Bowie's "Heroes," and was just out of rehab. Patrick had been her manager for years and we'd both hoped she might make an appearance tonight, but they'd fallen out and hadn't spoken for a decade. To be fair to Pat, she hadn't spoken to many people in the last ten years—and certainly no journalists. An interview would be a spectacular coup and would prove to my publisher that my vision for the magazine was right.

"I'm sure you'll find a way to get to Marcie," he said. "You're a very resourceful woman."

Patrick always knew the right thing to say, but before I could thank him for the faith he had in me, Justin, his partner of thirty years, appeared. "Sorry, Zoë, I need to steal Pat away from you."

"Uh-oh, sounds like I'm in trouble." Patrick winked at me. "We'll be at the vineyard in Crete at Christmas. Come for a break and drink yourself silly, then we'll find you a nice Greek man like your parents always wanted."

I'd given up on finding a nice man—Greek or otherwise. Music was a great industry to work in, but it made for a terrible dating pool. I dated the news editor of *NME* a few years back, but he kept wanting to know what I got up to on the nights I went out without him—and not because he was the jealous type. God forbid I stumble on a news story he'd missed because he was at home watching back-to-back episodes of *Star Trek* in his underwear.

Being single suited me just fine. It meant that if the mood took me I could stay in and watch the Federation's finest in my underwear too.

But Patrick was one of life's good guys, and I was going to miss him. Tears blurred my vision and I hastily swiped a finger under my eyes. God, what was wrong with me? In this mood, I may as well just go home—the last thing I wanted to do was descend into full-on blubbing. It had been a glorious July evening when I'd set off, but British summers being what they were, I'd wisely brought along my leather jacket for the journey home.

I made my way to the cloakroom and handed my ticket to the attendant, but instead of disappearing behind the velvet curtain to retrieve my jacket, he leaned forward and grinned.

"I fucking *loved* what you said to that pop star prick."

"Jonny Delaney? You heard it all the way out here?"

He shook his head. "I was doing drinks earlier. I passed by with a tray and lingered. No one notices waiters; it's like wearing an invisibility cloak." He pointed over my shoulder and grimaced. "Unfortunately, he heard it too."

A tall man in a dark suit was stalking toward me. Unlike the attendant, he did not look amused. His brow bone cast a shadow across his face, and as he moved, the lining of his jacket flashed angry red silk. He came to a rest beside me, his sleeve scratching the skin of my bare arm. He didn't speak or turn his head; he simply placed his hands flat on the counter, which the attendant took as a cue to hightail it behind the curtain.

He looked about my age and had one of those profiles you

usually see immortalized in marble in museums. The way his brow, nose, and jaw aligned would have made Pythagoras sing. This was good-looking on a mathematical scale.

"You're Zoë Frixos, editor of *Re:Sound.*"

His voice was gruff—it wasn't a question.

I squared my shoulders, tensing for a fight. "Are you going to tell me my bra size and blood type too?"

"I'm Nick Jones."

The name meant nothing. "Good for you."

He finally leveled his gaze at me. Impatience simmered behind bottle-green eyes. "I'm the publicist for Hands Down, and I'd appreciate it if you showed some professionalism when you spoke to my clients."

Wow. Another jumped-up posh boy who thought he was better than everyone else. I bet he spent ages every morning trimming those neatly squared sideburns. I shifted my weight, pushing back where his shoulder had encroached on my space.

"I see you went to the same finishing school as Jonny Delaney to learn your manners."

He drew himself up to his full height. He must have been six foot four, but I'm five foot ten without heels; tall men don't intimidate me.

"You want to talk about manners? Yours weren't much in evidence when you were talking to Jonny."

He had some nerve, standing there in his designer suit spouting self-righteousness.

"Well, if you were doing your job properly you'd have found a moment in between giving Jonny his afternoon milk and nap time to explain that we don't rewrite reviews because someone's feelings got hurt."

"*I'm* not doing *my* job properly? That's rich coming from the woman who reviews albums without listening to them."

He might have been gifted in the looks department, but the brains were seriously understocked—a lot like his client.

"I haven't written a review for months. That's what I've got a reviews editor for. I wasn't going to tell Delaney who wrote the review because then he'd set his thousands of Twitter twats onto her, but I've got a thick skin." Getting attacked on social media was par for the course, but Hands Down fans could be particularly rabid. "Anyway, as editor, I stand by that review."

"That wasn't a review—it was a hatchet job."

"You might be able to buy glowing reviews from music bloggers and teen websites, but we're part of the serious press."

A tendon in his jaw tightened. Good—I was getting to him.

"You think you've got the moral high ground? Your review said, and I quote: 'The best cut on the album is the two minutes of silence between the last song and the secret track.'"

I bit down a smile. I'd laughed at that line when Lucy filed her copy, and I still found it funny.

"It's one bad review. Surely you can explain that to your poor, wounded client? Every other review sang the record's praises. Oh wait, *every other* review was paid for by the label."

I wanted to spin round and march out triumphantly, but I couldn't leave without my jacket—it was a one-off I'd found in Camden years ago.

"You're not as different at *Re:Sound* as you think," he said. "Money doesn't have to change hands for a barter system to work."

Was he reciting Economics textbooks at me now? I really couldn't be arsed with this. Thankfully, the curtain whooshed back and the attendant materialized with my jacket. I thanked him, swung it over my shoulder, and marched out without another word.

The encounter had put me in a headstrong mood. So, when a taxi I'd flagged down was intercepted by a random bloke in a suit—probably a midlevel record exec—I marched over and glared him into submission. I swooped into the back seat, slammed the door behind me, and asked the driver to take me to Shepherd's Bush.

Uppity publicists were the bane of my life. They had no sense of perspective. Their emails were headed URGENT or BREAKING NEWS, but their content was always DULL or OLD INFORMATION. Well, luckily for me, I had no plans to feature Hands Down or any other autotuned upstarts in the magazine ever again.

Soon, the West End was behind us and we were zipping past Notting Hill and Holland Park. We crept along Shepherd's Bush Green, sandwiched between buses, and after we'd taken the Acton exit, I directed the driver to my road and my flat—the top floor of the stuccoed townhouse with the most cracks.

Snowy, my neighbor's cat, was sitting guard on the low wall, but as soon as she saw me she stretched up and demanded stroking. I scratched the soft white fur under her chin and she purred. You'd think a cat called Snowy would be white, but she was gray with a few white highlights—she was the color of *London* snow.

I unlocked the door and flicked on the light. I was picking my way past the junk mail on the floor when something buried among the ads for double glazing and pizza menus caught my eye.

I knelt down and picked it up. It was a postcard from New York: the Chrysler Building sparkling against an indigo sky. I turned it over and started to read.

Dear Member,

Great news!

Rumors of my demise have been vastly overstated.

A few bullets can't stop me! A surgeon was called to my home recording studio, and the pesky pellets were removed in between takes of guitar solos.

In unrelated news, art thief Vladimir Terribol was spotted boarding a flight from Moscow to Heathrow, so that's where I'm heading too—I'm coming to London, baby!

Keep doing the Fandango!

Zak x

When was this sent? I scanned the stamp, trying to make out the date, but the postmark was a blue smudge. I reread the postcard to make sure I'd understood it. I hadn't seen Simon for years, but now he was coming to London? My heart thumped double time as I digested the news.

Simon was coming to London.

3

NOTHING COMPARES 2 U

MY ALARM USUALLY WENT OFF at 8:00, but I woke up at 7:15 feeling refreshed and full of energy. It didn't make sense—I'd slept less than five hours. But as I lay in bed stretching my arms and wiggling my toes, it suddenly hit me.

I was happy.

I hadn't felt happy in ages. The stress of my job was pulling me under. It was obvious now—why hadn't I noticed before? One postcard, and it was as if someone had changed the soundtrack from Radiohead to Motown.

Simon always had that effect on me. We grew up next door to each other, but when he'd first arrived I'd been wary. I was ten and, having lived in the noisy cocoon of an extended Greek family, I didn't know what to make of a blond, blue-eyed only child with parents who didn't speak to one another.

My mum invited Simon over the day they moved in. Quick to notice the harassed faces of his parents as they directed the endless flow of cardboard boxes, she shepherded him out of the way of the moving van awkwardly parked in our Ealing cul-de-sac and shooed him down the side gate that led to our back garden. Mum suggested I show him our vegetable patch, so I left my bike, a Raleigh Chopper with worn-out tires, in the middle of the lawn and dutifully walked Simon to the end of the garden where my parents grew cucumbers, artichokes, tomatoes, and another leafy thing whose English name was a mystery to me at the time. Its Greek name, *lahana*, was met with a blank stare. (I later learned it was a type of chard.)

The Baxters were American, but this meant nothing to me until my brother Pete appeared and went googly-eyed over the accent and wouldn't stop asking if Simon personally knew the *Dukes of Hazzard* and Michael Knight. Poor ten-year-old Simon eventually said yes just to make a new friend. At thirteen years old, Pete still had that allure that high school kids held over juniors.

Simon didn't go to Hazelwood Primary School like I did. His parents—or rather his father's engineering firm—carted him off to a posh Catholic school all the way out in Hammersmith. Unsurprisingly, he hated it there and never really fitted in. The accent, however cool Pete claimed it was, singled him out as different. So he'd hang out with me after school.

For those first three years, everything was plain sailing.

That was, until we turned thirteen and everything changed. Or at least it changed for *me*. It was around the time I bought my first bra: I went straight to a B-cup because, being a tomboy, I'd been in denial about having boobs. But my new hormones came with an added complication: I started feeling awkward around Simon.

One early September day, after I'd gotten back from my annual four weeks in Cyprus staying with cousins, I found him leaning against the gatepost, waiting for me. He seemed taller, his shoulders wider, and it was as if a switch flipped inside me. I *fancied* him. Compared to the boys I'd hung out with all summer, he was James Dean. Where they were black-haired and scowling, Simon was dirty-blond and laid-back. He didn't wear high-waisted jeans or white terry cloth socks. He wore low-slung Levi's and Converse.

"Alright, Frixie," he called when I came to the front garden to meet him.

Thank God he was acting like nothing had changed, because I was barely remembering how to put one foot in front of the other.

"Hi, Si," I muttered, not daring to look him in the eye. He stood up straight, and I got a whiff of his Sure deodorant. Why was I suddenly weirded out by it? I'd been with him in Superdrug when he'd bought it, for God's sake.

"Something's different," he said.

Terror seized me. I forced myself to look at him. *Oh Christ, had his eyelashes always been that long?*

"What are we doing, then?" I said, ignoring his comment.

He leaned closer to me, and I got another blast of his heavenly antiperspirant. My own wasn't doing a very good job. My armpits were distinctly damp—thank God I was wearing my black Nirvana T-shirt.

He was peering at my nose and I thought: if there's snot hanging from my nostril I will *kill* myself.

He smiled. "Are those freckles?"

I smiled back, relief washing over me. In all the teen romance books I read, the heroine always hated her freckles. But I loved mine because they marked me as normal—all my English friends had them. They were usually very faint, but the Mediterranean sun had coaxed them out.

It wasn't just my complexion that had transformed. That summer had changed me in other ways too. Maybe it had something to do with going to my first nightclub, Careless Whispers, on the Larnaca beachfront, or the first alcoholic drink I had: a San Francisco cocktail that my cousin Elena said would taste great—*it didn't*. It was a cliché, but over one summer I'd experienced three revolutionary moments in my young teenage life: sex—a French kiss on the beach with Elena's friend Demetri; drugs—I was counting the half-shot of tequila in my San Francisco; and the Marks & Spencer bra-measuring service—why hadn't I realized I'd grown out of my bikini *before* I got to Cyprus? I looked indecent. No wonder Demetri was so enthusiastic.

So when I got back to London, I suddenly appreciated Simon for what he was. Where I used to see a lonely, shy misfit, I now saw a misunderstood, rebellious loner. How had I not noticed how intense he looked when he flicked up the collar on his biker jacket? How could I have brushed him off when he suggested the two of us skip school to see *Almost Famous* in the back row of the cinema? Luckily, none of my casual rejections had affected Simon. He still called me his best friend, but now "best friend" had a hollow ring to it. I wanted more.

The thing that cemented everything was my Year Nine dance recital. Usually, I quite liked our annual performance to the rest of the school. In Year Eight, we'd danced to a Beatles medley, which had the brilliant side effect of exposing me to the song "Norwegian Wood." But fast-forward twelve months and our teacher had fallen in love and was busy planning her wedding, which was the only reason I could fathom as to why the usually cool Miss Farrell—she wore a *nose ring*, for God's sake—had decreed we'd be dancing to Céline Dion's "My Heart Will Go On."

Was there a sappier song in the history of music?

No. No, there wasn't.

I remember fuming about it to Simon as we watched the episode

of *Friends* where everyone finds out that Moni
dating—my favorite, and not only because o
trope. But even that couldn't lift me out of my

"It's not such a bad song."

I gave him my best side-eye.

Simon, sensing he needed to do something drastic, got his guitar out, and plucked the melody to "My Heart Will Go On," singing along in his best falsetto voice. Except, because we were thirteen and easily amused, he changed the lyrics to "My *Fart* Will Go On."

I fell about laughing.

I wish my only problem with that recital had been the choice of music. Unfortunately, worse was to come. I landed badly on one of the jumps and twisted my ankle, but I had to bravely hobble on until the bitter end, red-faced and trying to ignore the sniggers of the Year Sevens in the front row.

Little shits.

Simon was there once I got home to help me laugh it off, and he even had a look at my foot. It was an awkward few minutes as I stripped off my sock, rolled up my jeans-leg, and he gently prodded the sensitive skin.

Please God, don't let my foot stink, I remember thinking. Closely followed by, *please God, don't let that random hair that sometimes sprouts on my big toe be there.* Being Greek and hitting puberty was a tough combination.

How could I not have fallen head over heels for him? He made me laugh, he made me forget my humiliations, and he tended to my swollen ankle with the thoughtful sexiness of Doctor Ross from *ER*.

I'd love to report that it all culminated in Simon reciprocating my feelings and eventually falling in love with me while gazing into es as we listened to Eddie Vedder's baritone on "Alive," but fate ely interrupted. His dad got a promotion, his parents divorced— the two were possibly linked—and a few days before his sixteenth birthday, Simon told me they were going back to America to live closer to his grandparents now that he was being brought up by a "single mom."

So he left, and I descended into a type of heartbreak that colored every relationship of my twenties.

No one could live up to the image of Simon. Or Saint Simon, as my best friend Georgia used to call him.

Maybe none of that should still affect me now that I'm thirty-four, but those early years mark you.

First love is brutal.

♪

Even the morning rush hour on the Central Line didn't drain the zip out of me. I emerged from Oxford Circus tube at 9:30 feeling virtuous, so I eschewed my usual Starbucks Americano and instead bought fresh orange juice from the café next to my office.

I swiped my key card to get into our building. Jody was already behind her desk at reception. She always looked pristine—perfectly straight blond hair that never wilted, no matter how humid the weather. I only had to look at a storm cloud for my hair to go frizzy.

"Did you have a good night?" I asked her.

Her cheeks reddened. "Stu wants to take me to Paris for the weekend."

I grinned. "Ooh la la."

Jody didn't have the best of luck with relationships, but thankfully her new guy, Stu, sounded like a keeper.

I ducked into the stairwell and started taking the steps two at a time.

We were on the fourth floor, but I avoided the lift because it broke down so much. However tired I was, it wasn't worth the risk.

The office needed a good paint, the carpet was threadbare, and the air conditioning was patchy. Hard to imagine that *Re:Sound*, established 1966 on Carnaby Street, had ended up like this. Back then, Jimmy Page used to play at the Christmas parties, and Keith Richards was introduced to his first dealer by the founding editor. In some versions of the story, he *was* Keith's first dealer.

But since the rise of the internet, print media had been a tough industry to navigate. *Re:Sound* was one of the biggest music monthlies in the business and we had a loyal readership, but each year our numbers were being slowly eroded by free online content and last year's circulation figures hit an all-time low. We had to cut costs and staff numbers, so new carpets and reliable air conditioning were luxuries we couldn't afford. As was triple-ply toilet paper, but I still managed to sneak it into the budget—Zoë Frixos: protector of bum cheeks.

The tune playing when I walked in was by a band that Gavin, my deputy, had discovered in Brighton on Saturday. Today was Friday, and he still hadn't let anyone change the album. His monitor was on, but he wasn't at his desk.

Lucy, the reviews editor, was also absent.

Still, it was barely ten o'clock and today was the most relaxed day of the month. Yesterday, the magazine had gone to press, which meant today we got to sort out our desks, reply to non-urgent emails, and generally relax, safe in the knowledge that the next deadline was four blissful weeks away.

I sat down at my desk and powered up my Mac. I unpeeled the sticky notes attached to the side of my monitor—all stuff from the issue we'd just put to bed—and threw them into the bin, just as Lucy barged into the office.

"Morning, boss," she said, flinging her canvas bag onto the floor by her desk. Lucy was twenty-three and a bit of a prodigy. She was making a bit of a name for herself, and not only for her pink hair. To be the reviews editor so young was testament to her amazing talent.

She started writing for us at twenty, sending in reviews of gigs, and after we published the fifth one, I offered her a job. Her well-to-do parents had been horrified that she'd chosen a career in music journalism over university and had promptly kicked her out.

"How was Patrick's retirement do last night?"

"It was okay," I replied. "He got a bit tearful when the speeches started, but apart from that he looked happy enough."

"I heard you were accosted by Jonny Delaney."

I was tipping back the last of my orange juice, but Lucy's comment made it go down the wrong way. I panic-coughed until my throat cleared. "How do you know that? Did he write something online?"

She went slightly pink, almost the same shade as her hair. "I bumped into Mike coming in."

"And how did *he* hear?"

"He had Jonny's new PR man with him. Who, for the record, is sexy as fuck."

"Nick Jones was here?"

"Yeah, with Mike."

As publisher, Mike looked after the financial side of things—he wasn't supposed to get involved editorially. But six months ago, the magazine had been bought by the Octagon Group, a corporation that made soft drinks, and our new overlords only cared about the bottom line. We'd been promised that things wouldn't change, but of course, they had. Our expenses were pored over, and there had been a freeze on pay rises. But worse was the fact that Mike had started encouraging me to put more commercial bands in the magazine to help reach a wider mainstream audience. I'd pushed back; it was at odds with why our readership had remained loyal for so many decades. But I'd finally relented with the Hands Down review, and the improved sales figures of that month's issue proved, frustratingly, that Mike had been right.

My eighteen-year-old self would have branded present-day Zoë a sellout, but teenage me never had to pay rent on a flat close to a train station.

My desk phone rang. Mike's name flashed on the display, but I let it ring. This needed a face-to-face.

Mike's office was tucked between the loos and the fire escape. The walls were lined with teak paneling untouched since 1970, and the glass in the windows was crisscrossed in that fireproof mesh that reminded me of school.

He was sucking an unlit e-cigarette as I entered his office. He may as well have been sucking on a Biro for all the satisfaction it was giving him.

"Lucy told me about your visitor this morning."

He removed the cigarette from his mouth and threw it into a drawer. "You seem upset."

"Let me guess: he wants more coverage in the magazine for his crappy boy band." He opened his mouth to speak, but I wasn't done. "That wasn't cool, Mike. You shouldn't have taken a meeting with him. You know you can't meddle in editorial." I was standing over his desk; its green leather top was pockmarked by ink and scratches.

"I thought, under the circumstances, I'd make an exception."

"What possible reason could—"

"He's just been appointed Marcie Tyler's PR."

"Oh. Shit."

This was some sort of cosmic joke. *Ha ha, universe—good one.* Mike was looking at me with suspicion. He had twenty-five years on me and had served with the Special Forces in the Falklands. He knew a thing or two about interrogation and could elicit a straight answer out of anybody simply by raising an eyebrow.

He was arching his left one now. "Anything I should know, Zoë?"

"We had a bit of a disagreement last night."

"What happened?"

I was surprised Nick hadn't told him—or maybe he had and Mike wanted my side of the story.

"He thought I was rude to Jonny Delaney from Hands Down."

"And were you?"

"We had a frank and robust exchange of ideas."

Mike shook his head, but the expected telling-off didn't come. "And you think it might affect our chances with Marcie?"

I nodded.

He picked up a fountain pen and absently balanced it across the pad of his index finger. Even gravity bent to his will. The tortoiseshell pen started to list to one side, but with a flash of his military-sharp reflexes, he flicked his wrist and righted it. "He seemed quite amenable to me. In fact, he said Marcie is considering giving her first interview in almost ten years, and he thinks we'd be a good fit."

I couldn't believe my ears. "*Good?* We'd be a *brilliant* fit!" I was already picturing the four-page spread: arty shots of Marcie in a run-down country house. Her wild hair black against crumbling Bath stone…

"…in exchange for something."

I hit pause on the movie in my head. "In exchange for what?"

Mike smiled tightly.

I groaned. Nick's lecture on bartering made sense now. "He wants us to redo the Hands Down review? I told him—"

Mike let the pen drop onto his desk. "A feature—double-page, plus the cover."

I pinched the bridge of my nose. "I see. And is he also going to tell us what font to use?"

"You saw what happened to sales with just one review of Hands Down. Why chase Marcie, who's practically a ghost?"

"Because *Re:Sound* has never been about boy bands. Can't you see the irony of it? Hands Down want our credibility to rub off on them, but every time we feature them they leach it away. I can't stand back and watch the magazine I've loved since I was thirteen turn into a celebrity rag."

"I sympathize, Zoë, but there's more at stake than just our credibility. We're talking about the survival of the magazine. I'm doing everything I can to keep the Octagon board happy, but if circulation doesn't hit their targets, they'll pull the plug."

The words made my breath catch in my throat. "They've threatened to close us down?"

He nodded.

I'd known this was coming, of course, but had tried not to think about it. I'd prayed that the magazine's reputation would be enough to keep Octagon off our backs a bit longer. But now the nightmare threat of closure was a sudden and glaring reality.

"I've told them we've got a major scoop in the pipeline, in time for the September issue, but we need to go back to them with increased ad sales and proof of increased circulation figures before the board meets in two months' time."

"No pressure then, Mike."

I tried not to let the enormity of what he was saying derail me. Concentrate on the next step forward—getting the Marcie interview.

"What was Nick like with you, by the way?" I asked, trying to keep my tone light.

"Seemed like a perfectly nice chap," said Mike.

I mentally rolled my eyes. Nick Jones was high-handed, rude, and arrogant. *Nice* was not the adjective that immediately sprang to mind.

"Where did he come from, anyway?" I said. "Why have I never heard of him?"

"He's been doing wonders for Pinnacle's artists in Latin America. Speaks Spanish like a native. French and Italian too, I'm told. He's trilingual."

"Of course he is," I muttered.

Mike frowned. "Except, when you add English, that's four languages. What's the word for that?"

"Tosser."

He smiled.

"It sounds like he moves around a lot," I said, brightening. "Maybe he won't be in London long."

"Play nice with him, Zoë; you don't have the luxury of time."

I left Mike's office with his last words ringing in my ears. If the magazine closed, it wouldn't be just me out of a job, it would be the whole team. They'd proved their loyalty by sticking by me, even when nothing in this godforsaken office worked properly—printers that constantly jammed, taps that dripped incessantly. How could I go back and tell them that their sacrifices had been for nothing?

I was gripped by a fear that cemented my feet to the nylon carpet. I steadied myself against the wall next to a dusty yucca plant, then sank to the floor. Its waxy green leaves had been here longer than me. I remembered seeing it on my first day ten years ago, when I'd started as a junior writer. I'd turned down a job at a national paper that paid almost twice as much. But my love affair with *Re:Sound* meant more than money. I'd once walked out on a blind date midmeal when he'd scrunched up his thick eyebrows in disgust, and opined that writing about music was rather lowbrow. As I left I'd "accidentally" knocked the table, toppling a glass of wine into his very rare Argentinian steak. Better lowbrow than monobrow, I'd wanted to tell him.

My relationship with *Re:Sound* had been the longest of my adult life. I'd been with it longer than any boyfriend.

It had been constant and loyal to me, and now it was my turn to be loyal to it. I needed to fight for what it stood for. Twelve editors had sat in my chair before me, and I could feel the weight of all of them on my shoulders. I was number thirteen.

Lucky me.

Back at my desk, I shoved a pile of proofs and two empty Coke cans out of the way and jogged the mouse to wake up my computer. I needed to learn more about my enemy.

Typing "Nick Jones" into Google was useless. I got over a million hits because it was such a common name. Adding "Pinnacle Artists" threw up loads of false hits too, because there were loads of "Nicks" and "Joneses" associated with the company. Facebook and Twitter were dead ends—pages of Nick Joneses scrolled down my screen. The only definitive information was a two-paragraph profile on the Pinnacle website, which was out of date because it listed his base as Mexico City and the artists he shepherded were Latin ones I'd never heard of. No mention of Hands Down or Marcie Tyler. The only useful snippet was that he'd been with the company a little over ten years.

I closed the browser, annoyed to have wasted my time. Forget Nick Jones; I needed to concentrate on getting to Marcie without him.

An hour later I was at the White Horse with Dawn Reynolds—Patrick's number two, who was now running Armstrong Associates as a subsidiary of Pinnacle Artists. She'd grown up a mile from me in Ealing, but was five years older. When Pat had introduced us six years ago, we'd immediately bonded over a shared love of gumshoe detective novels. Summer or winter, Dawn wore black, never having quite outgrown her passion for The Cure.

As we munched our Caesar salads, I asked her what she knew about Marcie's new team.

"Well, I secretly hoped that Marcie would come back to us now that Patrick's stepped down," said Dawn. "We're the best of both worlds—a boutique company with the clout of a bigger corporation behind us. But Marcie wants to carry on managing herself and just use Pinnacle for bits and pieces to control her publicity."

"I'm sorry, Dawn. I guess we were both pinning our hopes on her."

She forked a lettuce leaf and crouton and dipped it into the pot of extra Caesar dressing she always ordered. "We make a right pair."

I watched her chew, but my own appetite had vanished. "What do you know about Nick Jones?"

"Not much," she admitted.

"So how on earth did he get the Marcie gig?"

Dawn arched an eyebrow. "I guess he sweet-talked her."

"Are you saying what I think you're saying?"

"Marcie is flesh and blood like the rest of us, and he looks like a young Rock Hudson, down to that cleft in his chin—who wouldn't want him around?"

Me, for one. "Marcie wouldn't be that shallow."

"I can't see any other reason for it. Marcie hasn't bothered with a publicist for years."

Dawn had suddenly given me an idea. "Is there any way I can talk to Marcie directly—woman to woman?"

She frowned. "You know she hates talking to the press. And her home is like a bunker—she never goes out without tight security and is rarely photographed with friends or family. She doesn't seem to let anyone in."

"Surely she must get lonely?"

"From what I've heard, she's a loner, really. She's never been married, never had kids. But that's always been her choice. She's dedicated to her music."

We chatted some more, then said our goodbyes, maneuvering around the smokers standing by the door outside.

"See you in the gym on Tuesday?" It was the only day I regularly went, and having a gym buddy was probably the main reason for it.

"I'm sorry, Zoë, I can't. End-of-term piano recital—I promised to take the kids." She suddenly froze.

"It's okay, Dawn. I believe you. No need to look so guilty!"

"I've just remembered. I heard from a contact in Pinnacle that Marcie wants to take piano lessons."

"You're not suggesting I pose as a piano tutor, are you?" I laughed. "It's a bit Inspector Clouseau."

She swatted my arm. "No, she's buying a concert grand—my contact's organized a private shopping trip for her to the Steinway shop in Marylebone. She canceled the first one he booked for her, but then rearranged it. It's coming up, I think. I'll check."

This was promising. The shopping trip would no doubt be private, but surely I could wangle my way in. When else would I get the chance to approach Marcie in a semipublic place? And this way, I wouldn't have to go through Nick.

I was in a much better mood when I got back to my desk after lunch. If Dawn's tip about Marcie worked out, then I might be able to pitch an interview to her in person. If she really was intending to give someone an exclusive, *Re:Sound* was the obvious choice for her. And that way meant we wouldn't have to give in to Nick Jones's demands and sully the magazine with a double-page spread of Hands bloody Down.

The thought made me so chirpy, I even attempted to answer my logjam of emails. I would have gotten through them all if the phone hadn't kept interrupting me.

One particularly annoying call came from a publicist complaining that we'd called her client "English."

"He's *Welsh*," she huffed.

I told her I'd look into it and got off the phone as fast as possible.

"Gav," I called, craning my neck over my screen. "You described the lead singer of Stepping Stones as English."

"Is that against the law?"

"He's Welsh."

"Bollocks. He sounds English when you speak to him."

"Always use British. It'll save us a lot of hassle."

Lucy looked up from her screen. "Typical Gavin, always denigrating the Welsh."

Gavin swiveled round in his chair. "What are you talking about? I'm not anti-Welsh."

"Yes you are. What about that birthday card you bought me last year? It had a cartoon sheep on it, and as a proud Welshwoman, I was offended."

"You're from Leamington Spa," said Gavin. "You're about as Welsh as Lenny Kravitz."

"My nan's half Welsh."

"I didn't know," muttered Gavin. "And anyway, you said you liked that card."

"That was before I realized you were a racist."

"I'm not a racist!" He stood suddenly. "I'm going out for a coffee."

"A *white* one, no doubt," shouted Lucy to his retreating back. Gav halted in his tracks, his shoulders tensing.

"She's joking, Gav," I said, laughing.

He shrugged and left.

I turned back to Lucy, who was quietly giggling into her keyboard. "Gav makes it too easy."

"Go gentle on him, Luce," I said. "He's more sensitive than you might think."

She snorted. "Gav, sensitive? Give me a break."

Gavin might have looked like a hard man—shaved head, beefy build, and earring through one eyebrow—but he'd lost his mother at a young age and had been devastated when his grandmother passed away a couple of years ago. Lucy hadn't started with us yet, but I remember more than one evening staying in the office late with him, letting him sob quietly because his live-in girlfriend thought it outrageous that a twenty-seven-year-old man might visibly mourn the death of a grandparent. Needless to say, that relationship hadn't lasted, and he'd been single ever since. Gav never talked about girls, but recently I'd noticed that he held himself differently around Lucy—his shoulders seemed to unhunch and his back straightened.

Or maybe he'd just watched a YouTube video about posture.

Thankfully, the rest of the afternoon passed without name-calling or mickey-taking, then at 3:00, I got a text from Dawn that made me jump out of my skin:

It's your lucky day—Marcie will be at the Steinway shop tonight at 6:30!

Holy shit. I had a chance with Marcie *today*? I was about to announce it to the team, but stopped myself. Dawn had sent a second text, warning me that the shop was to close early and that Marcie would be traveling with security. *How on earth was I going to get even remotely close to her?*

My phone rang—unknown caller—but I grabbed it on the second ring in case it was Marcie-related.

"Zoë Frixos," I answered.

"I'm sorry, I must have the wrong number."

Something stopped me putting the phone down, something familiar in the vowels. "You're through to *Re:Sound*. Can I help you?"

"I hope so," came the male voice. "I'm looking for a Miss Zoë Frixiepants."

It had been a long time since anyone had called me that.

And there was only one person who ever did.

"*Simon?*"

"How the hell are you, Zoë?"

A warmth oozed through me that had nothing to do with the stuffy office. "I'm really well, Si. Zak tells me you're coming to London."

"He's right—I landed this morning."

"That's brilliant! Where are you staying?"

"At the Halson in Soho. I'm there now."

"That's round the corner from my office."

"I know." There was a pause and I could hear muffled voices in the background. "I'm in the bar and I've just seen a knickerbocker glory a foot high. Wanna play hooky and share one with me?"

"*Now?*"

"Now."

Air conditioning and ice cream sounded like bliss. I swallowed. Was the extra saliva due to the prospect of ice cream or Simon?

"I'll order extra whipped cream…" came his voice, low and tempting.

"I'll be there in ten minutes."

4

DAMN I WISH I WAS
YOUR LOVER

I HUNG UP. CHRIST ON a stick. First Marcie and now this? Someone was smiling down on me. I looked around the office to see if anyone had noticed that their editor was hyperventilating. They were all crowded around Ayisha, our digital editor, who was playing a video of a sleeping puppy whose ears were being blown about by a desk fan. I forgave all her non-work-related surfing because traffic to our site had skyrocketed since she'd taken over three months ago, when her previous role as my assistant had been made redundant by Octagon. Last month, she'd managed to make a story we'd run about festival food go viral—we'd even had a write-up in the *Telegraph*.

Instead of heading straight out, I detoured to the toilets. After checking the cubicles were empty, I rang my best mate Georgia. She'd listened to me talking about Simon endlessly at uni and was the only person who knew I'd carried a torch for him.

"*Fuuuuuck!*" was Georgia's reaction after I'd filled her in. "Simon fucking Baxter. No fucking way."

Since the birth of her twins ten months ago, Georgia had stopped swearing at home and now made up for it by swearing all day at work.

I'm not sure how happy her law firm was with the arrangement, but seeing as her billables had gone up, I suspected they were fine with it.

"That was sort of my reaction too," I told her.

"When are you meeting him?"

I checked my watch. "In about five minutes."

"What are you doing wasting time talking to me, then? Get a bloody move on!"

Things were always so black-and-white for Georgia: you liked someone, you told them, they liked you back—wham! You got married—albeit several years later. That's what had happened with her and Dean. They'd met on the first day of their law degrees and had been together ever since.

We said our goodbyes and I hung up. I'd been pacing up and down, but now stopped to assess myself in the mirror. I've never been one for preening, especially at work, but I wanted to make sure I looked presentable.

The black cargo pants and white V-neck T-shirt I was happy with. My hair, less so. I hadn't had time to wash it this morning, so instead I'd piled it on top of my head with a crocodile clip. Stray strands had fallen onto my shoulders, and the ends sprouted over the clip like the top of a pineapple.

On a good day I'd consider it windswept and insouciant; on a bad one, messy and neglected.

But what was it today?

Should I send a selfie to Georgia and ask her opinion? I held up my phone to click, but then stopped myself.

This was crazy—my hair was fine; it was just the lighting that was terrible. I rummaged in my bag for powder to blot my skin, wiped away some stray mascara, then left before I lost more time.

Striding down Great Marlborough Street and feeling the sun on my arms snapped me back to my normal self and not a moony teenager.

When Simon had first visited during the school holidays a year after he'd left, I'd barely slept the night before, and waiting for him had been agony. I had been in my bedroom pretending to read *Guitar* magazine when he bounded in with a goofy grin on his face. He was a foot taller and sporting cowboy boots and a much more pronounced American accent. To a seventeen-year-old girl, he could not have been more alluring. But I was older now; I'd evolved past the point where fancy footwear and a New York drawl were aphrodisiacs.

Five minutes later, I was standing at the entrance to the hotel. I stared up at the building and the warehouse-style windows stared right back. One of those bedrooms was Simon's. The thought sent a jolt through me.

Oh God. Perhaps I hadn't evolved at all.

I followed the hum of slackers starting their weekends early and found the restaurant. It was only half-full; the noise was down to five or six drinkers slouching by the bar. The room was dotted with people, some with drinks, some with food, but no sign of Simon. Then I rounded the corner, and there he was. He was relaxing on a bench by the far wall, lost in his smartphone, tapping his fingers on the table to the music.

His skin had a golden glow that belied his Scottish ancestry, and his dark-blond hair was cropped like a GI.

How could someone look so familiar and yet so alien?

He'd been on the wrong side of the Atlantic for years, and now that he was a few feet away, I couldn't move.

What if we had nothing to talk about?

I gave myself a stern metaphorical finger-wag. We might not have seen each other for five years, but we communicated on social media. I'd send him suggestions of bands he might like, and he'd start Twitter storms with me about how overrated *Game of Thrones* was. A couple of birthdays ago, he'd even sent me the twentieth anniversary Blu-ray of *Titanic* because somehow, unofficially and in a totally ironic way, "My Heart Will Go On" had become *our* song.

I forced myself to take a step toward him, and at the same time, as if he'd felt a ripple in the space between us, he looked up. He broke into a wide smile that lit up the room.

He stood as I reached his table and drew me into a hug. The muscles of his back stretched under my fingers as he squashed me against his neck. His skin was warm and smelled of citrus.

He pulled back to hold me at arm's length. "It is *so* good to see you, Frixie."

"It's good to see you too, Si," I said, marveling at how his eyes sparkled. That effervescent energy was still there. It explained why he could eat desserts in the middle of the day and stay so lean.

He tapped the seat next to him. "Sit on this side so we can people watch and everyone can see how amazing our ice cream is."

In the middle of the table was the most impressive sundae I'd ever seen: swirls of pink and white ice cream, adorned with flaked almonds, cream, and chocolate sauce, all topped with a juicy strawberry.

"You've got a good memory," I said.

He nodded. "Except now you're going to tell me strawberry's not your favorite anymore."

"Well, I didn't want to mention it…"

His smile faltered for a moment, but I couldn't keep up the ruse.

"It's still my favorite, Si. And you're right; it looks amazing." I sat down on his right and he handed me a long spoon. "For *madame*." He watched me as I brought a spoonful of ice cream to my mouth.

"Is it good?"

I swallowed and shivered. "Delicious."

I was absolutely talking about the ice cream, and not at all about how the low sunlight streaming through the window picked out the gold gleam of his stubble. It didn't help when he licked his bottom lip and raised his eyebrows. "Let's see if you're right."

He attacked the other side with his own spoon, taking a huge mouthful. He closed his eyes and when he swallowed his Adam's apple bobbed in a way that was *obscene*. I could have watched him eat all day.

He snapped his eyes open. "God, I feel eleven. Remember when you dared me to eat three Cornettos in a row?"

I forced my mind back to eleven-year-old Simon, who didn't have quite such distracting stubble.

Mum had bought a six-pack of the ice cream because we were expecting my cousins, but they'd canceled, and she'd given three to Simon to take home to share with his parents. Instead, I'd timed him to see how fast he could polish off all three.

"I thought that would have put you off ice cream for life," I said.

"How boring would that be?"

"They're not as nice as they used to be," I said. "Cornettos, I mean. They've made them smaller, and there's no chocolate sauce on the strawberry ones anymore."

"No chocolate sauce?" Simon shook his head in disgust as if I'd just reported a human rights violation. Then he took his spoon, scooped a layer of sauce from his side, and drizzled it onto mine. I watched the chocolate trickle down the pink and white ice cream.

"No one should be without chocolate sauce."

Oh God, how did he make that sound sexual? Is there alcohol in this?

His phone rang, and when he glanced at his screen, he grimaced. "I'm so sorry, Frix. I've got to take this." Simon dropped his napkin onto the table and stood. "I'll be right back—don't eat it all without me."

As he walked out of the restaurant, I touched the back of my hand to my cheek. It was searing hot, like I'd drunk a bottle of wine. What was wrong with me?

I took a mouthful of ice cream and closed my eyes. The cold helped. The only problem was, I had no appetite. After another couple of halfhearted spoonfuls, I took out my phone to distract myself. I was scrolling down my emails when Simon returned.

"Everything okay?" I asked.

He grinned. "It was my mom. Can you believe she was concerned that I hadn't texted to say I'd landed safely?"

I could, because my parents were huge worrywarts, although Dad had recently downloaded a flight tracker app so I'd stopped getting *that* phone call at least.

"How is Sandy?" I asked.

Simon's grin grew wider. His mum's name was Jenny, but when we were kids he'd convinced me that her real name was Sandy. This was just after I'd made him watch *Grease*. His dad's name was Danny and he claimed the movie was based on their lives, but that his mum had changed her name to Jenny because she was fed up with all the questions.

I believed that story for months.

To get him back, I'd made him watch *Grease 2*.

"She's great. She's getting married again, would you believe?"

"Wow. Was it unexpected?"

"No, she's been with Bill for years, but it's weird, you know, the idea of going to your parent's wedding."

It was something I'd taken for granted growing up—the permanence of my parents' marriage. "I can imagine," I said.

"How are your folks?"

"They're well. Chuffed to bits about Pete getting married."

"Your brother got hitched?"

"He's about to. The wedding's in six weeks."

"Good for him."

There was a hint of bitterness in his tone. "Are you okay, Si?"

"Louise and I separated. Actually, as of two months ago, we're officially divorced."

I'd suspected as much; I'd picked up bits and pieces on Facebook. Louise unfriending me was the final clue.

"Must have been a tough time for you."

"It was for the best, though. We got married too young."

I wanted to be generous, but I still remember the shock I felt when he emailed to tell me he was getting married. I hadn't allowed myself to say anything critical about Louise—ever—even when she'd professed on Facebook that she'd rather not vote at all than vote for Hillary.

It wasn't the only reason I'd never warmed to Louise, even though I'd never met her. All she posted on social media were pictures of herself or her rather ugly pug. Simon had always been a cat person.

"God, why did I propose six months after meeting her?"

"You got swept away," I told him. "I blame all those *Dawson's Creek* box sets. You always were a bit of a hopeless romantic."

"Unlike you. Please tell me that's changed?"

"As eighties rockers Twisted Sister once declared: love is for suckers."

He smiled. "So, I take it you're not seeing anyone?"

Did I detect a hint of hope in his question?

"Nope. I'm married to the job. I'll probably die an old spinster."

"No way. I bet there's a line of guys waiting to date you. You must be beating them off with a stick."

The compliment gave me a buzz. "Well, I didn't want to admit it." I smiled. This was a much better image to project than fusty old spinster. "It's quite exhausting, actually," I added, warming to my theme. "But my stick skills are excellent."

He laughed.

My phone vibrated in my pocket. The lull in the background music meant Simon heard it too.

"Duty calling?" he said.

I nodded. "I need to get back to the office."

Simon looked at his watch. "Dammit, I didn't realize the time. I've got a meeting in half an hour, followed by another meeting and then a conference call with New York at eight."

"Who says bankers don't know how to have fun?" I said.

"You do," he replied. "Often. And I've told you I'm a fund manager, not a banker."

I smiled. "Ah, yes, you shuffle piles of paper clips around. You start off with ten paper clips, and after you weave your magic, there are ten thousand of them."

He grinned. He'd tried to explain his job to me once using a paper clip analogy, and I'd never let him live it down.

"Minus my commission, of course." He gave me a playful shove. "What are your plans tonight? Suitably rock and roll, I hope, to make up for my lame evening."

"Oh, you know, the usual—coke-fueled orgies and animal sacrifices."

"Bit of a quiet one, then."

Neither of us moved. The idea of walking out and not seeing Simon for another five years pinned me to my seat.

"I've missed you, Frixie."

I wanted to tell him I'd missed him too, but I was suddenly breathless. "Let's not leave it so long next time," I said, lightly.

"That's what I wanted to tell you. The firm's moving me to the London office. I'm back for good."

I don't remember walking back to my office. My head was full of Simon. *He was back in the UK. Permanently. He was single. He missed me.* I was going to go crazy if I analyzed our whole conversation, the way I did when I was a teenager, even going so far as writing down my thoughts in secret notebooks I hid behind my Agatha Christies.

I needed a coffee when I got back, if only to shake away any dreamy thoughts about Simon.

God, he had good arms.

The dishwasher was on the blink again, which meant the sink was piled high with dirty mugs—not a single clean one remained. Normally I would have gotten annoyed by this, but I was in such a buoyant mood that I washed up the whole lot of them. And not once did I mutter under my breath that my colleagues were a bunch of messy bastards.

5

ONLY HAPPY WHEN IT RAINS

AT 6:15, I WAS STANDING in a doorway opposite the Steinway shop on Marylebone Lane. On the off chance, I'd tried the door, but it was locked. There was nothing to do now but wait for Marcie to arrive. The weather had turned—half an hour before I'd left the office, dark clouds had gathered and now rain was pelting down, but even that was a stroke of good luck. It gave me a reason to be standing here, waiting for the rain to stop. I would have looked way more conspicuous if it had been sunny. It also meant there were fewer pedestrians who might scare Marcie off. The few I'd seen had been hurrying purposefully to unknown destinations with umbrellas or at least a copy of the *Evening Standard* over their heads to keep the rain off.

The piano displayed in the window shone like vinyl and its white keys were dazzling, even on a gray day like this. It didn't have a price tag, of course; if you had to ask the price, your purchasing power probably only stretched to a Casio keyboard.

It was half past six now, and my nerves started to kick in. What if Marcie had canceled again?

A black cab pulled up. This looked promising. The back door swung open, but it wasn't Marcie, just a suited man opening a huge umbrella. He stepped into the road without looking and caused a Mercedes 4×4 to slam on its brakes to avoid hitting him. The suit didn't even look up; he just continued on his way, oblivious. What a dickhead.

If I'd kept my eyes on him a second longer, I would have missed the black-coated figure that spirited out of the 4×4's passenger seat and disappeared into the Steinway shop. A man wearing a dark suit exited the car a second later and followed her inside.

Shit. Was that Marcie? If it was, that was one hell of a distraction technique. The 4×4 drove on, and I stood on the pavement trying to think of the best way to proceed. The rain battering my scalp only added to my misery, so I trudged a couple of shops down to shelter in a doorway.

Should I wait for Marcie to come out again, then accost her in the rain? *Yeah, that would go down about as well as Justin Bieber opening for Slayer.*

When I was a teenager, I'd prided myself on talking my way into gigs for free. All it took was confidence, a cheeky smile, and a vague assertion that I was writing it up for my university paper. Somehow, I doubted this would work now. But acting like you belonged went a long way in subliminally convincing others they didn't need to challenge you.

A rattle caught my attention. A metal shutter was slowly rising, revealing a loading bay. I edged closer to get a better look. It was the unit next to the piano shop, but there were no signs. Still, pianos were big things; they certainly didn't get in and out of the shop via the front door. This had to be another entrance. An engine rumbled and a moment later a van nosed its way out. The loading bay was otherwise empty, save for a man in overalls checking a clipboard.

With a click, the roller shutter started to descend again, and I had seconds to decide what to do. Sod it—what did I have to lose? I ducked inside, trying to formulate a plan. I reached into my bag and grabbed my keys.

"Hi!" I said brightly to Mr. Overalls. "I'm the driver."

He peered at me, like he was trying to place me.

"You what?"

Luckily, he wasn't looking too closely at what was in my hand. If he were he might have noticed that I wasn't brandishing car keys, but a couple of Yales, the office alarm fob, and a key ring that proclaimed, "Drummers are people too."

"I'm the driver for Miss Tyler. It took me ages to park and now the front door is closed and no one's answering."

"Oh, right," he said, like I was making perfect sense.

I flashed him a smile. "Can I pop in this way?"

Without waiting for him to respond, I strolled confidently up to the door and brazenly walked in.

My mouth was dry and my heart was bouncing around my ribs. My ears were pricked, waiting for him to shout, "Oi!" but no sound came and when I turned round, the man was nowhere to be seen.

I was in! A little smile formed on my lips—I still had it.

Ahead of me was another door, but it yielded when I gave it a push, and I was inside.

It was darker here, and it took a few moments for my eyes to adjust. Oversized gold chandeliers gave off little light, but their glow was magnified by the polished surfaces of pianos. Everything smelled of new carpet and varnish.

The place was deserted, but I could sense movement in the furthest corner. I crept to the opposite wall and stopped to examine a portrait of

Beethoven. My interest lay less in the picture and more in the glass that framed it. It reflected a mahogany piano behind me where a woman sat at the keyboard. It was Marcie. I turned my head slightly to get a better look.

Her hair was pulled back into a loose ponytail from which a few dark curls had strayed. I knew she was in her fifties, but she looked ageless. Her complexion was smooth and pale and blemish-free. Eschewing summers in Saint-Tropez and Palm Beach had its upside. If being a recluse gave you such good skin, perhaps I ought to consider it. The flesh under her eyes maybe wasn't as taut as it had been when she'd released her first album at the age of twenty, but the heavier eyelids only made her face more magnetic. She was ridiculously beautiful. Those famous cheekbones and long neck could still turn every head.

Iconic was the only word.

Marcie had been sitting by herself, but now her black-suited security guard and a shop assistant in impressively high heels arrived. I ducked into an alcove, my heart beating furiously. This was it. Any second now, I'd have two iron grips hoisting me out of here by my armpits.

But then a miracle happened. Marcie shooed them away.

"Can I not have five precious minutes alone?" Her voice gave me goose bumps. Gravelly but smooth, like honey on toast.

I took a step forward, careful to stay in the shadows.

She was staring at her hands, which were resting on the keys. Her short nails were painted peacock blue. They were exactly the same shade as her leather ankle boots, which had silver buckles and a wooden spool heel. I recognized the designer—her shop was in Soho and I walked past her window often, coveting her handmade designs.

Marcie suddenly looked up. Her blue-green eyes were ringed

in dark eyeliner, her lashes heavy with mascara. I was caught in her laser stare, my mouth hanging open like a haddock in a fishmonger's window.

"Don't think I don't know you're there, young lady."

"I… I…" *Shit, say something, Zoë.* "I love…your boots," I said. "Suzi D'Arcy, right?"

She glanced down at her feet as if to check. "Yes. Not many people know Suzi."

"I walk past her shop all the time. Her stuff is beautiful."

"She made them in this shade especially for me."

"They're exquisite."

I felt lighthearted. I was having an actual conversation with Marcie fricking Tyler. She wasn't just telling me to get lost.

I thought about paying her another compliment, but then I'd sound like a crazed fan. I'd mean every word of it, but she didn't need to know the depths of my awe.

I gave myself a little shake, trying to get back into professional editor mode. "I'm Zoë Frixos, by the way, from *Re:Sound*. I'm friends with Patrick Armstrong. I was hoping to talk to you."

She seemed to shrink back on the stool. "An interview?"

"I know you don't like to give them, but you've got so much to say, and so much is written about you that you have no control over." Oh God, she was going to ask me what I was talking about, and I'd have to admit I had a Google alert on her name and knew about every bonkers rumor that had ever circulated about her. *Smooth, Zoë.*

"Where did you say you were from?"

"*Re:Sound.*"

She made a face. "Don't you usually prefer to interview man-babies who can only play three chords, yet think they're Jack White?"

She had a point. The magazine had tended toward whiny guitar-based bands who requested they be interviewed in lap-dancing clubs. It was the first thing I'd put a stop to when I'd taken over two years ago. "I'm the first female editor, and I want to take the magazine in a different direction. Go back to basics, talk to real musicians, and cover real issues."

Well, she wasn't laughing in my face, which was a win. Was she mulling over my offer?

"How did you know I would be here?"

Damn, it had started off so well. How to reply without getting Dawn into trouble? "My office is just round the corner." This was true, at least. "Sometimes I pop in here." Completely untrue.

"Do you play?"

"Piano?"

"No, chess." She rolled her eyes. "Yes, piano. What else?"

Oh crap, I was getting sass from Marcie Tyler. "Yes, but not very well. I'm a music journalist cliché—can't play well enough to be in a band, so I write about them."

I was hoping the self-deprecating shtick would raise a smile, but she didn't react.

"Play me something."

"Excuse me?"

"Play something. I want to hear how this piano sounds."

She'd obviously skipped over the fact I'd just explained I was a terrible pianist. But this was a command, not a request, and besides, I wasn't sure I could ever refuse Marcie Tyler anything. Panic welled up in my throat, but I forced myself to take a breath. This wasn't going out on the main stage at Glastonbury; this was a couple of minutes of tinkling on a piano. I could do this.

What could I still remember to play? Joni Mitchell's "Both Sides Now"? Carole King's "You've Got a Friend"? I'd played them constantly when I was younger, so hopefully the muscle memory would still be in my fingers.

Marcie stood up and nodded for me to take her place. I sat on the stool, trying not to get distracted by the fact it was still warm because my idol's posterior had just vacated it. She stayed behind me, where I couldn't see her. She was wearing a Chanel perfume; one my mum sometimes wore, except on her it always smelled musty and old-fashioned—on Marcie it smelled fresh and vibrant.

Sod it, I'd play one of Marcie's songs. Something only connoisseurs knew—"I Don't Believe in Love," from one of her early albums. I'd driven my family mad practicing it when I was a kid.

I readied my fingers on the keyboard, then began. The keys felt solid under my fingers, resistant and yielding in perfect proportion.

I hit a couple of bum notes, but I got through it passably—even the tricky coda.

When I finished, I heard Marcie clapping. Except when I looked round, I realized the applause wasn't coming from her. Standing next to her, a smug smile on his face, was Nick Jones. When had that fucker snuck in?

"A woman of many talents," he said to Marcie, as if I were an old friend he was introducing.

I faked a game smile. There was no point saying anything untoward to Nick, not if he and Marcie had a thing going.

"You just happened to be here at the same time as Marcie? That's quite a coincidence."

"Isn't it just?" I said, channeling my attention back to Marcie. "You were saying we could sit down and chat?"

Marcie looked at Nick, and I knew what was coming. "I'm sorry, but I've got to go. Maybe another time."

A man was striding over from the front door; I recognized him as the driver of the 4×4. He walked her out of the shop, and I was left to face off with Nick.

"That was not cool, Zoë."

"I saw a chance and took it. Any journalist would have."

"You were harassing a client of mine—and not for the first time. Do you want me to get the police involved?"

For fuck's sake. He was kidding, right? "I wasn't *harassing* Marcie; I was just—"

"Sneaking behind my back." His eyes glinted with anger.

"You're the one sneaking behind backs and cozying up to my publisher."

"It was a pleasant change talking to someone who understands the relationship between the press and an artist." He laughed bitterly. "As if Marcie would randomly give a journalist an interview, especially one who butchers her back catalog."

Ouch, that stung. "She asked me to—" I closed my eyes for a second, determined not to let him get to me. "I happened to be here and we struck up a conversation."

"Well, I hope you enjoyed it, because it's the last one you'll ever have with her."

6

EXPRESS YOURSELF

IT HAD BEEN AN HOUR since I'd left the piano shop, and I still wasn't feeling any better. I'd gone back to the office to kill time before going out. Rob, our art editor, had left some layouts on my desk, but I was too worked up to give them any attention. Instead, I was torturing myself on the internet, scrolling through job adverts on LinkedIn. Maybe it was time to smarten up my CV. There was a junior reporter's job going at *Shoe and Leather News*...

I closed my browser in disgust. Jesus, what was I doing thinking about jumping ship? If *Re:Sound* went under, what would happen to Lucy and Gav and everyone else who worked here? How would they pay the rent every month?

Failure was not an option. Not if I wanted to sleep at night. Too many people—*friends*—were relying on me.

There had to be another way to get the Marcie interview and save the magazine.

I just hadn't thought of it yet.

———

My plans for that evening weren't exactly setting me ablaze with anticipation. I was having drinks with Alice, my brother's fiancée.

It wasn't that she was boring; it was just that I didn't have much in common with her. She didn't eat fast food, she drank rooibos instead of normal tea, and her Facebook page was full of inspirational quotes against backdrops of sunsets.

But she meant well. In a fit of either devotion or madness, Alice had agreed to a traditional Greek wedding. She didn't have any Greek friends, and so she'd asked me to be her *proti koumera*—which roughly translates as "first best lady." And because I was officially only a "best lady," she could still have a maid of honor and bridesmaids. This placated her English friends, a couple of whom were put out at not getting the lead gig.

She'd planned a bonding evening so we could all meet. It was a pre-hen night, and although wearing angel wings while waving around plastic penises wasn't Alice's style, I couldn't rule out her friends bringing them. I was allergic to the female brand of shrieky fun that involved talking about sex and pretending to be Manhattanites à la *Sex and the City*, rather than denizens of Southall and Penge. They were having dinner at Pizza Express beforehand, but I'd arranged to join them afterward as I knew something would come up to keep me in the office late.

If I was honest, the other reason I wasn't looking forward to it was because I hated being reminded that people my age were happily pairing off. Pete was three years older than me, so it didn't matter he was getting married. But Alice was two years *younger* than me—barely out of her twenties. What was she doing waltzing up the aisle? I loved my brother, but had she seen the state of his toenails? Or heard his chainsaw snore? Was she really happy to tie herself to him forever?

It took all my willpower not to weasel out of going, and at 9:05,

I was outside the Anchor just off Great Portland Street. It was one of those old-fashioned pubs, stuck in a time warp where hipsters and hummus didn't exist. Gold lettering on the windows announced a saloon bar and taproom, for God's sake. But Alice had probably chosen it because it was quiet and we could actually talk to each other. She was practical like that.

As soon as I was inside, however, I realized my mistake. Blaring out was the Proclaimers' "500 Miles." But not the original—something much worse: a sea of smiley faces strumming ukuleles.

Hipsters had taken over here too.

We couldn't stay here. Alice must not have realized when she arranged this get-together. I pulled out my phone. If they were still in Pizza Express, I'd tell them to meet me somewhere else—somewhere quieter.

"Zoë!" came a cry from my right. Alice was beaming at me from the bar, a glass of wine in each hand. She wobbled over and hugged me, careful not to spill the drinks. "Yay! I'm so glad you're here."

Alice was a Pilates instructor and the fittest person I knew. Her lack of body fat meant she could get pissed on a glass of prosecco, and judging by her pinkness, she'd passed that milestone ages ago.

"Are we staying? Don't you want to go somewhere a bit more…" I swept my arm across the vista. "Ukulele-free?"

"Annette organized this," she said. "I don't want to hurt her feelings. Come on, I'll introduce you."

She led me to a table toward the back, where it was quieter, and slung her arm around a girl with long blond hair. She couldn't have looked more different from Alice, who had a dark pixie cut.

"Zoë, this is my best friend, Annette."

"The Double-A's," chirruped Annette. "We came up with that

when we were ten, when all it referred to was batteries. Now it sounds like a bra size." She laughed. "Nothing double-A about these puppies." She paused to indicate her ample bosom. "But it makes a good story."

Alice turned to a younger woman sitting beside her. "And this is Helen, my baby sister."

Baby was right—Helen looked like she was born this century.

"Zoë is my sister-to-be," said Alice proudly. "I'm so glad you've all finally met. You're the most important people in the world to me."

Alice wore her heart on her sleeve, but displays of affection made me uncomfortable.

"I think I'll go and get that drink now," I said.

"Don't be silly, Zoë. You just got here," said Alice. "Helen will go—white wine, right?" Before I had time to answer, she turned to Annette. "Same again?"

Annette nodded and Helen jumped up. "I'll get us a bottle," she said.

"Is she old enough to get served?" I asked, but no one seemed to hear.

Annette scooted closer to me. "Alice has told us so much about you," she said. "You've got the coolest job ever—and I bet you know loads of cool people. Do you know One Direction?"

I met Alice's eye and she mouthed, "Sorry." Then she gave her friend a gentle nudge. "I'd hardly call One Direction cool."

"But you love them," protested Annette.

Alice squirmed. "I listen to them in the gym sometimes," she said.

"Most of the time I'm stuck in the office or at boring meetings." I was only half lying. My job always looked more glamorous from the outside.

"You don't know the meaning of the word boring until you've worked in an accountant's office," said Alice. "I'm so grateful I got out."

Annette thumped the table with her fist, making me jump. "Tonight's not about work," she decreed, "it's about fun!" She ducked under the table and started rummaging through a handbag.

Oh God, she was going to produce a tacky bridal veil or worse, coordinating pink T-shirts with "hilarious" slogans. She reappeared, however, brandishing a ukulele. "Ta da!" She held it out to me like it was Excalibur.

"What am I supposed to do with it?"

"Play it, silly," she replied. "It's just like a guitar."

I looked at it uncertainly. "It's only got four strings."

"Even easier," said Annette, with the wisdom of the truly non-musical.

Before I could argue, a bloke appeared at our table. He was wearing a T-shirt that said "Ukes Not Nukes." He handed us a sheaf of sheet music before moving off to the next table.

I flicked through the pages. The music was in tab form, which meant it showed you exactly where to put your fingers on the frets. No musical knowledge required.

A quarter of an hour later, with a full glass of wine in me, I was poised with the ukulele and all four of us were watching the screen in the corner to read the ticker-taping lyrics. The song that popped my uke cherry was "Over the Rainbow," and against all odds, it was surprisingly pretty. A hundred strangers in a room all channeling our inner Judy Garland—albeit with significantly less skill than Renée Zellweger.

I have to admit, it was fun. Annette, Alice, and Helen were unexpectedly good singers, and once I got the hang of it, I made a pretty mean ukulele player.

By the time the break came, I was breathless. The fingers on my left hand throbbed from pressing down on the strings, but I didn't care. I was guarding the table while the Double-A's went to the bar and Helen went to the loo. I took my phone out to check on my messages and emails.

My breath caught—I had three texts from Simon.

Had so much fun earlier. We need to do this again. Soon!!

I grinned. Those double exclamation marks were so Simon—all bouncing energy.

God, I'm sooooo bored in this meeting. Am losing will to live…

This second text was sent an hour after the first. But five minutes later, he'd sent a third:

The only thing stopping me jumping out of the window is the possibility that you'll have dinner with me tomorrow night. My fate rests in your hands…

A frisson ran through me. Was he asking me out? Or was this just dinner with a mate? My thumb hovered over the keypad. What to respond? After a couple of moments I started typing:

That'll teach you to not pack your parachute. Oh well, I suppose I've got no choice but to say yes.

I hit send before I could change my mind. But when my phone didn't ping back after five minutes, I regretted my reply. I started to mentally word another message, but then Helen came back to the table and sat down opposite me, smiling shyly.

I pointed to the phone in my hand. "Sorry about this—I'm expecting a message about work." I felt a bit bad lying, but I wasn't sure how much conversation I could muster with a girl who hadn't lived through the Y2K computer panic.

The Double-A's came back from the bar—with another bottle of wine—and started refilling all our glasses.

"Are you okay, Zoë?" Alice was looking at me with concern. "You look a bit flushed."

"It's a work thing," said Helen. But a quirk in her lips made me suspect that she hadn't bought my story.

Just then my phone pinged, and I hastily swiped the screen.

YESSS!!! Meet me at the hotel restaurant at 8pm tomorrow. PS Should I admit now that I'm on the ground floor? S xx

I grinned and realized too late that Annette was leaning over my shoulder, reading my message.

"Oooh! Zoë's got a date!"

I stuffed my phone into my pocket, but my happy face must have been a dead giveaway.

"It's no one you know," I said breezily.

"Well, of course not," said Annette. "We've just met you! But the way you said that makes me think it's someone Alice knows. Who's the mysterious "S" who's texting Zoë so late at night, Alice?"

Oh God, when had Annette become so perceptive? A minute ago she was singing the rude version of Depeche Mode's "I Just Can't Get Enough."

I hoped Alice would nip this conversation in the bud, but she just sat there, perfectly upright with her Pilates-strength core muscles, sipping her wine.

"It's just an old friend who's visiting London," I said.

"A kissy-kissy friend?" said Annette.

"No."

"Are you sure? He signed off with three kisses."

"No he didn't."

It was just two, wasn't it? I wanted to pull out my phone and check, but then I'd give the game away.

"Ah! So it *is* a 'he!'"

Three wine-flushed faces looked at me expectantly. Sod it, why shouldn't I confide in them? It's not like they'd ever meet Simon.

"He was my best friend when I was a kid. But now that he's back, I think there might be a spark between us."

"That's so nice, Zoë," said Alice.

Helen clapped and Annette grinned. "You go, girl!"

With incredibly bad timing, Mr. Ukes-Not-Nukes rocked up at our table.

"Alright, girls?"

"Piss off, sunshine," said Annette.

Alice giggled. "We're in the middle of something, that's all," she said. "She didn't mean to be rude."

"Yes, I bloody did," said Annette, and I suddenly really, really liked her.

With one last roll of the dice, Mr. Ukes said: "Anything I can help with?"

Helen eyed his ukulele. "Yeah, can I borrow that?"

He looked at her uncertainly. "You want me to go away but leave you my uke?"

"Yes," she replied.

He blinked slowly, his reflexes visibly dulled by too many Jägermeisters. "No problem, dudette." He smiled, handed her his ukulele, then sidled off.

"Well played, Helen!" exclaimed Annette.

A bell rang to indicate that the second part of the singing experience was about to start.

Mr. Ukes wandered over a couple of times to sing with us, and to no doubt keep an eye on his £30 ukulele, but his voice was so bad it kept making us go off-key. Annette had no inhibitions telling him every time he hit a dud note, but we were too pissed to get annoyed and eventually his tone-deafness just made us laugh.

The lights blinked on and off to signal last orders. I checked my watch and was amazed it was already eleven.

"Last song!" shouted someone from the bar.

We all turned to the monitor to see what our swansong would be—"Bring Me Sunshine," announced the screen. It was a surprisingly emotional song, and having teased Alice for getting teary during the Everly Brothers, I found my own eyes filling with tears.

We hugged like old friends as the dying notes rang out. "Damn, that's a pretty song," said Alice, not trying to hide her sniffles. I had a lump in my throat so I couldn't respond, and Annette was touching up her eye makeup, although we all knew what was really going on.

We swapped numbers and emails and laughed on our way back to the tube. We were halfway down the stairs at Great Portland Street station before any of us noticed that Helen was still holding her borrowed ukulele.

7

IF I WERE YOUR WOMAN

IT WAS SATURDAY AFTERNOON AND I was due to meet Simon in a few hours. I was walking around my flat, trying to view it with fresh eyes. It's not that I *expected* Simon to end up here, but on the off chance that he did, I wanted the place to give the right impression.

In the kitchen was a poster of Elvis in black leather for his 1968 comeback special—kitsch or classic? Were the Diptyque candles on either side of the Victorian fireplace elegant or pretentious?

I threw myself onto my bed, and then all I could imagine was him standing in the doorway, undoing his cuffs and slowly walking toward me.

Stop it!

Who the fuck wore cuff links?

I needed a cold shower.

After spending longer than I normally did getting ready, I got the bus into town so I could avoid sitting in a hot and sweaty train carriage, and a breezy half hour later I was outside Simon's hotel.

The restaurant at the Halson was in the same room as the bar, but at night, the lights were dimmed and candles flickered on the tables, giving everything a warm glow. I was wearing indigo jeans and a black sequined top accessorized with a chunky silver bangle and ballerinas. The drama was upstairs: my hair was blow-dried glossy and my lips were MAC Red.

I was shown to an empty table, and I checked my watch as I sat down. Nope, not early. It was coming up to ten past eight. He hadn't canceled, had he? I felt a rustle of nerves in my belly. I was about to check my phone when Simon appeared, looking great in a blue shirt and dark jeans.

"Hope I didn't keep you waiting, Frixie." He kissed me on the cheek, and I got another blast of that citrus scent.

"Just got here, Si."

We ordered a bottle of wine, and the first sip went a long way in settling my nerves.

"I know it's been two years, but congratulations on being made editor," he said. "I think we can safely say you've fulfilled all your teenage dreams."

The top button of his shirt was undone, revealing the hollow of his neck. Plenty of my teenage dreams had involved that very spot of his anatomy. Admittedly a few other spots too.

"I've still got one or two more things to cross off my list." Christ, did I sound like a terrible hussy?

"Of course, I know all about one particular fantasy."

My hand was halfway to my glass, and I almost knocked it over.

He knew? I tried to sound breezy. "What's that?"

"You want to interview Marcie Tyler. You've worshipped her all your life."

I smiled, hoping it masked my disappointment. Of course, I'd told him as I was leaving his hotel on Friday about my grand plan.

"I won't lie. It would be an amazing career high. But I'm not sure I can pull it off." I shook my head. "She's a hard woman to reach."

He smiled. "I have faith in you."

"That means a lot. Thanks."

He held up his glass and chinked mine. "To Miss Zoë Frixiepants, the most determined woman I've ever met, and the first girl I ever kissed."

I nearly choked on my Sauvignon.

"We've never kissed," I said, with possibly a bit too much feeling. Unless he meant that kiss he placed on my cheek the morning he and his mum got a cab to Heathrow to start their new life in America. I'd wanted to bawl my eyes out, but had courageously held it in, feigning moderate sadness and blathering on about how internet phone calls and MSN Messenger meant everything could carry on just as before. I couldn't eat for twenty-four hours after he left. Mum was all set to take me to the doctor's until I finally relented and nibbled a piece of baklava she'd bought especially to tempt me.

"Maybe you're confusing me with the previous editor of *Re:Sound*. He had slightly less hair, but was quite a fox, if you like sweary Scots."

He clutched at his shirt over his heart. "Did it mean so little to you?"

I was ninety-nine percent sure he was joking, but as I was frantically trawling my brain for a stray memory, a waiter appeared to take our order. I'd never been so keen to get dinner ordered in my life. I literally asked for the first thing that caught my eye—a risotto—and Simon ordered duck confit. I really wanted to press Simon on this phantom kissing memory, although part of me didn't, because I suspected he was thinking of another girl. Specifically Harriet Smythe, his mum's hairdresser's daughter. I knew because my mum went to the same hairdresser and she told me.

The waiter hovered for a few more agonizing seconds,

flamboyantly shaking out our napkins and placing them on our laps.

When the waiter finally left, Simon leaned forward. "The time I'm talking about is when you'd just discovered your mum's lipstick. You wanted to conduct an experiment and you recruited me to help. How could I stand in the way of scientific progress?"

"Oh. My. God." I covered my face with my hands. "I did that with *you*?" I had a vague memory of trying out my mum's lipsticks, but in my head, I'd been kissing the back of my hand. I remember *wanting* to rope Simon into it, but never getting round to it.

Suddenly, however, it all came rushing back in excruciating detail.

My overly curious ten-year-old self had been intrigued that whenever actors kissed on screen, the woman's lipstick never smudged or transferred onto whoever she was kissing. It didn't make sense, and it *really* bothered me, but before I started writing letters to my favorite film directors—yes, I was *exactly* the sort of kid who did that—I wanted to be sure of the facts.

Sitting cross-legged on the green carpet of my parents' bedroom, in front of Mum's fake rococo dressing table, I had pressed my waxy lips against Simon's innocent mouth, held for a count of five, decoupled, then checked the results. A quick wipe with cotton wool doused in baby oil, and the process was repeated. We did this with every one of Mum's sixteen lipsticks.

"I'm so embarrassed. What was I thinking? And more importantly, why didn't you stop me?"

"Well, it *was* dumb that all those movies perpetuated the myth of the unsmudgeable lipstick." He grinned. "Hey, sometimes I wish my life was still full of girls wanting to make out with me in the name of science."

It was a casual quip—right? I sipped my wine, trying to cultivate an aura of serenity and mystique, but probably only succeeded in looking like I was ignoring him.

How had talking about childhood kisses turned into such a minefield?

I felt much more like we were on solid ground when Simon remembered a record-signing trip we made to Tower Records in Piccadilly Circus one afternoon—the one and only time I'd ever skipped classes. My parents were livid when they found out. I really should have hidden my signed Soundgarden CD a bit better.

I was in such a good mood that after dinner and coffee, I let Simon talk me into going to a club—and not one of my usual places. He picked a neon-signed monstrosity, far too close to Leicester Square, that promised "banging toonz."

We waited forty-five minutes to get in. I couldn't remember the last time I'd queued that long for anything. We stood alongside boys wearing too much Lynx and girls with thickly painted eyebrows. One girl muttered, "Wotchit, grandma" when I accidentally trod on her stiletto, but even that didn't dampen my mood.

Once inside, Simon burrowed his way to the bar and returned with two bottled beers. The music was loud, so his lips were brushing my earlobes as he tried to make himself heard. His breath made the hair on the back of my neck stand up. Before I knew it, he'd persuaded me to dance, even though they were playing "MMMBop."

But I didn't care. Simon's hand on the small of my back made me sizzle, and each time he twirled me, I felt a rush.

We danced to Bon Jovi, to S Club 7, and even to someone I suspected had recently won *The X-Factor*. Simon's energy was boundless. We bopped to Take That and Backstreet Boys, but when Hands

Down came on, my bubble burst. That's the downside to working in music—listening to it is how most people relax, but when it's your job it can intrude on your fun. Hands Down reminded me of Nick Jones, which reminded me of my failure with the Marcie interview.

"I need another drink," I mouthed to Simon and headed to the bar. By the time I got back to him, someone with taste had taken control of the DJ booth and "Under Pressure" was playing.

I hastily put down our drinks and grabbed his hands. We were jumping up and down and I was fifteen again, in my bedroom, listening to this song with Simon, bouncing on the carpeted floor till my mum came up to tell me we were shaking the bulbs out of their sockets. Bowie's voice going up the scale in the middle eight still gave me goose bumps.

We left the club at 3:00 a.m., and I was all set to get on the night bus when Simon objected.

He put his arm around my shoulder. "Your mum would kill me if she knew I'd let you get on a bus alone."

"Don't be daft, Si. We're not thirteen anymore. The bus practically goes to my front door."

"I'll come with you, then. You've got a couch, haven't you? I'll sleep on that."

"I've actually got a sofa bed," I said, mentally high-fiving myself for hoovering under it earlier. "But still, it won't be as comfy as your hotel room, which is a ten-minute walk away."

He held my eye for a second. Was that a coded invitation back to the Halson?

"I want the full London experience," he said. "A bit of night bus conviviality would be marvelous."

Our night bus experience on the 94 to Acton Green offered plenty of shouting, belching, steamed-up windows, and, just after Holland Park, a puddle of vomit.

Conviviality must have taken the N207.

We staggered through my front door just as the dawn light was beginning to creep over the horizon.

Simon slumped down at the kitchen table and rubbed his face. "I need another drink after that."

"Welcome to London," I said, opening the fridge, but the only bottles of wine I had had long since been consigned to the recycling crate. I prodded some sad-looking onions; I was sure an ancient Absolut Vodka was hiding in here somewhere…

"Not alcohol," said Simon. "I'm getting too old for this. I need a coffee. Actually, scratch that, Frixie, a tea would be great."

"Listen to you; you almost sound British."

"I can never win. Over there I'm a goddamned Limey, and here I'm a bloody Yank."

I moved to where he was standing to get to the cupboard. "The cups are behind you," I said.

He was leaning against the counter, but didn't move. I went up on my toes, and for a few seconds, my face was level with his collarbone. He'd undone a second button, and in those stretched-out moments, all I could think about was how close my alcohol-sensitized lips were to his tanned skin.

Then I remembered what I was here for and grabbed two mugs with my clammy paws.

I made us both tea, and we sat down at the kitchen table to drink. After a couple of minutes, Simon rubbed his eyes. "I don't know if it's late or early, but I am exhausted." He gave me a sheepish grin. "I guess my body can't take jet lag like it used to."

"Shall I make up the sofa bed?"

"I'll do it," he said. "Just show me where your bedding is."

I went to the cupboard in the hall, almost tripping over my own feet. I was drunker than I realized. Simon followed me and held out his arms as I pulled out the linen. My only clean pillowcase had "Cyprus—Island of Aphrodite" emblazoned across it. Talk about passion-killer.

Simon must not have noticed, however, because as I handed it to him, he leaned over and planted a soft kiss on my lips.

"Night, Miss Frixiepants," he said, his voice low.

I didn't find mine to answer him, and a moment later he'd disappeared into the living room.

Thirty minutes later, I was still feeling dazed. I lay in bed, my mind too full to sleep. I could just about act normal having Simon back in my life, but a single, gobsmackingly sexy Simon, whose preferred method of saying goodnight was a kiss on the mouth, was something else entirely.

8

EVERY ROSE HAS ITS THORN

THE NEXT MORNING, I WAS surprised to find Simon already up when I came into the kitchen. If I'd known, I would have brushed my teeth.

"Mornin', Frixie."

He looked remarkably poised for 9:00 on a Sunday morning. His clothes were crease-free, which must have meant that he'd hung them up last night and slept naked.

Oh God, I need to stop.

"Morning, Si," I said, busying myself with tea bags and mugs. "Did you sleep okay?"

"I did, thanks. I went out like a light. Last night is a complete blur."

If I looked disappointed, he couldn't see. I was facing the sink, refilling the kettle. What had I expected this morning? Certainly not a continuation of last night's kiss. Without the benefit of alcohol and tiredness, would it even have happened? What I needed was a plan for the day. Something the two of us could do together, something fun but subtly coupley. Maybe a trip to Hyde Park, and some boating…

I reached for the bread. "Want some toast?"

"That would be great, thanks. By the way, your mom called, she was going to leave a message on the machine, but I picked up when I heard her voice. I hope you don't mind."

Simon had always got on well with my parents, and they liked him, Mum especially. She mentioned him from time to time, and when she did, she'd get that faraway look in her eyes, as if he were The One That Got Away.

"She invited us over for lunch."

I was halfway between the bread bin and the toaster. I stopped, a slice of bread going limp in my hand. "You didn't say yes, did you?"

"Of course I did," he said. "It was so sweet of her, and I would love to see them. They're like family to me."

His eyes had gone glassy, and I looked away. When his parents' rows got really bad, he'd climb over the broken fence at the bottom of our garden and come and watch telly with us. Mum knew he was feeling scared and so was always extra nice to him, even when it was after our bedtime.

"They'd love to see you too," I said, feeling bad for my initial reluctance.

Simon stayed for a mug of tea, then left to go back to his hotel to shower and change. We agreed he'd come back around midday, and we'd go together to see my parents.

I finished the remains of my tea, then halfheartedly tidied the kitchen. Sharing Simon with my parents was the last thing I wanted to do, but he'd sounded so happy to see them, I didn't have the heart to cancel.

♪

A couple of hours later we were outside my parents' home in Ealing. My brother's Alfa was in the drive and my heart sank. Alice was most likely with him, and would surely put two and two together that Simon was the mystery "S" from Friday night. And to top it all off, if there were six of us it had officially morphed into a Proper Family Do. Mum would have rolled out the more expensive cutlery, and not the Ikea set that everyone preferred.

The smell of charcoal gusted over the fence, making me hungry. Dad's barbecues were famous, mainly for their frequency—neither rain, hail, nor snow could stop him. My Greekness had embarrassed me when I was young. I didn't like having darker hair than everyone in my class, or that my lunchbox was packed with strange food. Back then, even pita bread seemed exotic to my Anglo-Saxon classmates.

Mum was in the kitchen preparing a salad. She was swaying from side to side, in her denim skirt and FitFlops, singing along to something, even though the radio wasn't on. When she saw us, she rushed over, waving a half-peeled cucumber. I had to duck to avoid getting it in the eye. Then she swept her gaze up and down Simon. "Look at you! You've put on weight."

Personally, I didn't think that was a great way to greet someone you liked.

"Leave him alone, Mum." I glanced at Simon, but he didn't seem bothered.

"But it's a good thing," she insisted. "Simon needed to put on weight." She tapped his chest. "Now he's just right."

"Sorry," I mouthed, when Mum turned back to the cucumber. She finished slicing it, and added it to the salad. "Is this enough?" she said, pushing up her glasses as if she couldn't trust her eyes. The bowl was the size of a laundry basket. "You never eat enough fruit and vegetables."

"I eat plenty," I said. It wasn't a lie if I counted the bean sprouts in my Chinese takeaways.

She fixed me with an I-love-you-but-don't-believe-you stare, then surveyed her food mountain. "Maybe one more cucumber."

She swung open the fridge, and I took the opportunity to slink off to the garden.

Dad was barely visible through a halo of smoke. I could only see his bottom half. His jeans were the same color as Mum's skirt, which meant they'd gone on a recent spree in Marks & Spencer. He shook Simon's hand and asked: "Are you well?"

It had been more than fifteen years since they'd seen each other, but Dad wasn't one for outward displays of affection. "I'm very well, thanks," Simon replied. "Hope you are too?" Dad nodded. It was about as much as Simon would get out of him—he wasn't much of a talker. Dad now turned his attention to me. "How's work?"

The question threw me. It wasn't his usual line of inquiry. He preferred updates on more important things, like if my landlord had done this year's gas safety certificate and whether I was keeping an eye on that mole on my left shoulder.

"Work's fine, Dad." I felt ridiculously guilty, but I didn't want to burden him with what was happening at the magazine. "I mean, a few minor niggles, but nothing I can't handle."

Dad raised an eyebrow. Damn, he had a sixth sense for trouble.

"The dishwasher doesn't work," I blurted out.

"Get them to check the outlet pipe. Same thing happened to ours."

"Yes, good tip. Thanks."

He nodded, then turned back to the barbecue, prodding the whitening charcoal with a skewer. As the orange flames held my attention, my ears tuned into a familiar song playing on Dad's portable radio. A cover of Stevie Wonder's "I Just Called to Say I Love You" for saxophone and panpipes. Classy.

Dad's got bizarre taste, but I owe my own love of music to him. In my childhood, I used to relish going through his old 45s, because among all the Cliff Richard and Demis Roussos, he had some real gems, like Roy Orbison and Glenn Miller.

Simon nudged me and pointed to the shed at the bottom of the garden. "Do you remember we used to play soldiers in there?"

I nodded. "Until Pete decided he wanted to put in a pool table."

A second later, my brother emerged from the shed, carrying a cardboard box.

"Nice to see you, Simon," said Pete. "Mum mentioned you were over."

"Great to see you too, Pete," said Simon.

"What's in the box?" I said, trying to peer into it.

"Wedding stuff," he replied, as if it was perfectly obvious.

There was an awkward silence, which was only broken by the sizzle of the raw meat Dad slapped onto the griddle. A plume of smoke columned above us.

"Where's Alice?" I asked.

A moment later she emerged from the shed.

"Bet you they weren't playing pool in there," whispered Simon. Alice had a smaller, lighter cardboard box. She stopped when she saw Simon and held my eye for a second, then said, all innocence: "Are you a friend of Zoë's?"

I made the introductions, then Simon offered to carry Alice's box inside, which went down well with the Frixos males.

———

I'd been ordered inside to open the extending table when Pete cornered me. "How long is Yankee boy staying for?"

"Don't call him that."

"Did he stay over last night?"

I ducked under the table to find the lever that released the two halves.

"No, of course not," I said, my head level with Pete's knees. "Help me with this, would you?"

Without looking, Pete flicked the lever. The two sides of the table moved apart a few centimeters. I yanked one side toward me while Pete went to the opposite flank, and in one go, we'd heaved the table apart. "Mum said he answered the landline when she rang you this morning."

"He's staying up the road at Holland Park and had just popped in."

I didn't meet his eye. Instead, I unfolded the extra leaf, slotted it in, and clicked the lever back into place.

Pete didn't answer, which I took to mean he'd believed me. I just had to make sure the real location of Simon's hotel didn't come up in conversation later.

"Alice said you two had a great night out."

"She did?" *How did Alice know about last night?*

"Yeah, at a ukulele bar of all places."

He was talking about Friday night, of course. But had Alice mentioned the texts from Simon?

"Yeah, it was great," I said, casually. The conversation was veering into dangerous territory again. "These place mats are hideous—who buys cats in Charles the Second wigs?"

Pete shrugged. "Mum, obviously."

"I'll go and find the old ones."

———

Mum had a bit of a mealtime ritual: she didn't pick up her knife and fork until everyone had piled their plates with double portions of everything. I dropped a stone when I moved out for university, and Mum was the only one who'd never understood why. I shouldn't complain, though; we ate well as kids, and my parents still knew how to put on a spread. On a glistening stainless-steel platter they'd piled thick slabs of pork fillet, marinated overnight in red wine and herbs, and cooked perfectly over the charcoal—crisp on the outside, tender in the middle. On another platter were Cyprus potatoes, roasted in peanut oil until golden and crunchy. The salad was too big for the table so was relegated to the sideboard behind Dad. He kept reminding everyone where it was, in case we failed to spot the drum-sized bowl.

Apart from comments such as "Have some more meat" and "Plenty of potatoes still in the oven," my family's not big on talking when there's food around. Mealtimes are for the jaw, not the tongue, as Mum likes to remind us. When we were kids, she'd tell us off when she couldn't hear chewing—I had to seriously modify my noisy eating when I'd go over to friends' houses for meals. Simon came from the opposite school of thought, though. Polite conversation was a must over dinner—silence was a dangerous invitation for simmering resentments to boil over. He kept trying to resuscitate the conversation, regardless of the scant encouragement. In one of the longer pauses, the cat-flap swung open and Athena scampered in. She made straight for her bowl, which Mum had filled with finely cut pieces of barbecued pork.

Simon pounced on the opportunity. "So, Sophia, when did you get another cat?"

He knew how heartbroken Mum had been when our older cats died. We had two when I was growing up: Rocky and Rambo. Pete got to name them, and I was too young to argue.

"We didn't," said Mum, forking another potato onto her plate.

Simon frowned at me.

"It's the neighbor's cat," I said. "Mum sort of encourages her over."

Simon nodded. "With food?"

"And a cat basket, and a scratching post, and a new name," said Pete.

"She's free to go wherever she likes," said Mum. "She obviously prefers it here."

Alice had been throwing glances at me while we ate, but I'd refused to acknowledge them, mainly because Mum was so eagle-eyed she'd have immediately thought one of us had some huge news to impart— news that brought her closer to attaining her much-desired status of grandmother. But when there was a pause, during which Pete got up to make Greek coffee in a copper-bottomed pot and my folks made a start on the dishes, she addressed Simon directly.

"So, how long are you here for?"

"I'm kinda back for good," he replied.

Alice shot me another look, but I pretended to look at my watch— when had it become a quarter to three?

"Then you must come to the wedding," she said.

I looked up in panic to see Simon's reaction. He was shaking his head. "That's so kind, Alice, but honestly, I wouldn't want to screw up your seating plans or anything."

"Oh, we're nowhere near doing that," she said. "Besides, you're such an old friend of the family, it would be wrong if you didn't come."

"My mom's organizing her own wedding," said Simon, "and she'd hit the roof if someone she'd just met wanted to come to hers."

"Well, we should all get to know each other, then," said Alice, who was showing the kind of determination that explained how she'd achieved the sculpted body of an Olympian. "Why don't the two of you come over for dinner one evening? We don't have much on this week."

Oh God. I knew what Alice was doing and however well-intentioned, it had the cringe-inducing whiff of trying to set me and Simon up.

"That's incredibly kind of you," said Simon, "I would love to—but can we give it a couple of weeks? I've got so many work meetings to organize."

I tried not to feel a bit slighted. Because even though I didn't want to go either, Simon ducking out of time with me still stung.

"Oh, Zoë's like that," said Alice. "You either have to book her weeks in advance, or catch her on a night where her plans have been unexpectedly canceled."

An idea was dawning on Simon—I could see it on his face. "Are you guys free tonight, by any chance?" Alice was nodding even before he'd finished his sentence. "Not for dinner or anything," he continued, "it's just that there's a gig I was considering checking out."

My professional antennae twitched and not in a good way. "Gig?"

"I was chatting with Pete about bands we both liked, and this one happened to come up."

When had my brother discussed music with Simon? Pete's taste ranged from Bruce Springsteen to the Village People, with a dash of progressive rock for good measure. If Si was about to suggest we go on a group jolly to see Rush, I was going to scream louder than Geddy Lee.

"What's the band, Si?"

"It's actually the singer I knew from university. Do you remember Rydell and Jessica Honey?"

Her name was a blast of arctic air from the past. Jessica was the girl Simon had crushed on at university; how close they'd come to doing anything about it, I'd never been able to ascertain.

I'd been thrilled when Simon came back to the UK to do his degree, only to discover that he ended up at Edinburgh—about as far from Exeter, where I was, as it was possible to get.

And then he fell in with Jessica Honeywell. Or rather, Jessica Honey as the press soon dubbed her, because good-looking female musicians needed to be put in their place with infantilized nicknames.

"Are you still in touch with her, then?"

I might have sounded accusatory, but no one seemed to notice.

"No, I just follow her on Instagram," he replied. "She posted about this gig. I was up early because of my jet lag and was trawling social media to pass the time."

Pete returned with the coffees, followed by Mum, who was carrying a giant fruit bowl and motioning at me to offer it to Simon.

"Have some clementines, Si," I said, happy to distract everyone from Jessica Honey with citrus fruit.

"I couldn't," he replied, tapping his stomach.

"I have bananas and kiwis too," said Mum, undaunted. "And a watermelon in the garage." Without waiting for anyone to respond, she went on. "I'll tell your father to go and get it."

She called my dad over, who muttered something about the watermelon not being very good because Mum had gone to the wrong *bakali*. "I can drive to the Kurdish shop," he said. "His watermelons are the best."

"Only if you know how to pick them," said Mum. "You have to look at the stem. You never do unless I remind you."

"No, you have to tap it. A ripe one makes the perfect sound."

"You can't go round smacking every watermelon in the crate," said Mum. "That man in Wembley told you off last time you tried. That's why we don't shop there anymore."

"No, the reason we don't go there is because he gets his watermelons from Holland."

Mum nodded and muttered something in Greek that sounded suspiciously like: "Blessed Virgin Mary save us from Dutch watermelons."

"Why don't you get a *melon* melon instead," suggested Pete.

"I can't eat melon," said Dad. "Too sweet."

Pete rolled his eyes. "Says the man who mainlines Ferrero Rocher."

"Right, I'll go and get the car keys," said Dad, whose appetite had no doubt been whetted for a spot of chocolate too.

"Oh, please don't go on my account," said Simon, ever polite. My parents, however, didn't seem to be listening.

"I'll come with you. I need some fresh almonds," said Mum to Dad's departing back. "Then I can make some *halva* for when Simon next comes." She looked at me sternly. "I could have made it yesterday if I'd known he was coming. It's always nicer the next day."

Great, now I was getting shade from my mum because she'd only had time to make a *three*-course lunch.

"So, Simon, tell us more about the singer from Rydell—is her gig tonight?" Alice probably thought she was being polite, picking up the thread of Simon's conversation before Watermelongate. She didn't know about my issues with Jessica, so I smiled tightly.

"I loved that band," said Pete. I rolled my eyes. Pete had never liked Rydell—he'd just lusted over Jessica.

"Then it's decided—we'll go," said Alice. She aimed her brightest smile at me. "Oh, Zoë, this is going to be so much fun!"

Fun? One long drum solo would have been preferable. But it looked like I was going to have to suck it up and go.

9

LOVE IS A BATTLEFIELD

I REGRETTED WHAT I WAS wearing the moment I stepped into the club. We were in a converted factory—basically a room without windows, and very little ventilation. My kitten heels were sticking to the floor thanks to ten years' worth of spilled beer, and the yellow top with spaghetti straps that had looked so chic in my bedroom mirror made me feel like a half-peeled banana.

After eating some admittedly delicious watermelon, we'd left my parents' house and Simon had gone back to his hotel, while I'd returned to the flat. I'd then spent ages rifling through my wardrobe before deciding on black skinny jeans and a canary-yellow top that I'd bought last summer and never worn. I should have stayed in my usual clothes, but Jessica Honeywell brought out my insecure side, hence my attempt at a bit of glamour.

Simon had played bass in her first band when they were at university. When I'd gone up to visit him he'd seemed totally besotted with her. In fairness, most blokes were because she looked like a young Debbie Harry—with platinum hair and curvy white flesh poured into a Vivienne Westwood–inspired dress. I had stood at the side of the stage, clutching my Malibu and Coke, in my Topshop outfit, feeling like I'd rocked up at a royal wedding in a leper's castoffs.

She left university early when her second band, Rydell, signed with a major label. I anxiously followed her progress in *NME* and *Re:Sound*, secretly hoping her record would tank. But instead, it sold a million copies and she was invited on Marcie Tyler's last tour, ten years ago. I'd been green with envy because Jessica had never really been a fan. First Simon and then Marcie—it felt like she was appropriating everything I held dear.

She'd started to make inroads in America, but the second album, although brilliant, just never got the promotion it deserved and sales were dismal. Within months the label quietly dropped them. They'd fallen into obscurity, but then, about a year ago, one of her songs—a cheesy ballad—had been used in an ad for mobile phones, and there'd been an upsurge in interest in her. She'd appeared on a reality TV show, had a fling with a fellow castmate, and was now a tabloid darling. But no one ever talked about her music, preferring to obsess about her love life. I remember seeing an interview with her a few months back where she'd bemoaned the fact that everyone now associated her with wearing a bikini on TV and a stupid love song she'd written when she was nineteen. I felt for her, but the royalty checks probably made the burden easier for her to bear.

Simon was at the bar now, and I was making small talk with Alice while fending off insults from Pete.

"Blimey, sis, you've pushed the boat out," he said, as I hiked up my shoulder strap for the fiftieth time.

"Don't be mean, Pete," said Alice. "Zoë looks lovely—why shouldn't she look nice?"

Pete rolled his eyes. "Dunno, maybe because we're in a dive in Kentish Town?"

I was spared further sartorial advice from Pete by Simon, who'd returned from the bar carrying a tray of drinks.

"This is so exciting," said Alice. "Cheers, everyone!"

Simon was acting weird. He seemed unsettled, nervous even. His eyes darted back toward the bar. I couldn't work out why, but then I followed his eyeline and I realized what had prompted this change.

Jessica was at the bar.

I hadn't seen her for over ten years, but she looked just as poised and glamorous as she had then. She was still blond, but her poker-straight hair was several shades darker than the platinum tresses she'd sported in her twenties. She wore skinny leather trousers, a strapless top, and body glitter across her shoulders which at first glance looked like radioactive dandruff.

Pete noticed her next. "Fuck, is that Jessica right there?" The movement of the rest of the group turning their heads in her direction must have caught her eye because she suddenly looked up.

Simon awkwardly held up his beer bottle to say cheers, and she frowned. Then, when recognition hit, she threw back her head and laughed. She picked up her own bottle of beer and started walking over to us.

"Baxter!" She beamed, her eyes fixed on Simon.

Simon smiled right back, obviously delighted that she'd recognized him.

"Jess. How great to see you!"

I couldn't help noticing that her eyes were glassy from drink—she'd evidently started the after-show party early.

She gave him a kiss on the cheek, then blinked up at the rest of us.

"Jess, these are my friends," said Simon and introduced us all.

Pete had grown pale and was standing unnaturally stiffly. He'd been quite taken by Jessica Honey back in the day, but he needed to rein in the starstruck act. She wasn't Beyoncé, for God's sake.

"Pete, sweetie," said Alice, once Jess had shaken everyone's hands. "Could you get them to add some ice to my wine? I should have asked for a spritzer. I hate drinking on Sunday nights."

As Pete took Alice's drink back to the bar, she said to me in a low voice: "Pete was going to say something embarrassing—I thought it best to intervene."

She followed him to the bar, leaving me with Jess and Simon.

"You remember Zoë, don't you, Jess?"

"Of course," she replied. "You're the rock journo. I love *Re:Sound*. I should send you my new demo." Without waiting for me to respond, she downed half her beer in one go. "Right, I need to get moving. Not long till my set starts."

"Okay, catch you later," said Simon.

She took a couple of steps backward then changed her mind. "Come and keep me company, Baxter. You were always great at calming my pre-gig nerves."

Simon looked at me, as if to ask permission.

"Go ahead," I told him. I wasn't thrilled with this turn of events, but what else was I supposed to do?

Simon nodded, then followed Jess toward the stage door.

Great.

Alice and Pete had gone and now Simon. I was left by myself, feeling like a lemon in my yellow top.

Fun evening this was turning out to be. Why was I even here?

Professional curiosity was why. Jess had been a hell of a singer, and I wanted to know if she still had it. And however much she'd intimidated me with her natural confidence when we were nineteen, I had to admit she'd had a spark that should have sustained a much longer career. And of course, she'd spent time with Marcie, even jamming with her during a couple of gigs. I knew because I had the bootleg CD.

The club had swelled with people and the music had gone up in volume too, which meant we were getting close to showtime.

I usually like to stand in the center, about halfway to the front—it's where the acoustics are best, but tonight I didn't care. Instead, I burrowed my way to one side, till I was flush against the wall. Everything sounded muted and dulled, almost as if the gig was happening in another room.

How different tonight was from the last gig I'd been to with Simon. We'd been fifteen and had snuck into the Electric Ballroom, giggling like the schoolkids we were, sharing a bottle of blue Mad Dog. I still had the ticket stub—the Angry Crickets, with special guest Silver Finger. I don't remember what they were like because halfway through the first song Simon had rushed to the loo to throw up—the fortified wine had not agreed with him. Or maybe it was the four cans of White Lightning we'd bought from the corner shop beforehand.

Maybe a drop of cider would help this evening go a bit quicker. My wineglass was empty, and I was about to go to the bar when I stopped still.

There was a man in profile leaning on the bar who looked a lot like Nick Jones.

Shit.

He turned his head in my direction, and I slunk back into the shadows. He was the last person I wanted intruding on my Sunday night.

The music industry was a small world, but what would he be doing at a Jessica Honey gig? Could it be related to Marcie Tyler? I glanced back, but he'd disappeared. Or maybe I'd just imagined him.

A moment later, the lights went down, and figures stole onto the stage. A slow drumbeat began, accompanied by a thumping bass that I could feel from my soles to my sinuses. The club was only half full, but I could feel the tide of people being pulled forward, closer to the empty mic stand at the front of the stage. I'd been to hundreds of gigs, and no matter who was playing, the few seconds just before show time were charged with an anticipation that always made me hold my breath.

A brilliant flash of light announced Jessica's arrival, and she bounded onto the stage, a ball of energy against a white backdrop that announced her name in jagged lettering last popular with eighties metal bands.

Lead and rhythm guitars joined the bass and drums, then Jessica stepped forward and lifted up the mic. I'd forgotten how powerful her voice was. Even here, in the corner where it should have sounded muffled, the clarity of her voice gave me goose bumps. Without realizing, I had taken several steps forward, as if pulled by a magnet.

And there in the front row was Simon, one fist pounding the air, beaming at her like a proud father.

No, his wasn't the face of a proud father, it was something entirely different. He was smitten. The disappointment was like a shove in the chest.

I was being silly. Jessica was performing. It wasn't the real her onstage; it was a persona, one she'd honed from hundreds of sold-out gigs.

She barely acknowledged the audience, singing with her head tilted back and her eyes half-closed, as if she was performing to an empty room. Her body swayed to the music, but I could tell she was nervous. Her hands gave her away. Her pale fingers were coiled tightly around the microphone as if she were hanging on for dear life.

It took a lot of guts to put yourself out there. Lead singers needed swagger, but it was almost always bravado. They were often the most insecure person in the band. The spotlight hid as much as it revealed.

She sang four songs then, to my surprise, she was bowing goodbye. She couldn't have finished already; she hadn't sung any of her hits. I hadn't recognized any songs. Were they all new numbers?

She waved to the crowd as she headed off stage, but her smile faded before she'd disappeared behind the curtain. She looked sick with nerves. I felt a twinge of sympathy, but then she motioned for Simon to follow her backstage and the two of them were swallowed by the darkness.

Well, that was annoying. Should I go after them, or wait? The lure of alcohol won, so I got myself a drink, then schlepped up to the balcony where I'd have the best view of the stage door and found a table with an uninterrupted view of downstairs.

The wine had been pretty undrinkable so I'd switched to a bottled beer.

I took a sip and winced. The beer was horribly sour. It was a brand I'd never heard of, written in a Cyrillic script dotted with strange accents. I absently scored my thumb around the soggy label, trying to remove it in one satisfying piece and had nearly managed it when a voice cut in.

"Zoë?"

I turned.

Nick Jones. Dammit. It had been him. What was he doing here—apart from standing awkwardly under the low ceiling? And wearing a suit, for God's sake.

"Well, this is quite a coincidence," he said.

I shrugged. "I'm a music journalist. We're at a gig."

He looked incredulous. "You're here in a professional capacity? To see Jessica Honey?"

He had me there. "She's a friend." No need to get specific. "Why are you here?"

"I live nearby and pop in now and then—occasionally there are some diamonds in the rough."

It sounded like a blatant lie, but why else would he be here? It wasn't for the extensive wine list.

AC/DC's "Back in Black" was playing over the PA loud enough to prevent awkward silences, but we managed one anyway. No doubt he was still upset over Marcie. Well, sod him, I was here to enjoy myself. Except I was having a shit time—but he didn't have to know that. The last thing I wanted was to talk about work.

"What are you drinking?" he said eventually.

"I have no idea."

"I meant it along the lines of 'What can I get you?' but now I'm intrigued." He picked up the bottle. "Mongolian beer? No wonder you look so depressed."

That broke the ice. "It tastes truly awful."

He pointed at the empty seat next to me. "May I?"

"Really?" I hadn't meant to sound rude. I tried again. "What I mean is, I'm not going over the whole piano shop thing again. I did what any journalist would have done—a source told me she'd be there and I followed it up. You're not blameless either. You went over my head and cut a deal with my publisher. That's not on."

He sat down. "Marcie's quite a nervous character. All sorts of nut jobs follow her around. She doesn't like being ambushed."

"We were having a perfectly cordial conversation."

"Trust me, you'll get more out of her when she's expecting you."

I was taken aback. "Does that mean I'm off your shit list?"

"I was made aware of some new facts regarding your altercation with Jonny Delaney that night. He'd sworn to me that he hadn't provoked you. I was wrong to believe him, and I'm sorry about that."

Was my tinnitus playing up or was that an apology? "I appreciate that, thanks. Possibly I went too far, but I was feeling a bit emotional about Patrick leaving."

"You two are close."

Ridiculously, that brought a lump to my throat, so I just nodded.

"You and I need to make a fresh start." He pulled out a silver case from his breast pocket and handed me an expensively thick card. His details were embossed. No mere ink for Pinnacle's finest.

I gave him my own card, which was decidedly floppy and slightly worn, but he didn't seem to notice.

"So, how about that drink?" he said.

He wanted to stay? He'd cleared his conscience; why wasn't he off on his merry way?

I narrowed my eyes. "You want to buy me a drink?"

He held his hands up. "You're acting like I'm the first man to offer you a drink. Hell, I doubt I'm the first man tonight." He cast a glance at my outfit. "Yellow suits you."

Was the fucker flirting with me or taking the piss?

He smiled. "You might not like me, but I'm hoping to change your mind. Alcohol helps my case."

"I'll only be impressed if my senses are blunted by booze?"

"No, the alcohol's for me. I don't usually drink much, but I needed a whisky before I could come over."

"A music publicist who doesn't drink? Careful, or they'll lock you in a lab and study you."

"Well then, you'll have to keep it quiet."

Was he flirting again, or was I imagining it?

The beer was rank; a fresh drink would help while away the time it took Simon to return. But just as I was about to say yes, the man himself appeared, looking slightly out of breath.

"Oh, Frixie, thank God. I thought you'd left without me." He was grinning, but when he noticed Nick his smile faded. "Am I interrupting?"

"No, of course not," I said.

Nick stood. "Let's get that drink another time."

He sloped off, and I was left feeling distinctly puzzled. *He wanted to talk about work, right?*

Simon collapsed into the chair that Nick had just vacated.

"Sorry I kept you waiting. I haven't spoken to Jess for years and was hoping to have a catchup. But she's not on best form tonight. Between you and me, she was kind of a wreck. Her stage fright was so bad, she had to cut her set short."

"She's played Wembley and she worries about playing a dive like this?"

"She was just telling me how much her confidence has been knocked since she did that reality show. The press is merciless about her musical ambitions. I really feel for her, you know." He smiled shyly. "Maybe *Re:Sound* could do something to rebalance that?"

I felt for Jess myself. It was hard to be taken seriously as a female musician if you were even remotely attractive, dared to wear a swimming costume on holiday, or dated anyone famous.

However, I wasn't sure I could just stick her in the magazine as a favor to Simon. I couldn't say that outright though so searched for something suitably noncommittal to say. "I hope she's okay."

Simon nodded. "Shall we finish our drinks and go?"

He'd also ordered the Mongolian beer, but had evidently enjoyed it more than I had—only a couple of inches were left.

"I might leave mine," I said.

He tipped back his head, drained his bottle, then smacked it onto the table. It wobbled a couple of times, before righting itself.

"Was that guy hitting on you?"

"What?"

"You were sitting together for ages. I saw you from downstairs. Who was he?"

Was that a smidgeon of jealousy?

"It was no one," I said, smiling broadly. "Just someone from work."

10

YOU CAN'T HURRY LOVE

I SLEPT BADLY THAT NIGHT. My head was full of Jessica, Simon, and, bizarrely, Nick. I had hated seeing Simon fawning over Jessica, but my encounter with Nick had produced one unexpected benefit: Simon had been seriously irked by his presence. He kept asking faux-innocent questions about him on the tube ride home, which I'd nonchalantly brushed off. He apologized for not inviting me back to his hotel bar, citing an early start the next morning, and instead suggested we meet for dinner.

My goodwill toward Nick lasted only as long as it took me to turn on my phone the next day. At 8:37 a.m., as I was trying to squeeze out a bit of toothpaste from an almost empty tube, he was leaving me a voicemail about how we needed to talk about Hands Down. God, couldn't the man let me have breakfast before pestering me about that stupid band? I don't know what he'd been playing at last night—but in the cold light of day, I could safely say he hadn't been flirting.

I got to the office an hour or so later and went over the layouts Rob had left for me on Friday. He'd joined the magazine at the same time as me, starting as an assistant in the art department. Now he was art editor, and the department was just him. He was a gentle giant who never swore or raised his voice. He quietly got on with sorting out the look of the magazine by himself, issue after issue, never complaining. I found him by the kitchen, but before I could tell him how happy I was with his new layouts, he sailed past me, his tall frame even more hunched than usual.

"It's a war zone in there," he muttered, nodding toward Gavin and Lucy behind him. He sloped back toward his desk, while I went to investigate what the gruesome twosome were getting so worked up about.

They appeared to be having an animated conversation about getting stuck in a lift. Lucy was illustrating the drama by waving a teaspoon in the air and feigning a bout of mild hysteria, while Gavin was nodding and nervously running his hand over his shaved head. I didn't blame him. Lifts are scary enough without worrying about getting stuck in one.

"We've got a great idea to pitch to you, Zoë," said Lucy, brandishing the teaspoon in my direction.

"It was my idea," interjected Gavin.

"Was not!" said Lucy, shaking her head, which made her pink plait sway from shoulder to shoulder.

"Okay," I said, in my best United Nations negotiator voice, "conference room in five minutes."

"Conference room" was Lucy and Gavin angling their chairs toward my desk. The actual conference room was used as a stationery cupboard slash unofficial sick bay, pressed into service when someone's hangover required them to lie down with a ream of A4 for a pillow—personally, I preferred to use a folded-up jacket.

This conference was going remarkably well. The idea they were pitching was a new feature called "Stuck in a Lift with…"

Gavin was explaining how it would work. "We ask confessional questions, like what's the biggest lie you've ever told, or who's your secret crush."

"Yeah," said Lucy. "And the lift is hurtling to the ground so you're moments from death and these are the last things you'll ever say—it'll be fun!"

I wasn't sure "death-by-lift" and "fun" belonged in the same sentence, but I still liked the idea.

Gavin held up a finger as if he was about to announce world peace. "Or maybe it could be a plane that's about to crash."

Lucy nodded enthusiastically, and they both looked at me expectantly.

"It'd be easier and cheaper to photograph in a lift," I said, and I even felt a bit miffed at my sudden metamorphosis into a killjoy.

"Yeah, you're right, Zo," said Gavin. "And anyway, 'Stuck in a Lift' is catchier."

"Short and snappy," said Lucy. "That's why my original idea was so good."

"*Your* idea?" said Gavin.

"Let's just say you both came up with it," I said hastily, not wanting to get dragged into it again. "Let's move on to who we'd like to feature."

I opened my notepad and poised my pencil before it dawned on me: "Jonny Delaney's crappy boy band!"

Gavin's jaw dropped, and Lucy dipped her head and stared at me over imaginary glasses. Anyone would think I'd suggested cutting their baby in half.

"Hear me out," I pleaded. "I need a backup plan in case we get held over a barrel to put Hands Down in the magazine—this way it'll be tongue-in-cheek."

"I 'spose that makes sense," said Gavin.

"Yeah," said Lucy.

I felt a bit bad for deflating everyone's enthusiasm, but they weren't the ones fighting a publisher and a pushy PR man. Nor did they need to count sheep to sleep soundly, whereas the woolly fuckers kept me up all night bleating scary sales figures.

♪

When I got home that evening, Simon was waiting outside my flat.

Seeing him made my heart thump. He always looked so comfortable in his skin. He was sitting on a low wall in his faded jeans and white shirt, stroking Snowy under her chin. She looked ready to dissolve into a puddle of pleasure. Watching his hands move made me feel the same way. He had a way of holding himself that was so effortlessly sexy.

"Hey, Si. Great to see you," I said, trying not to sound too excited. "You should have texted. Have you been waiting long?"

He grinned. "Nah, and anyway, this little sweetheart has been keeping me company."

"Snowy's anyone's for a tickle under the chin."

By his feet were two carrier bags from Sainsbury's, and for a moment I wondered whether he'd been kicked out of his hotel and the bags were filled with all his worldly goods.

"What's with the bags?"

"I have the most amazing recipe for moussaka, and I wanted to try it on my favorite Greek."

He was talking about me, right? "You're going to cook?"

"Yes, and you're going to help, so come on—you've got potatoes to peel."

The first thing Simon did was turn on the oven. Except, it wasn't working.

"Yeah," I said, feeling a bit embarrassed. "I've been meaning to look into that."

He started laughing. "How long have you lived here?"

"Shut up. Maybe I don't use the oven because I make delicious healthy salads every night."

Simon knelt down to look at the oven's controls and after pressing a few buttons, the damn thing magically came to life.

He grinned. "You've got to set the clock, otherwise it won't work."

"Well, that's just dumb."

"Right, frying pan. We need to brown some onions."

This I could do. "Olive oil okay?"

He nodded—*thank goodness*—because I didn't have any other sort.

The kitchen was small and we had to keep moving around each other to get to things, which wasn't entirely unpleasant. The mince was simmering nicely in the pan, and even I had to admit we were creating some amazing smells.

At some point, Simon opened a bottle of wine, and we had almost drunk it all before we'd even got to the bechamel sauce.

"You want to make it from scratch?"

He looked mortally offended. "Is there any other way?"

"It comes ready-made in a jar. Even the Londis around the corner has it."

"Once you've tried my bechamel, you'll never go back to store-bought." He raised his eyebrows suggestively. Blimey, was he flirting over a jar of sauce? Who knew cooking could be fun?

"So, what do we need for the sauce?"

He reached into his carrier bags and took out flour and eggs. I snuck a peek at what else was there. Moussaka needed a surprising amount of ingredients. A packet caught my eye. I yanked it out and dangled it in front of him.

"Ready-made breadcrumbs? You are so busted!"

He held up his hands in surrender and laughed. "Okay, I admit it. I'm a total fraud. But I still win the adult stakes. Do you think I'm going to let you forget that you didn't know what "blanching" meant?"

"At least I don't call an aubergine an eggplant."

"Actually, the Brits used the word eggplant until the eighteenth century."

"You just made that up."

He'd opened the flour and had started sieving it. I did a double take—I had a *sieve*?

He caught me staring. "Yes, I bought a sieve. Now stop looking at me like I've grown a third arm."

He finished making the sauce while I peeled and sliced potatoes and aubergines. Then, we greased a Pyrex dish and layered in our mince, vegetables, and bechamel.

The final touch was grating some cheddar. Not strictly traditional, but he'd assumed I would have parmesan.

"You can't beat a good cheddar," I explained.

"I remember you were obsessed with it as a kid."

"Was I?"

"Yeah, you hated it when your mum made sandwiches with halloumi."

I frowned. "It's not that I hated other cheeses; I just hated standing out." When I was younger, I tried to wear my Greekness as lightly as possible.

He rubbed my arm. "Every kid goes through phases like that."

"I couldn't believe my uni friends grilled halloumi when we did barbecues." I shook my head. "All those years being embarrassed—what an idiot I was."

"I always loved that you were Greek—and not only because your parents always had eight different types of snacks to offer me when I came round. I should have told you more often. Your place felt more like home than my own. My folks barely spoke to each other, and when they did it was via screaming matches about whose life was shittier. The only time I ever heard your parents shout at each other was when your dad had added cinnamon to your mum's *spanakopita* recipe."

I smiled. "The *Cannella* Incident. We still can't speak of it."

The moussaka was lovely. But what made it lovelier was sharing it with Simon. We were sprawled on the sofa, our tummies full, and on our second bottle of wine.

"It's great being back in London," he said. "I should have come back sooner."

"It's great having you back, Si."

"After my marriage fell apart, I thought I would too."

He'd never really spoken about his divorce. "I'm sorry. I wish I could have been there for you."

"I was a fool for not keeping in touch. Only communicating through email or Facebook. I wasn't prepared to admit my marriage was a mistake. I avoided well-meaning friends who saw the end coming long before I did." He paused. "She cheated on me."

"Oh God. That's awful."

"She claimed it was because I was at work all the time, some nights till midnight."

"That's not an excuse for infidelity," I said.

He shrugged. "Maybe I was avoiding her, though. So, my motives weren't one hundred percent pure. I should have listened to my gut and owned up that the marriage wasn't working. But I've learned something about myself: avoiding my problems never works out."

"It's great that you can take something positive from it all."

"I wouldn't wish it on anyone, but it was a hell of a learning experience."

I picked up my wineglass. "To learning experiences."

"And old friends."

"Less of the old, please."

"To wonderful, amazing, inspiring friends."

His dark-blue eyes seemed so full of affection that I had to look away.

"Cheers" was all I trusted myself to say.

After a couple of minutes, my heart was almost back to normal beating speed.

"How long do you plan to stay at the hotel, Si?"

"The firm's put me up for a couple of weeks, but I want to find a place of my own before then."

"You could stay here if you like," I said, keeping my tone light.

"I couldn't impose like that."

"It's no problem," I said. "I could at least give you a key. That way, you're not hanging around outside in the heat."

"I know your game," he said, his eyes twinkling.

He did? "What do you mean?"

"You want to get out of cooking, don't you? And here I was thinking you were being nice, when really, you want me to have dinner ready for you when you're home from work."

I gave him a shove. "That's not what I meant!"

"Bit of tidying too? And start on the laundry?"

"Stop it," I said, trying not to squirm.

"Basically, an unpaid housekeeper."

"No!"

"Admit it, Frixie, you want me to be your slave."

Oh God, why did I hear the word "sex" in front of "slave"?

Simon's phone vibrated, dissolving the—probably imagined—sexual tension.

He read his text while I topped up our glasses, surprised to find that we'd reached the bottom of our second bottle.

"I guess I should call it a night," he said.

Before he left, I gave him a key, which he accepted without fuss. I mooched around the kitchen, rinsing our plates and glasses.

Were we finally on the cusp of something? The spark between us wasn't in my head. I really wanted to ring Georgia and tell her all about it. She was the one I always turned to when it came to relationship advice. But it was late and she'd be asleep. I needed to dampen my excitement. Simon was fresh from a divorce—the ink on his papers was barely dry. The last thing I wanted was to be his rebound relationship.

I twisted the taps off and dried my hands on a tea towel. Patience, I told myself. Then went to bed with that damned Guns N' Roses song drilling holes in my head.

11

HIT ME WITH YOUR BEST SHOT

THE TABLES AT THE CAFÉ near Georgia's office leaned like the Tower of Pisa, the lone fan on the ceiling did nothing to cool the place down, and the waiters didn't speak English, but Luigi's was always packed because it served the best penne all'Amatriciana this side of Naples.

It was Tuesday lunchtime and Georgia and I were squeezed around a table for one. Our knees kept knocking and if I twisted my head fully to the right, I'd be kissing the mug shot of Frank Sinatra on the wall. Before she had the twins, we'd see each other every week. Now, a monthly lunchtime catchup was the best we could manage. Thankfully, she'd been free when I rang this morning to convene an emergency session.

"So," she said, putting her phone on silent. "How's Simon?"

"Divorced and moving back to England."

Her eyes widened. "Pissing hell, you work fast!"

A waiter set down two mugs of sploshing tea. "Very funny," I said, mopping up the spillage with a paper napkin. "We're just friends."

"You've been grinning like an idiot since you got here. Come on, spill it."

"He came round last night."

She leaned forward. "Oh aye, keep going."

"He made me moussaka."

"Is that Greek for orgasm?"

I laughed. "No! He made the dish moussaka, from scratch. Or rather, we made it together."

"Sounds intimate, especially in your kitchen."

"It was…nice."

A waiter arrived with our pasta before I could elaborate. Georgia's eyes were as wide as the plates Luigi Jr. set down in front of us.

"Nice? Please tell me it was a night of unbridled simmering sexual tension."

Luigi was taking an age grinding parmesan onto our penne. I suspected his English was a lot better than he let on.

"No, of course not." Then, when Luigi finally left, "Okay, maybe a little. But we talked for hours and it was lovely."

"They're back, aren't they?"

"What are?"

"Your feelings for him."

If I was talking to anyone else I would have denied it, but this was Georgia. "Maybe."

I gulped down some tea to avoid her gaze.

"Did you have some kind of sexy food fight?"

"No, I told you, we talked."

"It never descended into sexy time?"

"Georgia, you've got a one-track mind, do you know that?"

"Oh, fuck off. I haven't had sex for months—everything's shriveled up down there. We're both so exhausted all the time. I want to live vicariously through you. So, am I going to get to meet Simon this time?"

The idea didn't immediately appeal. I wanted to keep Simon to myself for a bit longer. I couldn't explain it, though.

"He's really busy with work."

Georgia frowned. "That's not going to cut it, my dear. Bring him to Dean's surprise birthday."

She'd been planning a costume party for her husband, Dean, with military precision for months. Many a lunch had been taken up discussing the finer details: were cheese and pineapple sticks ironically retro or just plain odd? This was my chance to divert the conversation away from Simon.

"Have you picked out a costume?"

"Of course."

"What about Dean? He can't be the only one not in fancy dress, George."

"Got his sorted too. It's the white uniform from *An Officer and a Gentleman*. He'll love it. Or at least, he'll love it when he sees how hot I find him in it."

"You've thought of everything!" I said.

"I have to—I can't just have fun at the drop of a hat anymore. I haven't had a drink for two years. His mum's going to take the twins for the night, and we're going to bloody well enjoy it."

I had a quick glimpse of the old Georgia. The one who wasn't weighed down by having to keep two mini-humans alive. It was great to see her excited by something other than her babies' digestive tracts.

"Looking forward to it, Georgia."

♪

After lunch, I swung by Mike's office to give him an update on the forthcoming issue. But of course, after a few minutes, the conversation strayed toward the longer-term future of the magazine—and if it still had one.

"I spoke to Ed the Shred, earlier," said Mike.

My muscles tightened. Ed Fairbanks was the head of special projects at Octagon. No one really knew what he did, but his job mainly involved firing people and slashing budgets. Hence his nickname, Ed the Shred.

"What did he want?"

Mike rubbed the back of his neck. "He's set all of us new sales targets."

All of us included the two other magazines the company had recently bought—a car review monthly and a baking magazine. None of us had anything to do with one another, although I sometimes wondered whether I could swap some of my comp gig tickets for salted caramel cupcakes.

"What numbers are we talking about?"

"We'd need to double our ad sales."

If I hadn't been sitting, my knees would have given way.

"Why do they keep moving the goalposts?"

Mike sighed. "Rumor has it that Ed the Shred wants to come in as executive editor if these new targets aren't reached."

"He'd come in over my head?"

Mike pursed his lips. "You'd be out, and I suspect the rest of the team wouldn't be that far behind."

"But…" I went woozy for a second. "Ed isn't a journalist, and he knows nothing about music."

"I don't disagree, Zoë. What they aren't saying is that Ed's tenure would be short-lived. He'd come in, strip everything he can from the *Re:Sound* brand and then close the magazine. We'd be lucky if we ended up with an internet radio station."

I stared at him, dumbfounded.

"Are you sure you still want to focus all your energy on getting Marcie Tyler?"

"What choice do I have? Thanks to her reclusiveness and her recent stint in rehab, Marcie is the only artist that could generate the sales we need."

"Well, there's still Hands Down, and Nick Jones is rather keen."

Anger flared in my gut. "Are you and he planning something behind my back?"

"We've spoken a couple of times."

I shook my head. This wasn't like Mike at all—it had to be Nick's doing.

"I will hit those targets, and I'll do it the right way, Mike."

Back at my desk, I had a missed call from Nick and an email. Sod him. He'd made his bed with Mike; he could bloody well lie in it. I would find another way to get to Marcie.

I'd managed to get a couple of hours' work done when Jody called from reception.

"You've got some visitors." Then, without waiting for me to ask who, she added: "I'm sending them up."

I heard them before I saw them. My parents marching toward me in matching reversible jackets, making that swishing sound that only anoraks produce. I checked the sky out of the window. Not a single cloud. But that didn't stop the voice in my head scolding me for not having brought an umbrella today. My parents could smell rain two continents over.

"Mum, Dad, what are you doing here? Is everything okay?"

"We came to do some shopping and wanted to say hello," Mum replied. "You've got a big Marks & Spencer up here."

Dad was not known for his love of shopping, and it was only now that I noticed he was carrying something that looked suspiciously like a toolbox.

Gavin was staring at me with ill-concealed glee. Crap, what had I told the office about my folks that was about to bite me on the backside?

Before I could warn him to be discreet, he spun round in his chair to face them. "Hello, Mr. and Mrs. Frixos. I'm Gavin."

They shook hands, their expressions mirroring Gav's delight. I was racked by filial guilt that this was the first time they'd ever come to the office and I hadn't thought to make the introductions myself.

"Shall I give you a tour?"

Dad held up the plastic case he was carrying. "I brought my tools so I can fix your dishwasher."

"You don't have to do that, Dad." Surely there was some sort of health and safety directive he'd be infringing?

"Oh, that's great," said Lucy, who'd mooched over. "It was my turn to buy the washing-up liquid—now I don't have to bother. I'm Lucy, by the way."

I glared at her. "Maybe you could go and get some dishwasher tablets then."

"Oh, we've got loads of them," she replied. "We haven't been able to use them in weeks."

Dad shook his head in a "this is serious" way. I needed to get them away from Lucy before she accidentally let slip that last week I'd gotten a mild electric shock when I'd tried to sort out a paper jam in our dodgy photocopier.

"Why don't I make us all a nice cup of tea," I suggested, trying to herd them toward the kitchenette. *Please God, don't let there be a half-eaten curry in the microwave.*

"So, what have you been up to since the weekend?" I asked Mum as we waited for the kettle to boil. Well, Mum and I were waiting for the kettle; Dad had declined the offer of caffeine and was already unscrewing the sides of the dishwasher and inching it away from the wall.

"We went to see Father Michalis today to go over everything for the wedding. He asked about you."

I hadn't been to church for years, so I suspected I was about to get a telling off.

"That's nice," I muttered, hoping I could avoid what was coming. Perhaps I could develop a sudden interest in broken dishwashers and join Dad on the floor…

She looked at me hopefully. "He's not so young anymore, but he'd like to marry you."

What? I might have audibly gasped. The internet had gone gaga for the vicar in *Fleabag*, but Father Michalis had a ZZ Top beard and was no Andrew Scott. "He's a priest, Mum!"

She frowned. "Well, yes, who else would do it?"

I mentally thumped my forehead. Of course. He didn't want to *marry* me, he wanted to *perform* the ceremony.

Mum hadn't noticed and continued: "He's nearly eighty, you know. He baptized you, and he'll be very upset if he dies before you decide to get married."

This conversation was getting more and more surreal—and not

one I particularly wanted to be having at the office. I would have bet good money that Lucy and Gav were eavesdropping around the corner.

"Getting married is the last thing on my mind," I said, hoping to end the discussion.

"How is Simon?" came Dad's voice from the floor. "Will you be bringing him round again?" Mum grinned. My parents were a formidable double act sometimes. Dad may as well have inquired when Simon planned to propose. But I knew better than to indulge their fantasies.

"How's the dishwasher coming along?"

Dad shuffled upright. "All fixed. It was the outlet pipe. Run it empty a couple of times, then it should be fine."

Well, that was one piece of good news. "Thanks, Dad. I feel awful for hurrying you, but I've got a meeting in a couple of minutes."

They didn't seem too bothered by the fact that I was blatantly chucking them out. Sometimes they needed reminding that I wasn't a teenager anymore and was in fact—*shock, horror*—a grown woman. Although admittedly one that appreciated having a dad who saved her money on fixing broken kitchen appliances.

♪

With Dawn at her kid's piano recital, I was tempted to skip the gym that evening, but the idea that Simon might be seeing me naked in the near future made me drag myself to spin class. Except when I got to the gym I was informed by the chirpy, tanned receptionist that the spin class was full. Dawn usually remembered to book us in; it had completely slipped my mind to do it myself.

"We've got Boxercise starting in a bit," he said. "It's great for cardio, great for muscle tone. You'll love it."

His sales pitch worked, because fifteen minutes later, having changed into my Lycra gym gear, I was standing in a circle with about ten other people doing jumping jacks.

The instructor, who had arms like a spinached-up Popeye, had introduced himself as Carl, and was now shouting peppy platitudes at us over a soundtrack of nineties dance music. Fitting, because techno always made me want to hit something.

"You guys are awesome!" he declared. "Feel your blood pumping—doesn't it make you feel alive?"

Actually, Carl, I wanted to say, *it makes me feel like I'm about to die.*

We were only about five minutes into the class, but my heart was hammering like a four-armed drummer and my limbs felt as heavy as granite. I bet evil dictators used jumping jacks as a torture technique.

"Okay," cried Carl. "Now let's start running on the spot."

This was only slightly less taxing, as at least I could rest my aching arms, but Carl kept encouraging us to "get those knees up higher" like a deranged drill instructor. Any higher and my knees would be knocking my fillings out.

After what felt like fifteen hours or so, Carl decided we'd earned the right to move round in a clockwise direction. Everyone around me had mad grins on their mugs. Were they actually enjoying this, or had they all been smoking something before the class started?

"And now anticlockwise."

The circle now started jogging in the opposite direction. I was just about getting into the swing of things when Carl reversed the direction again.

"And double time!"

What?

I was practically tripping over my own Nikes, trying not to get overtaken by the person behind me. My lungs were burning and sweat was pooling into my sports bra. Thank God I was wearing black. Although how I looked was pretty low down on my list of cares. Topping that particular list was: *Help, I'm about to pass out.*

I could tell I was suffering from oxygen deprivation because a bloke who'd just joined the class looked a lot like Nick Jones.

He high-fived Carl, who slapped him on the back, and joined the circle opposite me. I rubbed my eyes, because clearly this couldn't be right.

He smiled. *Shit.* It *was* Nick. Was he bloody well stalking me?

"And stop," announced Carl.

My limbs throbbed, and I *really* wanted to collapse in a puddle on the floor, but I couldn't. Not in front of Nick.

I turned away to give myself some time to recover, but a moment later, Nick was at my side. He was wearing a light-gray T-shirt, which was tight enough to show off all the planes on his chest.

"Evening, Zoë." Annoyingly, his breathing was unaffected.

I willed my diaphragm to behave so I wasn't so obviously panting.

"Don't 'Evening, Zoë' me. How the hell did you know I'd be here?"

He shrugged. "How did you know Marcie would be at the piano shop?"

Dawn had known both things, and for a second I panicked that she'd told him.

"Have you been following me?"

"How do you know I'm not in Boxercise every Tuesday night?"

"Maybe I'll ask Carl," I replied.

"Be my guest."

My real reason for going over to Carl was because he was near the door. My instinct was to get out of here, but then I'd look like a chicken. And sod it, I'd paid for this class, why should I leave?

But before I could move, Carl was issuing fresh instructions. "Okay, pair up and get your gloves."

I scanned the room trying to find the other woman who was here, but she'd already paired up with someone. Everyone seemed to partner up quickly, assuming Nick and I were already a pair.

I was stuck with him.

"I swung by your office," said Nick.

"Excuse me?"

"That's how I knew you'd be here. Your receptionist told me you'd be at the gym."

What was Jody doing giving a complete stranger my whereabouts? She was always so trusting of everyone. Maybe I needed to give her the stranger-danger talk.

I wasn't going to tell Nick I was miffed, though. "Right. So, you just happen to be a member *and* have your kit with you?"

He dipped his head as if explaining something to a child. "It's the best gym close to both our offices. Why wouldn't I be a member?"

He was such a liar. I bet he'd joined on the spot. A discreet conversation with the receptionist when I left would soon settle it. If he wanted to waste his money that was his business, because frankly, I'd run out of energy to argue with him.

Carl was standing in a corner, stamping his feet like a bull and clapping his hands. "Everyone got what they need?"

"I'll get us some gloves," said Nick, before jogging toward where the equipment was piled in a corner.

I could still make a run for it. But something about Nick's demeanor had changed, a bit like it had at Jessica's gig. He'd stopped busting my arse about hassling Marcie in the piano shop. Why?

The only way to find out was to ask. And I'd feel a hell of a lot more comfortable having that discussion in my regular clothes rather than the sweaty Lycra I was currently rocking. The sooner we got down to our Marcie negotiations, the sooner I'd be interviewing her.

Nick came back with gloves. Was he serious? "You want to finish the class?"

"I find it very cathartic—don't you?"

"Are we actually going to hit each other?"

He grinned. "No. That's what we've got pads for." He handed me a wedge of blue Styrofoam. It looked like a book-shaped flotation device, the kind we had at school when we were learning to swim.

Next, he handed me a pair of red gloves. "These look like the right size for you."

I tried to take the gloves from him, but he stopped me. "I know you're angry with me, and you'd like nothing better than to knock my lights out, but you do know how to do this, right?"

"What do you mean?"

"Do you know how to put on a boxing glove?" He didn't wait for me to answer. "Make sure you tuck your thumb under your fingers, otherwise you'll break it."

Christ, that would be just my luck.

He dropped the gloves to the floor, then took my hand, startling me.

"What are you doing?"

His hand was cool against mine. Without saying a word, he folded my thumb against my palm and curled my fingers over my thumb joint.

"That's how to make a fist." He picked up a glove and held it out for me, his eyes fixed on what he was doing. I slipped my hand in, and he tightened the Velcro strap.

"How does that feel?"

"Tight," I said.

"Good. It's supposed to." He handed me the left glove. "Can you manage?"

Of course I could—

Wait. How was I supposed to put the other glove on with no opposable thumb? Come to think of it, why did boxing gloves even have a separate bit for the thumb—you couldn't move the damn thing.

"Are you going to tell me what you're doing here, Nick?" I said, buying time.

"I told you—I swung by your office and your receptionist told me Tuesday was your gym night," he said. "Lucky for me you're a creature of habit."

He made it sound like such an insult, and I nearly told him as much, but I suddenly had a eureka moment about getting the other glove on. I jammed it between my knees and triumphantly slid my hand in.

"So, you've used your amazing powers of deduction to track me down, because, you know, God forbid you email or phone."

"I've left messages—you're the one choosing to ignore me."

Oops. I'd walked straight into that one.

"Okay, we're here now. What do you want?"

He kept his gaze locked on my left hand and gestured for me to give him my hand, which I dutifully did. He pulled the glove fully up and tightened the strap. Funny, I'd thought I'd feel powerful with boxing gloves on, but I felt strangely vulnerable.

Nick keeping me in suspense about what he wanted only added to my unease. *What the hell was he after?*

Carl's voice sliced through the thumping music. He was standing next to us. "You all okay here? Do you need any help?"

The answer to that question was most definitely yes, but I was too concerned with finishing my conversation with Nick.

"We're good," I said.

"Great, let's see some punches."

Shit, he was going to stand here and watch.

Nick readied the pad in front of his chest. I swung my arm out and connected with it. It made a feeble "pfff" sound. "Great attempt!" said Carl. "But maybe I could give you some pointers."

A crack echoed around the gym. It sounded like a gunshot, but was more likely someone's fist making contact with bone. Possibly a nose.

"I'll be back in a mo," he said, worry clouding his features.

With Carl gone, I could grill Nick.

"You were saying?"

"Keep your arm parallel to the floor," said Nick.

"You want to teach me how to punch?" He was unbelievable.

"When you do it right, it will feel so good."

He sounded like he had a fetish.

I swung again. This time I made better contact with the pad, making Nick take a step back.

"Impressive," he said. "One more, and this time keep your shoulder low." He pressed his palm against the side of my ribcage. "It will engage the lats."

His hand barely made contact but it felt oddly intimate. He really was fixated on teaching me how to hit properly.

I planted my feet firmly on the sprung floor, relaxed my shoulders, and threw another punch.

Thwack. My arm vibrated all the way up to my jaw. Nick was propelled two steps back.

"How did that feel?"

I grinned uncontrollably, trying to find the right word. "Pretty good."

Nick nodded. "Let's keep going."

I swung my arm, and each time my gloved fist made a satisfying thud against the pad. I was getting into the swing of it, because I threw three punches in quick succession that made Nick recoil and drop the pad to the floor.

He shrugged. "You're imagining my face, I take it."

I smiled. "You're right, that feels amazing. *Now* will you tell me what you're really here for?"

He took my hands in his. "First, let's take these gloves off."

I let him. When I was safely glove-free, he put his hands squarely on my shoulders and looked me straight in the eye.

"Can you get me a date with Jessica Honey?"

12

THAT DON'T IMPRESS
ME MUCH

WE'D SHOWERED AND CHANGED AND were sitting side
by side at the gym bar. My post-exercise high was messing with my
hormones because Nick's aftershave was distracting me like catnip; a
woody-berry scent that I'd never smelled on anyone else. I inched my
seat away from him in an attempt to control the flood.

The man had some proper biceps on him, a fact I'd clocked when
we'd been sparring. He was broad-shouldered too.

Dawn was right: there was something old-school Hollywood about
him. He had a surfeit of masculinity that you didn't come across very
often. But he wore it subtly. He wasn't my type, of course, just like I'd
never go for a Jonny Delaney or a Harry Styles, but I could see why
Marcie might like having him around. Marcie, it turned out, was the
reason he wanted to get close to Jessica.

"They toured together ten years ago," he was explaining. "Marcie
didn't usually have much to do with her support bands, but she saw a
kindred spirit in Jess and took her under her wing. But they fell out, and
Marcie always regretted it. When I told her she was touring again, she
asked me to approach Jess to see if she was willing to mend those bridges."

"What did Jess do to piss her off?"

Nick shook his head. "Nothing. It was Marcie that let Jess down."

I couldn't believe what I was hearing. "*Marcie* wants to beg forgiveness from *Jess*? From all those years ago? What on earth happened that could still be bothering her?"

Nick met my eye. "I can't divulge that."

Of course he couldn't. "Why can't you talk to Jess directly?"

"I've tried, but she won't have anything to do with Marcie or people linked to her. Including me. We've never actually met, but she's rejected every request I've made through Pinnacle for a meeting."

"So what do you want me to do about it?"

"Introduce me to her as a friend of yours."

This was starting to feel a bit far-fetched. "Let me get this straight. You need to talk to her, but she can't know you're Marcie's publicist?"

"Exactly. Invite me along the next time you go out with her. You're friends, right?"

"She's a friend of a friend." Why was I being so specific?

"I think I saw you together that night. Tall guy with blond hair?"

"Simon, yes."

"Simon seemed pretty friendly with Jess."

"What do you mean?"

Nick was looking at me curiously. "That they seemed like friends. What else could I mean?"

Jess and Simon's rapport was a sore spot. Guess I'd just admitted as much to him.

"Yeah, they're friends."

"He's not your boyfriend, is he?"

"No. Of course not."

"So could you arrange a casual meeting, with a few people around, where I'd get a chance to chat to her?"

"But we'd be lying about who you are."

"If it gets you face time with Marcie would it really be a problem for you?"

At last, something concrete. "You'll give me Marcie?"

He nodded. "But you still need to do right by Hands Down."

"Meaning?"

"You need to personally interview Jonny Delaney."

Why did I get the feeling that Nick was enjoying this?

♪

The only small fly in Nick's request was that it meant I had to spend time with Jessica, or rather, Simon and Jessica together. She was always so flirty with him, and it rubbed me the wrong way. But I guess in the big scheme of things, it was a small price to pay.

At home that night, I ate leftover moussaka and scrolled through Instagram. Jess had posted something about another gig in London tomorrow night.

Okay, I could deal with that. Maybe a few drinks backstage, either before or after, nothing too intense. Nick could cast his magic spell on her, or whatever, and that would be that.

I texted Nick with the details, and he replied immediately, telling me he'd meet me there.

What to tell Simon, though? Should I mention Nick's real intentions or keep quiet about them? I'd ring him and play it by ear.

"Always a pleasure to hear your voice, Frixie," he said, which gave me a little buzz.

"What are you up to?"

"Boring work stuff. I've got a million spreadsheets to go through."

"I noticed Jess was playing another gig, and I've got a friend who was a fan back in the day who'd like to come."

"That's great! I was thinking of going too. It would be great to go together. You must have liked her the other night then?"

"She was pretty good."

"You know, it's amazing how many people loved Rydell. I'll see if Jess can put us all on the guest list. She told me off last time for not telling her we were coming. What's your friend's name?"

"Nick," I replied. No need to give second names.

Simon had gone quiet. Was he weirded out that I wanted to bring a bloke?

"It will be nice to meet your friend."

We agreed on a time to meet and I hung up.

Seems I'd made my decision quite easily—I'd be keeping Nick's identity a secret. I felt a smidgeon of guilt. Was I pimping out Jess to get to Marcie?

No, I decided. I was trying to heal a rift between the two of them. My motives were pure.

Sort of.

At the office the next day, I forced myself to work on a feature I'd been putting off. It had started off as a lighthearted piece about classic T-shirts, featuring album covers that had seeped into mainstream culture: the Rolling Stones' "tongue and lips," the Clash's Mick Jones smashing his guitar into the floor, the red and blue circles of the Who's *Quadrophenia*. But somewhere along the way, Mike had insisted we needed to add links to where readers could buy the T-shirts, and now the whole thing had turned into a messy advertorial that made me want to pull my hair out. Then Mike had told me how much the advertisers had paid to be featured, and I'd had to do my hair-pulling in private.

It was a long and frustrating day, and I wasn't exactly jumping up and down with joy at this evening's offerings—another Jess gig. I'd been so uncomfortable with what I'd worn at the last concert that this time I made sure to dress appropriately.

I went home to shower then changed into yoga-style linen trousers and a black vest. I blasted my hair dry, then applied mascara and eyeliner.

I stopped to study myself in the hall mirror before I left.

Maybe I'd overdone it with the MAC paint pot. I hadn't worn eyeliner this thick for ages. Why had I felt the urge tonight? A memory of something Simon had said years ago surfaced. He'd said he liked the fifties look. I was tempted to scrub it all off—the last thing I wanted was to look like I was trying too hard. But dammit, that tick along my upper lids was *perfect*. And anyway, it was almost eight and I needed to get going.

Simon had put my name on the guest list and suggested we meet backstage before the gig. I'd sent the same details to Nick, except I'd told him to come twenty minutes later.

The gig was in Camden again. A poster outside listed the artists on tonight—Jess's name wasn't among them, but I guess she must have been a last-minute addition.

Instead of going via the front, I detoured down the alley next to the club, to the stage door. The smell of urine reared up from the pavement. Was the hem of my trousers trailing in stale wee? Gross. I tiptoed as fast as I could to the threshold.

A goateed man in a Motörhead T-shirt was guarding the entrance. He held up his hand. "Have you got a pass, love?"

"I'm Zoë Frixos—I'm on the guest list."

"No, you're not."

"Try Simon Baxter."

"Is that name supposed to mean something?"

I frowned. This was odd, but not totally unexpected. Simon wasn't the most organized of people. I was obviously going to have to go via the front.

"She's with me, Stan."

I turned round to see Nick. He was early. And how had he managed to get into Goatee Stan's good graces so quickly?

Stan held the door open and gestured for us to go through.

"After you," said Nick.

I swept through, feeling confused. We went down a concrete staircase, which opened into a dimly lit corridor, and claustrophobia gripped my gut. I quickened my step—the faster I found the dressing room, the better.

"You don't think it's odd that the doorman didn't know who Simon was?" said Nick, who was close behind.

I shrugged, not caring if he could see me or not. The corridor was getting narrower, and my throat felt like it was closing.

"There's an obvious reason that you haven't quite grasped yet," he continued, from the shadows. "Neither Simon nor Jess is coming tonight."

I spun round.

Nick didn't stop fast enough, and my forehead hit his chin. For a second, I saw stars and started tumbling backward. But before I could fall, his hands were around my shoulders, pulling me toward him.

Woozy, I found my face flattened against his lapel. Embarrassing. I took a couple of steps back. "What did you say?"

He looked at me like I was speaking a foreign language—and not one of the seventeen he could speak. "Fine, skip the part where you thank me for saving you from cracking your head on the concrete floor."

Really? He was calling out my etiquette? "I wouldn't have run into you if you hadn't been pressed up against my arse."

"I wasn't pressed up against your arse." He said the words slowly. A bit distastefully, actually. Like my arse wasn't worthy of his time. "You stopped suddenly."

I wasn't in the mood to argue, partly because he had a point, but also because Simon had apparently canceled without telling me.

"I'd know if the gig had been called off," I said.

"Jess is on the other side of London."

I rolled my eyes. "How would you know that? Have you got a tracker on her?"

"I know a couple of people who are following her movements."

"What? Like stalkers or private eyes?"

He smiled. "No, of course not. Photographers. She's a bit of a minor celebrity."

"Paparazzi? Really?"

Nick tilted his head to one side, amused at my naïveté. "That's the power of reality television. She's got half a million Instagram followers, but not one of them realizes she's also a talented musician."

"The internet is full of idiots," I muttered, pulling out my phone. I scrolled to Simon's name. But when I tried to dial, I had no signal. Probably just as well. We wouldn't be able to hear each other. The muffled vibrations from a last-minute sound check were bleeding through the walls, and raucous male laughter was coming from a room nearby.

"Come and hear it from the horse's mouth."

"Simon's here?"

"No, the club manager."

"Oh."

Nick turned down a corridor to his left and nodded at me to follow. Within a few steps, the passage gave out to an office where a man with a long gray beard was sitting behind a desk.

"Tell her what you told me, Jim." How the hell was Nick on first-name terms with everyone? Had he been staking out the place since yesterday?

Jim looked up and steepled his hands. The tip of his little finger was missing. I tried not to stare. "They rang half an hour ago and canceled. Do you know them?"

I nodded.

"Well, you can tell them they're not getting their deposit back. And I'm keeping the buns."

Buns? I thought I'd misheard him, then he pointed to a pink-ribboned basket of pastries doing its best to brighten a dusty-gray filing cabinet.

"Got it," said Nick. "No refund, and the baked goods are impounded."

He nudged me, trying to guide me out, but I held fast. I needed to know something.

"Did they give a reason for canceling?"

"She's unwell. Food poisoning or something."

Well, that explained why I hadn't heard anything. I felt marginally less slighted.

Jim waved us out, and I followed Nick as he steered us into the next room.

I blinked as he turned on the light, and I realized we were in a small dressing room. A bare bulb struggled to banish the gloom, but it was better than nothing. And there wasn't much to illuminate: a fire extinguisher on the wall and a dark stain on the carpet tiles.

Nick held out his hand. "Pain au chocolat?"

I hadn't seen him take it. "No, thanks."

He finished it in three bites, then brushed the flakes from his hands.

"Maybe you should go back and distract him so I can get another one."

I didn't respond. Instead, I checked my phone again. Now, I had reception—and two texts from Simon. The first apologizing and the next suggesting we all meet up in a restaurant. Wait, wasn't Jess supposed to have had food poisoning?

I asked Simon in a text. The reply came back almost immediately.

"What is it?" said Nick.

"Simon says Jess had stage fright."

"Not food poisoning?"

"I guess that's the excuse they gave to the club."

My phone buzzed again. This time, Simon had sent the name of the restaurant where they were.

"Do you like French food?" I asked Nick.

"Why?"

"Simon's suggesting we meet them at a place by Piccadilly. If you still want to meet Jess?"

"A cozy meal, just the four of us? Won't that be a bit date-ish?"

He was right, and then it suddenly occurred to me that if Nick wanted to keep his connection to Marcie under wraps, then we needed to work out our cover stories.

"What do we say when they ask who you are? A friend from work?"

Nick seemed to think for a moment. "Let's tell them I work in your legal department."

"We don't have one."

He frowned. "What do you do when you've got a legal issue?"

"We use an outside firm."

"Okay, I can work for them."

"Why are you dead set on being a lawyer?"

"I trained as one. If anyone asks anything, I'll be able to fob them off."

"What's wrong with just saying you're a journalist? You know plenty about that."

"I was hoping to keep the lies to a minimum."

Really? He was suddenly developing a guilt complex? More likely he thought journalism was beneath him. *Arrogant prick.*

"Okay, we'll say you're a lawyer. God forbid they think you're a lowly hack."

Nick's guilt complex must have been contagious, because in the taxi on the way to Piccadilly I started worrying that I knew nothing about him and that it might be glaringly obvious we weren't actually friends—or even colleagues.

"So, what sort of stuff do you do in your free time?"

Nick was in the process of straightening his cuffs—was he actually wearing cuff links again?—and suddenly stopped.

"You're asking me if I have any hobbies?"

"It needs to look like we know each other."

"I wasn't being facetious. I was just making sure I understood you."

"Here's a question I always ask when I'm interviewing: what's something you like to do that I'd never guess? So none of that going for long walks, watching movies, and reading."

"Zoë, have you been checking out my Tinder profile?"

"Fine, don't answer me."

"Okay, here's something I don't tell many people. I've got three hobbies that all begin with the letter K. Care to take a guess?"

"What the hell starts with a K?"

"Knitting."

"You knit?"

"Is that weird?"

I peered at him. Was he taking the piss?

He smiled. "No, I don't knit. But I was just proving the point that a lot of activities start with the letter K."

"Riiight."

"Kick-boxing, karting, karaoke, karate, kung fu, kayaking, kite-flying."

"Who flies kites for a hobby apart from kids and Mary Poppins?"

"Okay, so you've ruled out knitting and flying kites. What about the others?"

He opened his mouth, but I stopped him. "I bet it's none of those." I thought for a second. "Kissograms, kleptomania, and kerb-crawling."

"Wow. You don't think much of me."

"You really wanted me to guess? I bet you're a martial arts nut. Karate, kung fu, and that other one you mentioned. Am I right?"

"Kick-boxing, kayaking, and karaoke."

"*Karaoke?*"

"Karaoke."

"Singing to a backing tape? In public?"

He shook his head. "Don't say you've never done it."

"I've never done it."

"You're missing out."

"I doubt it."

"I do a very moving version of Aerosmith's 'Angel.'"

Was he serious? "You're an Aerosmith fan?"

"Unfashionable, I know. But *Permanent Vacation* is a great album." He looked at me. "Let me guess. You only like their early stuff—the Columbia years."

"I get it, you think I'm a music snob—but actually, I agree with you. *Permanent Vacation* is a great album. The steel drums on the title track are a stroke of genius."

He looked surprised. "Well, who'd have thought we had something in common?"

He seemed genuinely pleased, like we'd discovered we were connected by an old friend. It wasn't such a big deal. Loads of people liked Aerosmith. But it was something I'd noticed over the years— music's peculiar magic to forge bonds between the unlikeliest people.

A few moments later, the taxi pulled up to the restaurant and Nick jumped out to pay the driver through the window. I tried to thrust some money at him, but Nick waved me away.

"Thanks," I said, once the taxi had gone. "But let me give you half the fare."

"You don't need to do that." He gestured toward the restaurant. "Shall we?"

13
ELEGANTLY WASTED

IT WASN'T A RESTAURANT I'D been to before, or even heard of. It was an upmarket French brasserie called En Grande Tenue, and the people going in and out looked moneyed and swanky. Guarding the entrance was a doorman, but we must have looked moneyed (Nick) and swanky (me) because he nodded us through.

My heart sank when I saw we needed to go down into another basement. Did Jess choose these places on purpose? The reception area was dimly lit, the walls lined with red velvet, topped by a low ceiling. The inside of my mouth was as parched as sandpaper, but I tried to swallow the panic down.

Then Nick's hand brushed my elbow, guiding me toward a door, and we emerged into a broad corridor, flanked by a cloakroom. It was brighter here but reeked of incense and almost shook from the thud of music, which seemed to just be a bass line.

The woman at the maître d's desk gave us a glossy smile. "*Bonsoir madame, monsieur.*"

Nick fired off some rapid French.

I blinked. My French class felt like an age ago, but I remembered enough to be able to tell that Nick sounded *properly* French. I mean, I knew he spoke all these languages, but he sounded native, not just fluent.

He spoke again, this time more slowly. "*Nous avons une réservation au nom de...*" He turned to me expectantly.

Sorry, was I supposed to join in? "Erm, Simon Bax-*tair*."

The hostess checked her list, then nodded and asked us to follow her. It was weird—Nick's vowels had always suggested minor public school, but I was suddenly curious about his upbringing.

"Where did you go to school?" I asked, as we were led through an archway painted in gold leaf.

Nick paused momentarily, nearly causing a waiter to go into the back of him. "I went to an international school near Nice." He sounded stiff, but then he seemed to relax. "Lessons were in French and English—some Italian and Spanish too. I can teach you all the cool swear words."

The conversation stopped as we entered a huge dining room. Mapped around us were at least a hundred tables, all draped with white tablecloths that reached the marble floor. Piercing the din of voices was the chime of cutlery and the chink of glasses.

Even from fifty feet away, I could see Simon and Jess sitting side by side, their heads bowed deep in conversation, oblivious to the world.

Simon was wearing a white shirt with the sleeves rolled up. His face lit up when he spotted me, and my stomach did a little flip.

"Frixie, you made it!"

Jess was sitting next to him, still dressed in her stage gear. Another off-the-shoulder top, this time in red. When she leaned forward to shake our hands, a silver pendant necklace swung against her cleavage.

I made the introductions. Neither Jess nor Simon asked any questions as to how I knew Nick or what he did for a living. They took my "This is Nick" as a simple statement of fact and moved on to other things.

"Are you okay, Jess?" I asked, mainly because it was the polite thing to say.

"I'm grand, petal," she said. She looked fine—no trace of nerves. Her eyes were a little unfocused, but that was probably down to a couple of drinks.

"Could you not go through with the gig?"

Out of Jess's eyeline, Simon frantically started to shake his head.

It appeared that Jess's stage fright was not something he should have shared with me.

She scrunched up her face. "They'd sold a grand total of seventeen tickets. I'm not going to play an empty club."

I nodded sympathetically, hoping she hadn't noticed my gaffe. Her tipsiness probably worked in my favor.

"We've just ordered a bottle of wine," said Simon. He poured a glass for me, but Nick declined.

"Nick must prefer the hard stuff," said Jess. "And I don't blame him. Tequila would be excellent right now."

"I'll stick to mineral water," he replied.

Jess made a face. We weren't off to the best start.

"So, Zoë." She smiled toothily. "What have you been up to all these years?"

Had she forgotten that we'd recently seen each other?

"I told you, Jess, she's the editor of *Re:Sound*," said Simon—with a definite hint of pride. "The most influential woman in music."

Nick coughed. "Is that so?"

Nick could fuck off. So what if Simon was happy about my career trajectory?

Simon didn't take kindly to Nick's comment either. He looked at him rather sternly, and in something not unlike a schoolteacher's tone, said: "So, what do you do, Nick?"

"Well, when I'm not moonlighting as a kissogram, I'm a lawyer."

Jess leaned forward. "Kissogram? Is that a euphemism for male escort?"

How drunk *was* Jess?

Nick took it in his stride, though. "The kissogram's a private joke between me and Zoë."

Jess gave him a flirty smile. "Shame. I'd hire you."

Simon gave me a wide-eyed stare that I couldn't quite read. Was he embarrassed or amused? "So what type of lawyer are you, Nick?" he said, wisely moving the conversation on.

This was Nick's chance to say something bland about contracts or whatnot.

"I specialize in defamation," said Nick, brightly. "But trying to keep Zoë on the right side of the libel laws is quite a job." He smiled a big, fat fake smile.

"Ooh, tell us more," said Jess, leaning forward.

I couldn't believe what I was hearing. "He's exaggerating."

"Well, that review of Hands Down was a bit iffy," he said, smile still firmly plastered on.

"But perfectly justified." I added a fake smile of my own. "You and your great legal brain agreed. Otherwise you wouldn't have let us run it, would you?"

"You reviewed Hands Down?" said Simon. "That's not the kind of stuff you usually cover, on account of they're shit."

I could have kissed him. "First and last time," I said.

I silently dared Nick to contradict me and glanced over at him, but

I guess even he realized that a thirty-plus man defending Hands Down would raise *way* too many questions.

Fortunately, a waiter appeared with menus, which put an end to the discussion. He rattled off the day's specials, but I wasn't really listening. Nick was being an arse, and it was ruining my appetite. Maybe Jess's suggestion to crack open the tequila wasn't such a bad one.

"So, how do you all know each other?" Nick asked, when the waiter had gone.

"Oh, these two have known each other forever," said Jess confidently. "Practically brother and sister."

I caught Simon's eye. Was that Jessica's assessment, or was that how he characterized our relationship too?

Nick looked at me for clarification. "We used to live next door to each other," I said. Then, probably just to annoy Jess: "We were best friends growing up."

"Simon and I played together at uni," said Jess to Nick.

"Before the big time came calling," added Simon.

"Of course," said Nick. "You toured with Marcie Tyler. How was that?"

I had to hand it to him—Nick had steered the conversation in the direction he needed pretty fast.

"Well, just between us, it was a nightmare," said Jess.

"How so?" I asked, my curiosity genuinely piqued.

"We're not going to find this splashed across *Re:Sound* next month, are we?" She was joking, but there was an edge to her voice, which was fair enough.

Simon sprang to my defense. "Of course not, Jess. You can trust Zoë."

She flicked a glance at Nick, whose expression remained impassive. Evidently, she trusted him without anyone having to vouch for him. The perks of having a pretty face.

"Marcie and the guy she was seeing kept having screaming matches. Honestly, it was a miracle she had a voice each night to sing with."

"She sounds like quite a fiery customer," said Simon.

"I think the words you're looking for are diva bitch," said Jess.

I bristled and I swear Nick bristled too. Was it because Jess had just insulted his girlfriend?

"Don't say that about Marcie," said Simon. "Zoë idolizes her."

"Jess can say what she likes," I said, stiffly.

"Was that Benedict Bailey?" Nick asked.

Jess frowned. "God, how do you remember his name?"

"He was a pretty famous guitarist in his own right," he said. "He came onstage with you one night, didn't he?"

She narrowed her eyes. "How would you know that? Are you some kind of stalker-ish fan?"

"I was at that gig."

She looked at Nick disbelievingly. "It was in San Francisco."

"I was living in the States at the time."

"Whereabouts?" asked Simon.

Was Nick telling the truth about working in the States? Was he about to get grilled on it now? "On the West Coast—I was doing an MBA at Berkeley."

Was that in addition to the law degree? I wanted to ask, but it wasn't really in my interests to question him.

"Right," said Simon, who was obviously satisfied. Then he turned back to Jess. "Wasn't that the tour I was supposed to come out and meet you on?"

"Yeah, the tour got canceled afterward," said Jessica. "We were just starting to get airplay in the States. It was a bad time."

I raised my eyebrows expectantly. "What happened?"

"Benedict died," said Nick. "Motorbike accident."

"How do you know so much about it?" said Jessica sharply.

I was pretty surprised that Nick was offering information that Jess would have provided anyway. He was sucking at all this deception stuff.

"Benedict was a rare talent. The music he and Marcie wrote together was amazing," said Nick. "The *Stars* album."

It was the first time I'd heard Nick sound like a genuine fan. It was my favorite Marcie album too.

"It's a great record," I said.

"Zoë's one of the few people I've met who loves Marcie Tyler as much as I do."

There was something behind that statement that I couldn't quite put my finger on. It didn't help that he made it sound like Marcie fans were rare. Like we were two trainspotters cast to the edges of society because no one understood our love for diesel engines.

"Loads of people like Marcie Tyler," said Simon, with a touch of defensiveness.

"Exactly," I added.

"When you meet her, like I have," said Jess casually, "you realize she's not that special. Even her voice was disappointing. Autotuned to the max every night."

"Interesting," said Nick. "They say meeting your heroes is always a bad idea." He sounded amused. How was he not pissed off to hear Marcie trashed like this?

It was taking every ounce of my willpower not to—*oh, fuck it*. "Have you not got anything positive to say about her?" I said to Jess.

Her eyes were still struggling to focus, but when she looked at me, I swear it was with pity. She smiled. "Let me think… She had good taste in men. For an older man, Benedict was sexy as hell."

"You guys had great chemistry onstage," said Nick.

"Are you implying I shagged him, Nick?" She giggled. "I'll never tell," she whispered, then winked, which contradicted her vow of silence as loudly as if she'd given us a rundown of times, places, and preferred positions.

Nick had told me that Marcie had wronged Jess, but it was becoming increasingly obvious that Jess had not been an angel either.

Nick leaned forward conspiratorially. "How was Benedict those last few nights of the tour? Were the arguments with Marcie as bad as ever?"

"Are you from a tabloid or something?" Simon hadn't said much so far, but it was like he'd finally smelled a rat. He looked at me, waiting for an answer.

Nick held his hands up in the air. "Sorry, I was just curious."

He'd pushed too hard and antagonized Jess. Could he not turn on a bit of charm? She'd flirted with him—all he had to do was flirt back. Was he really such a stiff?

Giggling from the next table distracted us. A couple of girls, or rather, grown women, were attempting to photograph Jess on their phones without her noticing, but they were doing a piss-poor job of it. When Jess clocked it, she grinned broadly—being the center of attention seemed to make her glow.

"It's so nice when actual fans want a picture. I can't abide it when the scumbag paparazzi do it. They're only interested in humiliating photos. I had one chasing me up Bond Street the other day," she said crossly. "I thought social media would put an end to the paparazzi."

Nick gave me a knowing look which said, *I told you.*

Jess didn't notice, though; she was too busy interacting with her fans. She waved them over. "Come and get a proper pic, ladies!"

A proper pic was a selfie, naturally. Each of them took about five turns to get a picture they were happy with, and it all took twice as long as it should have because they were telling Jess how great she looked: her lipstick, her hair, that darling little seahorse necklace that glistened under the lights.

Could she not see how self-centered and rude she was being? Simon raised his eyebrows when one of the women jostled him. I smiled in solidarity and he grinned back. For a moment, we were the only two people in the room.

I wasn't overly concerned with what Nick was doing while this was going on, but it dawned on me that he had turned to face in the opposite direction like he was embarrassed to be seen with us.

Jesus.

Yes, he was hiding his identity from Jess, but it wasn't as if the pics would go viral and expose him. And if he thought so, he was even more deluded about Jess's popularity than she was.

Jess noticed his reluctance to be photographed too. When her gushing fans were gone, she said to him: "Got a wife at home, Nick? Is that why you're avoiding the cameras?"

"I thought I saw someone I knew," he said.

"Oh?" said Jess.

"My wife," he deadpanned.

"Did you know he was married, Zoë?"

She thought she was such a comedian. "He was joking," I said.

"So, how long have you been going out?"

I blinked. Did she mean me and Nick? Her watery eyes were wandering from him to me, so I guess she was addressing us.

"Jess—" said Simon, but she didn't let him finish.

"They're so cute together, don't you think?" She was in a world of her own. "They both have that dark, Mediterranean look."

I was about to put the record straight, but then our starters arrived and the moment passed.

"This looks amazing," said Simon, eyeing his scallops. My salad seemed to feature eight different types of tomato.

"*Bon appétit*," said Nick, before picking up his knife and fork. Only Jess didn't react; she hadn't seemed to notice her food. She'd gone pale and was staring straight ahead, like she'd seen the ghost of dead guitarists past.

"Are you all right?" I said, but I didn't get to finish the sentence. Jess clamped one hand on her mouth, pushed Simon to one side, and threw up into the ice bucket.

I froze, transfixed, as much by the sounds she was making as the sight of her. She sounded like a weightlifter hefting a barbell that weighed a ton.

A hush descended, which only made Jess's moans echo louder. Simon, bless him, was the first to react. He put his hand on Jessica's back and asked if she was okay.

It was a bit of a moot question, and one she was too busy to answer, as a second wave of her stomach contents splattered into the ice bucket. With a bottle of wine and all the ice cubes, I was impressed nothing had spilled out. If you're going to hurl in a Michelin-starred restaurant, that was the way to do it. It was pretty rock and roll.

People at other tables had swiveled round to get a better look at the entertainment offered at ours.

I felt bad for Jess. I mean, it was self-inflicted—she'd clearly drunk way too much—but whenever anyone threw up in public I always had a "there-but-for-the-grace-of-God" moment.

"Maybe we should get Jess out of here," I said.

Simon gave me a grateful glance and helped her to her feet. "I'll get her home," he said.

It was the right instinct and incredibly noble, but I was still a bit crestfallen. We hadn't talked properly; I'd hoped we could ditch Jess and Nick after dinner and the two of us could go somewhere quieter afterward, but that obviously wasn't going to happen.

A couple of waiters appeared, and once they'd ascertained that Jess wasn't in immediate need of the ice bucket, they magicked it away. We'd have to tip them extra for that.

"I'll settle the bill," said Nick.

"Tell us how much we owe you," said Simon, who was now standing and supporting Jess with both arms.

Nick nodded, and Simon and Jess hobbled out. I thought it only fair to wait with Nick.

"Well, that was…a surprising turn of events," I said. "And a little bit funny."

"Alcoholism is a disease."

He'd said it with a straight face. Was he serious? "The girl had a couple of drinks too many," I replied. "That doesn't make her an alcoholic… And don't tell me you've never overdone it," I added. "The holier-than-thou act doesn't suit you."

"Of course I've overdone it before. But I choose my time and place."

He was starting to wind me up now. "Look, as far as Jessica knew, she was having dinner and drinks with friends, so stop being a Judgey McJudgey Pants. It's not like she threw up at a palace garden party."

I reached for my drink, then stopped myself. Nick's mineral water seemed to mock my half-empty glass of wine.

"Do I have to remind you that right now, she was supposed to be onstage in Camden?" he said. "Granted, it's not Wembley Stadium, but if she wants to build a following, she can't treat her fans like that. This business is not forgiving."

He had a point, which I charitably conceded by ignoring it.

Luckily, a waiter arrived with the bill to distract us. Nick whipped out his credit card before I'd unbuckled my bag.

"Let's at least split it," I said, not wanting to add to his God complex.

"You arranged this evening for me; I'm more than happy to pay."

Part of me knew it was a nice gesture, but most of me felt he was rubbing it in. First the taxi and now this.

I peeked a glance at the total. *Wow.* Three figures, and they'd only charged for starters. I should probably be a bit more grateful that Nick's expense account was soaking it up.

He put his card back in his wallet. "So, when are we going to do this again?"

"You want to do this again?"

"It's part of our deal, don't forget."

I hadn't forgotten, but maybe it was time to remind him of what he owed me. "I want Marcie for the September issue. And that means I need to sit down with her in the next fortnight."

Nick paused. "You need to interview Jonny first. You, not one of your underlings."

I rolled my eyes. "Seriously?"

He shrugged.

Depressed, I drained my glass. Nick's judgey eyes following my every move. He could sod off.

"Thanks for paying," I told him, getting up. "I'll talk to Simon and try to arrange something soon."

14

HEART OF GLASS

THE NEXT MORNING, I MESSAGED Simon to ask about Jess. He texted back saying she'd been okay apart from getting into a shouting match with a photographer who'd been waiting outside the restaurant and had snapped her unawares. But he'd found a taxi and had gotten her home safe and sound. My fingers itched to text again and ask what time *he'd* gotten home, but I stopped myself; he would have surely seen it for the pretext it was—to double-check he hadn't stayed the night at her flat. Not that he'd given me any reason to suspect anything, but my antennae when it came to Simon had a habit of tuning into phantom signals.

With heroic self-restraint I instead texted him to ask if he fancied coming to a fancy-dress party. His enthusiastic reply carried me smiling all the way to my tube stop at Bond Street:

YESSSS!!

♪

I wasn't going straight to the office today; I was meeting Alice at her dress fitting to choose a dress of my own for the wedding. She'd chosen turquoise for the bridal party, but each of us was free to pick our own style to match our taste and body shape. She was democratic like that.

I found the right shop in a warren of streets north of Bond Street and pushed open the door. But before I could charge through to where Alice was waiting, a surprisingly strong female arm stopped me in my tracks.

"Shoes *off*!" came the accompanying voice.

Had I somehow walked through a magic portal that had transported me back to morning assemblies at Hazelwood Primary?

"Excuse me?"

"We have a shoes-off policy," came the curt reply. The sales assistant slash Head of Shoe Policy added a smile, but it did little to mask the irritation in her voice.

I toed off my Converse and padded over to Alice in my blue-and-white-striped socks. She kissed me hello and told me to take my time choosing a style.

"I want you to feel like a princess," she said, before floating into a changing room where an alarming amount of white fabric was waiting for her.

I'd never been a princess-y kind of girl. Unless you counted Princess Leia, who could kick arse with a blaster and ended up a general.

I listlessly ran my hand along the rail where a rainbow of shiny bridesmaids' dresses hung. Several pairs of eyes were following me nervously, although I'm not sure what the sales assistants feared I would do—zip out a can of spray paint and graffiti the damn things? I wasn't in the mood for this, so I picked a blue dress at random and trooped into an adjacent changing room. I shed my clothes and put on the dress, then turned to assess myself in the mirror.

It looked bloody awful—it flattened my chest, and the skirt was far too poufy—but I felt a duty to show Alice in case she loved it.

I stepped out, trying not to grimace, but when I saw Alice I stopped dead in my tracks.

Her gown was something else. Ivory satin sheathed in a layer of fine lace from head to toe. Tiny crystals and pearls sparkled on the bodice and matching full-length gloves completed the ensemble.

"Pete's going to burst into tears when he sees you," I said.

"Is it that bad?"

"I mean in a good way."

Alice smiled. "I know; I was joking." She checked her reflection from the side. "It's not too revealing, is it? The back's lower than I imagined."

"It's the most elegant dress I've ever seen." I suddenly had a lump in my throat. "You look beautiful."

She smiled and came to stand by me. "You look beautiful too." She tilted her head to one side. "Maybe with the right shoes?"

I was still wearing my stripy socks, but that wasn't the main issue. The full skirt would have transformed Alice into Audrey Hepburn, but the only movie star I resembled was Shirley Temple. All that was missing was the lollipop and hair bow. I looked bloody ridiculous.

I must have been scowling, because Alice suddenly asked: "Do you not like it, Zoë?"

I tried to relax my furrowed brow. "Sorry, Alice, I'm a bit tired this morning. I'm more than happy to wear this if you like it."

"I want you to be comfortable, Zoë, and I'm not sure you are." She reached over to the rail and pulled out a full-length dress. "Why don't you try this one? You're tall and it will look amazing on you."

She was holding an amorphous mass of pink shiny satin. "Ignore the color, obviously," she said. "Just try it on for the style."

I wasn't sure that style and this particular dress had ever been introduced, but I didn't want to disappoint Alice. "No problem," I said, taking the dress from her.

Back in the changing room, I unzipped the blue dress and peeled off my socks. The pink dress had annoying little eyelet hooks down one side which took half my thumbnail off as I unfastened them.

It had looked like a scrap of material on the hanger, but as I shimmied into the dress it transformed into something quite nice. More than nice, actually. I twirled in the mirror—was there a hint of Marilyn Monroe there? Or at the very least Madonna circa "Material Girl"?

I poked my head through the changing room curtains.

"You might have landed on a winner, Alice."

"Well, let's see you then."

Alice now had a veil on. It trailed behind her, reaching the floor and fluttering on an imperceptible breeze that made her look like she'd just stepped out of a perfume ad.

"Okay, now you're going to make me cry," I told her.

She smiled. "It looks good, doesn't it?"

I nudged her. "Glad you can finally see it."

"You look amazing too, Zoë. I knew a column dress would look great on you. You even pull off the hot pink."

I grinned. "I wouldn't go that far."

With my dress chosen remarkably easily, we went to grab a coffee. I say coffee, but Alice's digestive system was a caffeine-free zone, so it was a latte for me and a dandelion tea for her.

"That dress shop really scares me," Alice whispered as we sat at a nearby café sipping our drinks.

"Really? But you looked so serene."

"The first time I went, they insisted I wear gloves before I touched any dresses."

"You're joking."

Alice shook her head.

"God forbid you defile them with a fingerprint," I said.

"It helped having you there, Zoë. You never let people intimidate you. And you always know how to act in every situation."

Is that what she thought of me? "I feel intimidated sometimes," I confessed. "But I make sure I don't show it."

"Fake it till you make it?"

I smiled. "Alcohol sometimes helps." I was flattered that Alice thought I was some sort of Teflon-coated superwoman, but the truth was, lately, I'd been feeling more and more wrong-footed. And Simon was the reason why. Would it help talking to Alice? Her trusting eyes waited patiently. "I get into plenty of situations where I don't know what to do," I said. "I'm in the middle of one right now."

"Has this got anything to do with a certain someone called Simon?"

For a second, I panicked that my darling brother had told Alice I had feelings for Simon, but I'd never told Pete and he wasn't the world's most observant sibling.

"How did you guess?"

Alice smiled. "The pair of you have a fantastic energy. It's like you both glow when you're together."

I felt my cheeks redden. No one had ever said anything like that to me before. "Is it that obvious?"

"Only to someone who knows what to look for," she said. "What's the deal between you?"

My coffee must have been strong, because I suddenly felt my heart beating faster. "I've never met anyone who makes me feel like Simon does."

God, had I really just said that out loud?

Alice smiled. "Sounds like love to me."

I frowned. "But he's got no idea that I like him. I've never so much as hinted because I'm terrified he'll run a mile."

"But what if he doesn't, Zoë? What if he feels the same but is paralyzed by the same fears? Your friendship means a lot to both of you, but sometimes in life you just have to take a leap of faith."

"I feel like I've got myself into such a mess, though."

"What's happened?"

I found myself giving Alice a rundown of Nick's request to get close to Jess on behalf of Marcie, and how I'd lied to Simon about Nick's identity.

"The problem is, Nick wants me to organize another dinner. I hated lying to Simon, and I can't bear to do it again."

Alice took a sip of her tea. "Nick is holding you to ransom over this?"

I nodded. "Although God knows what other hoops he'll make me jump through next."

"Well, I can't vouch for Nick, but it's obvious that Simon genuinely cares for you. He'd understand that you had no choice. I think you should just come clean."

"And admit I lied?"

"I'm sure he'll understand."

"You make it sound so simple."

"Often the simplest solutions are the ones we forget to consider."

———

Alice was right. Why hadn't I seen it myself? Of course Simon would understand. As I walked back to my office, I rang him.

He picked up after the third ring. "And how is the lovely Frixiepants this morning?"

"I'm great, Si. How are you?"

"Excited as a puppy. I've been googling fancy-dress shops."

I laughed. "I had no idea you had such a dramatic streak."

"We need to get our costumes sorted early, or they'll only have crappy ones left. The last fancy-dress party I went to I had to go as a court jester. No one looks good in yellow and red stripes, Zoë. And my hat had fucking bells on."

I laughed. "Well, we'd better get organized, then."

"Glad you agree. Meet me outside Covent Garden tube at six o'clock," he said. "I'll take you on a magical mystery tour of London's best fancy-dress hire shop."

♪

Our jaunt to the fancy-dress shop could not have been more different from that morning's antiseptic expedition for bridal wear.

First of all, they were playing Pearl Jam when we entered the shop. I loved Eddie Vedder more than was healthy, but his was not the voice to serenade you while you rifled through a technicolor display of sparkly costumes. Someone here had a sense of humor, as well as excellent taste in music. "Where did you see *PJ Twenty*?" said Simon. He didn't need to ask *if* I'd seen the film made for Pearl Jam's twentieth anniversary.

"Westfield. You?"

"I went to Seattle especially," he said proudly.

"You lucky sod."

"I won't lie; it was all kinds of amazing. I thought about you all the way through."

I grinned. "Same."

A gray-bearded assistant shuffled toward us. "How can I help you today?" He was American, and when he smiled he displayed an impressive set of teeth. I'd pegged him at near retirement age, because of the slow way he moved, but up close he was probably barely fifty. He wore a leather waistcoat and faded jeans and had the air of someone doing a job they loved, rather than just to pay the bills.

"Are you Ray?" asked Simon.

The man nodded, and Simon extended his arm for a handshake. "I'm Simon Baxter, we spoke earlier on the phone."

Out came the healthy teeth again. "Simon! Great to meet a fellow Knicks fan."

"Zoë, meet Ray. Before he opened up this place, he used to be a roadie for—among others—Jethro Tull. How cool is that?"

I shook his hand. "You must have some amazing stories."

He winked. "You wouldn't believe half of them."

"I don't know, Ray," said Simon. "Zoë is the editor of *Re:Sound*. I reckon she's heard a few of them already."

Ray's eyebrows shot up. "Always great to meet folk who appreciate good music. They just don't make them like the Tull anymore."

He led the way to where his best stock was hanging. The clothes available weren't polyester mixes and naff netting; they were heavy velvets and finely sewn silks.

This was going to get rather expensive. But then Simon, as if he'd read my mind, whispered: "This is on me—to thank you for inviting me to meet your friends."

I was about to object, but Simon held up his hand to shush me. "No arguments."

"Feel free to browse," Ray told us, "although some people prefer to look through the catalog. It's quicker that way."

I thanked him and took the catalog he was offering.

"Can I get you a drink? I've got bourbon in the back."

"Bourbon would be grand," said Simon, before I had a chance to think about it. "How cool is this place?" he whispered after Ray had gone to get our drinks.

"The most fun I've ever had in a shop in my life," I said, grinning.

"Wait till you get a load of the costumes."

Simon wasn't wrong. There were so many to choose from, the first thing we did was narrow it down to ones that had a film theme. This still left us oodles of options, but made life easier because we'd think of a cool film and then check if the accompanying costume existed.

Uma Thurman's outfit from *Pulp Fiction* was popular, Ray told us, but Simon immediately nixed it as too plain. "It's just a white shirt and black pants," he pointed out.

"What's your favorite film?" asked Ray. I looked at Simon and we both giggled. "What's so funny?" said a bemused Ray.

"Well, we've got a *real* favorite film and one we quote when we're asked, to make us look cool and sophisticated," said Simon, whose tongue the bourbon had really loosened.

"For example, when asked, Zoë will say her favorite film is *Citizen Kane*. But only I know it's really *Grosse Pointe Blank*."

"And Simon will say his favorite film is *The Shawshank Redemption*," I explained, "but really it's also *Grosse Pointe Blank*."

He smiled at me, and heat spread from my toes to my ears. And that wasn't just the bourbon.

Ray scratched his head. "You guys sure like John Cusack. Not sure any of those films feature great costumes. Although *Grosse Pointe Blank* has a heck of a soundtrack."

We both agreed.

Ray frowned. "Unless you want to go as a convict, Simon?"

"Nah, we'll have to put our thinking caps on," he replied. I giggled again. "What?"

"Who says 'thinking caps'?"

Simon pretended to be offended. "I do."

I turned to Ray and smiled brightly. "Do you have any thinking caps?"

"I'll leave you kids to browse," he muttered, wandering off to the back room, no doubt in search of more bourbon.

The first costume I tried on was a tan leather jacket and chaps combo, complete with gun belt and cowboy hat.

"Who's that?" said Simon.

"Calamity Jane," I said. "She's cool."

"Agreed," he replied. "But something about the leather and all those tassels screams cheesy extra from *Nashville*—not what you're trying to project."

Annoyingly, he had a point.

Simon tried on his own cowboy outfit, which he somehow managed to pull off without looking like a country music reject. He was all set to go with it when another outfit caught my eye.

"Si, how about this one?" I held up a pair of brown leather trousers, cream shirt, and leather hat.

"Is that Indiana Jones?"

I nodded. "How cool would that be?"

"There's a whip too," he said. "Kinky."

I hadn't noticed it, and now I found myself blushing.

"We can find you something else," I said, pushing the hanger back onto the rail.

Simon's hand was warm on my arm. "Not so fast, Frixie."

He gave me a look that sent even more blood to my face. "Why don't we concentrate on you?" he said. "I saw a rather lovely Catwoman outfit a couple of rails back."

"That's just a black rubber catsuit."

"You say it like that's a bad thing."

This was not the time to mention how it would probably set my cystitis off, or be horribly unforgiving to the couple of extra pounds I carried. I needed to respond with something flirty.

"I do like cats."

Oh God. I'm so out of practice with this.

Simon laughed. "Very true."

We carried on searching through outfits, but as time went on, the niggle of guilt that had felt like a pebble in my shoe was starting to feel as big as Indy's boulder. I needed to talk to Simon, but didn't want to do it here, so on impulse I decided to just go with Dorothy from *The Wizard of Oz*.

Not the most exciting of outfits, but the ruby slippers sort of made up for it.

Ray rang up our chosen outfits, and Simon offered to pick everything up on Saturday morning so we didn't have to lug them around with us now.

"There's something I want to talk to you about," I told Simon as we stepped outside. "Have you got time for a quick drink?"

"That bourbon's gone straight to my head," he said. "Maybe a coffee would be better."

Another drink would have given me an extra dose of courage, but an Americano would have to do.

We found a nearby Starbucks, bought our drinks, and sat down.

"What's up, Frixie?"

My nerves were strung tight and I paused, trying to decide the best way forward—was the direct route best? "That night when I brought Nick along to meet Jess—I wasn't entirely truthful about who he was."

"What do you mean?"

Here goes nothing. "He's not a friend of mine. He's Marcie Tyler's publicist."

I watched Simon's reaction but his expression remained blank. Did he not know about the bad blood between Jess and Marcie?

"What did he want with Jess?"

"Jess and Marcie fell out ten years ago, and now Marcie wants to make amends. But Jess doesn't want anything to do with her, so Nick's hoping he can change her mind."

Simon frowned. "How well do you know this Nick character?"

The question took me by surprise. "Not that well, admittedly, but—"

"He told you Marcie wants to apologize to Jess?"

"Yes."

Simon rolled his eyes. "And you *believed* him?"

He was looking at me like I was being slow on the uptake. "I didn't have any reason to doubt him."

Anger flashed across his face. "They 'fell out'? Is that how he describes it? Marcie sacked Jess in the middle of their North American tour—and it ruined Jess's career."

What? "Are you sure, Simon?"

He laughed bitterly. "I was one of the first people she rang when it happened. I'd been due to fly over and see one of the West Coast gigs."

It bothered me to hear that the two of them had been in touch over the years. But I couldn't tell Simon that.

"I'm sorry to hear that, but…I've been in the business a while and I've learned to trust my instincts, and right now, they're telling me to believe Nick Jones."

He didn't respond. Were we really arguing about this? I tried another tack. "Nick's holding me to ransom. I need that Marcie interview, and this is my way of getting it."

"And to hell with anyone else's feelings?"

Simon's anger wasn't abating; if anything he was getting more wound up. His passion in defending Jess was starting to grate on my nerves.

"*Re:Sound* is in big trouble. This time next year we might not exist. We might not even make it till Christmas if we can't dramatically increase circulation and advertising revenue." I paused to swallow down a ball of emotion. I needed to stay calm. "The targets are nearly impossible, but this Marcie interview is my one hope of securing the future of the magazine. Marcie just wants to make things better with Jess. She's been through a lot over the last few months. She's detoxed and she's straightening out her life."

Simon shook his head. "You heard what Jess said at dinner that night. She screwed Marcie's boyfriend. She's not proud of the fact, but the point is, Marcie might still hold a grudge. It's not redemption she's after; it's revenge."

I couldn't believe what I was hearing. "What on earth are you talking about? What sort of revenge?"

"Making sure any comeback Jess attempts fails."

This was getting ridiculous. "And how exactly would Marcie do that?"

Simon rolled his eyes. "You tell me; you're the expert." Without waiting for me to respond, he went on. "Marcie's got the ear of a lot of industry people. I'm sure it would be easy enough to convince them not to give Jess another chance."

I would have laughed if I wasn't so angry. Jess's career was a speck of mud on Marcie's shoe. "If what you fear is true, then Marcie could wreak any revenge from a distance," I said. "But if she wants to get close to Jess it means her motives are good."

"Or maybe that's just what you want to believe of your precious Saint Marcie."

I jerked back. That was low. "I want to believe the best in people—why is that such a problem for you?"

He shook his head. "Because your unquestioning belief in Marcie might hurt Jess. *That's* my problem." I wanted to ask him why he seemed more concerned with Jess than with me, but he wasn't done speaking. "And don't pretend this is all some altruistic act to help Marcie heal. You're doing this for your own career."

That blow landed too. But this one I wasn't going to take lying down. "You're damn right I am. I've worked for ten years to get here, and if the magazine fails it's not just my career that goes down in flames, it's the jobs and livelihoods of all the people who work with me. But maybe that doesn't mean anything in your industry, where it's every trader for himself."

I was breathing hard, trying to contain my feelings.

Simon nodded slowly and stood up. "Well, thanks for putting me in my place."

He walked out, and I was too dazed to stop him.

How the fuck had this conversation spiraled out of control? Alice had been so sure Simon would understand.

He was wrong about Marcie having ulterior motives. I knew it in my bones. And I'd been right to stand up for her. It wasn't because I was some obsessed fan defending the saintly image of Marcie Tyler.

But my feelings had run higher for another reason: Simon had been so quick to side with Jess instead of hearing me out. His blind loyalty to her clawed at me. It wasn't something I wanted to dwell on.

I stood up and downed the last of my coffee. I was fed up with going round in circles. I may have said a couple of things he didn't deserve, but Simon had given as good as he'd got.

15
I HATE MYSELF FOR
LOVING YOU

WHEN I GOT HOME I made another attempt to google Marcie's tour from 2009. But like last time, I found references to Jess's band supporting Marcie and nothing about the band being dropped. Supporting artists didn't always do full tours—they did legs, and then other bands took over. Nothing untoward was hinted at.

As a last resort I went to a trashy rumor site that kept changing addresses to stave off libel action, but even there the only story I found was about Marcie having had the secret love child of a long-dead, black-and-white movie star with the help of alien technology.

Whatever the facts about that particular tour, they weren't easily available on the net. You needed to have been there.

I was due at Patrick and Justin's for dinner that night and I was itching to ask Pat, but I knew I had to restrain myself.

We had a rule about not talking shop in each other's homes, and that was probably a good thing because, in all honesty, I didn't really care about Jess and Marcie. I cared that their ten-year-old ghosts had caused friction between me and Simon. Would he still want to come to Georgia's party tomorrow night? Going without him would be horrible, especially after we'd had such a lovely time choosing costumes.

♪

"Zoë my dear, you made it! And laden with gifts, I see." Patrick smiled and enveloped me in a hug. On the way to their Hampstead flat I'd stopped at a 7 Eleven and bought a bottle of red wine and a huge box of Bendicks chocolate mints—Pat's particular weakness.

"Let's not tell Justin about the chocolates," said Patrick conspiratorially. "Sugar's as deadly as nicotine, or so he keeps telling me. I've kicked the smoking habit—how boring would it be to cut out chocolate too?"

Something divine and garlicky was being concocted in the kitchen. Justin was a great cook who loved to make mouthwatering pasta dishes from scratch.

"You caught us in the middle of a domestic," said Patrick, ushering me through to the kitchen, where Justin was presiding over two sizzling pans. "We're having a ding-dong about olive oil. But now you're here, you can put the whole matter to rest as an impartial observer."

Justin turned from the stove to kiss me on each cheek. "Zoë, you know I love you, but you're hardly impartial."

I sat down at the solid wood kitchen table. "What's this all about?"

Pat sat down next to me and poured me a glass of wine without me having to ask. "Justin's annoyed that I only bought Greek olive oil this week, and he wanted Italian for his dish. I told him the damn pasta will only be improved by this marvelous Cretan oil I found."

I took a sip of wine, trying to weigh up my words. "Well, it's Justin's recipe, and if he thinks Italian olive oil is better, that's his call."

Justin humphed in satisfaction.

"Not so fast," said Patrick. "That's not what I'm asking." He turned to me. "In your opinion, my dear Zoë, which olive oil tastes better—Italian or Greek?"

I laughed. "I'm afraid Justin is right; I can't be objective about this. Growing up you get it drummed into you—the Greek version of *everything* is better."

Two hours later, with Graeco-Italian rivalries put to one side, we were relaxing in the living room, a second bottle of red wine open, and congratulating Justin on his delicious penne all'Arrabbiata. Although in Patrick's case, the wine had been swapped for his customary Gordon's and tonic.

"The trick is to get fresh Scotch bonnet," said Justin, and I nodded, pretending to know what he was talking about.

"It's a type of chili," whispered Patrick, noticing my blank stare.

The pair of them thought it was hilarious that my parents were in the restaurant business, but I was so terrible in the kitchen. But that's the thing about having great cooks in the family—you never have to learn for yourself.

"You seem out of sorts, my dear. Is everything okay?" Patrick was too perceptive not to notice that my quietness wasn't all down to not keeping up with Justin's culinary tips.

"Boy trouble," I murmured.

Justin winked. "That's the best kind."

"Too many to choose from?" said Patrick.

"There's only ever been one boy for me," I said, surprising myself. Wow. Was that the wine talking or how I really felt?

Patrick smiled. "You never seem that bothered about relationships and dating. I should have guessed it was because you'd already lost your heart to someone."

Hot tears welled, and I blinked them away. "I don't know what to do," I said. "He accused me of being too wrapped up in work to care about other people, and we got into an argument."

Patrick came to sit beside me and patted my knee. "I know that magazine is everything to you, but sometimes you have to sit back and look at the bigger picture. There's a world out there beyond work."

Justin chuckled. "It's taken me years to make him see that."

Pat nodded. "You're an amazing girl, full of spirit and passion, and the right boy will see that. It will all turn out well in the end. Just give it time."

Pat's pep talk helped—they always did—and I felt better on the tube home. But instead of going straight to my flat, I detoured to Soho. When I'd been in the 7 Eleven earlier, I'd added another item to my basket along with the wine and chocolates: a postcard. It was a corny tourist one, bigger than normal, featuring red phone boxes and Big Ben, but my options had been limited.

I sat in the reception of Simon's hotel to write it. I kept looking up, paranoid that Simon would randomly appear. I needed to put this down in writing; if we tried to talk it through again, we'd only get into another argument.

After half an hour, I was finally happy with it. I dropped it off at the front desk and went home.

Dear Member,

It's tough being a rock star, sometimes. The record label argues every expense (the magic just wasn't happening until we repainted the studio cerulean blue), that idiot session drummer is convinced that his sticks are cursed, and I need to practice throwing TVs out of windows. (I really did my back in with that last 50-inch flat screen.)

When you've got all of that to contend with, you forget about the important things in life. Like friendship.

I'm sorry we argued.

You're the last person I'd ever want to hurt. You mean the world to me, and I feel like I've been living life in mono without you.

I hope you can bring me back to stereo one day. I'll sign off now. That TV isn't going to throw itself out of the window.

Keep doing the Fandango,

Zak x

I woke early the next day, even though it was Saturday. I'd slept fitfully and any slumber I did manage had been full of dreams of Simon and Jess laughing at me.

My thumb ached from checking my phone. I was hoping that I'd hear something from Simon, but by lunchtime he was still incommunicado. I guess Zak hadn't worked his magic this time.

I toyed with phoning Georgia and faking a cold so I wouldn't have to go to her party tonight, but in the end my conscience wouldn't let me. Besides, a party was probably exactly what I needed to take my mind off Simon. I'd have to rustle up a costume myself, but that wasn't the end of the world.

By three o'clock, I'd vacuumed the living room, scrubbed the bath, and pulled an alarming amount of hair out of my shower, but I still hadn't worked off my restlessness, so I decided to go for a run. Hitting the pavement was my last resort when I felt antsy; I always found it so boring. But armed with my iPod, earphones, and Metallica playlist, running seemed to help.

I headed for the local park and settled into a satisfying rhythm. My breaths came hard, but each step calmed me. The sun was hidden behind clouds, so it wasn't too hot. But I was still slick with sweat by the time I got back almost an hour later. I opened a couple of windows and was just untying my Nikes when the doorbell rang. I tried not to get my hopes up. It was probably a delivery—my online clothes-shopping habit had grown worse—or Mrs. Hargreaves from downstairs needing help with her router again.

I swung open the door. It was Simon, holding two enormous bags.

I took a step back, suddenly wrong-footed. Was he still upset? His face seemed a bit red but more from exertion rather than irritation. Then he smiled, and a smidgeon of hope bloomed in my chest.

"Don't just stand there, Frixie. Give me a hand with these costumes. I've been carrying them around since this morning."

I took one of the bags, and we climbed back up to my flat. I felt self-conscious; my hair was a mess, and my sweaty Ramones T-shirt was sticking to my back.

"Do you want something to drink?" I said, keeping my tone light.

"I'm good, thanks," he said. "I've spent the last two hours with estate agents looking for a place to rent."

I did a double take. "You don't waste much time!"

He nodded, and I poured myself a glass of water to give myself something to do.

"Whereabouts?"

"Holland Park."

"That's just up the road."

He nodded. "I even saw a couple this side of the roundabout."

"You mean you'd stoop so low as to have a W12 postcode?"

"Yeah, I'd be roughing it. But Shepherd's Bush has its upsides."

"The shopping's good, and it's easy to get into town."

He held my eye, and I knew he wasn't talking about Westfield or the transport links.

"I'm sorry about lying to you, Si."

"No, I'm sorry for losing my temper. You didn't deserve it."

It was like a weight had been lifted from my shoulders. "Let's not argue again."

"Deal," said Simon. He pulled out his phone. "I'll give Jess a call."

I froze. Did he want me to apologize to her too? I slumped onto the counter. "Why do you need to ring her?"

"To arrange that get-together with us and Nick."

Relief flooded through me. This was more than I'd dared hope for. "You're okay with that?"

He walked over to me and clasped my hand. "I want to help you, Zoë. It's the least I can do after being a jackass."

I squeezed his hand back. "Thanks, Si. I appreciate it." I'd been leaning against the counter, but now I stood up taller. "I need to take a shower. Can you amuse yourself for a while?"

He nodded. "Of course. As long as you trust me with that open window and your TV."

The postcard had worked after all. I should never have doubted Zak.

♪

I'd showered, blow-dried my hair, and was eating a cheese and pickle sandwich that Simon had rustled up from the contents of my fridge. It gave me a warm glow that he was so comfortable in my flat.

By the time we were ready to leave for Georgia's, everything was back to normal between us. Simon looked amazing in his Indiana Jones getup. He hadn't shaved that morning, and his stubble added an extra layer of authenticity, not to mention sexiness.

His hotness contrasted with my sexless Dorothy costume. A baby-blue and white gingham pinafore—honestly, could I have chosen a more virginal outfit? *So* not the image I wanted to project tonight. I'd planned to style my hair into two plaits but—with apologies to Judy Garland—sod that. I'd wear my hair loose and wavy.

The sparkly ruby slippers did their bit to vamp up my anemic costume, but only just. I added a layer of gloss to my MAC Red lipstick, just to jazz things up a bit.

"You're looking mighty fine, Frixie," said Simon when he saw me frowning.

"Really? I feel a bit frumpy."

"Mother of God, you must be kidding. You're prompting a rather uncomfortable adult reaction to a favorite childhood character. And these pants are *tight*."

I felt my cheeks color instantly. He was joking, right?

Don't look at his crotch.

Don't look. Don't look. Don't look.

I looked.

Inconclusive. But I could only peek for a split second.

When Georgia opened her door to us twenty minutes later, she looked resplendent, and rather sloshed, in her Good Witch of the North outfit, complete with wand and tiara.

"Twinsies!" she yelled after she took in my costume.

I grinned. "Same film, different characters, but close enough."

She pulled me in to her pale pink satin. "It's so good to see you, Zo."

When we'd disentangled ourselves, she gave Simon the once-over.

"George, this is Simon," I said.

"Well hello, Doctor Jones," she cooed. "I've heard *so* much about you."

Simon smiled. "It's great to meet you." He held up two bottles of wine. "Where shall I put these?"

"Kitchen table—straight through to the back. Thanks, guys!"

Simon and I headed to the back of the house and added our two bottles to the alarming arsenal of alcohol on the kitchen table.

Dean appeared from a side door, carrying a bag of ice. "Hey, Zoë, great to see you. Who's your friend?" He obviously hadn't been briefed on who Simon was, thank God, because tact was not his forte.

"This is Simon."

Simon stepped forward. "Can I give you a hand?"

"Cheers, mate," said Dean, "Help me dump it into that ice box."

"Great outfit, Dean," I said, as they poured the ice into the box, with only a few cubes going astray. His military whites made him look pretty dashing. If Georgia wasn't careful, they'd be welcoming another bundle of joy into their lives nine months from now.

"Itchy as fuck, pardon my French," he said. "And George won't let me take the hat off. She says she pushed two babies out of her hoo-ha, so the least I could do is put up with a bit of hat-hair."

"You look very handsome," I told him. "Every inch an officer and a gentleman."

"Thanks, love. Help yourself to drinks, guys."

Dean flitted out of the room, scratching the nape of his neck.

"Red or white?" said Simon, picking up two plastic flutes.

"Better stick to white," I replied. "If I get red wine on the dress, we'll lose our deposit."

Twenty-odd people were crammed into the lounge. I scanned the room, taking in a couple of cowboys; an Al Capone, complete with violin case; a Sleeping Beauty, and as a foil to Georgia, her sister, Fliss, had come as the Wicked Witch of the West. "I'll get you, my pretty," she said to me in a crowing voice. Her green skin only added to the menace. Props to her for commitment.

Simon was a hit with everyone, including Georgia. I don't know why I'd been worried about her meeting him. One of the cowboys, Matthew, a credit controller at Dean's firm, challenged Simon to a shoot-out, and Simon had us in stitches when he used his whip to knock the gun from Matthew's hand in a reversal of the classic scene from *Raiders of the Lost Ark*.

"This wine is excellent," said Georgia, dropping to the floor beside me.

"Paint stripper would probably taste good after your pregnancy dry spell."

"This is only my third glass, and the room is already spinning. Is that normal?"

How the mighty had fallen. Georgia used to be able to drink pint after pint at uni. The rugby boys had made her an honorary member of their team.

Simon was on the opposite side of the room, talking to Al Capone. Our eyes met for a moment, and he raised his glass in a toast to us.

Georgia grinned, first at me and then him.

The music, which despite my best efforts had slipped into middle-class thirty-something dinner party mode—who else could have rocketed Ed Sheeran to number one?—suddenly changed. Someone had put on some Bruno Mars and people had got up to dance, blocking my view of Simon.

"So, will you be shagging Doctor Jones tonight?"

I turned round to Georgia. "Keep your voice down. He might hear!"

"Believe me, he's thinking exactly the same thing. He hasn't taken his eyes off you since you got here."

"He doesn't know anyone else, so of course he'd stay close to me," I said, trying not to jump the gun as quickly as Georgia had. But she was right; I'd noticed too.

Georgia's words had lit a spark I'd been trying to keep matches away from all night. His Indiana Jones outfit was proving lethal—I'd never fancied anyone so much in my whole life. I'd been trying not to drink a lot because that only fueled my libido, but Dean had been far too attentive as host and whenever my glass was less than full, he'd topped it up. Technically, I hadn't gotten to the bottom of my first glass yet.

Simon came over and dropped onto the floor next to me.

"Is it me or did it suddenly get hot in here?" said Georgia, theatrically. "I'd better go and check on the heating." She left, but not without first giving me a cheeky wink that I'm sure Simon saw.

"She's right, it is kinda hot in here," he said.

"Must be all that whip action," I replied.

"Do you want to get some air?"

"Sure."

A couple of smokers were hanging around the patio, but Simon led me toward the back of the garden to a bench by a magnolia tree. It was pitch black and silent apart from the distant roar of the North Circular.

We sat facing the house, my leg pressed against the length of his. I shivered and Simon wrapped his arm around my shoulders, which only made me want to shiver more.

"It's peaceful out here," he said.

"Yes, it is," I agreed, completely ignoring my racing pulse.

He took my hand in his. God, I hoped my raised heartbeat wasn't obvious.

"You look beautiful tonight, Frixie."

I didn't know what to say. The little voice that had always warned me not to read too much into his words was uncharacteristically silent.

"Yeah, I tend to look good in the dark." And there it was. Still scared to accept a compliment from him.

"I probably shouldn't tell you this, but I've been thinking about you a lot lately."

My eyes were adjusting to the dark now, and I could see his expression. Surely there was no way to mistake it? It's the way I used to look at him, the way I'd longed for him to look at me. My heart knocked against my ribs.

He twisted round to face me. "You make me want to do something bad."

I swallowed. "How bad?"

He leaned in close. "Pretty bad," he whispered.

"Maybe you should just do it."

He kissed me softly on the lips and pulled back.

"That's not so bad," I said, my breath raspy.

He leaned forward and kissed me again. This time his lips lingered longer.

"Is that bad enough?" His voice was low.

"Not even close."

He bent his head to my lips again, this time for a proper kiss.

I couldn't shut off the voice in my head. *I'm kissing Simon! With tongues!* I'd imagined this a hundred times, and here he was, flesh and blood and putty in my hands.

His arms were suddenly scooping me up off the bench and onto his lap. His hands were in my hair, and mine were roaming his broad back.

He broke off the kiss, and rested his forehead on my shoulder.

I stilled my hands. "Everything okay?"

He looked up. "I've been wanting to do that for a long time."

I smiled. "Me too."

He ran his thumb over my cheek. "You're beautiful."

I could sense a "but" coming and swallowed back a ball of lust and disappointment.

"What is it, Si?"

"I have all these feelings swirling around my head, confusing the hell out of me. Until a few months ago, I was desperately trying to make my marriage work. And now I'm in London with you, and I don't want to mess things up."

"You haven't messed anything up."

He hugged me closer. "You're amazing and sexy, and God, I feel like I could fly right now."

I grinned, even though he couldn't see me. "You're not too bad yourself."

"But I need us to take things slowly. Could you bear that?"

"Of course I can, Si. We can take all the time you need." *I've been waiting half my life*, I wanted to say, *what are a few more weeks?* I couldn't stop smiling as we walked back to the party, my hand in his. Fucking hell, I wanted to scream: Simon and me. It was finally happening.

As we reached the patio door, our hands uncoupled. Probably best not to give Georgia a hint of anything. Not when it was all so brand new. I went straight to the loo to give myself a chance to compose myself. My pink-faced reflection stared back at me. My hair was mussed up and the red lipstick was gone—hopefully not all over Simon's face.

I wanted to stay in my little post-kiss bubble for a bit longer. Simon's stubble had left a track of pink from my jaw down my neck, where he'd planted soft kisses.

A knock at the door made me jump. I guess twenty guests sharing two bathrooms meant my time was up. I flushed the toilet, ran the tap for a couple of seconds, then made my way back to the living room.

Simon was deep in conversation with Dean. They seemed to be discussing alloy wheels. Or at least, Dean was leading the charge, even getting his phone out to illustrate his question about whether to choose eighteen- or nineteen-inch rims for his new car.

Simon was the least car-crazy bloke I knew, but he was ably holding his own. His eyes locked on mine for a second and a smile played at his lips, but then his attention was back to Dean.

I could tell without looking that Georgia's eyes were burning a hole in me. She had a sixth sense like that. I kept myself busy chatting to others so she wouldn't get the chance to interrogate me. She only got her chance when we hugged just as I was leaving with Simon at 1:00 a.m.

"I will want every salacious detail, madam," she whispered in my ear.

Later, in the taxi ride home we sat side by side, my leg pressed against Simon's. The driver was listening to Smooth Radio, and it was nice to have soft, soothing music serenade us as we drove. I felt like I was in some sort of alternate universe, my head resting on Simon's shoulder, his hand stroking my knee. As we turned into my road, "My Heart Will Go On" came on.

I lifted my head, and Simon smiled.

"Sometimes I put this on when I want to be reminded of you." His voice was low.

"Same," I said, my heart feeling like it was going to burst.

A few short moments later, the cab was pulling up outside my flat. We got out slowly, the spell broken.

I looked up at him. "Do you want to stay for a nightcap?"

We both knew what I really meant.

His eyes drifted to my mouth. "I think it's probably better to avoid that particular temptation. I'll go up to get my clothes, but I won't stay."

He asked the driver to wait, and I opened the front door to let Simon up.

I preferred to wait outside, scanning the stars that crisscrossed the midnight sky, enjoying the cool night breeze against my skin.

When Simon returned carrying his bag, he stopped to kiss me just below my ear. I shivered. It was almost more intimate than a kiss on the lips. It took all of my willpower not to grab him and drag him back into my flat.

His car disappeared down the street, and I sighed. A bit too loudly. A passing bloke looked up and winked.

I hastily ran up the concrete steps to my front door. There should have been a light flashing above by my stoop. Next level unlocked! Shiny new world revealed! But everything was the same as before. The same peeling black paint on the door; the same tarnished brass on the lock.

We'd kissed!

So why was I on cloud eight-and-a-half instead of cloud nine?

The answer was already waiting for me: because Simon wanted to take things slowly. We'd been dancing around this for *years*. I was raring to go, so why did he still need time?

I walked into the kitchen, my ruby shoes clicking against the tiled floor. If I tapped my heels together three times, would they grant me my heart's desire?

I tried, but the clicks made hollow echoes in my silent flat. I got ready for bed, carefully hanging up my blue and white gingham dress. I was being melodramatic, I decided, as I brushed my teeth. We'd dressed as characters from the movies tonight, but real life wasn't like the movies; regular people didn't jeopardize everything for love—they made conscious decisions after carefully weighing up the risks and rewards. Simon worked in finance; he knew this better than anyone.

It was good to be prudent. Still, it was hard to go to sleep without imagining what it would have been like to have him sharing my bed tonight.

16

IF I CAN'T HAVE YOU

MY EYES SPRANG OPEN AT 8:00 the next morning. I lay in bed replaying the delicious memories from last night. How Simon's lips had been soft on mine, the hard muscles of his back under my eager hands. I felt better this morning about Simon's suggestion we take things slowly. He was moving to a flat nearby with plans to stay put. We had all the time in the world.

My improved mood paid off; after I'd showered I saw I had a missed call from him. Hmmm. Maybe he wanted to come over tonight and take things slowly again. The thought made me shiver.

"Hey, Frixie," he said, when I called him back. "I was just thinking about you."

Maybe he wanted to come round *right now* to take things slowly.

"How are you feeling this morning?" I asked. "Not too hungover, I hope." It would be just my luck that he'd been too drunk to remember what happened.

"Nope. I'm on top of the world."

I grinned. *Same*, I wanted to say. But didn't.

"I spoke to Jess."

I froze. "Oh?"

"To ask her about meeting up with us and Nick."

I'd almost forgotten about that. "Of course. What did she say?"

"She's really busy and is off on tour tomorrow."

My editor brain was finally catching up. Jess disappearing was a problem. "Damn."

"But we're in luck because she can do tonight. Are you free?"

I perked up. "Yes, of course."

"Pick a bar you like and we'll both be there. Shall we say eight o'clock?"

"That would be great."

"What about Nick?"

Simon sounded uncertain, but I wasn't. This was as important to Nick as it was to me. What earth-shattering plans could he have on a Sunday night that he couldn't cancel—was he washing his hair? "Nick will be there too."

Simon was silent on the other end of the phone. Did he want to talk about last night?

"Are you okay, Si?"

His voice was low. "I made an executive decision."

"What do you mean?"

"When I was talking to Jess—I told her Nick was your boyfriend."

I couldn't have been more winded if someone had socked me. He'd done what? "Why would you say that?"

"Because she seemed suspicious of him."

My mind was reeling. This was wrong on so many levels. "But we didn't say we were a couple the other night."

"I'm not sure she remembers much from that night," said Simon.

It was a good point.

"I'm not crazy about lying to Jess," said Simon. "But you've assured me it's for a good cause."

Another good point.

"I'm sorry about all this, Simon. It will be the last time—I promise."

We said our goodbyes, and hung up. I paced up and down the kitchen, feeling rattled. Did he really have to tell Jess that Nick was my boyfriend? It was weird, but something more was bothering me.

I took out a mug to make tea, mulling things over. As the kettle boiled, things slowly moved into focus. I hated the idea that Simon was happy to see me with another man. I wanted the idea to repel him, not for him to be the one suggesting it. Would he really be so sanguine if I announced I was actually seeing someone? And then on top of that, I would have to adjust my focus and act like I was with Nick, when all I wanted to do whenever Simon was in the same room as me was lock eyes on him.

Maybe I was overreacting. Simon was only asking me to *pretend.* There was a world of difference between faking a boyfriend and having one.

I poured milk in my tea and threw the tea bag into the bin. I still had one more hurdle to overcome: Nick had to agree to our faux relationship too. It was almost nine o'clock now—was that too early on a Sunday to ring him?

I scrolled through the numbers of my mobile and found Nick's. It rang twice before going to voicemail. Dammit. I had wanted to get this over with quickly. I hung up without leaving a message. I opened and closed cupboards, trying to find my emergency stash of Rich Teas.

I was in the middle of dunking my fourth biscuit when Nick's number flashed up on my mobile.

"Hi, Nick, thanks for calling back."

"No problem. What can I do for you?"

"This is kind of awkward, but Jess is going away for a couple of weeks so if you want to talk to her it has to be tonight."

"That should work. I can shift a couple of things."

Okay, now I needed to get to the hard part. "There's just one small detail. Simon thought it would be easier to explain your presence to Jess if we said you were my...um...boyfriend."

Silence.

"Nick? Can you hear me?"

"Not very clearly because it sounded like you said you want me to pretend to be your *boyfriend*."

He sounded offended, which was a bit rich. I mean, it's not like he'd never flirted with me.

"Yes," I said stiffly. "That's exactly what I said. She's more likely to trust you that way. It was actually a genius idea." *Did I just use the word "genius" to describe this harebrained plan?*

"Being your boyfriend—what exactly would that entail?"

Jesus, he sounded like a drama student with a walk-on part who insists on discussing his *motivation*. "Just act normal—like we did the first night. No one's asking you to act untoward."

"Is this something you do quite often?"

"Jesus, what do you take me for? No! But I can't see the big problem. What's the difference between friends and dating?"

He paused for effect. "Zoë, did your mother never sit you down and have that special talk?"

"Oh, for God's sake, you're making a big deal out of this. It's not like we have to prove to Jess we have carnal knowledge of each other."

Why did I just say carnal?

I tried again. "For all she knows, you're a born-again Christian who doesn't believe in sex before marriage."

Shit. Wrong again.

"Not that there's anything wrong with that if you are... Are you?"

Stop. Talking. Zoë.

"Am I what? A virgin or a born-again Christian?" He paused. "Is this something you ask all your prospective boyfriends?"

He was enjoying this.

I rolled my eyes. "No, just the fake ones."

"Lapsed Catholic, if you must know. And very few of us are virgins when we get married."

This discussion was featuring far too many sexual terms for comfort. "So, it's settled—drinks tonight?"

"I've got a meeting beforehand in London Bridge—if we could meet on that side of London that would be really helpful."

"Sure, no problem," I replied, relieved to have got the evening plans firmed up.

"I know a nice place. I'll send you the details."

"You owe me the Marcie interview after this. It's the only reason I'm going through with all this fakery."

"Noted: you don't like to fake it."

He hung up, no doubt congratulating himself on getting in one last double entendre.

♪

I had a busy morning ahead of me. Once a month on a Sunday, I invited the team over for brunch, and today was one such Sunday. It was nothing particularly fancy—but I'd got quite adept at frying sausages and eggs for half a dozen people at a time. And I only burned the toast *some* of the time. I set off for the supermarket to get bacon and eggs and tins of baked beans, and when I got back to the flat, I started sorting out the kitchen. I cleared the table because our get-together was usually an excuse for us to play board games—they sure weren't coming to sample my culinary skills. The oven was on the blink. Again.

Gavin and Lucy arrived first. He'd brought along a new game called Risk. Well, new to us, but it was a classic, he assured us. Rob arrived next, bringing with him a jar of artisanal honey.

"Got this at Borough Market earlier."

Bless Rob—he never arrived empty-handed. Last to arrive were Ayisha and Jody, who looked like she'd got less sleep than I had.

I was halfway through cooking when the doorbell rang again. When I went to answer it, it was Mike. I took a step back. He was always invited to these mornings, but he rarely came. And by the look on his face, I could tell that he had news to impart. And not the fun kind.

"Everything okay, Mike?"

"Of course," he said, but he didn't fool me.

"Spill it."

"It's nothing urgent. My more pressing question is: Do you know how to make French toast?"

The answer to that was an unsurprising "no," but Mike had suspected as much. He'd brought his own bread, eggs, flour, and cinnamon, guessing rightly that my own spice rack would be lacking somewhat.

After we'd eaten and had our mugs refilled with tea, Gavin painstakingly explained the rules of Risk.

I tried to pay attention, but my mind kept snagging on why Mike was here. What worried him enough to warrant a trip from Berkshire to Shepherd's Bush on a Sunday that couldn't wait twenty-four hours?

We played in three teams, and enjoyed—I use the term lightly—a fiery few hours playing Risk. Sadly, I wasn't a natural. Rob, Ayisha, and I came last, our poor little green soldiers getting their butts kicked wherever they went. But at least we didn't get into a nuclear showdown with anyone, unlike Jody and Lucy, who waged a fierce and expletive-filled campaign for Kamchatka against Gavin and Mike.

Lucy claimed that Mike's military background gave him an unfair advantage. He didn't usually talk much about his time in the army, but as we played he casually divulged that he'd once been on a mission in Kamchatka.

"How can *that* be fair?" asked Lucy.

Gavin tried to cool heads by reminding them that success in the game largely depended on the roll of the dice, rather than whether or not a player had seen action in the region they were trying to conquer. And he was proven right by the fact that he and Mike came second, crushed by Jody and Lucy's victorious yellow plastic troops.

"Beginners' luck," Gavin muttered, who was unlucky enough to roll three ones, which resulted in losing Western Europe to Lucy and Jody. It was a catastrophic retreat that he never quite recovered from.

Luckily, I had bought a massive lemon cheesecake, and after two slices, Gav's injured pride was restored.

I was in the kitchen making another round of teas and coffees when I noticed a text from Nick. He was asking for my address so he could pick me up later. I texted back without thinking much of it, but as I rinsed everyone's mugs, Nick's suggestion niggled me.

When I realized why, I rang him.

"Why would you want to come to Shepherd's Bush?"

"Excuse me?"

"You said you had a meeting in London Bridge beforehand."

"Oh, right. Yes. My meeting got canceled."

He sounded off, but I had no idea why. He wasn't really treating this like a date, was he?

"Let's just meet by the river at half seven."

"Whatever you prefer."

We rang off just as Lucy walked into the kitchen.

"Everything okay, boss?"

She must have noticed me frowning. "I'm fine."

Was Nick being weird or was I imagining it?

Lucy opened the fridge to get the milk. "He's such a sore loser."

"Who is?"

"Gav, of course. Who else?"

She then proceeded to give me a litany of Gav's complaints, the first of which was that he'd come without his lucky dice.

When we returned to the living room, we were shocked to find Jody in floods of tears.

"What have you done now, Gavin?" said Lucy, sharply.

I have to admit, I'd had the same thought. Ayisha and Rob had left soon after the game ended, and Mike had stepped out for a cigarette break. Gav was the prime—and sole—suspect.

He shook his head in protest. "All I did was ask if she'd like to finish my cheesecake—she hasn't had any and I felt bad having a third slice."

I went to sit next to her. "What's wrong, Jody?"

"It's not Gavin," she said, between sniffles. "I got dumped—by text."

I rubbed her shoulder. "Oh, sweetheart, I'm so sorry."

"What, just now?" Gavin had taken a new interest. "That's low."

Lucy arrived with a tissue. "Here you go, Jodes."

She dried her eyes. "I'm sorry. I didn't mean to ruin everyone's fun."

"You're not ruining anything," I told her. "You're allowed to cry if you feel like it. Do you want to talk about it?"

Her hazel eyes were ringed with red. Without makeup she looked so young—barely into her twenties.

"He said he didn't see any future for us because I didn't care enough about my appearance."

"What sort of bullshit is that?" said Lucy. "You are gorgeous, and you always look amazing."

"He said I had a nice face but that...I was *fat*."

I blinked in shock. "He said *what*? The problem is him, not your weight. You're better off without him. And if I ever lay eyes on him—"

Mike returned, trailing the scent of fresh cigarettes. "What's going on here then?"

"Jody has discovered that her ex-boyfriend is an arsehole," said Lucy.

"We might be in need of your green beret friends," I said.

Jody gasped. "You're joking, Zoë." Then, a touch wistfully: "Aren't you?"

"Just say the word," said Mike, winking. "No one will ever find the body."

We convinced Jody to try half a slice of cheesecake, because she was definitely not fat and because it was definitely the best cheesecake ever made, according to Gavin.

An hour or so later, it was just me and Mike left sitting at the table. Gavin had suggested a rematch, but when everyone had groaned, he relented, picked up his game, and walked to the tube with Lucy and Jody.

"Another coffee, Mike?"

He shook his head. "You did well with Jody earlier."

I shrugged. "I only said what anyone would say."

"You're a good leader, Zoë."

The conversation had taken an odd turn, and I found I had a lump in my throat. "They're a great bunch. They probably deserve an editor who's not taking such a big risk on the magazine's future."

"Your vision might actually secure a brighter future for *Re:Sound*."

"What do you mean, Mike? That sounds like good news, but your face when you arrived told a different story."

"A directive came down from Ed the Shred late Friday."

My neck muscles tightened. "What did he say?"

"He wants to trim the editorial team."

"Meaning?"

"Lose either Gavin or Lucy."

I felt myself go light-headed. "I have to choose?"

He shook his head. "I told Ed we wouldn't stand for it."

"And that was enough?"

He gave a wry smile. "Yes. That and me forgoing fifty percent of my salary for the next six months."

I gasped. "You can't do that, Mike. You've got a mortgage and kids."

"I'll cope. I did it to buy us more time. This is a campaign of attrition—they're going to keep coming back with more and more demands. We need that Marcie interview."

I hadn't told Mike that I didn't trust Nick to deliver me Marcie anymore, but now didn't seem the time to mention it.

"And I've worked it into our contracts that we get bonuses when we beat their sales targets."

I noticed he said "*when,*" not "*if.*" God, he really was full of confidence at the moment. Maybe we should all eat French toast every day.

After Mike had left, taking some leftover sausages, the weight of what he'd told me began to sink in.

Mike wouldn't be able to keep taking pay cuts. I'd offer to take one too if it meant I could keep both Lucy and Gavin, but after that...

He'd put a lot of faith in me. It was time to pay it back.

17

SMOOTH OPERATOR

MIKE'S NEWS GAVE ME FRESH resolve to do everything I could to make tonight go to plan. I stood in front of my wardrobe, trying to decide what sort of outfit a girlfriend of Nick's would wear. A dress, for sure. Something slinky, paired with high heels.

Well, sod that. I'd wear whatever I wanted. I tried on a couple of outfits before deciding on some black, high-waisted jeans, a wrap-around white shirt, and flats.

I was pretty happy with how I looked, but as I was applying eyeliner it dawned on me that I *did* know how Nick's girlfriend dressed. Because, according to the rumors, Nick's girlfriend was Marcie.

My hand slipped and I smudged black kohl on my brow bone. *Christ. Talk about impossible shoes to fill.*

I spent the next few minutes with a cotton bud and makeup remover, trying to erase the evidence of my shaky hand.

I was being silly. They were just rumors. Nick was far too strait-laced to be shagging his employer. He wouldn't be comparing me to Marcie all through our "date."

At 7:30, I found myself people watching from a bench by the river, waiting for Nick. The bar he'd suggested for our meetup was a couple of minutes away. It was surprisingly middle-of-the-road. I thought he'd have chosen something a bit fancier, not one that advertised live rugby games.

Fifteen minutes passed and still no sign of Nick. Had something come up? I checked my phone, but I didn't have any missed calls.

I was debating whether I should go straight to the bar, when I heard a voice in my ear.

"Hello, gorgeous."

I turned round to find Simon. "Hey, Si."

He grinned and sat down next to me. "Not like you to be early."

"I'm supposed to be meeting Nick. My *boyfriend*."

His grin faded. "Remind me whose dumbass idea this was? Oh right, mine."

He was wearing a charcoal suit rather than his more usual casual gear. "You dressed up for the occasion?"

Simon looked down at his shirt and tie. "Well, I figured I needed to keep up with Mr. Savile Row."

I tried to hide my smile.

He brushed invisible specks off one sleeve. "How well do you know this Nick guy?"

"What do you mean?"

"You know he's Marcie Tyler's publicist, but what's he like as a person? He might be some creep who'll use tonight as an excuse to get handsy with you."

I bit my cheek to hide a smile. Was Simon a teensy bit jealous?

"He's been with his company for years. Abroad mostly—most recently in Latin America. And I know he speaks eight languages."

"*Eight?*"

"Okay, maybe just three or four."

Simon didn't speak for a while, and we both watched the world go by.

I stifled a sigh. If only we could blow off Jess and Nick and do our own private thing tonight.

Simon was breathing deeply. Was he thinking the same thing?

"I guess it's almost show time," he said.

He sounded wistful. But he was right—it was eight o'clock. Time for the main event.

A couple of minutes later, we'd made it to the bar. It was about half-full and dotted with the usual muted Sunday-night drinkers. It was nicer than I'd imagined, with shining parquet floors, polished brass bar top, and arched windows.

"Jess is outside," said Simon, pointing to where a few tables were gathered on a thin strip between the pub and the pavement. A row of potted plants was doing its best to hide the busy road beyond it.

She was sitting in the smoking section, puffing on a cigarette. A Zippo lighter lay on the table next to a bottle in a cooler. I wasn't crazy about sitting among the swirls of stinky white smoke, but it seemed churlish to complain.

"Hiya," said Jess as we approached her. Simon leaned down to kiss her on the cheek, and I awkwardly followed suit. She was wearing a low-cut black top and her wrist was weighed down with jangling bracelets.

"Nick didn't come with you?" asked Jess, peering over my shoulder as I sat down opposite her.

"He's on his way." He'd bloody well *better* be on his way.

The cooler was housing a bottle of champagne. Simon reached for it and poured us both a glass. Jess's flute was still full; she must have only just arrived.

I was surreptitiously checking my watch when Nick arrived a couple of minutes later. Well, we'd cleared the first hurdle of getting the four of us into the same room, even if that "room" was an outside table in the middle of the city. Nick didn't bother to go round the front, and instead edged past a potted Buxus to reach us. He was wearing a dark-blue suit with a white shirt and red tie. It was the same outfit he'd worn the night we'd first met at Patrick's party. I wanted to tell Simon as much—to let him know Mr. Savile Row didn't have a limitless supply of suits.

Simon stood up to shake Nick's hand, then Jess struggled upright with a lot of chair-scraping and swearing.

"I don't do handshakes," she announced, leaning forward to smack a kiss on both of Nick's cheeks.

We now had a small problem. If he was happy to greet a virtual stranger the continental way, how would boyfriend Nick say hello to me?

For a horrified second, I thought he would kiss me on the lips, but without skipping a beat, he kissed the top of my head and sat down. He moved his chair closer to me and leaned to murmur in my ear.

"This is me greeting you with something unspeakably filthy."

I noticeably—embarrassingly—shivered, and he grinned like a Cheshire cat.

It wasn't his words that had goaded my goose bumps; his breath had been a feather down my neck. Anyone's breath would have triggered the same reaction. I had sensitive skin. Unfortunately, the person whom this show was for—Jess—wasn't even looking; she was busy peering at her phone. Nick's move hadn't escaped Simon's notice, however. He was staring at Nick with laser beam focus, his lips pressed into a hard line. It was sort of gratifying that Simon was struggling with this, but it had been his idea and we were in for a long evening if everyone was going to act so unnaturally.

I reached out to pat Simon's arm. Unfortunately, Jess chose that moment to put her phone down.

She looked from me to Nick then back to Simon. It had been a harmless touch; she couldn't really suspect anything—*could she?*

Without thinking, I placed my hand on top of Nick's where it was resting on the table. His skin was cool where his knuckles jutted into my palm. *Oh God, this was weird.* But I couldn't just snatch my hand away—that would look even weirder.

Nick didn't seem to notice. He looked perfectly at ease, sprawled in his chair. "So, what are we drinking?"

"Champagne," said Jess.

"Sounds great."

Well, at least Nick wasn't going to profess to prefer mineral water tonight.

I withdrew my hand to pour him a glass.

"Cheers," he said, and proceeded to drink half of it in one go like it was a bottle of Lucozade.

I stared at him. How thirsty *was* he?

"Rough day?" said Jess.

"Something like that," he replied.

I felt irrationally slighted. Great, I was the sort of girlfriend who drove her man to drink.

No one was saying anything and an awkward hush was descending. I glanced around, desperate to spot something to comment on. A cute dog would have been ideal, but the only animal nearby was a pigeon with a misshapen foot pecking at a crisp packet—hardly a red-hot conversation starter.

"So, Nick," said Simon, who hated uncomfortable silences more than I did, "Zoë says you speak loads of languages. How come?"

Bless Simon for trying.

"I moved around a lot growing up."

"Whereabouts?" asked Jess.

"I bounced around between England, France, Spain, and Italy."

"Must be a real headache during the Six Nations," she said. I didn't see Nick as a rugby fan, but he smiled gamely.

"Where do you prefer living?" said Simon.

"I like England, these days."

Jess leaned forward. "Is that because of Zoë?"

This was Nick's cue to say something suitably affectionate. Or make a joke.

He reached for the champagne and started refilling all our glasses. "She certainly keeps me on my toes."

It was hardly a ringing endorsement for true love, but Jess didn't seem to care.

The champagne ran out before Nick got to his own glass.

Simon frowned. "I meant to order another bottle."

Nick stood. "It's no problem; I'll go to the bar."

Once he'd left, Jess announced she was off to the ladies, leaving just Simon and me at the table.

I groaned and hid my face in my hands. "This is excruciating."

"But kinda entertaining."

"Nick's not even trying to get Jess to talk about Marcie."

"He seems kinda uncomfortable."

I nodded, impressed that Simon had sensed it too. "It's probably because I make a crappy girlfriend."

"Nah, it's Nick that makes a crappy boyfriend."

It was a throwaway line, but he said it with feeling.

I smiled, amazed at Simon's reaction. Initially, I'd been peeved that he'd suggested this stupid charade, but bizarrely this stupid charade seemed to have thrown things into focus for him. Like how maybe he'd quite like to try out the role of my boyfriend…

"You look very pretty tonight, Frixie."

I smiled again. I wished fourteen-year-old me could have been here. I'd spent years trying to work out how to get Simon to like me. I would have got here a hell of a lot quicker if I'd enlisted the green-eyed monster sooner. Simon was *hating* seeing me with another man.

"Nick should try to flirt with Jess a bit," I said. "I bet she'd start singing like a canary."

Simon frowned. "That would be kinda low, don't you think?" It jarred to hear his concern wasn't uniquely for me. Now he was getting all protective of Jess? I bit my lip to hide my disappointment.

"I just want all this done and dusted so none of us has to pretend any longer," I said.

"Hold on to that thought," he whispered. "They're back."

I turned round to see the pair of them walking back toward us. Jess was holding on to Nick's arm like a debutante about to be announced at court. In Nick's other arm was a fresh bottle of champagne.

God, were we all expected to buy such expensive rounds?

"You're not usually such a big drinker," I said, as Nick reclaimed his seat next to me.

"Champagne never gets me drunk."

"How weird," I said. "It gets me pissed faster than anything."

"I'll have to look after you, then."

Fake-boyfriend Nick was the overprotective type.

Jess elbowed Simon in the ribs. "They're so cute together, aren't they?"

Simon half shrugged, half nodded.

"Nick was just telling me how they met. It's such a darling story."

I twisted in my seat to gawp at Nick who was sitting there wearing an enigmatic smile. What on earth had he been telling Jess? Surely not the Jonny story?

"Tell Simon too," she said to Nick. "It shows a side of Zoë I bet he has no idea about."

I didn't like the sound of this.

"I'd better not," said Nick, the *Mona Lisa* smile morphing into a faux-sheepish grin. "It might embarrass her."

What the actual fuck had he been saying?

"They met in a boxing class," said Jess.

What did she just say?

"Boxing? I thought you knew each other from work," said Simon, looking alarmed.

I jumped in to reassure him. "Boxercise, there's a difference. We knew each other from work, then happened to be in the same class one night."

Nick leaned closer to me and bopped me on the nose. "And as the punches flew, so did the sparks." I stared at him openmouthed. Had he really just said that with a straight face?

Simon looked ready to throw a punch of his own. "Christ, Nick, you weren't hitting her, were you?"

"Of course not," I told him. "We just did a bunch of cardio exercises and practiced punches on Styrofoam boards."

Nick nodded emphatically. "Zoë isn't someone to mess with."

Too bloody right I wasn't, although he was skating on pretty thin ice right now.

I stood up. "You know what, there's no queue at the bar right now—I'll go and get another round. Nick, will you give me a hand?"

My mistake was in the wording, because Nick took the request literally and held out his hand. I thought about just pulling him up by the wrist, like an errant toddler, but it would have looked weird. I gingerly took his hand, hoping to get away with just the briefest of touches, but he wrapped his fingers around mine and held on with surprising force. We snaked around the tables trying to get to the bar, but with each step my palm grew hot in his grasp. Sweaty too, which was a bit awkward. I mean, I didn't give a toss about Nick, but the last thing I wanted him to think was that I was some kind of freak.

Zoë Frixos: The Incredible Sweating Woman.

Once we'd reached the bar, I let go and discreetly wiped my palm against my trouser leg.

"Did you have to tell Jess that Boxercise story?"

Nick shrugged. "Jess wanted details, and it was the first thing that came into my head. It's always easier to tell a lie if there's a grain of truth in it."

Nick's face was unreadable, but I suddenly felt uneasy. He was talking like he'd had a lot of practice skirting the truth. Was he a serial liar? And was I being suckered right now?

"We're here because you want to coax Jess into forgiving Marcie, correct?"

"Correct."

"So let's see some movement in that direction. I know you can't ask her point blank, so let's see some evidence of that silver tongue." I held up my hand before he could speak. "In plain English: flirt with her."

Irritation flashed in his eyes. "Well, by introducing me as your boyfriend, you've somewhat tied my hands."

"I'm suggesting you flirt with her, not shag her on the table."

He turned his head away and took a long breath, his chest rising and falling.

"What do you want to drink?"

Perfect. He'd changed the subject rather than answer me.

I huffed impatiently. "It's my round."

He shook his head. "You've gone to a lot of trouble to arrange this evening, so the next round's on me. What can I get you?"

"Surprise me."

I knew I sounded ungrateful, but I didn't care. I spun round and headed back outside. My legs were shaking and my senses felt heightened. The champagne was definitely having an effect because talk of Nick's tongue, tied hands, and shagging on tables had thrown up all sorts of racy images in my head.

God, what was wrong with me? How sexually frustrated was I?

It was all very well Simon wanting to take things slowly, but at this rate, I wasn't sure how long I could last.

I got back to the table and almost did a double take: Simon was lighting up a cigarette. And he'd always been such a rabid non-smoker.

His cheeks hollowed as he sucked in a breath, then he tipped his head back and blew out an elegant plume of smoke. *You're ruining your beautiful, beautiful lungs*, I wanted to say.

But damn, you look hot doing it.

Okay, that was definitely the champagne talking. Men who smoked only ever became attractive when I was a few sheets to the wind.

My eyes met Simon's as I sat down. "You're smoking."

He looked at the cigarette in his hand like he was just noticing. "Yeah. Helps me relax."

What had stressed him out so much? Talk of my Boxercise class with Nick? I guess Nick was right. It had convinced everyone—even Simon, who knew it was all an act.

"Where are the drinks?" said Jess.

"Nick's bringing them."

"I should go and help," she said.

When she was gone, I took hold of Simon's free hand. "Don't smoke."

He nodded and extinguished the cigarette in the ashtray that contained at least a dozen of Jess's butts.

"I'm sorry this is turning into such a shit night," I added.

He smiled grimly.

Before I could say more, Nick appeared, placing another bottle of champagne onto the table.

"Not much of a surprise, mate," I muttered, in a very un-girlfriend-like manner. But I didn't care. I just wanted to get to the end of the evening and fulfill my obligation to Nick. I couldn't give a rat's arse whether he was happy with the outcome or not. After tonight, he was on his own.

As Nick sat down, Jess came into view behind him. She was carrying a tray of four chasers.

"The surprise is the tequila," she sang.

This wasn't right. Getting Jess blotto might have helped Nick's cause, but it didn't sit well with me. She didn't deserve Nick's underhand ways.

"Whose idea was the tequila?" I asked.

Jess giggled. "It was a joint decision."

Concern mixed with anger was pooling in my gut. "Are you sure you're all right, sweetie?"

"I'm perfect, petal," she beamed. Her cheeks were rosy, and her lip gloss was smudged. She picked up her glass of tequila and poured it into her flute. Then she chinked her glass against mine. "Bottoms up."

Champagne tequila slammers were a lethal combination. A friend at uni had vomited lime green for two hours the last time I'd been anywhere near that particular duo.

She banged her glass down and looked pleased with herself. If Nick was right about Jess being a borderline alcoholic, it was damn near criminal that he'd introduced tequila to the mix.

I leaned closer to Nick and placed a territorial hand on his cheek. "You're a fucking psychopath," I whispered, a fake smile on my face so the others couldn't see that I was seething.

He unpeeled my palm from his cheek, and held my hand in a fake display of intimacy.

His grip was tight. "You're in as deep as me."

I wanted to snatch my hand away, but he held fast.

A man shouting nearby broke the deadlock. Nick let go of my hand, and we both looked over to where the noise was coming from.

Two men were waving at Jess from the pavement. "Wearing knickers today, Honeywell?" one of them leered.

Jess looked stricken. One of the men was holding a camera. It flashed twice. *Shit*. Were they paparazzi?

They got closer and Simon tried to shield Jess from the lens. "Piss off," he shouted, angrily.

"We're on a public footpath," said the one with the camera, although I could see now that the other guy had his phone out and was filming us.

"Let's get out of here," I said, trying to put myself in front of Jess.

Nick stood up and pulled us both toward him. "Follow me. I know a private exit."

I don't remember the route we took, or how we got out, but we found ourselves by a side alley, mercifully empty of people. Nick jogged up to the main road, and a couple of moments later, a black cab with a yellow light appeared at the entrance to the alley.

He waved us over.

I looked at Simon. "Should we get into the cab?"

"There doesn't seem to be any other option right now."

We hurried toward where Nick was waiting with the cab door open. I helped Jess and followed her in. "Are you okay, Jess?"

Her rosy complexion from earlier was gone—she looked ghostly pale.

"How did those guys find me?" she stammered.

Simon climbed in and sat on the foldout seat opposite Jess, then Nick got in and installed himself opposite me.

"Cayenne Court," he called to the cab driver.

"Where are we going?" said Simon.

"My flat is nearby—we'll be safe there."

No one said much on the journey. I spent it avoiding Nick's gaze and trying to dodge his knees—they knocked into mine every time we went over a speed bump.

Simon was looking behind us to make sure we weren't being followed. "I think we're in the clear," he said, after a while.

When we got to Nick's flat, there was some discussion about what to do. Simon was suggesting he just take Jess home, but in the end, we decided she should come up to have a cup of coffee and draw breath.

Nick lived in a converted warehouse with dark-yellow bricks and high windows. His flat was on the eighth floor, which meant taking the lift. He saw me pause to steel myself before I stepped in.

"You okay?" he whispered.

I nodded, then lifted my chin and forced myself into the lift just as the doors closed.

I concentrated on the numbered buttons lighting up as we swooped upward, trying to tamp down my burgeoning claustrophobia.

Then the lift doors pinged open and we were released. I let out a breath as we followed Nick down the corridor toward a two-tone wood door with silver numbering.

"Make yourselves comfortable," said Nick, letting us in. "I'll go and make the coffees."

Nick disappeared toward the kitchen while the three of us wandered into the living room. Like the hallway, the floors were light oak and the walls were stark white. Apart from a couple of candles in glass jars, and a chrome clock ticking the seconds away on the wall opposite, Nick's flat looked unlived-in; fake almost. Like a film set, waiting for someone to dress it and actors to breathe life into it.

We sat down on a creaking leather sofa, taking care to put Jess between us. My instincts were to shield Jess from Nick; something didn't smell right. Not literally—the place smelled of Jo Malone candles—but my gut was telling me that Nick wasn't being entirely truthful. He was hiding something.

He came back with four espressos and sugar. I hated black coffee, but asking for milk would have looked like weakness. I would drink the damn thing as it came.

Jess poured a teaspoon of sugar into hers. "Is there somewhere I could smoke, Nick? My nerves could do with a cigarette."

"Go ahead and smoke here," he said. He nodded to a crystal ashtray that looked like it had never been defiled by cigarette ash.

"No, it's okay, I'll leave it." said Jess. "You're a non-smoker. I don't want to make your home smell."

"It's really not a problem, but if you prefer there's a balcony off the bedroom—why don't you go in there?"

Jess smiled gratefully, then grabbed her bag and followed Nick to his bedroom.

When they were gone, Simon scooched closer to me and picked up his coffee. I took a sip of mine and grimaced.

"You hate black coffee," he said.

"Yeah, but I don't plan on staying long."

Simon looked at me. "There's something fishy going on."

I nodded. "I've got the same feeling."

"Do you want to say something, or should I?"

"What do you need to say?" Nick's voice made us jump. He strolled in and dropped into an armchair. He'd taken off his jacket and tie—he looked like an entirely different person without the rigid lines of a suit. Someone I didn't know.

Simon looked at me, as if asking permission. I gave it with a nod.

"Zoë told me who you really are, Nick," he began, his voice low. "I know what you do for a living, and it hasn't escaped my notice that whenever you're around, the paparazzi show up."

Nick frowned. "Wait, do you think I'm the one who tipped them off? That I organized the whole thing?"

"This was all your idea," said Simon. "Right down to the choice of bar."

Simon was right—Nick had been keen to meet by London Bridge; I hadn't questioned it at the time, but now it felt off.

"Now hang on a minute," said Nick. "Jess chose to sit at a table facing the road."

"But you knew she was a smoker," I said, with a growing feeling of unease. "She was always going to sit in that section."

He looked surprised. "You can't honestly think that I sent those paps, Zoë."

I wasn't sure what to think. But Nick had told me he knew the paparazzi who were chasing Jess, and Simon's theory was starting to make an awful lot of sense.

"I don't know, Nick. But lies seem to trip off your tongue mighty easily. The night I saw you in Camden at Jess's first concert, you told me you lived nearby." I looked around me. "Yet, here we are in Southwark, which is definitely not near Camden."

"That was a white lie. You asked what I was doing there, and it was the easiest explanation."

He leaned forward and picked up his coffee. Was he avoiding making eye contact?

Simon leaned forward too, anger squeezing his features. "You know what I think, Nick? I think you've been feeding us a load of bullshit. Marcie doesn't want to make amends with Jess; she wants to humiliate her and ruin any chance she has at a second music career. You're just her errand boy."

I searched Nick's face, hoping to find signs of shock or disbelief. But the seconds ticked by and he remained silent.

Simon stood. "Fuck this. I need a cigarette too." He stalked out, leaving me to deal with Nick.

"Are you not going to deny it, Nick?"

He sat upright. "Of course I deny it. You think I'm the one wrecking Jess's chances? She's the one drunk as a sailor every night, unable to go to her own gigs."

"But you bought the tequila earlier. You were encouraging her to drink."

He let out a hollow laugh. "I was just trying to break the ice. I might have suggested a few drinks and joined in myself, but last time I didn't touch a drop." He shook his head. "She's doing a perfectly good job of fucking up her career all by herself."

The swear word jarred; I hadn't heard him curse before.

Was he rattled because we'd figured him out?

"Can you tell me categorically that this isn't Marcie's payback for Jessica sleeping with Benedict?"

He laughed. "I can't believe what I'm hearing. This isn't a storyline from a damned soap."

I went cold. "That doesn't sound much like a denial."

He held my gaze. "Marcie wouldn't be that petty."

I stood up. "Maybe it was your idea."

"*My* idea?" He stood too and came toe to toe with me. He was flushed with anger. "I expected more from you, Zoë."

"Oh, save me the sob story about your hurt feelings. I know just how petty and humorless you can be. You proved it when you objected to our review of Hands Down. And what's more petty than insisting that *I* interview Jonny. You enjoy playing mind games. You're a sadist."

"Wow, you really don't think much of me."

"Look me in the eye and tell me you've told me the whole truth about Marcie."

He looked away and my shoulders sagged in disappointment. I'd wanted to believe him. But just when I'd started to trust him, he'd blown it.

"I've told you everything that's relevant."

I laughed. "Jesus, Nick. Listen to yourself—you're digging yourself deeper."

He didn't respond because Simon and Jess returned from their cigarette break.

"I've ordered a taxi," said Simon, ignoring Nick. "Come on, Zoë. We can leave now."

We didn't say much as we rode the lift down again. We'd agreed to let Jess take the cab, while the two of us got the tube, but she seemed so unsteady on her feet, I suggested maybe Simon should go back with her to make sure she got home okay.

"I'm sorry about all this," I told him, before he climbed into the cab.

"I guess he fooled us all."

Was he saying I was to blame? He closed the door before I could ask. I looked up at the top floor as the taxi drove away. If Nick was watching us, he was making sure he stayed hidden.

18

TEMPTATION

I WAS STILL FEELING ANTSY the next morning, brushing my teeth so hard that I made my gums bleed. I'd pissed off Simon, and now I didn't know if I could trust Nick to tell the truth, never mind stick to his promise to give me the Marcie interview. I had a missed call from him, but he hadn't left a message. When I did talk to him, I wasn't sure what I would say, or what he could possibly do to make me trust him again.

I owed it to Mike to tell him what had happened. So the first thing I did when I got to work was swing by his office. He smiled broadly when he saw me, and my stomach lurched. I'd bet the magazine on Nick's honesty; Mike had taken a personal financial hit—maybe telling him about this mess wasn't the best move.

"Morning, Zoë. I trust you've got over your catastrophic Sunday."

I was pulling back a chair and froze. He was talking about Risk—wasn't he?

"I'll get you next time," I replied, with fake bravado.

He shook his head. "I got a call from Nick Jones earlier."

Oh. He knew.

I had a moment of irritation at the crappy little bromance they had going on.

We had to talk it out now—walking away was no longer an option.

I slumped into the chair opposite Mike. It was a gorgeous old captain's chair, upholstered in green leather. I had no idea where it had come from; the chairs on my side of the office where all black plastic, and if you were lucky, they had a lever to adjust the height.

I wasn't lucky.

"What did Nick have to say?"

"You're doing a great job. He says you're interviewing Jonny tomorrow and Marcie next week."

What?

Was Nick telling the truth or just playing Mike? I could believe he'd set up a Jonny interview without giving me much warning, but was he really going to follow through with Marcie?

"I have to admit, Mike, this is news to me. I missed a call from him this morning. I'm just surprised that's what he wanted to tell me."

Mike peered at me. "Well, why else would he be ringing at the crack of dawn? Unless the two of you are having a tumultuous affair you're not telling me about."

He chuckled, and I tried to mirror his smile. "I did find a stray sock in my bedroom. I guess it must belong to one of my other lovers."

I went back to my desk and dialed Nick. I wasn't sure what to expect, but if we started arguing, with the office empty at least I wouldn't have an audience.

"Zoë? Thanks for returning my call."

He sounded cordial enough, but I wasn't about to let my guard down.

"I hear I'm interviewing Jonny Delaney tomorrow. Did you have a specific time in mind, or do I have to clear my whole day?"

I hadn't meant to sound tetchy, but it was breathtakingly arrogant of him to tell Mike before telling me.

"I tried calling, but you didn't pick up."

"Do you blame me, after the stunt you pulled yesterday?"

"You've made a lot of assumptions about my role in what happened. I've tried to explain, but it gets a bit boring when you won't listen."

"I *choose* not to listen when I'm being fed bullcrap, Nick. And I can smell yours from a mile away."

"You didn't exactly come up smelling of roses, either. If you'd played your part properly last night, we might have gotten somewhere with Jessica. But your head's not in the game; you're too preoccupied with Simon."

My breath stilled. Did he just use my feelings about Simon against me? The fucking *cheek* of the man. He knew nothing about Simon. I had a hundred comebacks, but didn't want to give him the satisfaction of rising to his bait.

"Why don't we stick to talking about Jonny?" I said, my voice even.

He paused, presumably weighing up his options. "Can you make seven a.m.? You'll be done by eight and then you can get to your office at your normal time."

Why did his reasonableness annoy me? Oh yes, because I couldn't trust him. "And what about Marcie?"

"Within the week."

I blew out a breath, frustrated at yet more vague promises. "I'll hold you to that."

He was silent for a couple of moments. "I won't let you down."

We'd see about that.

I tried to get on with the day, but I still couldn't decide how much to trust Nick. So, I rang the only other person who could help: Patrick. I was in luck because he was round the corner in John Lewis buying a new set of suitcases.

"Could we maybe meet for a coffee?" I said. "I won't take up too much time, I promise."

"Of course, Zoë, dear," he said. "I've always got time for you, and I could do with a second opinion."

We met in the cafeteria on the top floor, where I found him at a table by a window overlooking Oxford Street.

"You're looking great, Pat," I said, kissing him on the cheek before sitting down. "Retirement obviously agrees with you."

He pointed to the half-eaten slice of cake in front of him. "No, it's the chocolate that agrees with me." He sighed. "I'm going a bit mad trying to keep busy," he admitted. "I'm packing up the flat before we go to Crete, but all my cases are falling apart."

"All that time on the road, Pat," I said.

"I hate to get rid of them. They're like a record of my life—every knock, scratch, and tear tells a story."

"Like the time you were in Cupertino for a meeting with Apple and your case fell open in the lobby of their space-age HQ."

Pat smiled. "Oh God, the look on Steve's face when he saw I had more condoms than clothes in my bag. He wanted to run for the hills!"

"Not what most people bring to their meetings with tech giants."

"I'd come straight from the airport. The flight had been delayed, I was jet-lagged, and my breath stank because the only thing I'd eaten for twenty-four hours were Doritos, owing to an enormous hangover I'd been nursing since Heathrow."

I grinned. "You need to write your memoirs, Pat."

He tapped the side of his nose. "Ah, but I've been sworn to secrecy about so many things, Zoë, I wouldn't be able to put in any of the good stuff."

"You'll have to share some of those secrets with me one day."

He winked. "I'm sure when you come over to the vineyard, and the wine's loosened my tongue, you won't be able to stop me."

He took a sip of his tea. "So, what's going on with you, Zoë? You sounded quite perturbed on the phone. Is this about your new beau?"

I shook my head. "No, this is a work thing, I'm afraid. I wanted your advice on Marcie's new publicist. I can't get a handle on him, and my instincts are all over the place. His name is Nick Jones—he was at your party that night."

A small frown creased his brow. "There were so many people at the party, and I'm afraid I didn't get to speak to all of them."

I was so sure Pat would know him that I was thrown. "But you must have met him before," I said, smiling. "Come on, Pat. You know everyone."

"I must be slipping in my old age," he said.

There was no way Pat was anything other than razor-sharp. "You must know him. He looks like a matinée idol."

Patrick raised an eyebrow. "He sounds intriguing."

I tried not to let my disappointment show. "Could you ask around? I want to know if I should trust him."

"Has he been slippery?"

"It's unclear," I said. "I'm not sure if his actions and words match up."

"Sounds like a typical music publicist, if you ask me. And nothing you can't handle."

I guess he was giving me the young Padawan speech from *Star*

Wars; telling me to trust myself instead of thinking other people had the answers.

"Come on, then," I said. "Didn't you want me to have a look at the cases before you chose one? Justin won't thank you if you turn up with a suitcase covered in pink leopard print."

"It's okay, my dear," he said. "You get going—I'm sure you've got more important things to be getting on with."

"It's no bother, Patrick."

He reached over and patted my hand. "How about I promise to stick to black?"

I left feeling a little out of sorts. Pat seemed a bit off. Maybe he was finding retirement less fun than he expected. My parents had been like that when they'd sold the restaurant. Membership of the National Trust had helped, but I doubted a gift subscription would go down so well with Pat. Still, he had Crete to look forward to.

I was disappointed that Pat had nothing concrete to tell me about Nick. But I supposed he was right—I couldn't rely on him to keep giving me advice on everything. He wanted to step back from the business, and I needed to stand on my own two feet.

♪

My mood improved considerably when Simon rang. I'd been worried he was still upset about the previous night. But he didn't mention it and started telling me about a work trip he was having to take tomorrow.

"I'll be a few days," he said. "But the good news is that when I come back I'll have a flat."

"What do you mean?"

"I signed a lease today. I pick up the keys tomorrow morning."

"That's great, Si. Congratulations. Whereabouts?"

"Just on the other side of the roundabout."

I smiled. "Oh God, you're going to be banging my door down at all hours, demanding cups of sugar."

It was a shame he was going away for a few days, but at least things seemed okay between us.

"I'm sorry about how last night ended, Simon."

"No, I'm sorry I lashed out at you. I was mad at Nick—for lots of reasons. But mainly because I didn't like the way he was pawing at you."

"He wasn't pawing at me," I said.

"He obviously likes you."

"Don't be daft, Si. You've got absolutely no reason to be..." I stopped, unsure how to end that sentence. I'd been about to say "jealous," but that would sound presumptuous. Though how else could I interpret Simon's words? He'd been so upset on Jess's behalf, convinced that Nick was out to get her, it was nice to be the object of his concern for once.

"You don't need to worry," I said. "I've got no interest in Nick."

"Good."

The single syllable was delivered with feeling.

I smiled, grateful he couldn't see my grinning face through the phone.

"Let's not talk about Nick Jones. I don't want to think about work." Except now, of course, I *was* thinking about work, specifically, the Jonny Delaney interview tomorrow and whether Nick would be there.

"Want to come over for a drink?" he said.

It was tempting, but I needed to keep a clear head for the interview. "I've got an early start tomorrow."

"That's a shame. I thought we could celebrate my new flat."

"Let's do a proper housewarming when you're back."

"God, I'm so looking forward to having some space. I'm fed up with living in a hotel room. I don't care how great the bed is."

"What's so great about your bed?" As soon as the words had left my lips, I regretted them. Or rather, realized how laden with innuendo they sounded.

He chuckled. "After all these years, you're finally asking?"

I've thought about your bed a million times, I wanted to shout. But that would have been spectacularly uncool.

"Are you inviting me over to see your record collection?"

"It's my last night in the hotel. I thought maybe you'd like to spend it with me."

Blood was pumping in my ears. It was also making other parts of me pulse. But this was a decision my brain needed to make, and it was very strenuously advising *against*.

"You're off on a work trip, and I've got a big interview tomorrow morning." These were lame reasons, I knew, but I would have sounded even lamer listing my *real* objections: my armpits needed shaving, there was possibly a strand of tuna stuck in my teeth from lunchtime, and I was wearing lust-extinguishing underwear—knickers like gray flapping sails and a mustard-colored bra. (In my defense, it had been half price.)

"Another time, then."

My mouth was dry, but I managed to answer him. "Another time."

19
NOWHERE TO RUN

IT WAS 6:45 A.M. WHEN I got off the tube at Waterloo. I'd set two alarms, paranoid that one wouldn't work, so here I was, fifteen minutes ahead of schedule for my interview with Jonny Delaney. Nick had arranged it early so it didn't clash with my working day, but what I'd then taken for thoughtfulness now felt more like mind games.

It wasn't clear from Nick's text whether I'd be meeting Jonny alone or if he would come too, but I had my answer now.

Nick was leaning against a wall, his hands in his pockets and his head tilted toward the sun. His stillness was exaggerated by the bustle of commuters spiraling from the station.

He saw me approaching and straightened. His eyes were wary. "I wasn't sure you'd come."

"Couldn't disappoint Jonny." I looked around, trying to locate the man in question. "Where is he?"

"Let's walk."

I followed his lead, and we fell into step.

He cleared his throat. "I was snappy with you on the phone. I should have just told you what you needed to hear, which also happens to be the truth: I didn't send the paparazzi on Sunday night."

He seemed genuinely sorry, but what did I know? And anyway, did it matter if he was telling the truth or not? I was back on good terms with Simon and that was all I cared about.

"What's done is done," I said, keeping my voice neutral. "I'm here to interview your client, and then the next contact you and I have will be when you call to tell me where and when I can interview Marcie Tyler."

He raised an eyebrow. "What, no social calls?"

I frowned. "We're not friends, Nick. I'm sure you're a perfectly nice bloke, but we have a working relationship and that's all."

He tipped his head to one side. "I feel like I'm missing a page in this script."

"Never mind," I said, wishing I'd never let Simon's assessment of Nick's intentions toward me get under my skin. "If you got the wrong idea, it's partly my fault because I asked you to pretend to be my boyfriend, but that was a one-off. And it was an act."

He held up his hands. "I just did what I was told."

I nodded. "Great. I'm glad we cleared that up."

After a couple of beats, he said: "So, are you and Simon…"

"That's not really your business," I said. "But yes, sort of."

I'm not sure why I hadn't stopped talking after "business." Except I did know why; my curiosity was just too damned piqued, and my next question had already formed on my lips. "Are you and Marcie…"

His eyes widened in surprise. "No. Why would you say that?"

I waved my hand in front of him. "Because you've got the sort of face ancient civilizations built temples for, and Marcie's a legend." Not to mention all the rumors.

I was digging myself deeper now, but didn't know how to stop.

"No one would blame you." *Except, of course, everyone.* "Look, forget I said anything. I'm sorry."

He nodded. "Okay, well, at least that's sorted."

"Where's Jonny?" I said, happy to talk about *him* for the first time in my life.

"He's meeting us there."

I glanced around us. "Where is this mythical place?"

Nick nudged my shoulder with his and pointed to the sky.

A plane was flying high above Big Ben. "Jonny's on a plane? We're miles from an airport."

"No, I don't mean the plane. I mean the London Eye."

"You want to do the interview on the London Eye?"

"It was Jonny's idea and I thought it might be fun."

"It'll be busy, won't it?"

"I've reserved a pod."

Of course he had.

Nick looked at his watch. It was one of those sleek Swiss affairs, with too many buttons and dials. "We should get over there."

Jonny was waiting by the ticket office, along with our photographer David, whose number I'd given Nick yesterday. Two bodyguards were waiting discreetly to one side, while David watched something on Jonny's phone. He was grinning and nodding at whatever was on Jonny's screen, but suddenly stopped when he saw me, as if he were a schoolboy caught with a girly mag by a teacher.

"Jonny was just showing me his new bike," he said.

Yeah, right. Nick must have read my mind because he held open his palm, and Jonny duly dropped his phone into it. Nick frowned at the screen. "Who buys a Ducati in lime green? I had a cat who used to shit that color."

My jaw dropped at Nick's rudeness, but Jonny hadn't seemed to take offence because he was grinning. "It's a custom color, you fucker. Only twelve of them were ever made."

"Sweet," said David, who looked as relieved as I was that Nick's comment had evidently only been banter.

Jonny took his phone back and gazed once more at the screen. "I'm picking this beauty up in a couple of hours, so can we get started, please?"

"Follow me," said Nick.

A few people were milling around the embarkation pen; but surprisingly, no Hands Down fans. How had Jonny resisted broadcasting this on Twitter? A couple of Japanese girls seemed more interested in a police boat motoring along the Thames than this multi-million-selling pop star. Even Jonny's Day-Glo orange biker jacket wasn't attracting attention.

He was going to look a bloody sight on that Ducati.

The slow-moving wheel seemed to come to a complete standstill, and the four of us were shepherded into an empty pod. Once the door clanged shut, it was remarkably quiet in our glass cocoon.

David was maneuvering Jonny to one corner and getting off a few early shots, while Nick sat down on the central bench with his back to them, his eyes following a train rumbling over Waterloo Bridge.

I walked over to the corner furthest from them. The capsule's glass walls and steel supports made me feel like I was in the cockpit of the Millennium Falcon. Except instead of an expanse of stars, I had a blue sky overhead and a murky brown Thames beneath my feet.

Whoa. When had we gotten so high?

I pressed my hand against the glass to steady myself and planted my feet more firmly on the floor.

Was that a wobble?

The central arc of the wheel loomed above, and a hundred steel sinews cobwebbed around us.

I closed my eyes and took a deep breath. We weren't wobbling; we were barely moving. My mind was playing tricks on me.

"Zoë?" Nick was beside me. "We should get started with the interview."

I prized my eyes open then quickly shut them again. We were higher up now.

"Zoë? Are you okay?"

"I'm fine. Just a bit hungover."

I swung round to face the middle of the pod, but it was useless; I was surrounded by glass, so couldn't get away from the fact I was suspended God knows how many feet above ground in a spindly bauble that could come away from its hinges at any second. Sweat pricked the back of my neck, and my palms grew slippery.

"Oi, Nick!" came Jonny's voice from miles away. "There's a fat naked fucker on the bank who's about to go for a swim in the river!" Nick went over to Jonny, but I kept my eyes firmly trained on Big Ben. It was only ten past. We had forty more minutes of this. My knees started to buckle as I crept toward the central bench.

"Look, he's kept his trainers on!" shouted Jonny. "I've got to get a photo of this."

I sat down and sent a silent prayer to the skinny-dipper who'd bought me some precious moments to pull myself together.

This was crazy. I wasn't afraid of heights. And the hangover bit was a lie. Then it hit me: this was claustrophobia.

But it was absurd. It's one thing to be frightened in a lift—a small, enclosed space—but to be having a panic attack in a glass-fronted space the size of my bedroom was madness.

I was losing my mind. In front of Jonny fucking Delaney. I was damned if I was going to show him any sign of weakness. I needed to concentrate on the job in hand. My heart flapped like a panicked bird, but I gritted my teeth. This was for the future of *Re:Sound*. I could bloody well pull myself together for thirty-nine more minutes.

Jonny slid onto the bench next to me. He held up his phone to show me the picture he'd taken. I smiled gamely, not sure if the pixelated image was down to his lack of focusing skills or whether my eyes were refusing to play ball. He could have been showing me the Loch Ness Monster for all I knew.

I pulled my Dictaphone from my pocket, trying to concentrate on the screen that seemed to get blurrier the more I looked at it.

"Jonny, mate," said Nick from the other side. "David's got a great shot of the Houses of Parliament from here. We need you in the picture too. The Americans will love this."

Jonny got up and I swear the whole pod rocked. I looked up in panic, but no one seemed to have noticed. I clenched and unclenched my fists and exhaled. David was shouting encouragement to Jonny about where the light was best, but every click of his camera made my heart knock louder. I wanted to scream, but more than anything, I wanted to get out of here.

Nick walked toward me and the floor lurched up and down. Except Nick was acting like everything was fine. Why could nobody else feel this damn thing swinging like a seesaw?

He sat down on the bench beside me, as calm as anything. I closed my eyes and tried to breathe, but a weight pressed down on my chest, and like an over-zealous bouncer, was refusing air entry into my lungs.

"How good are your capitals?"

I jerked my head sideways, trying to calm my jumpy pulse. "Are you…are you…talking to me?"

Nick nodded. "I was at a pub quiz the other night. Can you believe that none of my team got the capital of Australia right? And before you ask, no, I wasn't there with the other members of Hands Down."

My mouth was dry, but I almost managed a smile. "It's Canberra."

"That's what I said, but I was shouted down."

"Right."

The pod rocked again, but still no one reacted. Nick seemed lost in thought about his damned pub quiz. I held my breath, waiting to see if the pod would move again. Maybe it had been a gust of wind.

"They put Auckland as the capital of New Zealand."

"What?"

"Auckland instead of Wellington. Can you believe that?"

I shook my head, and Nick continued, the indignation written on his face. "At least we all agreed that Rio was the capital of Brazil."

"It's Brasilia," I said, on a shaky breath.

He frowned. "Are you sure?"

"Yes."

"The quizmaster gave me the point, though."

"I bet she did."

He held my eye, and I realized that, for a couple of seconds, I'd forgotten my panic. All this talk about capitals had given my brain something else to do.

My lungs expanded, and I took a proper breath.

He was shaking his head. "I don't know what I'm more offended about—that you think I don't know Brasilia is the capital of Brazil or that I'd flirt to win a pub quiz."

"You won? The other teams must have been really thick."

"They were. You'd think Bono and the Edge would have known that Dublin was the capital of Ireland."

He's kidding, right? "U2 were not at your pub quiz."

He smiled, and I found myself smiling back.

Just as I began to feel like the sky wasn't about to fall on our heads, Jonny stomped over and the walls started closing in again.

"*Hello?*" he said. "Earth to the lovebirds. I've been finished for five minutes. Are we going to do this interview or what?"

I tried to stand, but my limbs weren't responding. Jonny was staring at me, waiting for an answer, but the only part of me willing to cooperate was my upchuck reflex. Oh God, that would be a disaster. I swallowed hard and looked at Nick, but all his attention was on Jonny.

"We're only here for the pictures. Zoë's not here to interview you."

I wasn't?

"Then why the fuck is she here then?"

Good question.

"Because, Jonny, you insisted you get face time with the editor of *Re:Sound*, which is what I arranged. That doesn't mean you get to choose who interviews you."

"So when do we do the interview?"

"Later."

Jonny pulled a face. "But I've got to pick up the Ducati later."

"The Ducati will have to wait."

I should have stepped in and told them I would do the interview, but Nick was so convincing, I half believed that this had been the plan all along and that Jonny wasn't the only one who'd been misinformed.

Nick peered over our heads toward the door. "We're nearly back on the ground, anyway."

He was right. We were only a few feet away from terra firma.

The capsule suddenly didn't feel quite so small and enclosed. A sea of people in the queue had their faces turned toward us. Among them were some very excited girls who'd arrived because Jonny had probably Instagrammed pictures of his naked swimmer.

When the door opened, the fresh air energized me like a hit of caffeine. I stepped onto solid ground, my legs less wobbly with each step. Jonny was immediately swallowed up by the crowd, but then his bodyguards appeared to ferry him toward a waiting Range Rover, leaving me, David, and Nick to fend off the disappointed fans.

It didn't take long. Most of the girls quickly realized their prey had sped off in the opposite direction, so they didn't waste time hanging around us.

One of the last to leave was a brunette girl in school uniform, who looked about thirteen. Her closing shot was to tell me in rather grown-up language that Jonny had no interest in "an old slag like" me and that I "should fucking well watch" my back.

Charming.

David promised to have some shots for me tomorrow morning and headed back to the tube, leaving me alone with Nick. There was so much I wanted to tell him, and this was the perfect chance. But before I could speak, Nick was moving toward the main road and raising his arm to hail a cab.

"Jonny has some crazy fans," I said as I followed.

He stopped abruptly and I almost went into the back of him. "You don't know the half of it." The taxi he'd been hoping to stop sailed past us. He glanced at his watch and grimaced. He was obviously in a hurry, but I couldn't let him leave without acknowledging what he'd done.

"I wanted to thank you," I said, "For...you know."

"Organizing the interview?"

"No. Well, yes. But not just that."

The words wouldn't come. It didn't help that he had his full attention on me now. The gaze that had darted up and down the road searching for a free cab was now searching me. The whites of his eyes were really white, and it made his stare even more intense. I wanted to squirm and wriggle free but couldn't. Where's a rabid Jonny fan when you need one?

I broke eye contact to check my watch. I could always thank him by email.

"You wanted to thank me for that refresher on capital cities."

I looked up. He still had that intense look in his eye, but he was also almost smiling.

"I appreciate it. It was very—"

"Timely?"

I swallowed. "Yes, exactly."

"Don't think about it."

A cab appeared and stopped without Nick making any kind of gesture. Did I need to add telepathy to his list of talents?

He opened the door. "Why don't you take it? Jonny will be ready for his interview at my office at six. Send someone else to do it. I'm sure you're too busy at such short notice."

I climbed into the cab and turned to thank him, but I didn't get a chance because he closed the door, and the driver took it as a sign to pull away.

The whole experience had left me feeling shaken, but I tried not to dwell on it. Back at the office, I asked Lucy to go and interview Jonny. She looked less than thrilled by the prospect.

After I came back from lunch, I heard her trying to palm it off on Gavin by challenging him to a game of Rock, Paper, Scissors.

"You must be joking, Luce," he snapped. "Why would I go from having zero chance of having to interview that twat to a one-in-three chance?"

"Because I'd be eternally grateful," she replied in a flirty voice.

Maybe it was just hot in the office, but I could have sworn Gavin went red at her reply.

20

EVERYBODY HURTS

THE REST OF THE WEEK passed without incident, and still no word from Nick regarding the Marcie interview. But my goodwill toward him had grown since the London Eye, so I figured he was working on it. Late on Friday afternoon, I boarded the train at Victoria for Alice's hen weekend in Brighton. Her other friends had caught earlier trains, and I was the last to check in to the B&B. It faced the sea, which was an unexpected bonus, but was closer to Hove than Brighton. Still, even a dyed-in-the-wool Londoner like me could take pleasure from waves breaking on the pebbled shore to a rhythm of satisfying whooshes.

Alice had texted me where they were—a bar on the pier. I dumped my case on the floor between the paisley curtains and the single bed—the only place it could fit—then sat and rechecked my phone hoping I'd find a message from her along the lines of "decided to call it a night." But it was barely eight o'clock on a Friday and even Alice was upping her rock and roll game for her hen weekend.

I left my jeans and Converse on, but changed into a cotton peasant top—which felt appropriately seaside-ish. I'd barely taken five steps out of the front door before returning to get my jacket. Walks along

British shores were not balmy strolls under shady palm trees, but hard slogs against gale-force winds. By the time I got to the pier, my cheeks were stinging and my hair had doubled in volume, as if it had been blow-dried by the jet engine of a 747.

Alice and Co. were bunched together in a booth that comfortably seated six and rather uncomfortably seated nine, as I discovered when I joined them carrying a fresh bottle of wine. I knew Annette and Helen, but the other five faces were new to me. Annette, who had organized the weekend, immediately stood up when I sat down.

"Everyone, this is Zoë Frixos, the sister-in-law." A polite cheer went up—thank God they weren't all completely pissed yet. "You know what to do, girls."

The girl to my left thumped the table, clapped once, and then the rest of the group sang "Laura!" The girl after her then thumped the table twice, clapped twice, while everyone announced "Seema." And so it went on, till we got to me, by which time I'd cottoned on that I needed to thump the table and clap nine times while they chorused my name.

"And back round again!" decreed Annette, so the whole process was repeated like a Mexican wave.

I had to admit it was a neat trick to remember names. I'd barely been here ten minutes and could correctly identify everyone: Laura, Seema, Flo, Sally, Vicky, Helen, Annette, and Alice. Maybe I should suggest it next time I was at a work dinner and struggling to match names to faces.

I was also pleased I wasn't the most underdressed of all the hens. Laura and Seema looked like they'd come straight from work—both were wearing buttoned-up blouses and sensible skirts. Most eye-catching was Flo, however. She was wearing earrings that reached her neck—a constellation of gold stars on delicate chains that caught the light whenever she moved her head. She must be the jewelry designer—Alice had mentioned her. Pete had secretly commissioned her to custom-make a necklace for the big day—an uncharacteristically thoughtful impulse from my brother.

"We got you a little something, Alice," said Annette. She reached under the table and brought up a rather phallic-looking package. Annette had shown remarkable restraint in not suggesting we all wear fake tits and tiaras; I could forgive her one dildo. I only hoped that Alice wouldn't be mortified.

She started unwrapping and the package got thinner and thinner; Annette must have bought something from the beginners' range. But when Alice removed the last of the wrapping, her gasp was echoed by my own. In her hand was a stick of rock candy, a swirl of lilac threaded with white. Inside was written: Alice and Pete. Not Alice luvs Pete, or Pete and Alice 4 EVA, just Alice and Pete.

"We had it made especially," said Annette to impromptu applause.

Alice looked happy to the point of tears—and not only because she wasn't having to thank us for gifting her a plastic phallus. She was genuinely moved.

"It's in the right colors and everything," she whispered.

Annette grinned proudly. "And that's not all. We've made one hundred and fifty miniature versions that you can give your guests as wedding favors."

Alice flung her arms around Annette and let the tears fall. "Thank you so much!"

The moment was topped off by the arrival of flutes and two bottles of champagne. Annette had thought of everything.

I was feeling rather less sympathetic toward her, however, when the disco started. She insisted we all dance, and kept requesting those annoying records that have tacky choreography that she forced everyone to do.

"YMCA" I quite enjoyed. "The Macarena" I was less happy with. "Achy Breaky Heart" was hopeless. *Who the hell remembered this?* I drew the line at "Gangnam Style" and excused myself to go to the loo.

I splashed water on my cheeks to cool down. It was quieter here, and it was good to catch my breath. The bar was heaving; I was a few glasses gone, but still had stray moments of concern that hundreds of us were drinking away our cares while suspended above the freezing English Channel supported only by a few rickety pillars.

Alice joined me a few moments later. "You're missing 'The Loco-Motion,'" she grinned.

"Damn."

"I'll make sure you get to dance to it at the wedding."

"I'm sure you will."

Alice went into a stall, and I checked my phone out of habit. I had a missed call from Justin, but no voicemail. I checked the time he'd rung: ten o'clock. Strange—were he and Patrick having another ding-dong about Italian olive oil? The phone rang again, and Justin's name flashed up.

"Hello?" The line was crackly, and all I could hear were muffled voices.

I hung up, but a few moments later it rang again. This time I heard someone say my name.

"Justin? Is that you? I can't hear you. Let me ring you back."

Alice had emerged from the cubicle and was washing her hands. She stopped when she saw me. "Everything okay?"

The string of calls was unsettling. Had something happened?

Alice was looking at me, waiting for an answer.

"I'm sure it's nothing," I reassured her. "But I'm just going out to see if I can get better reception. I won't be long."

I pushed through the bar and out into the night air. The wind was calmer, but the temperature had dropped. My cotton shirt did nothing to keep out the sea-cooled air, and goose bumps sprang up on my arms. My hand trembled as I dialed Justin's number.

He picked up immediately. "Zoë?"

The line was clear at last. "Is everything okay, Justin? I've missed a bunch of calls from you."

"It's Patrick." His voice cracked. "He's had a heart attack."

I walked back into the bar barely aware of anything around me. The dance floor was filled with people sitting in rows, pretending to paddle boats. A few bars from "Oops Upside Your Head" filtered into my consciousness. Annette was waving at me from her prone position on the dance floor, but I kept walking till I reached the table. Laura and Seema smiled at me, and I smiled wanly back and grabbed my bag and jacket.

"I have to go," I told them. But even as I said the words, I wasn't sure what I meant. Go where?

"Is everything okay?" I heard one of them say, but I didn't answer. I just kept putting one foot in front of the other. I needed to keep moving.

Alice found me when I was halfway along the pier.

"Zoë, sweetie, what's wrong? You're shivering." She prized the jacket from my hand and wrapped it around my shoulders. "You're in no state to go anywhere alone. Tell me what's happened."

"Patrick's had a heart attack. He's in surgery now. I need to get back to London."

"Oh my goodness. That's terrible. But you can't go alone. Let me come with you."

Her words snapped me back to the present. "It's your hen weekend, Alice. I can't let you leave."

"Well, I can at least go back with you to the hotel. Come on, I'll find us a cab. I don't want to hear any arguments."

The taxi reeked of greasy food. The stale stench of kebab made my stomach turn. If the journey had been even one minute longer, I would have thrown up on the back seat. Instead, I retched on the pavement as Alice paid the driver. All I remember thinking was how the splatter reminded me of the shooting stars on Flo's earrings.

The next morning, I felt numb. I'd bought a tea at Brighton station, but had only managed a few sips. The sachet of milk I'd tipped into it had barely affected the color; the dark brew sloshed against the cup, murky and unappetizing, as the train rumbled north toward London.

After we'd gotten back to the hotel last night, Alice had wrapped me in the single duvet fully clothed while she checked train times. I sat motionless on the bed, only coming back to life when my phone rang: it was Justin telling me Patrick was out of surgery. He was stable, but critical.

Patrick was alive.

The news was like oxygen; I could finally draw breath. I didn't want to stay in Brighton—I'd suck the cheer out of everything—but I'd promised Alice I'd wait till morning to go.

She'd knocked again on my door just before midnight. I hadn't been sleeping, just staring into space.

She handed me a slab of Green and Black's dark chocolate. "Pete said it was your favorite. When I spoke to him, he sounded pretty cut up."

My hands were shaking, making it hard to open the wrapping. Alice straightened the bed covers to give me a few seconds to compose myself before she sat down. "He'd mentioned Patrick before, but I didn't realize he was a regular at your parents' restaurant."

I cleared my throat to spare Alice the crack in my voice. "He rented the office above, but some days he'd spend more time with us than upstairs—especially in winter. The heat from the charcoal grill had something to do with that."

"Pete said it was the lure of your mum's homemade tzatziki."

I smiled for the first time since the phone call. It felt good to remember; the happy memories were as comforting as a blanket.

"He used to give me his copy of *Re:Sound* after he'd read it, and we'd talk about bands for hours. My life would have taken a very different turn if Patrick hadn't been in it."

"Pete says your parents wanted you to be a lawyer."

"Immigrants always want their children to train to get proper jobs, and I don't blame them. It helped that Pete was happy to go into accountancy, it took the pressure off me. So, when I announced I wanted to do an English degree, they reassured themselves that I could always be a teacher. They wanted more for us than the slog of working in a restaurant. But then, if it wasn't for that restaurant I wouldn't have met Patrick."

After she left I didn't manage to sleep at all. The hours ticked by, and it felt like I was just waiting for my alarm to go off.

I dozed a bit on the train, thankful it was the weekend, otherwise I wouldn't have gotten a seat, but for the last part of the journey back to London, I gazed listlessly out of the window.

I now found myself back at my flat sitting on a hard-backed

kitchen chair, my bones aching from tiredness, mechanically chewing toast and forcing back coffee in an effort to jump-start myself awake.

I wanted to go to the hospital—surely he'd be allowed visitors by now? But would I be allowed in to see him? I wasn't family, and I didn't know any members of Patrick's as he never talked about them. I only knew Justin.

It was only a few days ago that Patrick and I had been chatting in John Lewis, and he'd told me how much he was looking forward to spending more time at his vineyard in Crete. He was going to learn how to make wine, and I'd teased him that he'd spend his days content just to drink it. The idea that he might never make it back to Crete made me feel sick all over again.

I had to do something. I couldn't just sit here.

I googled the name of the hospital Justin had given me. It was somewhere off Harley Street. Whether I was allowed in or not was in the lap of the gods. I just knew I had to try.

It was spitting when I came out of the station at Oxford Circus. I pulled up my hoodie and cursed myself for not bringing an umbrella. I could have stayed underground, changed onto the Bakerloo Line and gotten off at Regent's Park—the tube closest to the hospital—but trains were so unreliable on the weekends, it was faster to walk.

Despite the rain, I found myself walking slowly. Every so often I'd chide myself to get a move on, but it still took me almost twenty minutes to reach the hospital. Then there was some confusion over which wing I needed, and by the time I'd found the right entrance, I'd been walking for a full half hour. My hands were frozen and my trainers were sodden.

The reception was empty, with only a receptionist and security guard sitting behind a curved mahogany desk.

I walked toward them, my sockless feet squelching in my trainers. "I'm here to see Patrick Armstrong."

The receptionist clicked a couple of times on her computer, but before she could speak, the lift doors slid open and Justin walked out. He didn't need to speak; his ashen face said it all. He caught my eye and shook his head.

I was too late. Patrick was dead.

I felt my body sway, and I swung out my arm to steady myself against the wall. Justin was walking toward me; I blinked furiously, trying to get my eyes to focus.

I realized Justin was talking and that his hand was gently touching my forearm. "Zoë," he repeated. "You're in shock. I think we all are."

His words snapped me to attention. "I'm so sorry, Justin. Sorry for your loss, and for not being here for Pat sooner."

"There was nothing any of us could do." His eyes were glassy. He had his own grief to deal with; I was just in the way.

♪

The next few days went by in a blur. I did what I always do when I'm stressed—I threw myself into work and drank too much. I played phone tag with Nick, trying to pin down a day to interview Marcie, but I didn't have the energy to get angry with him when he didn't pick up the phone. I guess I just needed to trust that he'd come through for me.

Simon was still away, and we Facetimed as much as possible, but some nights, I was out too late to catch him, and we'd just send each other a series of texts.

On the fourth day after Patrick died, I got a postcard from Zak Scaramouche.

> Dear Member,
>
> I'm just a humble rock and roller, taking life one bottle of Jack Daniel's at a time, but I've learned a couple of things over the years: life is precious and we need to cherish every moment, and the people around us.
>
> I'm not very good at sharing my feelings—I prefer to let my guitar do the talking—but I want you to know that I'm thinking of you and that my heart breaks imagining that yours is breaking.
>
> Sometimes it's hard to keep doing the Fandango.
>
> Sometimes it takes all our effort just to keep putting one foot in front of the other. But I'm here walking beside you.
>
> Always.
>
> Zak x

I rang Simon the night before the funeral and asked if he could come with me.

"I'm so sorry, Frixie. I wish more than anything I could be there for you, but I just can't get back to London tomorrow."

I tried not to feel too hurt by it; it wasn't a personal rejection, and after all Simon didn't know Patrick.

I think he was surprised his death had affected me so much.

I tried to explain it to him. "I owe him so much. I'd never have considered a career in music journalism if I'd never met him."

"I understand, but you've got to look to the future, Frixie. That's what Patrick would want."

He was right, but it wasn't what I wanted to hear.

I was dreading the funeral more than I let on to anyone. Part of me wanted to bail, but I knew I'd never forgive myself if I chickened out.

I was struggling to grieve for Patrick and I felt awful. I hadn't cried once. What sort of monster did that make me?

The funeral was on Friday morning, but I got up early and went into the office first to make sure nothing urgent needed my attention. Mike was in too, which first surprised and then worried me.

I popped my head around his door on the way out. "Everything okay, Mike?"

He didn't look up from his monitor. "Yep, all good here. You?"

"I'll be fine."

He stopped typing and turned toward me, frowning. "Shit. I'm sorry. You're wearing black. It's the funeral today, and I forgot."

I tugged the hem of my skirt down. "It's okay. I won't stay too long."

"Take all the time you need, Zoë. Not much happening." He leaned forward. "Is Marcie going to be there?"

"I honestly hadn't thought about it."

"If she is, will you talk to her?"

"You want me to doorstep her at a funeral?"

Things must be worse than he was letting on; Mike wasn't usually this cold.

"You said you'd do whatever it takes."

"While still being a decent human being."

He didn't seem to hear me, much less notice my anger. He went on: "What does she care about Patrick? She bloody well fired him, didn't she?"

I took a breath to calm myself. "Well, I doubt she'll come to his funeral, then."

I was still irritated when I arrived at the chapel in Kensal Green Cemetery. What the fuck was wrong with Mike? How could he suggest such a thing? But my anger was being slowly filtered through dread. The finances must have been more desperate than I thought. I wanted to run away, not be at the funeral of my mentor with the almost certain demise of the magazine we both loved hovering on the horizon.

But I was already in the chapel now; people had seen me, and the service was due to start any moment. There were fewer people than I expected, and a quick glance around confirmed that Marcie was definitely not here. I was relieved, but sad at the same time.

Had they fallen out so badly?

Of course, there would be press here, and being in public was the last thing Marcie wanted. She probably couldn't have come even if she'd wanted to.

Justin led the humanist service, his voice strong and unwavering. He was a former singer, used to masking unwanted emotions. He not only managed to keep his tears at bay, he made a couple of jokes that pierced through even my grief.

I didn't get too close when we all trudged out to the burial plot. It was windy now, and gray clouds were gathering overhead. This was the real business of death. Not the flower-filled chapel, but here, in the cold, as six pallbearers solemnly lowered Patrick into a hole in the cold, hard earth. How could this be right? How could a man with such energy and vitality be snuffed out? My limbs felt heavy with grief, but my own tears still didn't come.

The wake was in a nearby pub. I hovered awkwardly, a small glass of wine in my hand, attempting small talk with people I usually laughed and got pissed with. But not today. After half an hour I left. The mood was too jolly; I needed quiet.

Instead of heading toward the bus stop, I retraced my steps back to the cemetery.

I walked slowly, reading the names and dates engraved on the headstones. Vera Edwina Edmunds, loving wife and mother to James and Rosemary, was thirty-four when she died—the same age as me.

I kept walking, not caring which direction I went, but after a few minutes I realized that I was approaching Patrick's grave. It had been filled in now; a brown rectangular scar on the green grass around it. A woman was standing in front of it with her back to me. She was wearing a long dark coat and her hair was hidden under a felt hat that looked familiar. She turned her head slightly, and I gasped.

It was Marcie Tyler.

21
TORN

NO ONE ELSE WAS WITHIN a hundred meters of us. It was just me and Marcie, standing with her back to me a few precious steps away.

I closed my eyes, in the vague hope that I could magic her away. If either she or I weren't here, then I wouldn't have to make this horrible choice. Because, however angry I had been at Mike's suggestion, now that she was in front of me, I couldn't just walk away. Nick had left me promising voicemails, but he had yet to come up with the goods. So while there was a chance, however small, that all my professional troubles could be solved by one short conversation with the woman standing in front of me, was it so wrong to approach her? All I would be asking for was sixty minutes, at a place and time of her choice.

I took a step forward, then stopped. She was grieving. I couldn't intrude.

But I might never get this opportunity again, and I'd kick myself if I didn't try.

I took two more steps, but she must have heard me because she spun round like a startled cat, her green eyes narrowing.

I froze. I couldn't move forward, but I couldn't back away.

She broke the silence first. "What are you doing here?"

Her voice sounded raspier than last time, and the words I was about to say died on my tongue.

She raised her eyebrows, waiting for me to speak. The sun had come out now, and it caught a tear that was halfway down her cheek.

"I, um, thought I'd left my umbrella here, that's all."

Marcie frowned, but I didn't wait for her to respond. Instead, I started walking in the direction I'd come from, my fists in my coat pockets and my heart thumping against my ribcage.

I went back to the office, not caring that I was still wearing my black skirt and blouse, or that my heels were pinching my feet. It was lunchtime, and most people were out—including Mike. I hadn't decided yet whether I'd tell him I'd seen Marcie or not. I wouldn't bring it up myself, but if he asked me directly, was I prepared to lie?

The afternoon passed slowly, but the others could tell I didn't want to talk and they left me in peace. Ayisha popped out at one point and came back with a Mars Bar, which she quietly slipped onto my desk. Someone from the trade press phoned to ask me to write an obit for Patrick, but I let it go to voicemail.

By six I was the only one left on the floor. It was just me and the hum of sleeping computers.

The ping of the lift meant the cleaners were arriving—my cue to leave. But to go where? I didn't want to sit in an empty flat. My head felt numb, but my body felt electrified, like the two were disconnected.

There was a tap. The door between us and the corridor was always open—why would anyone knock?

I looked up. Nick was leaning against the doorframe, wearing a black suit and tie—funeral attire.

Shit. He had been there too.

Was he here to give me an earful for daring to address Marcie?

He didn't look annoyed, but he rarely wore his emotions on his face. The professional side of him was always in control—never a speck on his shirt or a wrinkle in his suit. A man with his life in order, while mine was in chaos. I wasn't sure I had the energy to deal with him.

He walked over and pointed to Gavin's empty chair. "May I?"

I nodded—what else could I do? But instead of sitting behind Gavin's desk, he slid the chair round until it was level with my desk. And it was only as he sat down that I noticed he was holding a bottle of Gordon's gin.

"That's Patrick's favorite," I whispered, my throat tight.

"I thought we could pay our respects to him." He reached into his inside pocket and pulled out two plastic cups. "It's all I could muster at short notice. I don't suppose you have any crystal glasses lying around?"

"All the crystal's being polished, I'm afraid."

He smiled. "Then we'll just have to rough it."

He placed the cups on the edge of my desk, next to a proof of "Shit Lyrics." The gaudy headline made me wince; it suddenly felt disrespectful. Had Nick noticed? He hadn't appeared to; his eyes were on what he was doing: unscrewing the bottle and pouring us both a generous measure.

He handed me a cup. "To Patrick."

"To Patrick."

I wasn't a fan of neat gin, and it burned as it went down, but at least its fire was melting some of my numbness.

"I saw you today," he said, swirling his drink, "in the cemetery."

Here it was, the reason he'd come—to tell me off about hounding Marcie.

"We must have missed each other," I said, tensing.

Nick watched me as I took another sip of warm gin, but his own cup stayed on my desk. "I appreciate it."

He was thanking me? "What do you mean?"

"Marcie needed her privacy today, and you respected that."

I'd done the right thing by Marcie, that was what mattered, but for some reason, it also felt important to get his acknowledgment.

He looked tired today; not quite as perfectly clean-shaven as usual. "Marcie's in a bad state."

Without thinking, I placed my hand on his knee. "I'm sorry."

Nick didn't flinch; he didn't blink. His eyes were the same emerald green as the bottle of Gordon's, and they suddenly felt achingly familiar—like we'd known each other in a different life.

His gaze was unsettling; I needed to concentrate on something other than his face.

"We've done this funny feature called 'Shit Lyrics.'"

Nope. Not better.

He broke eye contact and downed the rest of his gin. His Adam's apple moved as he swallowed. "You're busy," he said. "I should go. I just wanted to make sure you were okay." He stood, and I suddenly really wanted him to stay.

"I might need one more shot, before you go."

"It's yours," he said. "It was Patrick's—"

"—favorite drink, I know."

"No, it's his actual bottle."

Everything went still. "This is...*his* bottle?"

He nodded. "He gave it to Marcie years ago. I snuck it out so you could have it."

A ball formed in my throat. I couldn't breathe.

Hot tears welled but before I could stop them, they were streaming down my face. I dropped my head so Nick couldn't see me cry.

He was standing, but instead of moving away he took my hand, pulled me to my feet, and wrapped his arms around me.

I clung to him, properly sobbing now. But each falling tear made me feel lighter. It wasn't the grief that was lifting, just my resistance to showing it. I was finally crying and the relief was overwhelming. I hadn't realized how much I'd needed a simple hug. At the funeral, people had pecked cheeks and patted backs, but the contact had been fleeting and unfeeling. Nick's embrace was warm and solid.

His pristine suit jacket was getting wet with my tears, but he didn't seem to mind. After a couple of minutes, he pulled back gently.

"The gin's better off with you than Marcie—a recovering alcoholic."

I managed a smile and wiped my clammy cheek.

"Thank you, Nick."

I stayed in the office an hour after Nick left, dumbly staring at my screen, but not managing to work. Every time I looked at the bottle of Gordon's I felt peaceful, but I couldn't explain why. The dread that had pooled in my stomach was easing, and even though I'd originally wanted to stay at work because I didn't want to go home to an empty flat, I now craved sanctuary—away from an office that was full of things that reminded me of how close the magazine was to folding.

I had a bunch of missed calls on my phone, including a couple from Simon, but I didn't have the energy to deal with anyone. For once, I just wanted to look after myself. A warm bath and an early night sounded like bliss.

I must have needed sleep more than I realized because I nodded off on the tube home and only woke up at the end of the line in Ealing Broadway. I then had to backtrack to Shepherd's Bush, and I was ready to collapse as I pushed open the door to my flat at eight o'clock.

But with a sinking heart, I realized I wasn't alone.

I should have checked my messages because then I might have known that Simon was back early. Instead, I was only finding out now that he was standing in my kitchen and simmering onions in my new Jamie Oliver frying pan.

"What are you doing here, Si?"

"Making a crappy Bolognese." He grinned boyishly. "I had a spare twelve hours so took a flight from Edinburgh. Got to be back by six o'clock tomorrow."

I felt a rush of gratitude. "That's so sweet, Si. Thank you."

His kindness, not to mention the tempting smell, made me feel guilty about momentarily resenting his presence.

"I'm sorry I couldn't get back in time for the funeral, Frixie."

"It's okay. Zak helped."

He closed the distance between us and folded me into a hug. It was comforting to feel his arms around me, and unlike the night at Georgia's, there was no heat between us. But it was exactly what I needed.

"You look exhausted," he said when we stepped apart.

"I am."

"Why don't you go run a bath? This needs at least half an hour."

"Are you sure?"

"Go, and when you come back this will all be ready."

I squeezed his hand. "Thanks, Si."

A bath would only send me to sleep, so I opted for a hot shower. I found some grapefruit body scrub and rubbed my limbs until they tingled. I toweled myself dry, taking the edge off my tiredness.

The temperature had dropped, so I dug out some flannel pajamas and wrapped myself in the terry cloth dressing gown I only ever wore when I was unwell.

I joined Simon at the kitchen table. He'd set it with a steaming bowl of tagliatelle and chilled wine. The combination of the rich sauce and crisp Sancerre was exactly what I needed to feel part of the human race again.

After we'd eaten, I surprised both of us when I refused a second glass of wine.

"Mug of tea instead?" he asked.

I nodded and was about to get up, but he insisted I go and relax on the sofa while he made it.

I put on a playlist of mellow nineties hits. The old-school tunes reminded me of being a kid again, a time without responsibilities, when the biggest worry I had was whether that red splotch on my chin was going to turn into a zit or not.

All Saints' "Never Ever" was playing when Simon returned with two mugs of tea.

"Great song," he said, sitting down next to me.

"How's your trip been so far?" I said, aware that we'd only talked about me since he'd gotten here.

He took a sip of tea and frowned. "Let's not talk about work. I'm getting boring in my old age, because I was dragged to a heavy metal concert in Stockholm by a client and I actually heard myself announce 'This isn't music!' just like your dad whenever we played 'Smells Like Teen Spirit.'"

I smiled. "We played that a *lot*."

"And who knew metal was so big in Scandinavia?"

"I did, actually."

He grinned. "You don't count."

He left by 10:30. I'd offered him the sofa bed, but he'd insisted he leave.

"I've got to be up in…" He checked his watch. "Four and a half hours. No need to wake you up too. Sleep tight, Frixie."

♪

Over the next couple of days I wrote two obits for Patrick—one for a trade paper and one for *Re:Sound*.

Then, on Tuesday morning as I arrived at work, I received a text from Nick:

Marcie can see you today at 6pm—can you make it?

Holy cow.

I typed back a feverish YES and stared at my computer screen, trying to decide what to do. I opened a document I'd created months ago with possible questions to ask Marcie. Was it finally going to happen?

A few minutes later, my phone buzzed with another text from Nick. It was an address in St. John's Wood—her home, as far as I knew. This was getting more and more surreal.

Then a third text:

Will text you today's password protocol later.

When the rest of the team arrived, I stood up and called for their attention.

"Guess who's got a hot date with Marcie Tyler?"

Gavin frowned. "One of the *Love Island* guys, according to the tabloids."

Lucy gave the back of his head a friendly thump. "Oh my God, Zoë. It's you, isn't it?"

I nodded and the room erupted into whoops and cheers. It brought Mike running to join us, which saved me a trip to his office.

"I'm going to sleep well tonight," he said, before slipping out again.

By 4:30, I'd checked and rechecked my Dictaphone was fully charged and had enough available memory. I printed out my questions, then headed off.

I got to St. John's Wood at 5:30. Every other house was being renovated; architects' boards hung from wrought-iron gates while diggers shifted earth to carve out basements. Paul McCartney was rumored to have a house around here. Did he and Marcie ever bump into each other at the corner shop that charged £3.60 for a small bottle of water? Of course, Marcie probably had assistants to nip out for her when she ran out of toilet roll. But famous people are like everyone else. I once bumped into Jerry Hall buying Häagen-Dazs in a Richmond convenience store at midnight. A sweet tooth is a great leveler.

I kept checking my phone, paranoid that Nick was going to cancel, or that he'd forget to send the password. However, at ten to six I got a single text from him:

You're Bonnie—ask for Clyde.

I texted back a thank you, then turned my phone to silent.

From what I could tell, Marcie's house was surrounded by an eight-foot-high red-brick wall. It was innocuous enough, until you noticed the security cameras angled high above. It wasn't the biggest house in the street, but then again, you couldn't really see it from the street. A black wooden door in the wall was the only point of entry, and even then, it would only grant you access to the front garden.

I pressed the button on the intercom at exactly six. It made no noise; it simply flashed blue.

Seconds passed and nothing happened. My finger hovered over the chrome box, poised to press again, but then I heard a crackly voice. "May I help you?"

It was a male voice, which threw me. But had I really thought Marcie would answer her own bell?

Time to test Nick's trustworthiness. "It's Bonnie."

"I beg your pardon?"

A faint barking came from the tinny box.

I cleared my throat. "It's Bonnie and I'm here to see Clyde."

Silence. Any second now, I was going to be told the police had been called. *Any second now...*

"Come in, Bonnie."

The door clicked open. I couldn't believe it and half expected it to slam shut again. I pushed against it tentatively, and it swung open. The barking was growing louder. Great. They'd released the hounds, and I was about to get mangled by a pack of angry dogs.

I moved stiffly along the graveled path, trying to remember what all those dog-whispering shows said about asserting dominance over dogs and avoiding getting mauled to death. Then a female voice issued a sharp "Down!" and the noise stopped.

The path led to a stuccoed building with Georgian arched windows and a glossy black door. On either side of me was striped grass, and out of the corner of my eye, I caught an ancient stone sundial.

I climbed two steps and raised my hand to knock on the door, but before I could, it creaked open, and a Staffordshire bull terrier stuck its face around it. Its mouth was the width of its head, and its teeth shone with saliva. It growled at me, and I froze.

"Come back here *now*, Saffron."

The dog backed away, and in its place, a looming figure in a long-sleeved black dress and bare feet appeared.

"Don't mind Saffie; she's harmless."

Marcie was taller than I remembered. Thinner too. When she turned to let me though the door, her collarbones jutted out under her fair skin.

We were in a cavernous hall with a herringbone wood floor that shone like a chestnut and was probably over a hundred years old. Every single one of my musical idols had probably crossed this floor. One was here in the flesh now, offering me a drink.

"I've just opened a bottle of wine."

Wait a sec.

She was just out of rehab; she shouldn't have been drinking. Saying yes was enabling her, wasn't it? Perhaps it was non-alcoholic…

"What sort of wine?" I blurted.

She frowned in concentration. "Red, I think."

She's joking, right?

She motioned for me to follow her, and I found myself in a corridor lined with gold discs. We were heading to the back of the house, toward an even bigger garden than the one out front. I peered discreetly through every doorway we passed.

Was that her seafoam green Telecaster propped up against a

bookcase? The one she had slung low on her hips on the cover of *Day By Day*—the first album I ever bought? Bloody hell.

I hurried to catch up with Marcie and found her in the kitchen. Saffie the Staffie was now curled up in a dog basket next to a double-sized Aga oven. Marcie was sitting at a black granite breakfast bar, and she nodded for me to sit opposite her, where a glass of red wine was waiting for me.

The bottle was almost empty. She clearly hadn't just opened it.

I slid onto a bar stool and knocked my knees against the table. The impact made my nerves tingle and produced a loud whack, but Marcie didn't react. My bag hung limply from my shoulder. I moved it to my lap, unzipped it, and took out my recorder. "Is this okay?"

Marcie smiled and I was struck by how beautiful she was. High cheekbones, perfect skin, unfussy, dark, glossy hair. "You won't need it."

I didn't like the sound of this. I'd done interviews before without my Dictaphone, but it wasn't ideal. It didn't look like I had much choice, though. "No problem, I'll just make notes."

"No notes, either."

My hand was in my bag, searching for a pen and notepad. I stopped. "No notes? You want me to rely on my memory?"

"You're not going to repeat anything we say."

What did she mean? "Nick said you'd agreed to an interview."

"I've done no such thing."

My heart sank. I was going to bloody *kill* him. "So, why did you agree to see me?"

"This is a pre-interview interview. We're simply going to chat, and if I decide I like you, I will allow you to interview me."

Okay, maybe this wasn't so bad. "So I can get you on the record afterward?"

She took a slug of wine. "Well, I'll need some time to decide."

My neck muscles tensed. "How much time?"

"A few days, a couple of weeks. We'll see."

Shit. I didn't have a couple of weeks. And Nick had expressly told me I would be interviewing her. He was going to have some serious explaining to do.

"We've met before, haven't we?"

I nodded. Was that going to count for me or against me? "At the piano shop, I played a tune for you." This wasn't the time to mention we'd seen each other at the cemetery too.

She didn't respond. Instead, she drained her glass then reached for the bottle. There was only enough left to fill half her glass. She turned the bottle upside down, tapped the bottom, and eked out a few more drops.

Oh boy.

"I'll go and get another bottle. Give me two seconds." And with that, she floated out of the room.

I let out a long breath. I really needed a drink. And she really *didn't* need a drink. I massaged my temples, trying to think straight. What the hell was I supposed to do? I grabbed my phone and was halfway through dialing Nick when I heard footsteps. I hung up and swiveled round. But of course, it wasn't Marcie. She'd been barefoot. This was a bloke I'd never seen before—most likely the person whom I'd spoken to on the intercom. He was wearing white cotton yoga pants and clogs.

He nodded at me then set about opening a tin of dog food. "I'm Ronan, by the way," he said over his shoulder as the meaty smell of Pedigree Chum wafted toward me. "I'm the chef." He was dividing the dog food into two bowls. Saffie must have had a little doggy brother or sister. "I hope you're hungry."

Was he talking to the dogs or me?

"I ate before I came," I deadpanned.

Ronan slumped his shoulders. "Oh, shame." He turned back to his task.

Something brushed by my leg, making me jump. A white poodle was looking up at me expectantly, but at the sound of cutlery tapping a bowl, moseyed over to Ronan.

"There you are, Noodle. I knew you'd appear when you smelled food." He turned to me. "He sleeps all day, this one."

Saffie was stretching in her basket, her nose twitching in the air. "Come on then, beautiful," said Ronan. "Let's have dinner outside. Marcie's got a guest today." He headed out through a patio door, and both dogs trotted after him.

I checked my watch. *Shit.* Thirty minutes had passed, and I was officially only allowed an hour. Where was Marcie?

For all I knew she'd fallen asleep somewhere. It was obvious that she was well and truly pissed. She wasn't just nervous or a bit tipsy, she was hammered. However much I didn't like it, I needed to pass her pre-interview interview, and she needed to be sober to remember it. A shiny red Nespresso machine caught my eye. If I could make her a coffee or something, and help her sober up, I might be able to salvage things.

I got up and made a show of stretching. I couldn't see Ronan in the garden, which hopefully meant he couldn't see me. Maybe if I just went through the door Marcie had left by, and called her, she'd remember I was still waiting for her.

The doorway led to a living room. The carpet felt plush underfoot. It was thick-piled wool, not the crappy nylon stuff that covered my floors. In the center of the room were two cream leather sofas facing each other and not the TV—the way they're arranged in glossy magazines. And a chest below a sash window looked like it belonged in Hampton Court Palace—the wood was almost black with age. Everything was natural and traditional; no designer Perspex chairs or ultra-modern cabinets.

It was a grown-up's room and however much of a bust this interview was turning out to be, it was still nice to know that Marcie had taste.

And just as I was admiring how classy everything was, Marcie appeared in the doorway and belched. She'd added a tartan ski hat and Arsenal scarf to her ensemble and was cogent enough to notice me staring.

"Got a bit cold in the cellar." She held up two dusty bottles of wine like trophies. "Go and get a corkscrew, Bonnie, love. There's one in the kitchen somewhere."

"I was thinking maybe let's leave the drinking for now."

"Oh, don't be such a prude. Wine's barely alcohol." She thrust the bottles at me. "Get a move on. I'm thirsty, and we haven't got all day."

22

GOODBYE YELLOW BRICK ROAD

I LUMBERED TO THE KITCHEN carrying the wine. The labels on the bottles were coming unstuck—much like I was.

What was I supposed to do?

Okay, my priority was to keep a clear head, but not *look* like I wasn't drinking. My untouched glass was sitting on the counter; I emptied it into the sink, refilled it with water, and drank it in one go, hoping it would dilute any alcohol I was going to have to consume.

But what about Marcie? I didn't want to encourage her to drink, but would she listen if I tried to stop her? She'd most likely kick me out.

My best bet was to bring her one glass and try to distract her from drinking any more by keeping her talking. The only problem was I wasn't sure how much sense I'd get out of her—she'd called me Bonnie, for God's sake.

I fixed the drinks and went back to the living room. Marcie had sunk into one of the sofas with her feet tucked underneath her. Her eyes were closed, but they opened when the wineglasses clinked against the coffee table as I set them down.

"I was beginning to think you'd gotten lost, Bonnie."

I sat down. "My name's not Bonnie, it's Zoë, and I'm here to talk about an interview for *Re:Sound*."

She heaved herself upright. "I know perfectly well who you are." Her tone was sharp. "But there's no hurry. We can have a drink first."

"I thought I only had till seven and it's almost a quarter to."

"Who told you that?"

"Your publicist."

"Well, it's poppycock. I've got no other plans, and Ronan won't have dinner ready till at least eight. You have to stay—he's making scaloppini."

She was asking me to stay for dinner? I guess that boded well.

"I'd love to—thanks."

She humphed with satisfaction and reached for her glass.

Not good.

"Maybe we can save the wine for dinner," I said quickly. "I'm a bit of a lightweight."

She waved dismissively. "For heaven's sake, child, what harm can a couple of glasses of wine do?"

To the liver of an alcoholic? Plenty.

I looked around, searching for a neutral conversation starter. "You have a beautiful house."

"Thank you."

I was hoping she'd elaborate.

"Do you collect art or antiques? That chest in the corner looks Jacobean."

"That's because it is."

"How long have you had it?"

"Years and years. It was a present from some count or other."

Hello, this was promising. "A count?"

"Yes, I forget his name. Italian. Had alopecia."

His lack of hair seemed a side issue. "Was there a particular reason for the gift?"

She reached for her wine. "I probably sang for him at a party or something. It was the eighties—we did that sort of thing."

"Where was this party?"

She seemed to go into a daze. With any luck she was remembering a masked ball in a centuries-old castle in the Dolomites and an infatuated bald count in rapt attention.

"A function room in a hotel in the Midlands."

Oh. I tried not to show my disappointment.

She glazed over again. "Did Nicky send you?"

I went blank. *Nicky?* Who was she talking about? "Do you mean Nick Jones?"

She nodded. "He said he was sending someone."

Was she having a memory lapse? I thought keeping her from the wine would be my biggest problem. "Yes, that's right. Nick set this up. My name's Zoë, and I'm hoping to interview you for *Re:Sound.*"

"Zoë?"

"From *Re:Sound…*"

"There's no need to talk to me like I'm an imbecile." She drank from her wineglass. "I might be fifty-eight, but I'm not an idiot." She smiled. "Well, fifty-three according to my Wikipedia page."

"Sorry, I didn't mean to—"

She suddenly looked sad. "You knew Patrick."

I flinched and tried to hide it by picking up my glass.

"Dear, dear, Patrick," she whispered. "It was so sudden."

I took several sips for Dutch courage because I had a question I'd always wanted to ask.

"Why did you part ways?"

"He was retiring."

"But you left years before that."

She shook her head. "Could we talk about something else?"

Under other circumstances, I might have pushed her to dish on her ex-manager, but not when that manager was a dead friend of mine. It was a moot point, though; she clearly didn't want to talk about him.

Unfortunately, she didn't look like she wanted to talk about anything else. She'd leaned her head back against the sofa and closed her eyes. Had she fallen asleep?

I coughed politely.

Nothing.

Then I noticed one of her fingers was tapping a rhythm against her thigh. I tried to think of something polite to say to wake her up.

The skirt of her dress was bunched up to her midcalf; she had a little tattoo on her ankle I'd never noticed before.

"That's an interesting tattoo. Have you had it long?"

She opened one eye. "Yes."

"What is it?"

She heaved herself upright; mercifully I'd landed on a subject she wanted to talk about. Who'd have known ink floated Marcie's boat? Funny, I knew so much about Marcie, but I didn't know she had any tattoos.

She pulled her skirt to one side to give me a better view. "It's a little seahorse. Gorgeous, isn't it?"

It was dark green with red eyes, almost dragon-like. But there was something benign about it and slightly familiar.

"When did you get it?"

She waved her hand. "Oh, a long time ago."

"Does it have a special meaning for you?"

She frowned. "Dammit, my glass is empty. Are you not drinking yours?"

She leaned forward and took my glass before I could stop her.

I needed to know more about the tattoo. Every instinct I had was urging me to keep her talking about it. "Why a seahorse?"

"I just like them. I had a necklace with the same design. But I lost it."

An image floated into my mind. Jessica had worn a necklace with a seahorse at the French restaurant when she'd thrown up. But surely that was just a coincidence.

My heart thumped. "When did you lose it?"

I mentally crossed my fingers that she'd keep talking.

"About ten years ago. I was touring."

I was starting to have butterflies in my stomach. That was around the time Jessica was touring with her. There's no way Jessica would have stolen it...was there?

"It must have meant a lot to you."

She nodded and looked strangely vulnerable. "I haven't written a single song since I lost it. Some things once lost are lost forever." Tears were welling in her eyes. She hastily wiped them away. "I want you to leave now. I'm tired."

Her words were like a punch in the gut. "I thought you said I could stay for dinner. Now you're kicking me out?"

"It's not my job to feed you, young lady."

Before I could protest, I heard the front door slam and the sound of urgent male voices. Had she hit some sort of invisible alarm? Was security about to boot me out?

Marcie hadn't seemed to notice the noise, only looking concerned when she heard excited dog barks.

"What's all the commotion about?"

The sound of footsteps grew nearer, then through the doorway marched Nick, followed by Ronan and the skipping dogs.

Nick didn't seem to notice me. His eyes were focused on Marcie and the two empty wineglasses on the table in front of her. The dogs went straight toward her, noses to the carpet, intent on sniffing her bare feet.

"Nicky," she cried, getting up. The dogs backed away, sensing that their mistress was unlikely to be steady on her feet.

She gave an exaggerated wave that tipped her off balance, and she toppled back onto the sofa. The leather whooshed as she landed. If they gave out Oscars for pretending to be drunk, she'd be a slam dunk. Unfortunately, she wasn't pretending.

I got up to help her but froze when Nick turned his gaze toward me. He was *furious*. The air around him was sizzling from his anger. And all of it was directed at me.

"Now, hang on." I was *not* going to take the blame for this.

He ignored me and instead helped Marcie up to her feet by himself. Ronan joined in and the two of them steered Marcie out of the room, all the while acting like I wasn't there. Only the dogs acknowledged me, sniffing at the hem of my jeans.

I bent down to stroke Noodle. Nick had a bloody nerve getting pissed off at me. If anyone had a right to be angry it was me. The stairs above me creaked, and both dogs took that as a cue to investigate. As they trotted out, Nick came marching in again.

"Did it ever occur to you that Marcie drinking might not be a good idea?"

My blood pressure spiked. "Of course it did. What do you take me for?"

"So why suggest it?"

I let out a hollow laugh. "Christ, Nick. How little you know your own client. She was half-cut when I got here."

"I don't believe you."

"I don't care what you believe."

"Ronan's under strict instructions to make sure Marcie doesn't drink."

"Then you should be talking to him, not me." I didn't mention that Ronan had been too busy with the dogs to know what Marcie was up to.

"I spoke to her an hour before you arrived. She seemed fine."

My anger swelled. "Then you weren't paying attention. She was drunk before I got here. Don't you dare try to pin this on me."

A look of doubt flickered across his face. He broke eye contact to adjust his cuffs. I waited for him to acknowledge his mistake, but as the seconds ticked by, he didn't speak.

I was just about ready to explode. "You're the liar, Nick. Marcie never agreed to an interview, did she?"

"I got you in the same room with her. If you didn't win her over, then that's your problem."

My patience snapped. "So now it's *my* fault? I lack the necessary charm? You're supposed to be her publicist, you're supposed to facilitate things, but it seems you lack the necessary skills."

He bristled. I'd obviously hit a sore spot. Maybe I was being unfair, but his words had hurt. I didn't need my interview subjects to like me for me to be able to do my job properly, but it was always a nice bonus if they did. Right now, I'd have swapped everyone's good opinion to have Marcie's. That I hadn't charmed her enough to give me an interview was a difficult pill to swallow.

Nick hadn't responded yet. He smoothed down his tie, then stroked the back of his neck. When he reached for his cuffs a second time, I'd had enough.

"Thanks for the clarification," I said drily. "If you think that Jonny interview is still going to press, you're dreaming."

"Well, I guess we've got nothing else to say to each other. You know where the door is."

Exactly one hour after I'd been granted entry, I found myself reeling on the pavement outside Marcie's house, frustrated and lost.

I dug out my phone and sent a text to Mike:

We need to talk.

Almost an hour later I was only just beginning to relax. The Crown was an old-fashioned boozer near Paddington where Mike got the train home. If you ordered anything other than a pint you got weird looks. I'd gotten a few tonight because I'd ordered wine—white or red were the choices—but out in the beer garden, most people were minding their own business. The "garden" part was a bit optimistic: we were on a tiny patio, and the only flash of green sprang from the moss growing in the cracks between the gray paving slabs.

Mike was nursing a pint of bitter and reflecting on what I'd just told him. It had taken me the better part of forty-five minutes to recount my meeting with Marcie. I'd kept going back and adding details I'd forgotten, and he'd questioned some of the more bizarre events.

"Why did she keep calling you Bonnie?"

"It's how I got through the door; I had to say I was Bonnie, and I was there to see Clyde."

"The name must mean something to her."

"I hadn't really thought about it. I assumed it was something that Nick came up with, but come to think of it, she had a framed poster of Warren Beatty and Faye Dunaway from the film *Bonnie and Clyde*. She must be a movie fan, because she had *Gone with the Wind* and *Butch Cassidy and the Sundance Kid* posters too."

"Interesting."

"Is it?"

"Always good to have intel on the enemy," said Mike.

He wasn't joking; Mike's military background gave him a unique perspective, and I'd learned to trust it over the years. "I haven't gotten to the weirdest part, though."

Mike leaned forward. "I'm all ears."

"Before she kicked me out, and before Nick came marching in, she mentioned a lost necklace."

"It had some significance?"

"Yes, it was the same as a tattoo she had, although she didn't say much about it. I pushed her on it, and that's when she decided she'd had enough."

"You hit a sore spot?"

I nodded. "My Spidey sense was tingling. The thing is, I've seen a necklace just like the one she mentioned."

"Coincidence?"

"Possibly, but the person I saw wearing it had spent time with Marcie around the time it went missing."

We both said nothing for a while, the rattle of bus engines filling the void.

"Look, you've got an interesting story about a necklace and a tattoo," he said eventually. "Why not write up what you've got?"

"She expressly told me that our meeting was off the record. She said she would decide whether she wanted me to interview her or not."

"Well, I'm sure you made a good impression. Surely you'll soon hear from Nick to arrange a proper interview."

I nodded. The problem was, I didn't share Mike's confidence.

It was almost eight o'clock when I left the pub. A lead weight was pressing against my stomach, but I willed myself to stay optimistic. Maybe I could portray Marcie sympathetically. Would she still object to publishing her off-the-record remarks if it showed her in a good light?

It gave me a glimmer of hope. But it was quickly extinguished. It might save my job for now, but if she sued us, I'd be in even bigger trouble.

And anyway, who was I kidding? How could I write up Marcie as anything other than a drunk? My only chance was Nick—to get him to see that I wasn't to blame for Marcie drinking. And to sort out a proper interview. Fast. He owed me as much, didn't he?

I took my phone out and dialed.

He answered on the second ring. "Zoë? I was about to ring you. I wanted to apologize."

"Oh." I hadn't expected him to cool down so quickly.

"Where are you?"

"Heading back to the office," I replied.

"At this time?"

"It's where I go when I'm stressed."

"Do you want to grab a bite to eat?"

I hadn't thought about food for hours, but I realized now that I was famished. "Okay."

"There's a noodle place off Golden Square."

"I know the one," I said. "I'll be there in twenty minutes."

I was there in under fifteen and seated by the steamed-up window, a pot of green tea in front of me on the crisp white tablecloth.

My stomach growled as the scent of chicken noodle soup wafted past. There was only one other couple in the restaurant; most of Soho had moved on to pubs or gone home.

The door swung open and Nick appeared on the threshold. He paused to scan the room and when he saw me, came over.

There were dark circles under his eyes I hadn't noticed earlier, and his collar wasn't sitting quite right over his tie.

He sat down opposite me. "How are you?"

"I'm well, thanks." It was an automatic response; well was not how I felt.

A waiter appeared with two single-page laminated menus, but I didn't look at mine.

"The noodle soup that went by smelled delicious—I'll have that."

"Make that two," said Nick.

"How's Marcie?" I said, after the waiter had left.

"Sleeping."

"It's not my fault she was drinking, Nick."

He exhaled. "I know."

Well, at least he was no longer being combative.

I sipped my tea, comforted by its warmth.

"I'm sorry about how things went today, I really am. But you've got to let me have another chance with Marcie."

"I'm the latest in a long line of publicists who can't convince her to talk to the press. Marcie's just not interested in being interviewed."

My fragile nerves jangled. "So, you've been playing me all this time? All those hoops I've jumped through, and you knew they would count for nothing."

"They weren't for nothing. You had an audience in her house, didn't you? It's a lot further than any journalist has gotten for a long time."

"I went for an interview, not to admire her soft furnishings."

"The more you can do to get Jessica on speaking terms with Marcie, the better your chances for a proper interview."

"Do you think I still believe this story you've been spinning?"

"It's the truth," he said.

"Well, give me the whole truth, then. Why are you so cagey about what Marcie did that she needs to atone for?"

Nick flattened his tie against his abdomen. It was a tic; but was it also a tell that he was about to lie?

"After she found out that Jess and Benedict were sleeping together, Marcie dropped Jessica from the tour. Patrick tried to talk her out of it, so she sacked him too."

The mention of Patrick's name was like a flame to a raw wound. "You'd better not be lying."

He held my gaze. "I wouldn't. Not about Patrick."

He flattened his tie again—maybe it was his tell that he was being honest.

"Marcie got Jessica and her band blacklisted—with promoters, music publishers, record labels. She ruined Jessica's music career—on purpose. And she's had to live with that ever since."

I sat back, absorbing what he'd said. It sounded ridiculous, but it also made perfect sense.

"Marcie must trust you a lot to tell you all this, Nick."

He frowned. "It's not some big secret, Zoë. Her inner circle has always known. I'm surprised Patrick never told you."

Had he not told me because he knew I idolized her? And that she would be tarnished in my eyes? It was touching, but sometimes Pat forgot I wasn't the starry-eyed fourteen-year-old he'd met all those years ago.

"Why didn't you tell me all this from the start?"

"It's not the sort of thing I wanted all over the music press."

"Why hasn't Jessica come forward with any of this? It would be a hell of a launchpad story to restart her career."

"Probably because she did sleep with Benedict. She basically admitted as much when we were in that restaurant." He paused. "Did you notice the necklace she was wearing that night?"

Nothing, it seemed, got past Nick.

I nodded. "It didn't mean anything to me at the time, but Marcie said she'd lost one just like it. I guess she mentioned it to you too. How did Jessica end up with it?"

He shrugged. "I don't have proof but I suspect she stole it from Marcie to get back at her. And given the circumstances, do you blame her?"

I found myself agreeing with him. "So, how do we go forward?"

"I'm persona non grata with Jessica now," said Nick. "But if you can persuade Jessica to talk to Marcie, she'd be your friend for life. Hell, she'd give you an interview a week if you wanted it."

"Is Marcie's conscience plaguing her that much, Nick?"

"Losing Patrick brought back all the memories of losing Benedict," said Nick. "And what she did to Jessica all those years ago."

The waiter returned with our soup, but I could tell that Nick had been about to say more. It didn't help that the waiter came back three more times, bringing two different sauces and taking and refilling our teapot. I started eating while all this was going on, happy to find the soup tasted as good as it smelled.

"Patrick died before Marcie could make amends with him. His death has affected her more deeply than you can imagine."

Did Nick's voice crack, or had I imagined it? "Are you okay, Nick?"

His chest rose and fell slowly. "Marcie's in a dark place. We don't leave her alone for any length of time and not only because she drinks."

"What are you saying?"

He swallowed. "We found her in the bath with a razor blade. The blood…" His voice dropped. "I'd never seen anything like it."

I gasped. "Nick, I'm so sorry."

"Marcie needs help, Zoë. And you've got a chance with Jess that none of the rest of us have. You'll be saving a lot more than just your magazine."

23

I CAN'T MAKE YOU LOVE ME

IT WAS PRESS WEEK AND I had a hundred things to deal with: proofs waiting for final corrections, facts needing last-minute checks, not to mention a missing album review that a freelancer had yet to file. It would come together in the end—it always did—but the next morning, I kept thinking back to my conversation with Nick. *Marcie had tried to kill herself? Is that why she'd been wearing long sleeves?* It made my own stresses pale in comparison. I felt awful for her, and Pat too, who'd wanted so much to reconcile with Marcie and now never could.

I'd never fully believed Nick's story about Marcie seeking redemption with Jess, but now it felt terrifyingly real. Nick may have burned his bridges with Jess, but I could still reach out to her. And for once, rather than going through Simon, I texted her directly to ask if we could meet at some point. She replied almost immediately, inviting me to her flat on Sunday for lunch. Her keenness made me feel a bit guilty; she probably assumed I wanted to interview her for the magazine, not bring up painful memories.

By five o'clock, Ayisha had subbed the remaining proofs and Rob had finalized the first batch of files to send to the printers. Still, for a press-week Tuesday, the office was abnormally subdued. Lucy and Gav had been quiet all day, and I'd only just noticed. The two of them usually provided a commentary on what they were doing in spectacularly vulgar language. When Lucy left early without wishing her twat-faced colleagues goodbye, I knew something was off.

Gavin watched her leave, a mournful look on his face.

"Everything okay, Gav?"

A red flush had crept up his neck, clashing with his orange T-shirt.

"I got a call from a mate who works at the picture desk of a national," he said. "She told me she'd come across some photos of Jonny Delaney that I'd want to know about."

The hairs on the back of my neck stood to attention. "Why's that?"

"He's with a girl who's got pink hair."

"Is that so bad?"

He shifted in his seat. "This pink-haired girl and Delaney are kissing."

I frowned. "Lucy and Delaney *kissed*?"

Surely that was ridiculous.

He shrugged. "Bit of a coincidence, don't you think? She interviewed him last week."

"Yes, but she was at Pinnacle's offices. There's no way she'd have gone off somewhere with Jonny, snogged him, *and* been snapped in the process." *Would she?*

"Maybe you don't know her as well as you think you do, Zoë."

He sounded really glum. "Have you tried asking her?"

Gav picked up the jacket on the back of his chair. "No, because it's none of my business, is it? But what I am going to do is get very, very drunk tonight. If you need me, I'll be in the Coach."

Things were bad if Gav had chosen that particular pub to drown his sorrows in. It was depressing as hell and only ever frequented by old guys with suspicious stains on their trousers.

Adrenaline buzzed in my veins. The Lucy pictures were potentially a big problem. We'd been trolled on Twitter just for writing a couple of uncomplimentary things about Jonny's music. How would his sizable fan base react to any woman who dared to kiss him? His fans were split into two groups: those that wanted him single so they would stand a chance with him and those who shipped his relationship with actress Jeanette Jerome and made creepy digital pictures of what their babies would look like. Both gangs were equally rabid. Lucy would have petrol bombs through her letterbox. And then things would really escalate.

I thought about ringing her myself, but what exactly would I say? Better to get the facts straight first.

If these pics existed, Nick would know.

I dialed and he picked up just before it went into voicemail. "Zoë?" He sounded out of breath. "If you're calling with good news, I'm very impressed."

"I'm afraid not, Nick. This is about an altogether different matter."

"Go on."

"I've had reports of some rather alarming photos."

"Photos?"

With any luck he would laugh me off the phone, but that didn't stop a knot forming in my stomach. I ambled to the kitchen. "Photos featuring a couple of people you and I know quite well—and they're kissing."

Three tea bags were piled on top of a spoon in the sink ringed by a stain of brown water. Nick was taking a long time to react, and my unease grew as the silence stretched.

"Shit," he said, eventually. "How did you find out?"

I slumped against the counter. "So it's true?"

"I'm sorry, Zoë. Who told you?"

I scooped up the tea bags and flicked them into the bin. "What does it matter who told me? If you knew about these pictures, why didn't you tell me?"

"That would have been cruel, don't you think?"

"*Cruel?* Giving me advance warning wouldn't be cruel. It's the least you could have done. The tabloid press will make mincemeat of her, and God knows what Jonny's army of rabid fans will do. Lucy's not as tough as she seems."

"*Lucy?* What are you talking about?"

"Pictures of Jonny and some pink-haired girl snogging. You mean it's not Lucy?"

"I don't know anything about that."

"Then what pictures are you talking about, Nick?"

He groaned—he'd revealed something he didn't want me to know, and my first instinct was to shout "hah!" in triumph. Except, I didn't feel too triumphant.

"Nick?"

Silence.

"What pictures, Nick?"

More silence.

"For fuck's sake, Nick."

"Pictures of Jess and Simon."

I swallowed. "I see."

"I'm sorry."

I grabbed the scourer and started rubbing at the brown ring mark in the sink. "When were they taken?"

"I don't know."

I stopped scrubbing. "Was it that night we were all together at London Bridge? They were standing very close, I remember, but they definitely didn't kiss."

He didn't immediately respond.

"Nick?"

"They're more recent than that."

"How recent?"

"Does it really matter when they were taken?"

"I was just curious, that's all."

"I can find out, if you want."

"No. No, it's okay." I ran the tap to rinse off my hands. I really wanted out of this conversation.

"I'll see what I can dig up about those other pics. But I have a hunch about what they might be and if I'm right, it's not Lucy in those photos; it's Jeanette Jerome in a wig from a party a couple of weeks ago. I'll check and get back to you, if it will put your mind at rest."

The other photos felt like a lifetime ago. "Yes, thanks, Nick. I'd appreciate that."

I lumbered back to my desk and collapsed into my chair.

Simon and Jess kissing.

Fuck.

With clammy fingers, I opened Twitter and did a search for Jess.

Nothing.

Then I navigated to her Instagram, but all I found were her usual images of outfits she'd just bought or gourmet food in hipster pubs. I was about to close her page, when one of the locations made me pause.

When had Jess been in Stockholm? Wasn't that one of the stops on Simon's trip?

The knot in my stomach tightened. The evidence was piling up.

Part of me had always suspected there might be something more between the two of them, the savvy part of me. The stupid part of me had been in control, however, and she had set sail for Denial Central.

On a whim, I texted Simon to see if he fancied catching some late sun after work on Golden Square. If he said yes, then I would ask him point-blank. If not, it was a sign I should just let things play out naturally. I mean, one kiss didn't mean anything, did it? We'd shared one kiss too, and he'd downplayed it immediately. The thought was supposed to comfort me, but thinking about the night in Georgia's garden only made me feel worse.

My phone pinged back almost straightaway:

Great! See you there at 6:00.

Shit. Now I had to actually talk to him.

Movement to my left stirred me. Ayisha and Rob were packing up for the day too. I caught up with them and asked if they could check on Gav in his misery pub. I didn't like the idea of Gav drowning his sorrows by himself.

I ended up getting to Golden Square late because I'd stupidly picked up the office phone at ten to six, only for the caller to launch into a long-winded query asking how he could get hold of a high-resolution life-size cardboard cutout of Lady Gaga. *Go away*, I'd wanted to scream, *the path of my true love needs some serious smoothing over here. All you need is a photocopier.*

When I got to the square, Simon was lounging on the dry grass, hemmed between a gaggle of sweaty bikers who were sweltering in their leathers and a trio of girls in breezy summer dresses paying more attention to their phones than to each other.

"Hey, Frixie." He got up and kissed me on both cheeks.

He smelled divine, even in the hot weather. One of the girls looked up from her phone and gave Simon a quick once-over. I didn't blame her; he looked gorgeous in a dark-blue shirt and chinos. His hair was standing up at odd angles, in an adorable way rather than a geeky kid way, and a sprinkling of stubble completed the look.

I sat down and tried to eke out a little more space so we could have a bit of privacy. He talked about work and his recent trip, and I tried to nod at the right places like I was paying attention. But a neon sign flashing "Jess" was lodged in my brain, blinding me to everything else.

He asked me about my day, and I bought myself some time by telling him about the Lady Gaga phone call. He smiled politely, even though it made a piss-poor anecdote. The fake smile had barely died on his lips when I launched into my interrogation.

"Simon, I know this is going to sound out of the blue, but what's the deal between you and Jess?"

His smile faltered. "What do you mean?"

"She was away for some of the time you were—did you see each other?"

He shifted his gaze to a daisy sprouting out of the yellow grass. "Funnily enough, she was in Sweden when I stopped over during my trip. She did a couple of gigs. The Scandis were crazy about Rydell."

I swallowed. "Did you guys…" *God, why hadn't I rehearsed this?* "Was it a case of what happens in Scandinavia stays in Scandinavia?"

"Frixie, you're not making any sense."

He looked so stumped that for a second, my hopes revived. Maybe Nick had been wrong about the photos.

"This is going to sound crazy, but there are paparazzi shots of the two of you kissing."

It definitely sounded crazy. This was all going to turn out to be a big misunderstanding.

"I'm sorry. I should have told you."

What did he just say? Why wasn't he laughing at my ridiculous rambling? And why was he looking at me so seriously?

A hysterical giggle escaped me.

I never giggled—and not hysterically, for fuck's sake.

"It was one kiss; you don't have to tell me everything," my voice continued; my brain was still two steps behind: *Can I interest you in a Lady Gaga anecdote?*

"It wasn't one kiss, Frixie."

Everything went still. My brain had finally caught up.

"Oh."

"We had a fling at university, and it always felt like unfinished business. I guess we're just exploring if it's got legs."

But what about me? I wanted to shout. *Don't you need to check my legs too?*

"I thought you were all about taking things slowly?" I tried not to sound bitter but failed miserably.

"This thing with Jess has taken me by surprise."

Really? I wanted to scream. Everyone else could see it coming for miles.

I swallowed, not trusting myself to speak. But the words bubbled out of me against my will. "But what about us, Si?"

He looked surprised. "You and I are best friends, Zoë. That will never change. I value you too much. I mean, I know there was that night at the fancy-dress party, but we decided not to take it further."

My heart sank with the weight of a hundred tiny daggers.

We decided to take things slowly, I wanted to tell him. *When had he decided we weren't going to take it further?* I couldn't say any of it out loud, though. I'd sound churlish, and the look of shock on his face if I told him I wanted more would be too humiliating to bear.

I nodded and tipped the corners of my mouth into a smile. If he saw how much this was hurting me, I don't think I'd ever be able to face him again.

I was pathetic.

And suddenly, crushingly alone.

I got out of there as quickly as I could, citing a forgotten meeting. I hated myself for running away, but if I'd stayed a moment longer, watching Simon's face as he reminisced about his history with Jess, I would have died.

My urgent meeting was with a bottle of wine in the same miserable pub as Gavin. Rob and Ayisha were there, keeping Gav company, and for a while their conversation distracted me. Ayisha, who happily drank non-alcoholic drinks whenever we went to the pub, was explaining that Ramadan was about to start, so this would be her last trip to the pub for a month.

By 9:30, it was just me and Gavin, brooding on a ripped leather bench and trying to avoid the gaze of a cross-eyed man playing snooker with an imaginary cue.

The good thing about Gavin was that he didn't always feel the need to fill silences with conversation. So we sat and drank and gave Snooker Man a thumbs-up every time he told us he'd just sunk the black.

If I hadn't asked Simon, when would he have told me about Jess?

It's not like he'd promised me anything, but there had been unspoken assurances—*hadn't there?* I hated that I was so thrown by this. I wasn't an insecure teenager. I was a confident, insouciant woman who only occasionally tried to win arguments by flicking her hair. Okay, that one was a bit childish, but still. Confident. Insouciant. Mature. Attractive(ish). *Right?*

I needed to snap out of it or I was going to end up mired in self-pity. I was already in it up to my knees.

Gavin looked even more depressed, and after I'd gotten our fifth round, I found out why.

"I love her," he announced as he slammed his glass on the table. "But she's not interested."

Poor Gav, I'd suspected as much. "Lucy?"

He nodded glumly. "I've loved her since she first strolled in with that ridiculous coat of hers. Do you remember it?"

I could see why Gav had fallen for her. On her first day she'd worn a floor-length sheepskin coat that reeked. I remember thinking, *How could sheep smell that bad?* Gav had greeted her with a bleat, and I'd waited for her response, convinced she would either start crying or thump him. She did neither. Instead, she'd thrown her head back and laughed. I think we all fell in love with her a bit that day.

I rubbed his shoulder. "Have you talked to her?"

"I don't need to. She'd never go for me. And besides, she's interested in someone else."

I sat straighter—this I could help with. "It's not Lucy in those pics with Jonny, Gav. I should have told you sooner." It would have saved his liver. "I checked with his publicist."

"Maybe not, but she's definitely got the hots for him."

"No way. I've got good intuition about this stuff." Not when it came to my own love life, evidently, but we weren't discussing that.

"Well, why did she leave early today?"

I laughed. "That's your proof? She could be anywhere. It doesn't mean she's out with Jonny Delaney."

"You wait—he'll put something up on social media tonight."

"You're being daft. He's very publicly dating that superhero actress."

"Jeanette Jerome? That's a smokescreen to cover up certain same-sex proclivities."

"If he's gay he can't be interested in Lucy."

"Jonny's a beard for Jeanette—*she's* gay."

He'd stumped me there.

"She wouldn't stop talking about him after the interview. He played her some new tracks, and she thought they were brilliant. This is Lucy we're talking about. Then they went for dinner together."

This was news to me, but for Gav's sake, I tried to not look surprised. "I doubt it would have been just the two of them. She probably tagged along to something he was going to with his entourage."

Gavin didn't look convinced. "Her write-up was full of sexual chemistry."

"You're imagining things."

"She banged on about the turquoise orbs of his eyes and the way the light played over the freckles on his arm."

"She most definitely did not."

"She did in the first draft she showed me. And it's all implied in her finished copy."

"She was having you on, Gav. There were no smoldering yearnings in her piece, trust me."

Snooker Man sank another black and gave us a toothless grin. We both held up our drinks to salute him.

For a couple of minutes, neither of us spoke. Then Gav shook his head. "I should just give up. She only thinks of me as a laugh."

He really liked Lucy. And I'd been too wrapped up in my own stuff to notice. "You should talk to her."

He shook his head. "How do you think that would go?"

"You don't know till you've tried." I was being a hypocrite—I'd never managed to tell Simon.

"She probably thinks I'm too fat or bald or short."

Gav was really wallowing now.

"You're none of those things." I turned to face him. "But if it helps, I'm sort of smitten with someone who only thinks of me as a friend."

His eyes widened. "Really? Is it that Nick bloke?"

"No, of course not."

"Who then?"

"No one you know."

"What a couple of saddos we are."

Jesus, you try to help someone…

"Anyway, it will all be forgotten in a couple of days."

He looked at me sideways. "If you like this guy, it will take time to get over him. There's no shortcut. You have to feel your feelings."

But what if I didn't want to feel my feelings?

I attempted a smile. "Or there's always alcohol."

Gav didn't smile back; he looked pensive. I didn't want pity, so I tried to hide my hurt by widening my smile. The effort made my mouth ache. Still, as far as he was concerned, I was A-OK. Feelings safely boxed away; nothing to see here.

He awkwardly patted my knee. "You're always here for us; you need to know that we're here for you too."

Why wasn't he letting this go? "You're overreacting, Gav. It's nothing I can't handle." If I could convince him, maybe I could convince myself.

"Bullseye!" came a shout from the corner. Snooker Man had moved on to imaginary darts. He spun in a circle, pumping his fist. The fool looked so happy in his little dream world.

Any chance there was space in there for two?

24

DON'T SPEAK

TOO SOON IT WAS SUNDAY, and at 1:00 p.m., I found myself, wine bottle in hand, ringing the doorbell of Jess's Clapham flat. Things with Simon had gone pear-shaped, but at least I could try to salvage the Marcie interview. All I had to do was convince Jess to see her, even though for ten years she'd steadfastly refused.

Simple.

Jess answered the door holding a wooden mallet wrapped in plastic. Christ. Had she deduced my true intentions and come to chase me down the street?

I must have looked startled because she pulled me into a hug with her free arm. "I was just tenderizing the veal. It's great to see you, Zoë."

I followed her through the corridor, along a warm current of rosemary and into the kitchen, where all the appliances were German and the worktops granite.

"Do you want to pop the wine in the fridge or open it now? I've made punch if you prefer."

She nodded at a ruby-red pitcher. Segments of peeled orange floated on its surface. It seemed like a lot for two people. Come to think of it, there seemed to be a lot of everything: two pans on the stove, a couple in the sink, and something in the oven. She either had my mother's tendency for overfeeding, or she was expecting more people.

Like Simon.

Balls. As if this wasn't going to be hard enough, I now had to do it pretending I was peachy that Simon and Jess had paired up.

"Can I help with anything?" I asked. Normally, I'd hope for a "no," but I felt antsy and a task would give me something to do other than scan the place for evidence of a recent male presence, like a pair of scuffed trainers or a rogue black sock.

The idea of them as a couple made my breath catch. Had he stood in this kitchen in his boxers, making her breakfast in bed?

Stop it! Concentrate on why you're here, Zoë.

"I'm all good, thanks," said Jess. "I'd hate for you to get your dress dirty. It's so pretty, and violet is a great color on you."

It was brighter than what I usually wore. Girlier too—sleeveless with a V-neck and a full skirt. Nothing to do with trying to compete with Jess. Nope. She was wearing skinny black jeans, a black tank top, and heels. Effortlessly sexy, basically. No jewelry. I'd held out a vague hope that she'd be wearing the seahorse necklace so I could ask her about it naturally.

Oh well. I was sure I could slot it—and Marcie—into the conversation suavely.

I poured myself some punch. "You were wearing a really pretty necklace a couple of weeks back."

"Which one is that, then?"

"I think it was a little shell or something."

She turned her back to me to start chopping parsley. "I don't have a shell necklace."

I took a breath. "I think it might actually have been a seahorse."

Smooth, Zoë, really smooth.

"Oh, that old thing."

"Where did you get it?"

"It was a present."

"Who from?"

Her chopping arm stilled. "I don't remember."

She was definitely uneasy.

I took a step closer to her. "Is that really true?"

She spun round, the knife glinting against the kitchen spotlights. "I know exactly where these questions are going, Zoë."

"Why the big secrecy around this necklace?"

"I'm not being secretive. Benedict Bailey gave it to me. Though what it's got to do with you I have no idea."

"Marcie thinks you stole it."

Jess let out a hollow laugh. "Right, and whatever Saint Marcie says is gospel, is it?"

It had been a mistake to start with the necklace. I was here to try to build bridges between her and Marcie, not accuse her of anything. I hated going in cold, but I had to get this done fast. When Simon arrived he was bound to put the kibosh on this conversation.

"I know what Marcie did to your career all those years ago."

She ran the tap to rinse her knife. "Ancient history now."

"She feels terrible about it, and she'd really like to make it up to you."

Jess turned to face me. "*She* feels terrible? How fucking rich is that? Does she have any idea how *I* might feel about it?"

This was going from bad to worse. "She wants to make it up to you, Jess."

She laughed bitterly. "Can she turn back time? I'm thirty-five in a couple of months. Do you think there's much demand for a female singer heading toward forty? I was twenty-five on that tour; it was my *one* chance. I wasn't perfect. I made mistakes. I was young and foolish and flattered by Benedict's attention. And yes, somehow you know that Benedict gave me that necklace. But that's got nothing to do with Marcie. Do you know how many other people Marcie was sleeping with when she was supposedly being faithful to Ben?"

"I'm not defending her. But she genuinely wants to make amends."

"Why is this so important to you? You're acting like you've got something to lose."

I reached for my glass to avoid her eyes. Had Simon told her? The idea stung, but I couldn't stand here feeling indignant; it wasn't altruism that had brought me to her door.

I tried a different tack: "Marcie has so much clout. Why not let her help you now?"

"*Help* me? She hates me. She wouldn't spit on me if I was on fire." She let out a breath and smoothed down her tank top, trying to calm her temper. "Let's not fall out over this, Zoë. I don't know what sob story she's spun you, but there's nothing she could do to ever make me forgive her and if you think I would, then she hasn't told you the full story of what happened on that tour."

She held my eye and I suddenly glimpsed the full depth of her pain. She was hurting about more than her career. Marcie's sins had sounded so grave that it had never occurred to me that I'd been told the cleaned-up version.

Jessica was shaking. I poured her a glass of her punch, and she took it with a wobbly hand.

"I'm sorry. It was none of my business."

After a couple of sips of her punch, she smiled. "It's okay. Your heart was in the right place. But no more talk of Marcie—I'd like us to have a nice meal."

The doorbell chimed, startling her. Was this Simon? She pointed to a peeled cucumber on the counter. "Could you chop this while I get the door?"

The knife handle was warm in my hand, and the cucumber ice-cold under my fingers. I'd made a pig's ear of this. Sticking my size eights into things wasn't going to get Marcie her longed-for closure from Jess.

As I sliced I tried to make out the bits of conversation floating from the front door. It didn't sound like Simon. Whoever had arrived seemed to be arguing with Jess.

Should I go and help?

Before I could move, a red-faced Jess burst into the kitchen. "I need my purse and keys."

She didn't make eye contact and instead grabbed her bag from the back of a kitchen chair. "I have to go and get some cash. I'll be ten minutes max."

She barreled out again, and I was left to gape in her wake. After a stunned couple of seconds, I hustled to the front door and opened it. Jess was already revving her ancient Renault Clio, the exhaust rattling as she pulled away.

What the hell was going on?

A white BMW was parked across the road. It was newer and shinier than all the other cars on the street. Its engine was idling and the driver had a tattooed arm hanging out of the window.

Was that her *drug dealer*?

I knew she liked to party, but was she really about to go and replenish her stash on a Sunday afternoon in the middle of preparing lunch?

I went back to the kitchen and finished my glass of punch. As I was refilling it, the door opened again and a male voice shouted, "Hello!"

This time, it *was* Simon and he had a key to Jess's flat. My already low mood sank further. It was a bit soon, wasn't it? He still hadn't given me back my key yet.

"Oh, hi," he said. "Jess told me you were coming over to interview her for the magazine. How exciting."

I wasn't in the mood to correct him, so I just nodded.

"Where is she?"

"She's gone to get cash for her drug dealer."

I waited for Simon to laugh or ask if I was kidding. But evidently, a Sunday afternoon drug deal was not an unusual occurrence in the Baxter-Honeywell household.

"Something smells good," he said, nodding at the oven.

"Yes," I replied lamely.

"Look, I know you meant well, Frixie, but Jess mentioned that you'd brought up the whole Marcie Tyler thing again."

That was barely ten minutes ago. Did they speak to each other every thirty seconds?

"This is turning into an obsession," he said. "You're like a scratched record."

His choice of words stung. "You know how important it is for the magazine."

"But you know it upsets Jess. Why keep bringing it up? It's like you've got some weird fetish about it."

Why was he suddenly acting like this—implying my interest in Marcie was unhealthy? I'd grown up listening to her, and Simon had been there hitting the repeat button on the CD with me. He should understand better than anyone.

Stupid, ridiculous, humiliating tears threatened to fall. I turned toward the counter, determined not to let him see how much his words hurt.

Simon poured himself a drink without asking if I wanted a refill. It was like I was invisible, and I was actually relieved when Jess's rattling car came to a halt outside.

"I'm back!" she singsonged from the hallway, banging the door behind her. She had a big—and possibly chemically induced—smile on her face. "Who's up for some grub?"

The rest of the afternoon was pretty lousy. I had to feign a headache to account for my quietness, and Jess's famed cookery skills proved hugely lacking. I don't know whether she'd taken a couple of pills or lines of coke, but she was too far gone to care that the veal was rubbery or that the rice was soggy.

Even the apple pie in the oven hadn't defrosted properly and turned out to be shop-bought, its Waitrose wrapping tossed carelessly on a counter.

It's not that I was being a massive snob, but Simon praised every fucking dish. His assessment of her culinary skills was tainted either by his feelings for her or his own lack of sobriety. His eyes were ringed red, which led me to believe that he'd partaken in whatever goods Jess had procured from her earlier gentleman caller.

In fairness, Jess had asked me if I fancied a little "help" too, but I politely declined and she didn't push it.

Around the time when normal guests would have readily agreed to coffees, I got up. "I'd better get home."

No one tried to talk me out of it.

We said our lukewarm goodbyes and then I was out, the door closing before I'd even made it to the pavement.

I looked up and down the street, trying to remember which way the train station was, but it was still early and I didn't want to go home.

When I pulled out my phone, searching for someone to recount my horrible afternoon to, my fingers scrolled to "N" without any help from my brain.

Was it weird to ring Nick on a Sunday?

A couple of rings before it went to voicemail, he picked up.

"Zoë? Is everything okay?"

"Everything's great," I replied automatically.

He paused. "Would you like to talk about it?"

He'd obviously heard something in my voice, because his had a note of concern.

I suddenly felt overwhelmed. "I'm in Clapham. I've just left Jessica's flat."

"Do you want me to come and get you?"

"No, no, nothing like that. I just wondered if you were around to talk."

"That train comes into Waterloo, doesn't it?"

I nodded, then realized he couldn't see me. "Yes, that's right."

"Okay, I'll meet you at Waterloo in half an hour. Then we can go somewhere to talk—I promise it won't be on the London Eye."

"I appreciate this, Nick. Thank you."

My train took about ten minutes to get to Waterloo, so I sat in the station coffee shop and sent Nick a text to let him know where I was.

I drank my tea staring into space. *What a bloody disaster.* It was bad enough that Simon was so oblivious to how hard it was for me to see him with Jess. But then he'd told me I was acting crazy about Marcie.

He'd sounded so callous, and that was hard to forgive. Had he spoken in frustration and now regretted it? I didn't know because we'd barely spoken for the rest of the meal.

I was lost in thought when Nick walked in, and I almost didn't recognize him. "You're wearing jeans," I said, as if this fact had somehow escaped him.

"You didn't mention a dress code." On top he was wearing a collared polo shirt with the first couple of buttons undone. "Can I get you anything?"

I shook my head and he went to the counter to order.

It was so odd to see him out of a suit, but it was a welcome distraction from my ruminations about Simon. Nick's blue jeans were faded and well-worn; I bet if I stroked them they'd be impossibly soft. Although why I was thinking about stroking Nick's legs I had no idea. The young woman serving him giggled nervously as she took his order. Nick flashed a wide smile of thanks, and her giggles got louder, making the other baristas shake their heads. Nick's hair was different too. Wilder. He must use gel to tame it during the working week, but I'd never noticed before.

He sat down opposite me with his lovingly made double espresso, his admiring barista no doubt disappointed that she could only see the back of his head.

"What have you been up to today?" I said, suddenly curious.

He shrugged. "I got up, went for a run, did some laundry."

"Are all your suits at the dry cleaners?"

"Contrary to what you might think, I don't live my job twenty-four-seven. Sometimes I can go a whole hour without thinking about it."

It was a bit mean to accuse him of never clocking off. He was here now for work because of me, wasn't he?

"You don't play football on Sunday mornings or veg out on video games with a buddy?" Why had I picked those two things? Not all blokes were as lame as my brother.

"Playing football is a British thing."

"So what did you do at school for sport?"

"Badminton and tennis, mainly."

"Have you ever done any dancing? Like ballet or something?"

I don't know where all these questions were coming from. Probably because I'd never really thought about what he was like away from work. Or more likely, I was avoiding talking about my failure with Jess today.

"Why do you ask?"

"Something about the way you move."

"I do a bit of yoga."

That made much more sense. Why had I said ballet? And now I had an image of him and his muscular legs in tights and a codpiece. What was wrong with me?

"So what happened with Jessica today?" he said, deftly changing the subject. He really didn't like talking about himself. "I take it she isn't winging her way to Marcie's place ready to hear her apology."

"No, unfortunately."

"Go on."

"I rushed it—I dived in and was shocked by her reaction. She implied that there's more to the story than Marcie has told us. Or rather, more to it than I know."

I paused, checking if this rattled him. His face remained impassive, but didn't it always?

"I've told you what Marcie has told me." He sounded genuine, but what did I know? "Why did you have to rush? Did she have to go somewhere?"

I squirmed. "No, I wanted to get it out of the way before Simon arrived. He doesn't approve of me raking all this stuff up. Especially now that he and Jess are seeing each other."

Nick nodded. "How do you feel about that?"

I smiled tightly. "They're two consenting adults; what difference does it make what I think?"

"Because you're in love with him."

Heat scorched my cheeks. I took a sip of my tea, hoping the mug would hide my reddening face. "No I'm not. We're best friends, that's all."

Most of that sentence was true.

He finished his espresso and stared into the distance.

If he was going to impart some romantic wisdom, he could piss off.

"I've been thinking these last couple of days," he said. "Reflecting, really."

"About what?"

"I'm quitting as Marcie's publicist."

25

SOMETHIN' STUPID

I SLAMMED DOWN MY MUG. "Are you serious? You arrive from halfway across the world, land this dream job working for Marcie, and you want to walk away?"

A flash of irritation passed across Nick's features. "*Dream* job? The reason I was burdened with Marcie is because no one else would go near her. They knew too well what the position would entail."

I didn't like hearing Marcie was a nightmare. She was an icon.

"Where will you go?"

He shrugged. "Somewhere new, I guess."

Neither of us spoke for a couple of minutes. Only the artificial voice of the loudspeaker announcing train departures punctured the silence.

Now that my initial shock had worn off, I could begrudgingly see Nick's point. She was demanding—and unstable.

"Do you want another tea?" he asked.

"No, thanks. I should probably head off."

"Let me give you a lift."

"You drove?"

"I've borrowed my boss's car, and I'm looking for an excuse to drive it."

I was intrigued. "Why's that?"

"Come and see."

We walked toward the parking garage, and very quickly the answer was obvious. Nick had a beeper in his hand, and when he pressed it, the lights of a racing-green Aston Martin blinked.

"Wow," I said. "Is that a DB9?"

"You like cars?"

"My brother does. Some of it rubbed off on me." I walked round to the passenger door. "I've never been in an Aston before."

"Hop in."

I didn't need a second invitation. "Drop me off at a Central Line station," I said. "Holborn is pretty close."

"No problem."

The interior was as plush as I'd imagined. The soft leather seat hugged me as I sat; the display was edged in polished wood, and even the dash was covered in leather with contrasting stitching.

Nick slid into the driver's seat and when he pressed the start button, the roar of the engine ricocheted against the concrete walls of the underground car park.

We turned to look at each other, guilty smiles on both our faces. "It's like music," he said.

He put the car into reverse and swung out of the parking space.

The car smelled of him, I suddenly realized. Or maybe it was that we were sitting very close to each other.

When we came out into the daylight, the engine didn't sound quite so brash. Above the snarl, Marvin Gaye was playing on the stereo.

When Nick reached across to open the glove box, his forearm grazed my knee and it was like a bolt of lightning.

Shit. Was that chemistry? This wouldn't do. Not if we were going to be cooped up in this sex-wagon for the next twenty minutes.

Marvin singing "I Want You" didn't help.

"Looking for your driving gloves?" I said, resorting to humor to defuse the situation. Not that Nick looked like he needed any sort of release. The chemistry was all in my head. Probably.

"Sunglasses," he said, fishing out a pair of Oakley's.

Unsurprisingly, the addition of dark glasses did nothing to lower my levels of discomfort. Did he have any idea how good-looking he was right now? Good job he wasn't my type.

"Do you have a girlfriend, Nick?"

How had *that* slipped out?

The car jerked as if he'd released the clutch too fast.

I couldn't tell what he was thinking now that he had sunglasses on. Maybe he hadn't heard me.

"I was seeing someone in Mexico."

Past tense. "What happened?"

He glanced at me. "Is this a therapy session?"

"I was just making conversation."

More silence.

"She ran off with a bullfighter."

"Bloody hell!"

"Well, he was an actor in a telenovela who played one. But bull-fighter sounds better."

"Mexican soaps sound fun."

"I used to think so too."

I couldn't suppress a smile. Nick glanced at me. "Glad you find my pain so funny."

"I'm sorry, Nick. You're right. It's not funny. But it could have been worse. If you were in England and she'd run off with a British soap star, you'd have to tell people she left you for a pub landlord."

"Gee, I feel so much better."

"You have to laugh, though, don't you? What's the alternative?"

"Throwing yourself into work. Swearing off relationships." He looked over at me. "Having the occasional hook-up."

I kept my eyes forward. "Sounds like pretty good advice, if you ask me."

Had I just told him I was up for hooking up with him? The idea was suddenly very appealing. No-strings sex with Nick so I could forget this Simon-shaped knot in my stomach.

He didn't speak and instead concentrated on the road. My eyes drifted to his hands; one on the gear stick, the other loosely resting on the wheel. He had good hands. Hands that knew what to do. Hands that could grab you, but not too roughly. Caress you with light touches, then build to something more insistent, more urgent...

Jesus, I was having a heart attack in my knickers.

I peered out of my window, trying to clear the images in my head. They involved lips as well as hands. And skin. Lots of skin.

I cleared my throat. "Want to grab a drink somewhere?" I tried to sound casual, but to my ears I'd just asked him back to my place to shag his brains out.

The sun disappeared behind a dark bank of clouds. I tried not to read too much into it. We stopped at a red light. He removed his sunglasses and hooked them into his breast pocket.

"Or we could do something else." His voice was low.

I swallowed. Was he thinking about my skin idea? Even without the dark glasses I couldn't read him.

He shoved the gear into first, and we burned the other cars. *Easy tiger*, I wanted to say, *I haven't said yes yet.*

Spoiler alert: I was definitely going to say yes.

"What did you have in mind?" I said.

"You'll have to trust me."

My neck prickled. "Can you be more specific, please?"

"I don't want to scare you," he said, "but how do you feel about doing something…public?"

Bloody perv. That's it, I was going to jump out of the car at the next set of lights. He wasn't the only one with hands. I had a couple of my own and a nice private bedroom.

"You know what, Nick. I'm flattered and all, but you can find someone else to play with tonight."

We'd been going at a steady 30 mph, but he suddenly swerved into a side road and braked to a stop. I had to brace myself against the dash to stop from flying forward.

He took off his seatbelt and leaned his elbow on the central console. It meant his whole body was tipping toward me. He looked up at me through thick lashes. "You'll wake up tomorrow a different woman."

Oh my God, this was the corniest seduction routine I'd ever been subjected to. I was actually embarrassed for him.

"Now hold on one minute, Nick—"

I didn't get any further. He was smiling. Grinning, actually.

Oh.

There was a teensy possibility I'd jumped to conclusions and Nick had been playing me like the damn fiddle in "Come On Eileen."

"Karaoke. I'm going to take you to a karaoke bar." He smiled again. "What did you think I meant?" He was really enjoying this.

"You know exactly what I was thinking," I told him, but my indignation had dissolved. "And you did it on purpose."

His eyes went wide with fake innocence. "I have absolutely no clue what you're talking about." He flicked his gaze to the back seat then slowly back to me. His eyes were far from innocent.

Oh my.

My breath quickened. This was bad.

Or he was having me on again.

"Come on, then," I said, playing it safe. "Where's this karaoke bar of yours?"

The answer to that question was a basement near Victoria. A well-lit basement, I was pleased to note. It had padded walls, but in a cozy way, not Hollywood-mental-hospital style. The only problem was that everything was in Japanese.

"A bit of help with this menu, Nick? I'm sure you can read Japanese."

"Tell me what you want, and I'll order it."

"White wine would be great. The drier the better."

"They don't serve alcohol here."

Was he serious? "The drinks menu runs to eight pages. What's it filled with, every version of Coke ever invented?"

"Actually, they make a green tea cola on the premises. Coke developed it for the Japanese market, but it never took off. I'll order us both one."

I grabbed his arm before he could turn to the barman. "You can't expect me to sing sober? In front of all these people?"

I waved at the room. My plea was somewhat undermined by the fact there were only three people in here. Two of them were on their phones, and the third appeared to be either asleep or in a cola-induced sugar coma.

"Oh come on, don't tell me you're chicken? Live a little."

"I live plenty. And I'm not scared."

"Prove it."

I folded my arms. "I don't need to do anything."

He tipped toward me on the balls of his feet. Closer than he'd been in the car, close enough for me to get a lungful of his catnip aftershave. "It's exactly what you need."

Would he shut up about my needs?

Suddenly, his hand was warm in mine. "What are you doing?" I asked.

He smiled and started walking, and I had no choice but to follow. Fuck, he was leading me to the stage. One of the blokes on his phone jumped to attention. He had an open laptop in front of him, and I realized he was the DJ. Three mics on leads were also arranged on the table.

Nick still hadn't let go of my hand. He handed me a mic then picked up one for himself.

"I'm not going to sing," I protested.

"No, I am," he said. "But you're going to join in on the chorus."

Before I could ask what the song was, the opening riffs of Def Leppard's "Pour Some Sugar on Me" were blasting through the PA.

The barman started nodding his head in time to the beat, but no one else seemed to notice what was going on.

Nick released my hand, but before I could make a run for it, he wrapped his arm around my waist and pulled me to his side.

His ribcage vibrated against mine as he sang, and his voice was a low growl; it was a spot-on impression of the lead singer of Def Leppard. The only thing missing was the mullet.

I watched the lyrics zip by on the screen in front of us. The words didn't make sense and were eye-rollingly cheesy, but their meaning could not have been clearer. The whole song was about sex. And being pressed against Nick's taut body as he channeled his inner rock star was doing funny things to my lady parts.

Shit, we were at the chorus. This was my cue. "*Pour some sugar on maaaaaaay.*"

I swear Nick winced. Well, sod him, it was his fault my mouth was so close to his easily offended ear.

He started on the second verse with extra swagger, his voice warming up now. I was swaying from side to side in time with the music, my hips perfectly synchronized with his. We got to the final crescendo; my one-line chorus bouncing around Nick's lament on how hot, sticky, and sweet he was.

We punched the air at the same time for the final drumbeat. And then it felt like the most natural thing in the world to hug.

His cheek was cool against mine, but his body was warm. I could feel waves of heat coming off him. Or maybe it was my own body heat pulsing between us.

I was smiling and breathless when I pulled back.

He grinned back at me. "How did that feel?"

I tried to find the right words. "Better than—"

"The next word out of your mouth better not be 'sex.'"

Look whose mind was in the gutter now. "Better than I *imagined.*"

"Good."

"It's a hell of a song," I admitted.

"Well, you get to choose the next one," he said.

I groaned. "Oh, come on, Nick. You want to go again?"

"Did you really think I was a once-a-night man?"

His expression knocked the breath out of me. Right now, I was hoping he was an up-against-the-wall man. They were padded, after all.

I kept that thought to myself and instead said: "Do I get to have a drink first?"

"Nope."

What was wrong with him? My seduction game was always better with a bit of lubrication. It was his own fun he was ruining.

"Just one," I said, trying not to sound desperate.

"I told you, this a dry bar."

He was serious about that? "No wonder this place is empty."

"I'll make you one concession," he said.

"What's that?"

"We'll go to a private booth."

He had a chat with the barman, and a couple of minutes later, was ushering me into a side room with its own karaoke machine. The padded walls, I was just realizing, were for soundproofing.

Once Nick had closed the door, I couldn't hear the music from the main bar. It was just as well, because as we'd left someone had started singing "New York, New York" in a key hitherto unknown to the human ear.

For a private room, it was pretty big. The padded leather banquettes that lined the sides could have easily seated fifteen people.

Nick sat by the screen and started scrolling through the computer to find a song.

"Do you want me to choose one for you?"

"Are you serious? You want me to sing?"

"Well, why else are we here?" This time, the flirty note was absent. "You said you enjoyed it. You'll enjoy it even more if you sing by yourself."

"You're going to just sit there?"

"I could stand if you prefer."

He pressed a few buttons and suddenly the room was alive with the intro to "Love in an Elevator."

Oh, very grown-up; he knew I hated lifts.

He handed me a microphone. "Thought you might like this one."

"Very funny," I muttered as he went to sit at the back of the room.

As well as being a *hilarious* joke, it was another raunchy number, full of double entendres about "going down." He evidently had a predilection for naff eighties hair metal that I secretly shared.

What followed wasn't pretty. Steven Tyler is one of the great voices of rock, and anyone would sound bad trying to imitate him, but I was truly terrible. I couldn't hit the high notes and didn't do much better with the lower ones either. I'd obviously been singing the lyrics wrong all my life, because the ones that were coming up on the screen were new to me. *What the hell was a "sassafras"?*

At last, the instrumental break arrived, and I'd never been so happy to hear a second-rate Joe Perry guitar solo in my life. It was precious breathing space. I'd kept my eyes fixed on the screen the whole time but now stole a glance at Nick.

He had his eyes closed and was thumping his hands on his thighs in time with the music.

Now that I knew he wasn't watching me, I felt a bit less self-conscious and threw myself into the rest of the song. I even added some dance moves. I couldn't sing, but no one could accuse me of not knowing how to shake my booty.

When I next looked up, Nick's eyes had snapped open.

Great, now it looked like I was doing a private dance for him. I turned away and tried to finish the song with the same level of confidence.

My vocal cords felt shredded by the end, but there was something cathartic about filling my lungs and belting out a damn good tune.

Nick clapped when I finished. "Brava!"

I did a mock bow. "Thank you very much."

"I mean, you sounded like someone was prizing off your fingernails with a flat-head screwdriver, but top marks for trying."

My mouth dropped open. "Cheeky bastard!"

He grinned. "Encore?"

"After that ringing endorsement?"

"I'll put it on random and see what it comes up with."

The machine whirred for a couple of seconds, then the slow swing of "I've Got You under My Skin" filled the booth. Nick's smile faded, and instead he was staring at me as if trying to decide something.

I squirmed, suddenly feeling I was being examined under a microscope.

He walked over and pulled the mic from my grasp. "Enough singing."

I swallowed. "Is this because of the flat-head screwdriver thing?"

He tossed the microphone onto the bench. "Dance with me."

Without waiting for me to respond, he took my hands, placing one on his shoulder and wrapping the other in his. Meanwhile, his right hand was skimming the small of my back, and I could feel his featherlight touch through the thin cotton of my dress.

He was close enough for me to make out the black flecks in his green irises. Close enough to see the furrows on his bottom lip. Close enough to count the black dots of his five o'clock shadow.

I was starting to feel out of breath, so I turned my head and rested it on his breastbone. I'd done it so I wouldn't have to gaze up at him, but I hadn't realized how intimate it would feel. Or how good.

The rise and fall of his chest was slow, but I was struggling to keep my breathing light. I wanted to take great lungfuls of air; there wasn't enough oxygen in the room. There wasn't anything in the room. There was only Nick.

My first mistake was to look up. My second was to let my eyes wander to his mouth. His lips were parted, and something in me snapped.

Instantly, I was pulling his head toward me. Then his arms were wrapped around my body and our lips touched. Desire surged through me, as I deepened the kiss and my hands scrabbled down his back, feeling the heat and the hardness and the longing as he leaned into me. My fingers reached under the bottom of his shirt and found warm skin and then I think I lost time.

Jesus Christ, the man could kiss.

The part of my brain that was still working wasn't surprised by that. What *was* shocking was my own reaction. My knees were shaking, and my heart skipping beats. And was it me making those little mewling noises? Probably, because after a particularly loud one, Nick broke contact and lifted his head.

"Are you okay?" His voice was so raspy, it made me want to tear off his shirt with my teeth.

Before I could act on that, or any of the other impulses I was having involving a naked Nick—preferably back at my flat, but here in the booth wasn't a deal-breaker—the door opened, and a barman walked in.

We jumped apart.

Shit, were there cameras in here? Had he come to kick us out? The barman didn't look particularly fazed; he was too busy concentrating on the tray he'd brought in. Of course, the drinks we'd ordered—about twenty-seven hours ago.

Carefully, he placed a pitcher of what looked like cola with mint-leaves floating in it on the table, then added two coasters, two glasses, and two metal straws. But instead of leaving, he poured the cola into the glasses, managing to spill ice cubes all over the table.

I snuck a glance at Nick, who was struggling to contain his laughter. He looked so relaxed; his hair was mussed and dimples framed a bright smile.

God, how could he go from sexy to adorable in five seconds?

Hang on a minute. Had I really just thought Nick was adorable? That wasn't right. Tonight was supposed to be about getting something out of my system. And with any luck, that's all it was with Simon and Jess too.

The barman finally left, so I grabbed a glass and gulped it down. Anything was better than standing here with all these confusing feelings. The cola was ice-cold where Nick's lips had been red-hot.

The karaoke machine moved on to a new random song. The opening penny whistle from "My Heart Will Go On."

I froze.

Oh God. This was a sign.

Suddenly, I wasn't confused anymore. I knew exactly what I had to do.

I slammed my glass onto the table. "I...I have to leave now."

He looked stunned. "You're leaving?"

I was so overcome with the need to get out I couldn't even form a coherent excuse. "I've got a thing."

"A thing?" I nodded, avoiding his eye. "That you have to do right now?"

I knew I sounded insane, but I didn't care. "Afraid so."

I turned to leave, but the gentle tug of his hand on my arm stopped me.

"What's going on, Zoë?"

I couldn't bear how kind and patient his voice was. If only he'd sounded annoyed or flippant, I wouldn't have had a problem flouncing out.

I finally turned to face him. "This has all been a terrible mistake."

He smiled ruefully. "It felt pretty right to me."

Why couldn't he be an arsehole about this? I knew where I stood with him when we argued.

"I'm just not interested in you. Sorry if I gave you the wrong idea."

It took all my willpower not to bolt. Instead, I muttered a goodbye then strode out, forcing myself to hold my head high.

Once outside, I picked up my pace, getting to the tube in what felt like a matter of seconds.

I passed the barriers, flew down the escalators, and arrived at the platform on autopilot. A blast of hot air announced a train was about to arrive.

The doors opened, and I shuffled inside, finding a seat far from the other Sunday evening travelers.

The motion of the train jolted me out of my stupor as I relived the past few minutes.

Sorry if I gave you the wrong idea?

Jesus. How had Nick not laughed in my face? My tongue had been rammed down his throat. What other idea was he supposed to form from that?

Seeing Simon with Jess had fried my common sense. Luckily, that song had come on in the nick of time. I smiled, feeling a twinge in my ankle, like I always did, along with a warm feeling in the pit of my belly.

What the hell was I thinking, kissing Nick?

You not-so-secretly enjoyed every second—that's *what you'd been thinking,* came a sneaky voice inside my head.

Well, I also secretly enjoyed watching *Most Haunted* with a tub of cookie dough ice cream. It didn't mean I wanted to do it every night.

I didn't go straight home. Instead, I got off the tube a few stops after mine and made my way to my parents' house. It was after eight now. I knew they'd have eaten dinner and would be watching telly. *The Crown*, probably—they really loved Her Majesty.

After a plate of reheated *tavas*, a favorite of mine: pork, potatoes, onions, and tomatoes roasted to perfection in the oven, I sat with them in the front room that used to only be for guests when I still lived at home. I knew they were a bit stressed about Pete's wedding; I hadn't ever looked at it from their perspective—their eldest kid getting married was a big deal. Thinking about someone else's problems was much more appealing than my own whirlwind emotions.

"How are you both?"

"Oh, fine, fine. We're fine." This was Dad's stock response to questions about his well-being.

I tried again. "Anything you need help with? Your phones or your computer?"

"I think the Facebook's broken," said Mum. "We keep seeing the same people over and over." My parents were very fond of their joint Facebook account that I'd set up for them—Frixos1234. Mum had been miffed that her preferred handle of Frixos123 had been taken by a bloke in Melbourne who, judging by his pictures, was a headless torso with impressively tanned abs.

"That's just the way Facebook is these days," I assured her. "Maybe unfollow people who post too much."

"Also, only me and your auntie Styliani liked the thing I posted about a goat dancing a sirtaki to 'Zorba the Greek.'"

My parents' internet surfing was eight percent looking up National Trust properties' opening times and ninety-two percent funny farmyard animals.

"I'll go and like it later, Mum," I said, feeling guilty.

We didn't always have to talk to feel comfortable together, I realized. It was nice just being in the same room as them. I was lucky having my parents so close. Loads of my London friends had families who lived hundreds of miles away or had horribly dysfunctional parents. It played a role in why so many stayed in unhappy or middling relationships—loneliness was too great a price to pay.

Having my folks so close probably explained why I wasn't as obsessed as some of my peers with finding a partner. Of course, Mum and Dad wouldn't be here forever, but it was all the more reason to appreciate them while they still were.

I gave them both an extra-hard hug before I left.

I still felt hurt by Simon, and my feelings for Nick were too weird to try and unravel. But by the time I got home, I felt much better about the crazy day I'd had.

26

I DON'T WANT TO
TALK ABOUT IT

I DRAGGED MYSELF TO THE office early on Monday morning and forced myself into crisis-management mode, but this time I directed my attention to where it was most urgently needed—the magazine. Being busy with work helped me to cope with my feelings for Simon. Because, even after all that had happened, the ache in my heart was for him. He was the last thing I thought about at night and the first thing I thought about in the morning. Gavin had been right. Sometimes you just had to feel your feelings.

I needed to talk to Mike, but I sat at my own desk first to gather my courage. I reread Lucy's interview with Jonny Delaney to double-check that she hadn't gone all fangirl on us, the way Gavin had suggested she had.

Of course she hadn't. I should never have doubted her.

Lucy had gotten some pretty good stuff out of him. He almost sounded sensible, which only proved what a great writer she was.

I put the proof down and took a long breath. Then I slowly walked to Mike's office.

He always looked so cheerful in the mornings; despite the fact that he got up at 5:00 and did a five-mile run before getting into work. I hated that I was here to wipe the smile off his face.

I walked in and he checked his watch.

"Goodness, Zoë. Did someone change your alarm clock for a joke? It's not even eight."

I shook my head and sat down. "We need a Plan B. The Marcie interview isn't going to happen."

"I thought you were getting along with Nick Jones."

"He has his limits. Marcie doesn't want to talk, and I've been a fool thinking I could be the one person to convince her otherwise."

I was on the verge of tears. *Oh come on*, I chided myself. *Pull yourself together*. "I'm sorry, Mike. I've let you down."

Mike's expression didn't change, but his face seemed to drain of color. "Any ideas for this Plan B?"

"Only one. We go big on Hands Down—make them the cover story." Christ, had I really just suggested that? I gritted my teeth to carry on. "Lucy's done a great interview with Jonny Delaney. We need to talk to the others and pray they've got something interesting to say."

"I thought you were dead against that?"

"I've grown up."

"All hope for Marcie is gone?"

I sighed. "Maybe when her new publicist takes over they'll be able to persuade her."

Mike frowned. "Nick is out?"

I suddenly faltered. "I probably shouldn't have told you that. He told me in confidence."

"Okay," said Mike. "Let's get our boy band game on."

———

A couple of hours later, when the rest of the team was in, I called an impromptu meeting. It was harder telling them than Mike because I'd never let them see how furiously I'd been paddling to get Marcie, all the while keeping up a calm exterior.

"That's a bummer," said Lucy.

"It sucks donkey's balls," added Gavin.

I tried to rouse their spirits, reminding them that it was Lucy's birthday in two days and we were going to have a small party in the office. Her proper celebrations would take place during the weekend, but she was turning twenty-four on Wednesday and I hated the idea of not marking it.

It might be the last birthday we all spent together.

I'd staked the magazine on Marcie and I'd failed. If the Hands Down issue didn't push up our circulation, our days were numbered. The idea filled me with dread.

"I could bring some games," said Gav.

"Only if you want me to cut your nads off," retorted Lucy.

"Luce, will you ring the Hands Down PR guy and set up the interviews? And give him David's number too, so they can liaise about the photoshoot."

I pretended to search for something in my drawer, bracing myself in case she asked why I wasn't ringing Nick myself. But she agreed without a fuss and got back to her work of terrorizing Gav.

♪

The night before Lucy's birthday, I declined all invitations to go out and get pissed because I had my own plans: I was going to make a birthday cake. I'd bought a cookery book in Tesco on a whim, thrown a few ingredients into my basket, and was all set to dive right in. Thirty-four years old and it would be the first cake I'd ever made from scratch. Was that lame or impressive?

It was all going swimmingly until I realized I only had plain flour—not self-raising. Would it make that much difference? To be safe, I rang Alice to check.

"Sorry, Zoë, the line must be bad because it sounded like you said you were baking a cake."

"I know it's unbelievable, but you heard right."

She suggested I add lots of baking powder to compensate, but when I broke the news that I was all out of that *too*, she warned that the cake would end up completely flat.

It meant another trip to the supermarket, but I had no choice. .

"Why don't I bring some over?" she said. "I can be there in ten minutes."

"Really?"

"I need to check with my own eyes that my sister-in-law is cake-making. In fact, I might need to get photographic proof because Pete is never going to believe me."

Two hours later, we were licking the bowl and the cake was rising nicely in the oven.

"How are things at work?" asked Alice, while I started on the washing-up.

"Not great." I let out a breath. "We're running a big feature on Hands Down."

"But that's really cool!"

I smiled. I'd forgotten that Alice was secretly a fan.

"Well, it will improve sales in the short run. Whether it will convince our parent company to keep faith in us is another question."

"I believe in you," she said.

Her words brought a lump to my throat.

"Enough about me," I said. "Tell me about Pete's latest groomzilla meltdown. Mum mentioned that he'd ordered the wrong *stefana*."

Alice frowned. "The wrong what?"

"They're like wreaths, and they're placed on the happy couple's heads during the wedding sacrament—surely Pete has mentioned them."

Alice giggled. "He's been calling them 'crowns.' He bought them online and prided himself on getting a bargain. Turns out they weren't crowns, but napkin rings. He's promised to go up to Southgate at the weekend to buy them in person."

♪

Baking, especially with company, turned out to be a lovely mood-booster, because the next day I felt remarkably positive. The cake had survived the journey on the Central Line and was now safely hidden in Mike's office.

Jody and Ayisha had brought balloons and poppers, and Rob had designed a "birthday girl" banner.

At lunchtime, Gav took me to one side to have a word.

"I must be a glutton for punishment," he said. "Because I've organized a surprise for Lucy's party tonight."

"Don't say you've bought a new board game."

"No, like I said, I'm a glutton for punishment. You know Lucy and I shared the interviewing for Hands Down? Well, I just spoke to Nick

Jones about it, and he's going to persuade them to come and sing for Lucy tonight."

"That's very sweet. So, Lucy is a convert then?"

He nodded. "Check out her Spotify playlist—it's full of Hands Down. The guys are okay, really. It's just Jonny who's a bit of a prick—probably because he gets all the extra attention, thanks to his famous girlfriend."

"How are things generally?" I looked around to check no one was within earshot. "Have you told Lucy how you feel?"

Gav shook his head. "I'm still working up to that."

Later, I popped out to buy candles and rang Alice.

"Want to come by the office this evening?" I asked her. "You may as well come and try some of the cake you helped make."

"But I don't know the birthday girl."

"That doesn't matter. Anyway, it will be nice to introduce you to everyone. You're the first sister I've ever had."

Alice sounded quite emotional by the time I rang off. I hadn't told her that Hands Down would be there because I wanted to surprise her. I knew she'd be thrilled, and the thought made me very happy. And God knows how miserable I'd been the last couple of days.

Gav and Rob nipped out and returned with wine and nibbles, and by six o'clock, we'd all switched off our computers and were huddled around Gav's desk as he poured the drinks. I hadn't had any alcohol since Sunday, but I knew it would look churlish if I refused a drink tonight, so I drank very slowly and kept my cup far from Gavin's enthusiastic refilling arm.

Alice arrived and I made the introductions. She chatted to everyone and found she had a friend in common with Rob's girlfriend.

Alice helped me light the candles then followed me back into the main office and started off the first round of "Happy Birthday."

Gav had been liaising with the Hands Down boys—minus Jonny—and as soon as Lucy had blown out the candles they burst in.

Lucy was bouncing up and down with joy, but my eyes were on Alice, who went bright pink and had to sit down. She looked over at me, mouthed "thank you," then turned her gaze back to Guy Williams, who I happened to know was her favorite Hands Downer. They'd moved on to a very pretty version of Seal's "Kiss from a Rose"— although I doubted any of them had been born when it came out.

I was so busy looking at Alice's happy face that I hadn't noticed Nick arrive. He was sitting on the far side of the room next to Mike. He was back in his usual uniform of a suit and tie, and beside him was a bouquet of flowers, which he presented to Lucy when she bounded up to him after the song finished.

Unlike Simon, he'd rung several times since Sunday, but I'd never picked up and he hadn't left a message. Things were too weird between us, and I had enough on my plate. But I had to admit it was nice of him to come and persuade the boys to sing for Lucy.

The last time he'd been here had been the night of Patrick's funeral. I swallowed back a lump in my throat. I missed Pat so much. Part of me felt that I deserved to lose my job because without Patrick's wise advice, I was bound to fuck up sooner or later. Why delay the inevitable?

My attention was caught by a flashing light, and I turned to see David, our photographer, snapping the Hands Down boys. Pics of them in our offices would add a nice touch to the issue. Thank God someone—most likely Mike—had thought to invite David and his camera.

Nick had moved and was talking to Gav. There were now only ten meters between us, instead of twenty. It felt far too close for comfort so I took myself off to the ladies to kill time. I wanted to go home, but it was far too early to leave.

By the time I got back, Lucy and Gav were arm wrestling. How could she not realize he liked her? He'd done everything except pull her pigtails and run away. Wisely, he let her win, and she stood on a chair proclaiming herself Queen of the World.

I smiled and at that exact moment my eyes met Nick's. He didn't quite smile back, but at least I'd inadvertently broken the ice. The next moment, Alice was by my side.

"Nick seems nice," she said. She'd seen me smile, then.

"You've talked to him?"

"Yes, he was very interested in my Pilates studio. He told me he trained with a yogi in India."

"You must have a knack with him; he's never opened up that much to me."

"Probably just making conversation," she said. "He doesn't seem all that comfortable to be here."

I didn't know how to respond to that. This wasn't the time to fill Alice in on our smooching in the karaoke booth.

"You seem to be enjoying yourself," I said.

She beamed. "Thanks for inviting me. I even got a couple of selfies with the band. I was shameless!"

"It's nice to see you looking so happy."

We left soon after. I hadn't spoken to Nick, but luckily, no one had noticed or commented on our lack of communication.

♪

I was glad of the early night because the next evening was the one black-tie event I went to every year: a ball held by the record label Sigma.

I was always surprised that people didn't buck the dress code. It was as if music journos secretly coveted a reason to ditch their usual uniform of jeans and trainers and dress like grown-ups.

I was wearing a floor-length red number I'd bought in the January sales. I'd swooped on it when I'd seen it on the rack even though I'd only popped in to buy socks. It was rather gorgeous: red velvet with a built-in corset, so after I'd showered and done my makeup there was no mad rush to find the one strapless bra I owned whose elastic hadn't given up the ghost.

I like to think I'm not easily impressed, but this year the ball was at the Natural History Museum, and standing under the skeleton of a blue whale, its jaw as big as my flat, had me staring in openmouthed wonder. I would have felt a bit stupid, but at least four other people were doing the same thing, including a minor royal.

Gav was by my side, scratching his head at the size of the damn thing, but then his attention slid over to Lucy, who'd gone to check our coats and was now coming back. He was mesmerized by her fifties-style dress; as she approached, the black netting of her full skirt bobbed up and down. He was so obviously smitten—poor guy.

Would Lucy notice him tonight? Dinner jackets did wonders for a man's sex appeal, and Gav was carrying off his penguin suit with panache—even if he had paired it with vintage Adidas trainers.

As Lucy approached, Gav leaned in to me: "Off to find booze before the good stuff runs out."

When Lucy reached me, she had a frown on her face.

"Everything okay, Luce?" I said, trying to glean if the frown was due to Gav's departure or something else. "Gav's gone to get you a drink."

"He could have asked what I wanted first," she replied.

"It'll be alcoholic—that usually covers it." I gave her an affection-ate nudge, but the movement caused me to rock on my rarely worn heels, and I had to grab her shoulder to right myself.

"Blimey, Zo, how much did you drink before you came?"

"Don't you think Gav looks good in his suit?"

She eyeballed me. "Now I definitely know you're pissed." She paused. "And overdue an eyesight test. Did you see the horrors he's got on his feet?"

I smiled, but before I could reply, she stalked off and I found myself alone and drinkless.

So, I went in search of vodka.

Armed with a double, I roamed the Hintze Hall, marveling at the pillars that rose to meet an impressive glass-vaulted ceiling. The windows were arranged in a trinity of arches—a church to science. The scale of it had taken my breath away when I'd first come as a ten-year-old on a school trip. To be here now as an adult, and to see it bathed in mood lighting, white-clothed tables circling around me, made me feel ten all over again. And I was transported to a simpler time, a happier time.

It had been four days, and I still hadn't spoken to Simon. He hadn't rung, and that hurt. I didn't know what to do about it because I was too scared to ring him. It was hell in this limbo, and I couldn't see a way out.

It would have been nice to let my hair down, get pissed, and forget about everything, but there was a good chance Nick would be here tonight, and the thought made me antsy. Still, there were several hundred guests, so even if he were here it would be easy enough to avoid him.

I chatted to friends and contacts, and by the time I sat down to dinner, I was feeling more like myself. I spotted Nick on the other side of the room, with a willowy blond standing next to him. A little too close.

After dinner and coffee the crowds thinned, and he seemed to have vanished. It was probably for the best. Whether the blond had vanished with him, I wasn't sure.

Lucy was sitting on the other side of the table, and when Mike got up to go for a cigarette, she came over and slumped into his chair.

"Everything okay?"

"Where did Gav get to?" she asked.

I hadn't noticed Gav leave, but his seat was empty. "Maybe he's dancing?"

A DJ had set up in another room, and people had been drifting toward the dance floor.

She rolled her eyes. "Gav *dancing*? He'll knock over some priceless exhibit, and we'll all be banned for life."

I smiled. Her digs at him were surely a cover for her feelings. Would Gav hate it if I tried to move things along a bit?

She sighed and reached for the chocolate mint Mike had left in his coffee saucer.

"You and Gav make a right pair," I said, matching her jokey tone. "One might even say a nice couple."

She frowned. Had I gone too far? She hadn't burst out laughing, which was a good sign.

"The problem with Gav is he's Darcy."

What did she just say? "You're comparing Gav to Mr. Darcy from *Pride and Prejudice*?"

"Yeah," said Lucy, oblivious to how odd she sounded.

Since when did a man being too much like Darcy constitute a problem? Did she mean that Gav was overly proud or arrogant? "You've lost me, Luce. I don't see the similarity at all."

"He's so serious all the time," she said. "He doesn't have a playful bone in his body. Cute, but a bit dull, you know? He's Darcy, and I've always had a thing for the devilish Wickham."

She should have sounded mad, sitting here comparing Gavin to a breeches-wearing Jane Austen hero, but she was making perfect sense. Playful and fun always attracted me way more than solid and reliable. But look who Lizzie Bennet had ended up with.

Lucy went off to dance. Our conversation had unsettled me, so I went in search of a bit of peace and I found it, quite unexpectedly, at the bar. With so much wine at the dinner table and an embarrassment of waiters hovering to refill glasses, most people didn't need to get their own drinks, so I sat on one of the bar stools and ordered a vodka.

As the bartender prepared a highball glass with ice, tonic, and lime, a woman in black satin trousers and backless top climbed onto the stool next to me. She had long fair hair, and I recognized her as Nick's blond from earlier. She gave me a weak smile, and I couldn't help noticing the smudged mascara and watery eyes. When she started to sniffle, I couldn't ignore her.

"Is everything okay?"

The girl extracted a tattered tissue from her expensive-looking clutch, then blew her nose quite unselfconsciously. Good for her.

"You'd think I could come to this amazing place and enjoy myself." She was American.

"I'm sorry," I said, like a British cliché. But what else was there to say? I was madly curious to know if she was Nick's date.

She leaned toward me. "Never get involved with an unavailable man."

"Too late."

Why had I just said that? She grinned. "I'm Ashley."

"Zoë. Pleased to meet you."

She sighed. "Men should come with warning labels, don't you think? 'Commitment-phobic,' 'Heartbreaker,' 'Secretly gay.'"

Now I was interested. Was I being unsisterly if I didn't disclose the fact I knew who she was talking about?

She frowned, like she was weighing up asking me a question. Then her eyes shifted to something behind me. "Can I borrow your drink?"

She didn't wait for an answer. She curled her hand around my glass and sprang to her feet.

I swiveled round just in time to see her throw my vodka tonic into the face of a very surprised—and now very wet—Nick.

27
TOTAL ECLIPSE OF THE HEART

THE BARMAN CRASHED A GLASS into a sink, but even the sound of it breaking didn't distract me. Ashley placed the empty vodka glass on the bar. Then, with excessive politeness, she said: "I'm so sorry about your drink, Zoë." She nodded at Nick. "That asshole will pay for a replacement."

Then she walked coolly away, while the rest of us picked our jaws off the floor.

Nick reacted first. He shook his head a couple of times—either in shock or to flick away the last dregs of vodka tonic. He was drenched, from his hairline down to a single drop pooling at the cleft of his chin. His neck was shiny, and dampness had even seeped into his collar and down the front of his shirt.

A splotch of green made me pause. I peered again.

Lodged between his bow tie and the starch of his collar was a wedge of lime.

I lost it.

I turned back to the bar, so he wouldn't see how much I was laughing. Lung-bursting belly laughs that strained the seams of my dress. *Oh God, I was going to rip it.* I tried to distract myself by picking out the names of all the designer gins lined up against the back wall of the bar.

A figure moved in my peripheral vision and when I glanced to my left, Nick was sitting next to me. He hooked his finger between his Adam's apple and collar and tugged his tie free. The lime tumbled to the floor between us.

It rolled in a lazy arc, holding our attention as if it were a grenade with its pin pulled out.

I chanced a look up and when Nick caught my eye, his face erupted into a smile and a roar of laughter escaped me.

This time, the giggles were even more violent. I bent double, my face practically on the bar, taking big gulps of air. I was half-aware of yanking my thumbs under my dress at the armpits to stop myself spilling out. The poor barman didn't know where to look, and suddenly found a stack of napkins that needed rearranging.

Soft laughter was coming from Nick, as he beckoned the barman over.

"I owe this woman a drink."

The barman looked from him to me uncertainly. "Vodka tonic?"

I nodded, not quite trusting myself to speak. "Make it two," Nick said. "With extra lime."

That set me off again. Nick sighed and shook his head. "I'm never going to hear the end of this."

"From what Ashley said, it sounded like you deserved it."

His eyes widened. "What did she tell you?"

"We had a pretty long chat." It was a blatant lie, but Nick didn't know that. And anyway, I was enjoying watching him squirm.

"You didn't want to hear my side of the story?"

"Maybe you should be worrying less about filling me in about your lovers' tiff and more about making it up to your date."

"She's not my date."

"She confused you with someone else? I guess all the blokes here are dressed the same, so it's an easy mistake to make. Next time, maybe come in a clown's outfit."

"We had a spare ticket in the office, and I asked if she wanted to come. It was never a date."

"You keep saying that. But it makes no difference to me—why should I care who you hook up with?"

There was a hardness to my voice that he didn't deserve.

He kept his eyes forward and didn't reply.

The barman faffed around making our drinks, which gave us something to concentrate on other than our stilted conversation. First, he placed two paper coasters with frilly edges in front of us, then he went back for the two vodka tonics—both with lime—and then he returned with two clear plastic stirrers.

"Would you like some olives?" he asked.

I shook my head and Nick said, "No, thank you."

"So, what have you been up to?" I said, after a couple of beats.

"I'm no longer Marcie's publicist."

I gasped. "You really resigned?"

He held my eye. "I didn't like the person I had become working for her."

I didn't know what to say. The silence was weighed down with a barrage of unspoken things. Feelings I'd pushed away, not daring to examine. Like how I'd felt at the brush of his hand against my leg in the Aston Martin; when I'd been pressed against him as he sang; when he'd kissed me. The memory made my blood surge. I felt hot and light-headed. I broke eye contact to take a sip of my mercifully strong drink.

I braved a glance back at Nick, whose attention was on his own glass. The top button of his white shirt was undone, his bow tie hung unknotted around his neck, and his damp hair glistened in the low light.

He was stunning.

I'd always known that, but his good looks suddenly felt dangerous.

My breathing quickened, a response to the danger. Fight, flight, or freeze instincts vying for control.

But I didn't want to do any of those things.

When he did speak, he didn't look at me. "Zoë, there are things about me you don't know…"

I waited for him to continue, but his attention had snagged on the rows of spirits in front of us. Or maybe he was looking at the mirror behind the bottles, because there seemed to be a rather animated scene unfolding behind us.

His jaw clenched. "Fuck."

He spun round and I twisted to see what he was looking at. A guy in jeans was arguing with a woman in a fifties dress. I hadn't seen anyone wearing casual clothes, but the dress was definitely Lucy's.

Then the man turned round and I froze. *What was Jonny Delaney doing here?*

Jonny must have felt his ears burning because he suddenly looked over. I could see Lucy pulling him back to her, but he shrugged her off and started to make his way toward us.

Nick rose and put himself between me and Jonny, which was a bit annoying because I wanted a clear view of him. What was Jonny's beef? I was about find out.

"I want a word with you," he blustered as he approached the bar.

I was holding my drink, and for a brief moment, had a vision of myself chucking it over Jonny's annoying floppy hair.

"A pleasure, as always." I added a fake smile in case he wasn't au fait with sarcasm.

Nick looked from me to Jonny, trying to read the room.

"Oh, you take a pleasure in ruining careers, do you?"

"What on earth are you talking about?"

He rolled his eyes theatrically. "Don't play dumb."

Nick inched forward. "Leave it, Jonny."

"No, don't leave it," I said, annoyed. "What stupidity has your tiny mind invented and blamed on me?"

"Lucy denies it, but I know it was you. You've always hated me."

Behind him, Lucy and Gav had appeared, looking rather shocked.

"It's true, boss," said a red-faced Gavin.

"What's true?" Nobody was saying anything remotely useful. "Can someone *please* explain what the hell is going on?" A few suits had turned to see what the fuss was, but I didn't care.

"Shut it, Gav," hissed Lucy.

Again, not helpful. "What's true, Gav?"

"Lucy's in love with Jonny."

This explained precisely nothing.

"*What?*" said Jonny.

"Don't be daft, Gav," mumbled Lucy. "It was just a snog."

"You snogged Jonny?" I directed the question at Lucy, but then cut my eyes to Nick. He hadn't reacted very much so far, and his face stayed blank now. Why had none of this surprised him?

"Can we get back to the point, for fuck's sake," said Jonny. "Which is that Zoë Bentos is trying to ruin my life."

One day, the little shit would get my name right. "And how exactly am I doing that?" I retorted.

"You leaked the fact that I'm leaving the band."

"*What?* That's preposterous—I had no idea."

"You overheard me on the London Eye."

"You're delusional. Where exactly am I supposed to have leaked it?"

"It's all over the internet—BuzzFeed even has a quiz about it."

"And why would I do that?"

"You've always had it in for me."

Nick took a step forward. "Jonny, enough."

Jonny turned to Nick and laughed. "And where were you when all this was going down?"

A vein in Nick's jaw was pulsing. "Zoë didn't leak anything."

Jonny seemed oblivious to Nick's anger. "Oh really? You're sure? Or were you too busy boning the bitch to notice?"

There was a collective gasp from my team. Whether it was because of Jonny's choice of epithet or his insinuation that I was sleeping with Nick, I was unclear.

Nick shook his head then turned to me. He was smiling, but his eyes were black. "Remember that session with Carl?"

What was he talking about? The only Carl I could think of was our Boxercise instructor.

Oh.

Oh.

Jonny had no idea where this was heading. Rather pathetically, he seemed to have decided that goading Nick was the best plan of action.

"Come on then, ya nancy." His accent seemed to have magically reverted to its Mancunian origins.

"You can't call him a nancy after implying he's sleeping with a woman," muttered Gavin, who was taking things a bit too literally.

Nick had his right first curled, but his arm was hanging by his side. Jonny's taunt hadn't pushed him over the edge—yet.

"Apologize to Zoë." Nick's voice was calm.

"Or?"

"I won't ask again, Jonny."

"Go fuck yourself."

Nick shrugged, like he'd just been told the barista was out of his favorite hazelnut syrup.

The single punch that knocked Jonny to the floor seemed to come in slow motion. Nick's elbow swung backward, then his fist smashed into Jonny's face. Jonny collapsed to the floor as if someone had removed all the bones in his legs.

Carl would have been proud.

I stared openmouthed, dimly aware of how ridiculous this all was. A man had just hit another man, defending *me*. I was like Maid Marian or Guinevere.

Nick stood looming over Jonny, almost daring him to get up and attempt a counterblow. "*I* leaked it."

"*What?*" The word was on my lips too, but Jonny had beaten me to it.

"I leaked it," said Nick again. He wasn't even out of breath, but mine was coming out in raggedy gasps. Nick had leaked Jonny's defection from Hands Down?

"You fucking shit!" Jonny screamed. "You're so fucking fired!"

Jonny was probably trying to intimidate Nick, but from his prone position, he looked ridiculous, especially since his nose was looking mighty red and both his cheeks were swelling. He looked like an angry hamster.

From somewhere to my left, two enormous blokes rumbled toward us. Jonny's expression changed from fury to satisfaction as the two men, in low-slung jeans, pristine white trainers and a lot of gold jewelry, approached. They were Jonny's bodyguards; I recognized them from the London Eye. Without saying a word, they flanked Nick, grabbing him by the armpits and without breaking stride, started dragging him toward the exit.

The whole place stopped and stared. This was so not fun anymore. What were they going to do once they got him outside? This wasn't right. And it was my fault.

I followed them, but they moved at a fair old clip, and I only caught up when they were through the huge revolving door and outside. These bloody shoes—not to mention my dress—were not designed for sprinting.

My concerns were justified. As I pushed through the door, I saw Tweedle Dum hold Nick upright while Tweedle Dee socked him in the gut. Nick doubled over but made no sound—unlike the whimper Jonny had emitted.

"Hey, leave him alone!" I shouted.

The one who'd punched him whispered something to Nick, then they loosened their grip on him and he dropped to his knees, winded. With blank stares in my direction, they sloped past me.

I rushed to Nick's side and knelt beside him.

"Are you okay?"

He nodded.

"Are you sure? That guy hit you pretty hard."

"I deserved it."

"Jonny should have hit you himself, not rely on his goon squad."

"They apologized afterward."

"How civilized."

He grinned, but it quickly morphed into a grimace. "My ribs are *really* going to hurt tomorrow."

"Well, at least they didn't hit you in the face," I said. "Jonny's going to have a corker of a black eye."

"I should have done that a long time ago."

"Is it true what you said, or were you just winding Jonny up? Did you leak that story?"

He nodded.

I shivered. "Why?"

Nick leaned forward, trying to slip his jacket off, swearing under his breath.

"What are you doing?"

"You're cold," he said, like that explained everything. "I'm giving you my jacket."

"Can you just answer the question? Leaking that story—that would have cost you your job with Hands Down. And after Marcie, it's like you're self-destructing."

"I did it for you."

"Excuse me?"

"Those pictures you rang me about. They were of Lucy and Jonny. I begged the picture editor at the *Post* not to run them. But they wanted another story in return."

"Why would you do that?"

"It's like you said, Lucy's life would get turned upside down if the tabloids found out she'd come between Jonny and Jeanette. The world's press would be on her doorstep, never mind the bile she'd get from the fans."

"That's noble of you, Nick, but why risk your job for Lucy, someone you barely know?"

"I did it for *you*, Zoë."

I frowned. "What are you talking about?"

"I saw how protective you are of everyone at the magazine. You treat them like family. If one of them hurts, you hurt. You're loyal, courageous, and honorable, and I've never met anyone like you."

Where was this coming from?

He saw my confused look and shook his head wryly. "For a smart woman, you're being a bit slow." He looked away briefly, then back to me. "I love you, Zoë. I love everything about you."

28

LOVE IS FOR SUCKERS

FOR A MOMENT, I COULDN'T speak. He *loved* me?

"I don't know what to say." Stating the obvious, a bit. I tried again. "I'm very flattered, of course."

His face fell, and a tiny piece of my heart cracked. Flattered was a stupid choice of word. I was an idiot. I wasn't flattered; it was more than that, but I couldn't quite pinpoint what.

He was looking at me without expectation, but I couldn't find the right words. His declaration was so unexpected, I didn't trust myself to spew out any more immediate reactions.

Loyal, courageous, honorable—had he really said all those things about me?

"Thank you," I said. Because I meant it, but even those two words were inadequate.

"Zoë, I—"

Before I could speak again, Gavin and Lucy were rushing over.

"Oh my God," cried Lucy. "That was kinda awesome. Jonny is such a prick."

Even Gav looked impressed. "The little fucker deserved it," he said, quietly. Lucy didn't react, but maybe she hadn't heard him.

Nick stood up slowly, and I positioned myself by his side in case he needed support.

"Where did Jonny go?" I asked. If he dared come near us, I'd hit him myself. I felt like a lioness, protective not only of my team, but of Nick too. I didn't want to analyze this feeling too closely.

"Not the best career move for you, Nick," said Lucy tactlessly.

"I knew I'd get fired over the leak. Getting to punch him was a bonus."

"Why did you do it, then? The leak, I mean?"

Nick glanced at me, and I held my breath.

"I thought it was the best strategy for his solo career. The coverage is going to be unbelievable."

Gav nodded wisely. "Makes sense. Although I'd rather see Delaney fall flat on his face."

"I've been a bit of a fool," said Lucy. "That's why I'm going to get well and truly hammered tonight."

"It's nearly midnight," I said.

"Exactly. The night is young," she announced. "A bunch of us are going to Old Street. Want to come?"

"I think I'll pass."

"What about you, Nick?" said Gavin. He looked at me as if it was my decision.

"No, I think I'm all partied out tonight."

Gav and Lucy left, looking relieved, leaving me alone with Nick. How many times had I stood this close to him and not thought twice about it? Now, I didn't know what to think, other than trying to stop myself from shivering. But I wasn't cold.

Nick assumed I was, because he put one arm around me. But then he wrapped his other arm round me too, until I was cocooned in his embrace. Our foreheads were centimeters apart.

"You're all I think about," he whispered. "I've gone half-mad these last few days thinking you hated me."

"I don't hate you, Nick."

My nerve endings were on fire. The nearness of him, the warmth of his jacket, his scent, all of it was making me light-headed.

My hips shifted forward, of their own accord. The length of his body was pressed against mine. His hands were curled around my waist, and my own arms were nestled into his sides.

I breathed him in, overcome by a peace I hadn't felt for a long time.

But then a buzzing sounded from my bag.

It snapped me back to reality. I needed some air, to hit pause and think.

I took a step back. "Sorry, I need to check who's ringing…" It sounded lame, I knew, but I needed to break eye contact with Nick. I pulled the phone from my bag: the caller ID said Simon. Why was he ringing now after days of silence?

A feeling of unease muscled out my earlier serenity. I swiped my finger to accept the call. "Simon?"

"Zoë, thank God. It's Jess." She sounded tense, and I immediately held my breath.

"Is everything okay?"

"It's Simon," she said. "An ambulance came. He's in hospital. He wasn't breathing."

Panic squeezed my throat. "What happened? Is he breathing now? He's not…" I couldn't finish the question.

"He's stable but unconscious. I thought you should know. I waited with him for a couple of hours, but I hate hospitals. Maybe you could go and check on him."

"Jess, which hospital?"

Nick had been biting his lip, but now he frowned in concern.

"That one in Paddington."

"St. Mary's?"

"Possibly."

"Had you guys been drinking?"

"Hmm?" Jess sounded distracted.

"Did Simon take something? Were there drugs involved?"

"You're a sweetheart, Zoë. I have to go now."

She rang off, ignoring my question.

"*Fuck.*"

"What's happened?" said Nick.

The embrace we'd shared felt like a lifetime ago. "It's Simon. Sounds like an OD or something." My breathing was shallow, barely enough to push the words out. "He's at A&E in Paddington—as far as I can make out. Jess wasn't clear."

I tried to focus. *Yes, St. Mary's—that's what she'd said.*

Nick's eyes were full of concern. "Is he okay?"

"I don't know. I need to get to him."

"Of course. Let me take you."

"No, no." I was already scrolling through my phone looking for my Uber app. "It's okay. You need to go and rest your ribs." I was prattling. I just wanted to know Simon was okay. The idea of him not being in the world was filling me with ice-cold fear.

I needed to get to him.

In the end, I chanced on a black cab and because traffic was so light, we crossed the park from South Kensington to Marble Arch without stopping once. Minutes later, I was being dropped off outside casualty at St. Mary's in Paddington.

Ordinarily, I would have felt a fool hauling arse in a ball gown down a linoleum-lined hospital corridor, but I didn't care how ridiculous I looked.

After a breathless conversation at reception, I found out Simon had been taken to a private room, that he was resting, but I could visit for a few minutes. It took me a while to find the private wing and then his room.

I paused at the door before entering. What would I find inside?

Simon looked asleep; his chest was rising and falling rhythmically. He looked paler than usual, but otherwise okay. I crept toward him, scared to wake him, but also scared that he might never wake. No one had told me anything about his prognosis—would he have long-term effects?

A wooden chair with a padded seat was backed up against the wall, under the TV. I picked it up and placed it close to the bed, so I could see him properly. Was I his first visitor?

I sat down, arranging the folds of my dress onto the chair.

"Si?"

He didn't stir, but then, I'd barely whispered.

I reached to touch his hand. It was cool but clammy.

I cleared my throat and tried again. "Simon?"

I squeezed his hand and his eyes fluttered open.

The relief was overwhelming. If I hadn't been sitting, my knees would have buckled.

It took him a moment to see me, but then he parted his cracked lips and smiled.

"Frixie." His voice was a coarse whisper. "You came."

"Of course I came, Si."

He looked down at my ball gown. "Nice dress."

"Thought I'd make the effort."

"You look great."

"You look bloody awful." I laughed nervously.

He smiled wanly. "I've been a fool."

"What happened, Si?"

"They pumped my stomach." He winced. "Not fun."

"How did you get into such a state?"

"I don't remember much. A few beers, some wine, then Jess suggested some pills. They asked me when I got here, but I didn't know what they were. How fucking stupid did I feel?"

"Don't think about it. The only thing that matters is that you're okay now."

"Don't pity me, Frixie. I couldn't bear it. They even sent a shrink, who asked if I was depressed and had OD'd on purpose."

He started to cough. I got up and poured him some water from a jug by the side of his bed.

He sipped the water until the coughs subsided.

"I felt too ashamed to tell the shrink I was just trying to keep up with Jess—to impress her—although God knows why. She's crazy. Why has it taken me so long to figure that out?"

"Is that a rhetorical question?"

"I'm genuinely stumped."

"It's not rocket science. You were besotted. From the moment you met her. It happens to the best of us."

"But you've been here for me all along. Why couldn't I see what was right in front of me?"

Another rhetorical question, but this time I didn't trust myself to answer him.

He shuffled upright so he was almost sitting. "You're wonderful, Frixie. Do you know that?"

"You're not so bad yourself."

"I'm being serious, Zoë. I realize now what I should have realized years ago. I love you. I *love* you."

I couldn't breathe. Was it the drugs talking?

"I'm not sure you're quite yourself right now."

He sat further upright and grasped my hand with both of his. "Is there still a chance for us?"

A nurse bustled in before I could reply.

"Back in bed, Mr. Baxter. No exerting yourself."

"I'm not exerting myself," he told her. "I'm in love."

I blushed as red as my dress.

"Well, congratulations," she said, looking from him to me. "You make a lovely couple." I pulled at a stray thread on the seam of my dress while she took his pulse. She tutted, and I looked up. "Still a bit weak. Probably better if you got some rest, Mr. Baxter. You'll have lots of time to see your girlfriend when you're released tomorrow morning."

Simon looked at me expectantly.

I nodded. "Of course. Rest now, and I'll see you tomorrow." I left before he asked me to answer his other question.

I got a black cab and was home just after 2:00 a.m. I slipped off my heels and wandered into my kitchen feeling dazed.

What an evening. Was I losing my grip on reality or had two men actually declared their feelings for me? Honestly, it was like waiting forever for a bus to show up, and suddenly, beep beep! Two bloody buses pull in at the same time.

Nick's declaration felt like a week ago or like something from a dream.

Guilt niggled me. I shouldn't have walked out on him like that. It was too late to ring him to apologize, but should I send a text? I found my phone and scrolled to his number.

My thumb hovered over his name. What on earth would I say? I'd sleep on it. Maybe the right words would come to me tomorrow.

I got undressed and threw on the old oversized T-shirt I slept in. I padded to the bathroom and attacked my makeup with cotton wool and makeup remover.

Why was I thinking about Nick?

After all these years, Simon had finally told me what I'd so longed to hear. Surely that should have been uppermost on my mind.

So why wasn't it?

Maybe it was because even though he'd said all the right things, I still felt like his second choice. And for all of Simon's protestations about learning from his divorce, he'd dived headlong into a relationship with Jess, after kissing me but then acting like it had never happened. And only when things had gone sour with Jess had he suddenly remembered me. Those were the actions of someone acting out of fear, not love. Was Simon one of those people who didn't feel comfortable in their own skin unless they were in a relationship?

At the other extreme, Nick had admitted that he avoided relationships. Was a commitment-phobe any better?

Maybe neither of them was right for me. Maybe I needed to wait for the next bus. Or rely on my own steam.

♪

I was up the next morning at eight. I was tired, but sleep had slipped from my grasp all night. Groggily, I carried out my usual routine, only noticing after I'd showered and dressed that I had a voicemail from Nick.

I stared at the screen. Did I want to hear it? He'd left it at six in the morning—timed for when he knew it would go straight to voicemail.

Sod it.

I hit play.

His voice sounded raspy and low, like he hadn't slept for a week, reminding me of Marcie's cigarette-abused voice.

"I hope you're okay and that Simon is on the mend. I got hold of Jess last night, who told me what happened. It sounded like they got him to hospital in time and that he should make a full recovery. I'm sorry you had such a fright."

A pause.

"I guess you won't be surprised to hear that I've been relieved of my duties at Pinnacle. I've got a few contacts in Mexico who'll still hire me, so I'm heading back."

Another pause.

"Take care of yourself, Zoë."

There was no mention of The Conversation.

Maybe he didn't mention it because he regretted it. Maybe his feelings had been tainted by wine and the romance of the venue. Maybe this morning he was congratulating himself on escaping. For a second, I wished he wasn't leaving and that we could carry on as friends. But we couldn't carry on as normal, pretending he hadn't said what he'd said. And anyway, would Nick want that?

I had taken the morning off work as I was meeting Alice for the final fitting of her dress and mine. On the way to the dress shop, I had a text from Simon:

Wanna hang tonight, Frixie? We could do a Marvel marathon on Netflix?

Was he implying we Netflix and "chill," or did he actually want to watch *The Avengers*? I didn't know how to reply, so very maturely, I didn't respond at all. I turned my phone off, then hurried to make my appointment.

Alice looked so happy as she twirled in front of the mirror. She was a picture of bridal bliss, looking stunning in her ivory lace. I stood next to her in my long satin dress while assistants fussed around both our hems.

"Do you not have your shoes?" asked the lady crouched on the floor by my bare feet.

"Shoes?"

"So we can get the length right?"

I looked guiltily over at Alice. She had reminded me to bring the heels I'd be wearing on the day for this very reason, but in the whirlwind of last night and this morning, I'd clean forgotten.

"No, I'm sorry," I replied sheepishly.

"Maybe Zoë can borrow mine?" said Alice.

Alice was almost a foot shorter than me and so had opted for terrifyingly high heels to compensate. Plus, her feet were tiny. I doubted I'd get more than my toes into them.

"It's okay," said the assistant, whose name was Eloise. "We have a selection, if Zoë would like to pick the pair that most closely resembles the shoes she'll be wearing on D-Day."

They all had a habit of calling the wedding day D-Day and I kept wanting to make a joke about fighting Nazis, but it never quite seemed appropriate.

After I'd picked the shoes with the lowest heels, I was back at Alice's side.

"So, how are things with you? You seem tired," she said, as we studied our reflections.

A wave of nausea made me flinch. Eloise was sticking a pin into my dress, but my sudden movement made her miss and the pin scraped my skin.

I flinched again.

"Sorry," she trilled. "But you must keep still."

"Is everything okay, Zoë?" asked Alice.

Eloise was busy with her pins, but I still didn't want to discuss this in front of a perfect stranger.

"I'm fine," I said brightly.

"Is there something you're not telling me?"

I couldn't keep up the pretense any longer. I glanced at Alice and nodded.

Eloise got to her feet. "All done."

Thank God.

I slipped off my heels and dragged myself back to the changing room with Alice in tow. She waved away the assistant and asked me to help her undress.

"So," she said over her shoulder as I began unlacing her, "what happened last night?"

"Simon got rushed to the hospital."

Her eyes widened. "Oh my goodness, why? Is he okay?"

How much should I tell her? Simon might not want people to know what happened.

"He had an allergic reaction to something, but he's fine now."

"Have you got time for a coffee? I want to hear all about it."

Twenty minutes later we were installed in the Nordic Bakery round the corner. Alice was watching what she ate so only ordered a rooibos tea. But I needed real sustenance and had armed myself with an Americano and a muffin bursting with blueberries.

"So, tell me everything," she said.

"I had a weird night. Even before I got the call about Simon."

"You weren't with him when he had the allergic reaction?"

I shook my head. "I was at a work do—a ball of all things—and there was a bit of a ruckus, an actual fist fight. Sort of...over *me*."

Alice's eyes were wide. "What happened?"

I glanced around to check if anyone might be listening. But it was okay—we were the only customers here, and the steaming espresso machine was making enough noise to ensure we wouldn't be overheard by the baristas.

"You know Jonny Delaney?"

"Of course."

Stupid question. "He gatecrashed the party to shout at me, and my friend Nick sort of punched him."

"Sort of punched him?"

"Knocked him flat on his arse." I grinned; I couldn't help it.

"Hang on, I met Nick, didn't I? Is he your deputy editor?"

"No, you're thinking of Gav."

She looked at me, waiting for more. After a couple of moments, I started feeling uncomfortable. "What?"

"Who is this guy who jumps to your defense like that? He must really like you."

"I didn't think he liked me at all, not after last week when I..."

"When you what?"

"I kissed him, then ran out on him."

Her eyes widened. "He must like you quite a bit."

I picked up my coffee, then put it back down again without drinking.

"That punch cost him his job—maybe his career. He got manhandled, and then hit, by Jonny's bouncers afterward, and when I went to find out if he was okay, he told me he had feelings for me."

"Good grief!"

"That was my reaction. With added swear words."

"And this was *before* you heard about Simon?"

"There's more."

"Did something happen at the hospital?"

"Simon told me he regretted his time with Jess. He asked if there was still a chance for the two of us, because he'd suddenly seen the light."

"So let me get this straight—you had *two* men tell you they're in love with you in one evening?"

"I know; it sounds unbelievable, doesn't it?"

"Let's take them one by one. What did you say to Simon?"

"He was groggy, and a nurse came in before I could answer him. But the truth is, I have no idea how I feel about him. I don't want to be his second rebound after his divorce."

"What did you say to Nick?"

"Not much. I was speechless."

"Zoë Frixos lost for words?" She smiled. "That's a first."

My guilt came flooding back. "I should have reacted better, told him something kinder. But then I got a call from Jess telling me Simon was in hospital, and all I could think of was getting to him."

"It was a medical emergency; surely he'd understand?"

"But my reaction was awful before that. What on earth can I say to make things go back to the way they were between us?"

"Are you close friends?"

It was a good question. "Half the time he drove me mad, but he made me look at things differently; and sometimes I felt he was the only person who got me."

"You're talking about him in the past tense."

"There's no going back for us. He's leaving the UK anyway. He's worked abroad most of his life. I'm sure he'll get over me pretty fast. He doesn't strike me as the type who lacks female company."

"I'm sorry."

"I'm okay, I promise. Anyway, enough about me, what's happening with you?"

"I had a bit of a blow-up with my parents," she said.

I couldn't imagine Alice blowing up at anyone. "About what?"

"We're serving chicken at the wedding, and they want lamb."

My first instinct was to laugh. She was winding me up, wasn't she? How could they have fallen out over this? But from the look on her face, Alice wasn't joking.

"Can you elaborate?"

"We settled on lamb months ago, even though Pete hates it. I talked him round because my parents insisted that chicken was a bit, well, *common*." She looked embarrassed. "They were being terrible snobs."

"So, we're having lamb—is it really a problem?"

"Pete shouldn't have to eat something he hates at his own wedding. I was wrong to side with my parents, or rather, avoid going against their wishes."

"Pete would have been fine with the lamb—it's one meal."

"But the principle of it bothered me and I told them that. I should never have made Pete agree to the lamb. I should have persuaded my parents to accept the chicken."

Alice was talking about menus, so why did I find myself tingling?

She was getting up now and gathering her stuff. But I was still trying to work out what she'd said that had affected me so much. This was madness.

"See you tomorrow," she was saying. "For our Greek night."

29

I CAN SEE CLEARLY NOW

ALICE AND I SAID OUR goodbyes, and I still didn't know what she'd said that had set my heart racing. But I knew enough to follow my gut, so instead of walking south from Chiltern Street to Oxford Street, I found myself heading north to Baker Street tube.

Then it came to me: I was overwhelmed by the conviction that I had to talk to Marcie again. Her house was only a couple of stops away on the Jubilee Line. I wasn't sure what I was going to say—it sure as hell didn't have anything to do with chicken or lamb. But I just knew I had to speak to her.

Then suddenly, everything pulled into focus, and Alice's story made sense. I should never have tried to talk Jess round into forgiving Marcie; I should have persuaded Marcie that she didn't need Jessica's forgiveness.

Just as Alice had been intimidated by her parents and initially taken the easier path, I'd let myself be intimidated by Marcie.

Excitement bubbled in my gut. Could I pull this off? My hope faltered when I remembered I still had to get past the intercom password.

As I waited on the platform for the tube, a woman walked past me carrying a Bonnie and Clyde tote bag.

I froze.

What if the same password I'd used a couple of weeks ago still worked? Could it really be so easy?

My confidence surged. What was the harm in trying? What did I have to lose?

The train arrived and I calmly boarded. I got off one stop later at St. John's Wood, then, on autopilot, I retraced my steps to Marcie's house.

Before any doubts got the better of me, I pressed my finger to the buzzer.

"Hello, who is it?" came the disembodied voice.

"It's Bonnie, and I'm here to see Clyde."

I held my breath as I waited for the response.

Please, please, please.

"I'm sorry, you must have the wrong house."

Damn.

The password had changed. Nick had warned me that they rotated. I kicked the wall in frustration.

But what if they were all based on films that Marcie loved? I pictured the other posters she'd had up: *Gone with the Wind* and *Butch Cassidy and the Sundance Kid*. Not a fan of happy endings, then.

But who did Marcie most relate to—southern belles or outlaws?

I cleared my throat and on instinct I announced: "It's Butch Cassidy, and I'm here to see the Sundance Kid."

Long, long moments passed. But then the door buzzed and clicked open.

Success!

Amazed, I slipped through the widening gap and hurried to the front door. Ronan was standing at the threshold with both dogs on leads. They barked as I approached.

"Hi," I said confidently, both for his benefit and so the dogs wouldn't sense my anxiety.

"Most people don't get two attempts at the password," he said. "But I figured I'd bend the rules because I owe you. I screwed up when you were last here. I should have been watching Marcie, not trying out new recipes, and she got drunk. But you didn't tell anyone, and I appreciate that. After this, though, we're even."

"Thank you, Ronan."

He stepped aside to let me pass, and the dogs growled but this time, only for show.

I hesitated in the hallway. I'd been so focused on getting in, but that was only half the problem. Yes, I was in Marcie's house, but would my words have any effect? I turned to Ronan, who nodded toward the lounge.

"She's in a good mood." He leaned forward and whispered, "She had a late night visitor, if you catch my drift." He winked in case I hadn't. Then he froze. "Shit. Don't tell anyone. I'll get fired, and I'm already on thin ice."

"You can trust me," I said, and sent a silent thank you to Marcie's secret Romeo, who might just have tipped the balance in my favor.

Ronan waved me to the living room. "Go through. You'll soon know if she wants to talk to you."

I walked to the doorway and stopped. Marcie had been shopping since I'd last been here because slap bang in the middle of the room stood a mahogany grand piano, exactly like the one I'd played for her at the Steinway shop. It had looked huge on the shop floor, but in Marcie's high-ceilinged drawing room, it looked normal-sized.

And sitting behind it, her bowed head peeking above the lifted lid, was the woman herself.

I took a step forward and she looked up. She had a yellow pencil tucked behind one ear, but it didn't distract from her heavily made-up eyes, which were boring into me with a ferocity that made my knees shake.

My mind suddenly went blank.

Why was I here again? Oh yes, to suggest the chicken not the lamb.

Oh God. This was crazy. Maybe I should just turn around and make a run for it.

"You've got a lot of nerve turning up, young lady."

My courage faltered, but I stood straighter. Never show weakness. Never let them see they intimidate you. Sometimes, those mantras were worth living by.

"I know what you did to Jessica Honey," I began.

She narrowed her eyes. "*What* did you just say?"

"She told me that you blacklisted her band ten years ago. Out of petty jealousy."

Marcie stood, the piano stool screeching against the wood floor. "How dare you!"

Shit. Was I making a mistake?

I breathed deeply. No, it wasn't a misstep. I was here to drop some truth bombs. That were long overdue.

"You have to own what you did, Marcie. You can't let your peace of mind rest in someone else's hands. If Jessica hasn't forgiven you after ten years, then you have to accept she never will. Learn from your mistakes. Find another young musician to take under your wing, if you have to, but for God's sake, let it go."

She walked around the piano till she was a couple of feet from me.

She still looked mad, but she'd dialed down from nuclear meltdown angry to plain ol' white-hot fury.

"Take back the word 'petty.'"

My whole speech and she was stuck on that?

Perhaps she was allowed a little appeasement. If not for her current behavior then for her *Stars* album. Every track on that record was gold.

"Okay, I take back 'petty.' But you were jealous of a meaningless girl. You were the most talented musician on the planet." Appeasement had steadily morphed into sycophancy, but this was Marcie effing Tyler. She'd taught *God* to write songs.

"He was the love of my life."

"Benedict Bailey?"

She nodded, and a little more anger melted away. "I knew I would fall in love with him from the way he held a guitar."

That was possibly the most romantic thing I'd ever heard.

She seemed lost in her memories as she floated to the sofa and sat down.

I joined her, making slow movements so I wouldn't startle her. "Do you want to talk about him?"

"This isn't an interview. Everything I'm going to tell you is still off the record. But seeing as you've got such strong opinions about my life, you should at least do me the courtesy of hearing my side of things."

"It's off the record, I promise."

"I met Benedict in a recording studio—it was 1985, and my last album had flopped. Although, in today's terms, it would have hit number one. Anyway, it was decided that I needed fresh blood. Patrick brought him in. He wanted to shake things up a bit. Told me not to get involved with him." She laughed. "Benny was a session player. When I heard him play 'Never Let Me Down,' I knew I had to have him for my band. Then when I met him, I knew he was the one."

I nodded, not wanting to interrupt her reverie. But for long moments, she didn't speak.

"Can you tell me about your tattoo?"

It was a risk asking such a direct question, but this might be my only chance. I was amazed she hadn't kicked me out yet.

"Benny and I went on holiday in Bermuda," she said. "We were burned out after two solid years on the road—we were like zombies, sleeping all day and drinking all night. But one day, someone persuaded us to go snorkeling. We were as hungover as dogs—God knows how we didn't drown—but we were taken to this amazing reef and spent an hour swimming beside these exquisite seahorses.

"That holiday saved us. Seeing nature up close put everything in perspective. We decided to get clean and got matching tattoos to remind us of that feeling, but after I'd gotten mine, Benny confessed he was terrified of needles and had been too scared to tell me.

"I told him I hated tattoos too, and had only done it because I thought he liked them. We laughed so hard."

She paused, remembering happier times. With her lips parted, her face appeared softer and she looked a decade younger.

"That's not what you told me last time, Marcie. You told me you got the tattoo to remind you of a necklace you lost."

She frowned and the lines on her face returned.

"When he couldn't get the tattoo, I had the necklace made for him. He told me he'd always treasure it."

"It was your present to him?"

"A woman giving a man jewelry—is that too feminist for you?"

"No, of course not," I said. "But why did you lie?"

"I lost him when he lost the necklace." She laughed bitterly. "Turns out, few things are as permanent as tattoos. At first he told me he'd lost it, but then one night, after we'd been arguing, he told me he was through with me, and that he'd given the necklace away. Can you believe that?"

"He gave it to Jessica Honey?"

She nodded.

So, Jess had been telling the truth.

"It damn near broke my heart," she said.

"I'm so sorry, Marcie."

"Then he died and I learned what real heartbreak was."

Tears filled my eyes, but hers stayed dry. There was so much pain in what she was saying, but her voice was even; it was like she had numbed herself to it. Who could blame her?

"And now he's gone I can never make up for the things I've done to him."

Jessica had told me that Marcie and fidelity hadn't been closely acquainted—I guess she'd been right about that too.

"You need to forgive yourself. You might sing like an angel pickled in whisky, but you're still human."

"What did you just call me?"

Oops. Maybe that was a step too far.

"Sorry, I just meant you're larger than life."

"I'm nothing. I haven't written a single song since I lost that necklace."

It was like she was stuck in a loop—she'd told herself that lie so many times, she was starting to believe it. "But you didn't lose it, Marcie. He chose to give it to someone else. I know that hurts, but frankly, it was a bit tacky of him."

Her eyes widened in shock.

Oh God, I was dissing the love of her life—not a clever move. But dammit, she was holding him up like he was blameless.

"How dare you talk to me like that in my own home." She got up and stumbled to the door. "Ronan! Ronan! Get this woman out of here!"

I didn't need to be told again. Ronan might have seemed like a nice guy, but if he was forced to defend Marcie I didn't doubt he'd be happy to use his fists.

I edged to the hallway, my fingers grasping at the front door. The damn thing had seven locks on it. Which one did I need to turn?

Footsteps were pattering upstairs. I only had a few seconds.

"It's not the missing necklace that's been holding you back, Marcie. You've deified Benedict, and now you can't move on."

"Get out! Get out! Get out!" she screamed, her voice breaking on every word.

The locks finally twisted free. I yanked the door open and ran.

The door slammed shut as I reached the end of her path. I chanced a quick glance behind me to check no one had followed.

I was safe, but in my hurry to look back, I didn't see what was in front of me and stubbed my toe on the base of a concrete urn.

I landed heavily on my hands and knees.

The pain was sharp enough to make me gasp. Blood was slowly oozing from my palms where I'd grazed them and a telltale wetness was forming around my knees under my jeans.

I slowly turned myself till I was sitting. The urn housed a thick topiary which hid me from the kitchen window.

Movement from it made me catch my breath.

A shirtless man with his back to me was opening the fridge.

He was tall and broad-shouldered with shower-wet hair.

The fridge door closed, and he turned round.

Nick.

My heart almost stopped.

He was pouring a glass of orange juice. A sobbing Marcie appeared by his side. He slid the glass toward her, but she shook her head. Then, as if it were the most natural thing in the world, he wrapped her in his arms and kissed the top of her head.

I ducked down.

I couldn't breathe.

Marcie and Nick. He was her midnight booty call. Just as I'd always suspected.

He'd resigned as her publicist, but he'd found another position pretty sharpish. Or had they been together all along?

I swallowed hard. Where did I fit in? Was anything he said to me the night of the ball true? I'd rejected him. I had no reason to feel jealous. But still, it hurt.

I crawled the rest of the way to the gate.

And then ran.

I was numb as I sat on the train heading to my office. My palms and knees were burning, but they felt like someone else's body parts. Two images were seared behind my eyelids:

Marcie, white as a statue, screaming at me and Nick with his golden torso locked in an embrace with her.

♪

All day, I tried not to think about Marcie. But that night, after I'd had dinner, I couldn't stop myself from unpacking what I'd seen. The Nick thing didn't matter. He was free to spend the night with whomever he pleased. The fact that he'd told me he loved me twenty-four hours ago didn't matter. I'd rejected him, hadn't I? And I didn't regret it. I regretted the *way* I'd rejected him, but that was a different thing altogether.

But that kiss in the karaoke booth…

Damn. Here I was again, letting Nick hog all my attention when there was so much more to be worrying about.

Poor Marcie. What the hell had I been thinking? Who was I to tell her how to feel?

An icy shiver ran up my spine. She'd tried to kill herself once. What if I'd given her the impetus to try again? How irresponsible I'd been.

It was a blessing Nick was there. He'd make sure she stayed away from razor blades or whatever else she might try to hurt herself with. If anything happened to Marcie, I would never forgive myself.

There was that word again. Forgive.

But what did I know about forgiveness? How much of it had I shown Simon? Even when he was lying half-comatose in a hospital bed?

I needed to ring him. I'd been a coward not to answer his calls.

"I'm sorry it took me so long to get back to you," I told him. "I was with Pete and Alice helping with their wedding prep." I crossed my fingers behind my back. He didn't need to know that I'd spent half my evening crying at episodes of *Queer Eye*.

"Don't sweat it. I'm sorry for putting you through last night. I was scared you wouldn't want to see me." He sounded exhausted.

"Never think that again. I'll always be here for you."

There was a pause at the other end. "I know I've been shitty, Frixie. I still hate myself. What can I do to make it up to you? You're the most important person in the world to me."

I found myself swallowing back tears and couldn't speak.

"Maybe I could come round tomorrow night. Cook you another moussaka?"

"I've got Alice and her friends coming round for a girly prewedding get-together. Sorry."

"What about in the afternoon? I could help you set up?"

He sounded so sincere and so desperate to see me—how could I refuse?

30

THIS AIN'T A LOVE SONG

IN THE END, SIMON CAME round at five to help me prepare for my Greek night with Alice and the girls. I put him in charge of food, and he happily emptied the shelves of my local Waitrose of anything resembling Greek food. His overzealousness had resulted in some samosas sneaking into his basket, but they were delicious so I couldn't complain. He even made an extra trip to Tesco, because he knew I preferred their taramosalata.

It was such a sweet gesture, but my feelings for him, which had once run so hot, could barely reach lukewarm levels.

Give it time, I told myself. I just needed a bit of fun to lift myself out of this slumped mood, and then everything would be back to normal.

♪

Alice and Co. arrived exactly on time, and Annette made a beeline for the dining table, where Simon had laid out the finger buffet.

"I'm starved," she announced. "I skipped lunch so I could stuff myself tonight." She turned to Alice. "I love you, but hate dieting for your wedding."

"We should have ordered the fourteen—you never looked overweight to me."

"Nah, size-twelve Annette will be unstoppable. I'm planning to get lucky at your wedding, Alice. Lock up your menfolk, Zoë!" I thought of my cousins coming over from Cyprus. Annette was going to terrorize them.

When we'd all piled our plates high, Alice sat next to me on the sofa. "How are things with you, Zoë? Any more men fighting over you?"

"A couple of duels and a sword fight, but no fisticuffs."

She smiled. "Is that your way of telling me you don't want to talk about it?"

Her perceptiveness disarmed me. I hadn't even realized I'd dodged her question; I fell back on humor so often, I'd forgotten how not to.

"I will talk about it with you. But not tonight. Tonight is about you."

Annette, who was sitting nearby, and who'd clearly been eavesdropping, made a face. "Less talk and more prosecco!" She got up to refill our glasses. "Now, are we going to bust some Greek moves or what?"

I'd decided to teach them two dances: a fast one and a more sedate number that the bride's female friends performed together.

"It's called *Kalamatiano*," I explained. "And before anyone asks, yes, it's related to Kalamata olives—it means 'from Kalamata,' a place in Greece. You see them dancing it at the end of *My Big Fat Greek Wedding*."

We pushed the furniture to one side till we'd cleared a decent-sized space on the carpeted lounge floor. Then we all held hands in a circle, and I walked them through the steps, which basically involved, well, walking in a twelve-step pattern.

We ran through it a couple of times then I put the music on. But it was way faster than we'd practiced and had us all bumping into each other.

Helen, who'd done a lot of ballet and tap in her not-so-distant youth, was a natural, and I let her lead so I could stand between Alice and Annette and help guide their wobbly legs.

"No, the back step is on the two and six," Helen admonished on our third attempt with the music.

I let the girls practice while I scrolled through my playlists to find a slower version and came across a classic tune from my childhood.

"Okay, let's try it to this," I said. "The lyrics are a bit bonkers—it's called 'Maria in Yellow,' and it's about a woman who wishes her husband would turn to stone because she's in love with her neighbor."

The bonkers Maria song turned out to be much catchier, and on only our second attempt, we danced the whole way without anyone putting a step wrong.

"That was brilliant!" said Alice, collapsing to the floor in a tired and happy heap.

We popped open another bottle of wine and once we'd been suitably refreshed, I walked them through the steps of a second dance.

"This one's called *Sousta*, which means 'spring' or 'bounce.' It's a traditional dance, but you can do it to "Zorba the Greek," which will get everyone going. I have to warn you, though—it's fast and jumpy."

"Ooh, lucky I've got my sensible Marks & Spencer bra on, then," said Annette.

When I'd walked them through the steps, which were, again, just a series of forward steps with some back steps to keep everyone on their toes, I put the music on.

"Blimey, that is fast," said Annette, then she grinned wolfishly. "Gonna be interesting in heels and a strapless dress."

She had a point. "I'll make sure we get a slower version."

It was quite a cardio workout, and probably one that was best attempted without quite so much lubrication, but we were having fun. And it was exactly what I needed. I was going to make sure I kept up my friendships with the girls even after the wedding. Hell, I might even suggest another ukulele night.

By ten, we decided that we were as good as we were ever going to be and too tired to keep going. I was also concerned that all the bouncing on my floor would keep my downstairs neighbor, Mrs. Hargreaves, from sleeping. So, we opened another bottle and flopped down on the sofa to watch *My Big Fat Greek Wedding*—Annette's idea. I kept sneaking glances at Alice, worried the movie might spook her. But she seemed fine.

We all cried during the wedding scene, which proved just how drunk we were.

The girls left at midnight, and I shuffled around the flat putting things away and humming to myself. I was loading the last plate into the dishwasher when the doorbell rang.

Odd.

Had one of them forgotten something? Or had Simon decided to come back? If it was the latter, my first urge was to ignore it.

But I'd promised myself to cut him some slack, so I bounded down the stairs and opened the door.

Standing on the step was Marcie. With a large guitar case.

Oh. My. God.

For a second I thought I was imagining things. But I wasn't that drunk.

"Good, you're in," she said. "I knocked earlier, but no one answered."

I gulped. "Marcie, how did you know where I live?"

"We know plenty of people in common. And really, is that your most pressing question?"

She had a point. "What... What are you doing here?"

"I'm here to give you your interview."

She pushed past me and headed up the stairs, her guitar case banging against the bannister as she climbed up to my flat. This was surreal. What was weirder than having Marcie Tyler arrive at your flat at midnight? Having her arrive with a guitar.

She burst into the living room.

Oh God, it probably smelled of fish. I'd accidentally smudged a bit of taramosalata on the dining table earlier and hadn't wiped it off properly.

"Erm, can I get you a drink or something?" *Shit. She was off alcohol.* "I mean, I've just put the kettle on if you want a tea or coffee."

If someone had told my younger self that at the age of thirty-four I would have Marcie Tyler sitting on my Ikea sofa, drinking instant coffee out of a chipped University of Exeter mug, I would have laughed.

But here she was, larger than life. Nerves were getting to me, and I thought I was going to erupt into manic laughter any minute.

I pinched the soft flesh under my arm. *Get a grip, Zoë.*

"So, are you serious? You're here for the interview?"

"It depends."

I let out a slow breath. Another catch? I was so close it was killing me. "On what?"

She opened her guitar case. Inside was a 1970 Zemaitis acoustic. Only around three were ever made. It was scratched and scuffed, but that only added to its value. In fact, just having it in the flat probably voided my contents insurance.

"I wrote a song."

I swallowed. "Really?"

"Some of what you said got through to me. Maybe I didn't need that damn necklace, maybe it was a cop-out I gave myself whenever I tried to write and nothing came out."

Pure pleasure spread throughout my body. Something I'd said had broken through ten years of writer's block for one of the most famous singers in the world. I could die happy; tombstone engraving sorted.

She put her mug down. She'd barely drunk it and I didn't blame her. God knows how long that jar of Nescafé had been open.

"I'm going to play that song for you now. And if you think it's any good, you can have your interview. But if you don't like it, I will leave."

This was getting crazier by the minute. Of course I was going to love Marcie's song. She'd never recorded anything I hadn't immediately loved, including an ill-advised album of duets with Perry Como.

She fixed me with her blue-green eyes. "You have to tell me the truth. I'll know if you're lying."

She picked up the honey-colored guitar, passed the strap over her head, and placed her left hand on the fretboard, her index finger resting on a heart-shaped mother-of-pearl inlay.

She started to strum, her fingers picking out a haunting melody that made the hairs on the back of my neck stand up.

Then she started to sing.

Her voice was crisp and clear on one phrase, then raspy and raw on the next. She sang about letting go. She was saying goodbye to a lover because she knew her future was without him. And at the end of the song, her lover was wishing her love and luck on her journey. She was letting go, and he was giving her his benediction.

The song ended and my ears buzzed in the silence.

Marcie reached forward with her hand outstretched. Her thumb slowly wiped my wet cheek; I hadn't realized I'd been crying.

She smiled. "I'm glad you like it."

She put her guitar back in its case. "Now, let's start this interview."

It was light when Marcie left. We had talked till four in the morning, then she'd rung Ronan to come and pick her up. I'd waved her off like an old friend as they rattled down my road in a surprisingly battered old Mini. I knew I wouldn't be able to sleep, so I powered up my laptop, sat down at my dining room table—mercifully free of taramosalata—and began typing up the interview.

When I was done, I emailed it to Mike and closed my laptop.

I was exhausted but happy. But as I sat dazed on my sofa, not quite able to bring myself to wash the mug Marcie had used—*it had her lipstick on it!*—I knew there was something I had to do.

Something that had been niggling at me, which I'd pushed down and tried to ignore. But Marcie's song had pulled everything into razor-sharp focus.

I needed to talk to Simon.

I showered and changed and got ready for work. It was still barely seven o'clock, but I knew Simon would be up.

As I passed Mrs. Hargreaves's flat, I stopped to stroke Snowy, but all of a sudden her door swung open.

"Morning, Zoë. It's going to be a hot day."

I'd chosen to wear a summer dress because for once I'd checked the weather app on my phone.

"Can't wait," I said.

"Was that Marcella Taglioni who came round last night? She knocked on my door when you didn't answer."

I frowned because the name was familiar. *Shit, it was Marcie's birth name.* "Tyler" was a stage name.

"I hope we didn't keep you up, Mrs. H."

"She was a naughty one," she continued. "Never used to eat her greens and insisted on playing the wireless all night."

What was Mrs. H talking about? "Are you sure you're thinking of the same person?"

"Oh yes, my memory's still pin-sharp. I used to babysit her."

I wanted to stick a finger in my ear to make sure there wasn't a giant lump of wax blocking it. "You…You used to *babysit* her?"

"Yes, back when I was a student living in Hampstead." She picked up Snowy, who'd been mewling by our feet. "Let's get you fed, madam." She turned to leave. "Imagine seeing Marcella Taglioni here," she said. "I wonder what she's up to these days."

Her ignorance seemed absolutely genuine. "I'll fill you in another time, Mrs. H."

I laughed. *Mrs. H and Marcie had known each other all this time?* It was preposterous, but given the surreal night I'd had, it somehow all seemed perfectly plausible.

♪

"Frixie!" Simon looked happy to see me. "How great that you stopped by. I was just thinking about you."

He ushered me into his kitchen. "I took your advice and bought some Yorkshire Tea. It's amazing. Let me make you one. The kettle's only just boiled."

I nodded and let him fuss around the kitchen. He was whistling to himself as he worked.

What was I doing here? I was sleep-deprived, and I wasn't thinking rationally. How could I be sure this was what I wanted?

But the answer came to me almost immediately. I'd known it last night as Marcie had sung her song. She'd been singing it to Benedict, but she could have written it for me and Simon.

"Here you go." He sloshed the mug down on the table. "Not too strong, just as you like it."

My hands were shaking as I reached out to take the mug.

"You okay, Frixie?"

Maybe I needed longer to think about this. I could tell him I'd popped by because I was passing; I could drink my tea and then be off on my merry way.

But it was too late to back out now. His eyes were searching mine— he'd already realized something was different.

Oh God. Was I about to mess everything up?

I couldn't imagine my life without him, but I needed to be honest with him. And he needed to know the truth.

I reached out to grab his hand. "You're the greatest; do you know that, Si?"

"Well, actually, I think Muhammad Ali is the greatest." He grinned. "But I'll take second greatest."

A lump formed in my throat. "I've loved you since I was thirteen. You've been there for me all my life. When you arrived in London all those weeks ago and we shared an ice cream sundae, I was the happiest I'd been in a long time. You do that to me. You're fun and funny and can always make me laugh, and I never want that to change."

His face stiffened. His lips were still curved in a smile, but the happiness had left his eyes. Those beautiful, marine-blue eyes looked scared.

"What are you saying, Frixie?"

"It's not going to work between us. I'm sorry."

For long moments, he didn't speak. "But you and me are the dream team, Frixie. Please don't give up on us."

"You were all I wanted for so long, but I realize now that the image I had of you in my head wasn't based on reality. It got fixed there when I was thirteen. I'm no better than the girls who are crying over Jonny Delaney leaving the band. I fell in love with an image I created, not a real person."

"You were always real to me, Zoë." His voice was soft, and I hated that he was using my name and not Frixie. It was like he was putting up a hard shell.

"You told me once we were better off as friends. And as much as I hated hearing that, I realize now that you were right."

His soft expression suddenly hardened. "Is there someone else?"

I closed my eyes. "I think I'm fated to be single forever."

Simon smiled sadly. "I'm starting to think that you and Twisted Sister were right all along: love *is* for suckers."

"I'll always be your friend, Si. If ever there's a day I'm not, you can send Zak Scaramouche to hunt me down."

That raised a smile. He leaned forward in his chair. "But how can you be sure? Maybe you just need time to adjust to this new aspect of our friendship. Call it V2.0."

"But real love—love that inspires you to write songs or stops you from sleeping or makes you risk everything—is either there or it's not." I felt more sure of myself now. "You don't have to adjust to it; you don't grow into it. We've known each other long enough. If you'll have me, I want to be your friend, your *best* friend. The sort of friend who'll help you bury the bodies and not ask questions."

"Is there nothing I can say to convince you that you're wrong?"

I shook my head sadly. "One day you'll see I'm right."

I got up because there was nothing left to say. My tea stayed undrunk on his kitchen table, and we didn't hug or say anything as I stood on his doorstep. I gave his unyielding hand a tight squeeze and walked away.

I don't know how I got through the day. The high of interviewing Marcie helped a bit, especially when I told Gav and Lucy about it.

"Fucking hell," said Lucy. "You do realize that you're the first person to hear a new Marcie song in ten years."

She was right, but it hadn't sunk in at the time. I'd been too lost in the music to think about anything other than the pain in her voice and the pain that echoed in me.

Rob had already designed the Marcie spread. It was four pages—twice as long as a regular feature. But the truth was I'd struggled to stop writing; I could have filled the whole magazine with Marcie.

Mike had spoken to the board, and they were drawing up fresh contracts and pay rises for everyone now that the new investment was guaranteed.

Our normal print run was fifty thousand, and I rang Mike to see if he thought it needed changing.

"Shall we increase it?" I asked. "Sixty thousand or maybe sixty-five to be safe?"

Mike's chuckle came down the line. "We're estimating a print run of a hundred thousand—and even that might be conservative."

A *hundred thousand*? This was unbelievable—it was comparable to the heyday of the magazine in the seventies. Except, at least these days, the paper came from sustainable sources.

Okay, so the print runs would return to more modest sizes, and maybe *Re:Sound* wouldn't survive another thirty years, but I'd given it the best possible chance.

And when the day came for me to hang up my boots, at least they'd still be there for editor number fourteen.

31
DON'T KNOW WHAT YOU'VE
GOT (TILL IT'S GONE)

ON THE FRIDAY NIGHT BEFORE the wedding, I met Alice in Selfridges to get a few last-minute things. She wanted to buy some underwear, and I'd gone up with her to the first floor thinking she needed a more supportive bra or a spare pair of tights. I couldn't believe my eyes when she eschewed the usual brands and made a beeline for Agent Provocateur.

"Alice, I'm shocked," I told her, only half joking. This stuff was next-level racy; everything seemed to come with matching blindfold.

She smiled. "You only have one wedding night."

"Knock yourself out, but you're on your own. I'm not going to stand here while you pick sex outfits for my brother. And have you seen the prices?"

I left her among the sheer teddies and peephole bras, and took the escalator back to the ground floor. I could do with another MAC lipstick; mine was running low, and it was always nice to have a spare.

Of course, I ended up buying loads of other stuff, including primer and setting spray, which I'd never worn in my life, but the lady was so convincing, and wow, her eye shadow was amazing.

LOVE SONGS FOR SKEPTICS 361

No, I'd never tried blue with gold highlighter, but go on then, ring those up too.

Credit card still hot, I was wandering around the fragrances when I caught the scent of something divine. What was that smell? It made me feel happy and sad at the same time. It was so familiar, yet…

Oh.

Nick. It was Nick's aftershave.

Another blast of fragrance, this time stronger. I spun round. A woman behind a counter was spraying a scent onto a card for a customer.

I edged closer to her. Three tall angular bottles were lined up on the glass counter. The one she'd just put down was on the right. The name "Serge" was printed on the amber glass in discreet black lettering. It wasn't a brand I knew.

"Would you like to try one? They're unisex." She picked up the middle bottle. "This is our newest fragrance."

I shook my head. "Could I try the one on the end? The one you just sprayed?"

"Of course. On a card or on your wrist?"

"On a card," I said quickly. I couldn't bear to have the smell of him on my skin. It would feel too intimate.

She pumped the top and a fine mist blossomed onto the card. "It's got a woody base with top notes of musk, leather, and blackcurrant," she said.

Blackcurrant? Nick didn't smell like a throat lozenge. I took the card from her, brought it to my nose, and closed my eyes.

I couldn't smell the individual notes. They all fused together to form one glorious sensation. I breathed again, and my spirit soared. Silken and smoky. Velvety and visceral. It was Nick.

But not quite.

"Do you like it?"

I came back to earth with a bump.

"I need to think about it," I said, hastily tossing the card into my shopping bag.

I went to the coffee shop and ordered a chamomile tea—caffeine was the last thing I needed. I sat down at a corner table trying to compose myself.

Jesus, I'd almost had an orgasm in the middle of a department store.

What the hell was wrong with me?

I missed Nick. That much I was prepared to accept. We'd spent a lot of time together these past few weeks. It had been stressful at times but satisfying trying to help Marcie.

But it wasn't only that I missed him. When I'd caught that first hit of his cologne by the MAC stand, for a second I'd felt a magical burst of joy. And that wasn't because I missed him.

It was something more.

When I'd told Simon we couldn't be together because something was lacking between us, I wasn't talking about some mythical, undiscovered magic.

I knew about it because I'd felt it with Nick.

It had crept up on me slowly, though. My first inkling had been on the London Eye when he'd calmed me down without drawing attention to my distress. It had been such a selfless thing to do, and I'd been too shocked to even thank him. But there had been a spark between us from the moment we met. I hadn't acknowledged it because it had been so bloody inconvenient.

But my subconscious had known.

And I'd blown it. Now he was spending his last few nights in another woman's bed before jetting back to Latin America, his sojourn in the UK and his fleeting feelings for me consigned to a bin labeled Big Mistakes.

Alice dropped into the seat next to me in a heap of yellow Selfridges bags.

I quickly blinked back the looming tears. "Blimey," I said, in a teasing tone, "those are big bags for a load of smalls."

She grinned. "I also bought a few other bits and pieces." She leaned closer. "Looks like someone else went shopping too."

She tried to peek into my bag, but I jostled it out of the way. I didn't want her to smell the card with the cologne on it. I felt stupidly embarrassed that she would recognize it and see how pathetic I was—getting my kicks from an overpriced chemical concoction.

"What's wrong, Zoë? Is something on your mind?"

I shook my head. It was the night before her wedding; I wasn't going to unburden myself on her. I wanted to be there for any last-minute nerves she might be having.

"I'm a bit tired, but in a good way. Did I tell you I interviewed Marcie?"

"That's amazing!"

I tried to mirror her smile. "It really is."

We didn't speak for a few moments. I took a sip of my chamomile tea and wished it was a glass of wine.

"There's something else."

"Nope, there's nothing."

"Please tell me. I need to take my mind off tomorrow. Give me something to think about other than tripping while I walk down the aisle or having a coughing fit during the ceremony. It happened to Annette's sister. It was awful; the poor thing went purple."

How did Alice always know the right thing to say?

"I told Simon I didn't love him," I said eventually.

Her eyes went wide. "I'm so sorry. Are you okay?"

"Well, apart from feeling awful for doing it to him, I know it's for the best."

She rubbed my arm. "Are you sure you're okay? You look like you're about to cry."

Oh God. She was right. My face was getting hot, and suddenly I was blinking back tears.

Alice gave me a hug while I held my breath, trying to stop sniveling.

Hold it together, Zoë. This is not the time.

But it was no good. It was like a dam had burst, and I was helpless to hold back the flood.

She let me sob for a good five minutes. Then she gave me a tissue and a stern look. "Talk to me, Zoë."

"It's Nick," I said.

"You've got feelings for him?"

I nodded, and then another round of sobs overtook me. She waited patiently for them to pass, listening to the whole sorry story.

"Have you tried ringing him?"

"No, but since he left he's only left me one message—he's hardly bursting to hear from me."

"But he doesn't know how you feel. How can he? You've only just realized yourself."

I blew out a breath. "What would I say? 'Hi, Nick. Sorry about laughing in your face that night and running off with another man. And in other news, I'm crazy about you.'"

Alice smiled. "That's exactly what you need to say. But word it slightly differently, of course."

"There's no point. He's left the country. He was never really keen on living in England."

"I bet he'd like England a whole lot more if he knew how you felt about him."

For a second, it seemed so simple. It was one phone call… I pushed the thought out of my head before it took root.

"He's with someone else."

Alice frowned. "Really? So quickly?"

"It was a badly kept secret in the industry that he was sort of seeing someone he worked with. Someone rather high-profile."

Alice's eyes went wide. "*Marcie?*"

I nodded.

She'd left her phone on the table, and it suddenly buzzed angrily. "Sorry, Zoë, I need to check who this is." She frowned as she read the message, then put her phone down again. "I'm sorry, but I need to go. I'm staying at Annette's, and apparently I'm late for the evening of pampering she has lined up."

"Get going, then, woman. You've got a big day tomorrow."

She hopped off the stool and gave me another hug. "Ring him. Tell him how you feel. If you don't do it now you'll always wonder."

I stayed in the coffee shop after Alice left, trying but failing to not think about what she'd said.

Should I tell Nick how I felt? It was just asking for humiliation, wasn't it?

Thankfully, Pete rang, so I didn't have to think about it anymore.

"Hey, bro," I answered, with forced cheerfulness. "What's happening?"

"Arma-*fucking*-geddon," was his grim reply.

32

I GUESS THAT'S WHY THEY CALL IT THE BLUES

ONE EXTORTIONATELY EXPENSIVE CAB RIDE later and I was at Pete's front door. Over the phone he'd explained in expletive-filled language that there had been a double booking with the band, which meant they had no music at the wedding tomorrow.

Pete ushered me into the sitting room and offered me a steaming mug of tea so strong I could feel it stripping the enamel off my teeth.

"There's no need to tell Alice," he said. "It will only worry her."

I sat down while he detoured via the kitchen. He appeared a couple of minutes later, carrying a plate of *pastichia*. The almond macaroons were traditional at Greek weddings, and I suspected I would be eating gut-bursting quantities tomorrow.

"Want one?"

"I'm okay, thanks."

He sat down on the sofa, next to an open Yellow Pages.

"What are you doing with that?" I asked. "Did you steal it from a museum?"

"I'm trying to save my wedding," he answered gruffly.

"I'm not sure how many bands advertise in the phone book."

"I'm not looking for bands. I'm ringing every DJ within a fifty-mile radius. Not that I've got anywhere. They're all booked up."

He was losing it and I needed to do something. "Pete, we don't need a DJ. We can make playlists on a laptop and plug it into the hotel's PA."

"Oh, I didn't think of that."

I patted his arm. "The other benefit of my idea is you won't have to endure some mullet-haired moron talking over the intros of your favorite tracks. Leave everything to me. You will have music tomorrow, I promise."

Pete looked at me weirdly. Did he have something in his contact lens? Or was he about to get soppy? Then he pronounced my name the Greek way—with the accent on the second syllable—and I knew the answer: "I don't know what I'd do without you."

Oh God, if Pete started blubbering he'd set me off again too, especially after my outburst in Selfridges.

Displays of affection between us were as rare as classy Christmas number ones. But just because we didn't show it, it didn't mean we didn't care.

"Ditto," I replied.

Pete laughed. "How are we both missing that Greek gene that should make us excessively affectionate with our loved ones?"

I pointed at my mug and the plate of biscuits. "We show affection with food and drink."

He nodded.

"I'm really proud of you, Pete."

"Why? I didn't make the *pastichia*. I got them from Green Lanes."

I thumped him. "Not about the *pastichia*. I'm proud that you met an amazing woman and that you had the sense to ask her to marry you. You've got this whole love thing sorted, and I couldn't be happier for you."

"You'll find someone too, sis. Once you get your head out of your arse and realize Simon isn't right for you."

I stifled a gasp. "What are you talking about?" I had every intention of denying everything, but from the look on Pete's face—a cross between exasperation and pity—I wasn't going to brazen this one out. We might never have spoken about it, but he obviously knew all about my feelings for Simon.

"How much did Alice tell you?"

"She hasn't told me anything—she didn't need to. You've always carried a torch for Simon, though I could never for the life of me see why."

I frowned, not quite ready to hear anyone bad-mouth Simon. "What's wrong with Simon?"

"He's a bit boring, isn't he? I mean, he tucks his shirts into his jeans, for God's sake."

I smiled. "Who died and made you the fashion police?"

"He's flighty."

"Excuse me?"

"*Flighty*—he doesn't stick at anything. Take that time he saw my Panini sticker album for the '94 World Cup. The next day he'd bought his own, and I was looking forward to having someone new to do swaps with. I was desperate for a Zinedine Zidane, and all I kept getting were Thierry Henrys. England was a state that year—apart from Michael Owen—honestly, it almost made me give up on football."

"I think we're getting a bit sidetracked, Pete."

"All I'm trying to say is, a week later he'd forgotten all about the album. That's what he's like—always jumping from one thing to another. He doesn't ever commit to anything—or any*one*."

The old need to defend Simon was too strong to resist. "That's a bit harsh, Pete. He got married—that shows commitment."

Pete shook his head. "I've had bouts of athlete's foot that have lasted longer than Simon's marriage."

"Simon's had a tough life."

"Oh yeah, all those years working down a coal mine. I forgot." Pete rolled his eyes. "Look, I get it. His parents divorced when he was a kid; it must have been hard. But I could always tell you liked him more than he liked you. And then when he was salivating over Jessica in front of you, I wanted to deck him. I still will, if you want me to."

I wiped my eyes roughly before Pete noticed how emotional I'd become.

He was right. I'd never held Simon to account for how he'd treated me.

But right now, I had more pressing issues, namely saving my brother's wedding.

"Enough about me, Pete. Get your laptop, because we've got playlists to make. But I warn you—there's only so much Genesis I'll allow at this wedding."

After a while, we'd compiled an hour-long Greek dancing playlist and a general five-hour playlist that I promised to fine-tune at home.

As I was about to close the computer, one of Pete's playlists caught my eye. It was full of great songs, i.e., not his usual taste. They were mostly slowish, mellow tracks, and among them was my favorite Marcie song: "It's Too Late for Love." Even just seeing the name of a Marcie song made me think of Nick, and I was overcome with sadness again. Would I ever be able to listen to her again?

"What's this?"

He smiled. "It's one of your playlists. I followed it on Spotify ages ago. Thought I'd use it to impress Alice when we were dating, because you always said I had shite taste in music."

The playlist was cryptically labeled "LSFS."

"Did I give it that name?"

Pete smiled again. "Nah. Once I'd listened to it, I renamed it."

"To what?"

"Love Songs for Skeptics."

"Why?"

"There's nothing joyful or uplifting in these songs. They're all a bit, well, jaded. Look: 'I Hate Myself for Loving You,' 'Everybody Hurts,' 'Love Is a Battlefield.' Would it kill you to listen to a bit of Abba?"

I frowned. "You think I'm a skeptic?"

"Not in a Scully way, just when it comes to love."

"You psychoanalyzed me from a flippin' playlist?"

"No, I psychoanalyzed you from being your flippin' brother."

Was he right? Deep down, did I not believe in love?

I'd made jokes with Simon about love being for suckers, but if Pete thought it too, then perhaps I needed to address this. Maybe he had a point—I'd mucked up my chances with Nick in a way that bordered on sabotage.

"I guess it's a form of self-protection."

"A healthy dose of skepticism is a good thing, if you ask me. I'd rather have a sister who was cautious about romance than one who fell for every muppet who turned up with a drooping bunch of cheapo flowers. You'd sooner kick a boy's arse than let him break your heart. And thank fuck for that. It cuts down on the number of arses I need to kick on your behalf."

A little later, I was heading home. But as the bus wheezed back to Shepherd's Bush, I was starting to feel less and less satisfied with my playlist idea. Maybe we'd have to resort to that for a bit of Greek music, but surely I could find a band to fill in for the main gig? I knew enough of them. I had just over eighteen hours. Someone out there owed me a favor or two.

I must have rung twenty managers, promoters, and musicians. Then I roped Mike, Gav, and Lucy into it, and they promised to make a list and share phone duties. Altogether, we must have spoken to over fifty people.

When I was in professional mode, I got shit done. It wasn't lost on me that there was a personal issue I was too chicken to address. But after I'd done all my ringing round, I felt wide awake, and I knew it was too early to try and sleep. It wasn't quite eleven o'clock—not so late that I couldn't ring Simon. I wasn't sure what I would say exactly, but there was an itch in me to speak to him, and I knew that I wouldn't sleep till I had.

I suddenly worried that maybe it *was* too late to call, so I sent a text instead.

Can you talk?

To my relief he texted straight back.

Need some company? I can be over in 10.

For once, I didn't spend the next few minutes worrying about the tidiness of my flat or how I looked. I spent the time trying to work out what I needed to say.

It was now or never.

"Nice flowers," said Simon, as I led him into the living room exactly seven minutes later. He must have left his place as soon as he sent that text. Seven minutes had been precious little time to figure out what needed to be said—I was going to have to wing it.

"Thanks," I said, admiring the bouquet of roses and lilies—a present from Alice for the Greek dancing lessons. "Can I get you a drink?"

Simon shook his head. "I'm glad you texted. I've been wanting to talk to you."

I held up my hand. "Would you mind if I said a few things first?" I swallowed, and I could tell from Simon's expression he was nervous. It was reassuring, in some ways, because my heart was knocking weirdly in my chest. Like I was having a bout of stage fright.

I twisted in my seat, my eyes focused on Simon, who was sitting upright on the sofa opposite. "When I came round that morning and told you we couldn't be together, there was something I should have said. Something you tried to admit, but I wasn't ready to hear."

He nodded, and I went on. "The whole time you were telling me you felt something for me, you were hedging your bets and telling Jessica the same too. And when we kissed that night, we said we'd take things slowly. We never talked about it again; we never agreed to pretend it never happened. You decided that by yourself. And that hurt, Simon. It *still* hurts."

His eyes were shining. I hated making him feel shitty, but if I didn't vent these emotions they would fester. And I wasn't prepared to hold on to this feeling, as if it were dirty or something I should be ashamed of.

I took a shaky breath before I continued. "You and I aren't right for each other, I get that now. But that doesn't mean that I can laugh off how you treated me. I'd like to think our friendship meant more to you than that."

Tears were running down his face. "I never meant to hurt you, Frixie. Your friendship has always meant the world to me. For half my childhood, you were my only friend. You were a safe haven in the storm of my parents' fucked-up marriage. Having you around made those years bearable. I can't imagine what a mess I'd be now if we hadn't moved into 27 Priory Lane."

He smiled and I smiled too, because I couldn't imagine what life would have been like if he hadn't grown up next door either.

"I behaved terribly," he said, sadly. "I know that now. I was so freaked out after Louise left me, it's like I reverted to being a teenager again. Not thinking of anyone else. You've always been there for me, so I stupidly assumed…"

It was hard to listen to what he was about to say, so I said it myself: "You assumed that I'd always be here?"

He nodded glumly. "I'm so ashamed of myself."

"When it comes to you, I was a glutton for punishment. It was hard seeing you with Jess, worse even than seeing you get married and having to put on a brave face and congratulate you."

"I wish I'd known."

"I should have said something. But I wasn't brave enough."

His eyes widened in surprise. "Zoë Frixos, you're the bravest person I know."

We both started bawling after that. But they were happy tears. I was a bit worried we'd wake up Mrs. Hargreaves downstairs, but thankfully there was no angry knock at the door.

33

I CLOSE MY EYES AND
COUNT TO TEN

THE DAY OF THE WEDDING dawned with torrential rain. I rang Pete to make sure he'd slept okay. Actually, that wasn't true. I rang to make sure he hadn't overslept or been the victim of a late-night visit from best man Alex that had ended with Pete stranded in a ditch on the side of the M1 with his eyebrows shaved off.

He sounded very chipper. "I just spoke to Mum," he told me. "She said that back in the village they always said it was good luck to have rain on your wedding day."

This was bollocks, but it was sweet Pete had believed it. If that were really the case, English summer weddings would be the most blessed on the planet.

I showered, had a slice of toast and cup of tea, then went to get ready. I opened my Selfridges bags to retrieve my new makeup and a wave of Nick's cologne hit me, along with an overwhelming sadness.

I let myself cry for a good couple of minutes.

God, I really was taking Gavin's "feel your feelings" thing to heart.

Either way, I figured it was best to get any tears out of the way early. Waterproof mascara never lived up to its name.

I was ready half an hour before my parents' taxi came to pick me up. I sat rigidly on my kitchen chair, conscious not to get too many creases in my long satin dress. Time on my hands was a bad thing. Alice's suggestion to ring Nick kept echoing in my mind. My fingers itched for my phone, but every time I picked it up and tried to make the call, I chickened out. What would I say?

Oh, hi, Nick. If ever you get bored with Marcie Tyler keep me in mind—I'd love to be your consolation prize. Sorry I passed you over for another man. My bad.

I replayed this fake conversation in my head ten times, before another conversation—this time a real one—from last night muscled it out. Simon had said I was the bravest person he knew. It was time to live up to that and talk to Nick.

I took several deep breaths, hoping courage would fill me.

Okay, not really much courage in the air of my kitchen. Maybe I needed to open a window.

I stopped myself. I was being daft. What was preventing me?

I wasn't very good doing things ad hoc—maybe I should write out what I wanted to say.

I rummaged through the kitchen drawers to find what I needed, then I sat at the table, pen poised over an A4 pad, waiting for the right words to come.

Any second now.

Just be patient.

Oh for God's sake. I was a journalist; I was supposed to be good with words.

Maybe it was the pen that was throwing me. I hadn't written anything by hand for years. Maybe sitting at a keyboard would help.

I checked the clock. Crap, did I really only have fifteen minutes? I was running out of time to have a last-minute wee, check my makeup, and recheck I had everything packed in my ridiculously small handbag.

There was no time to write anything. I would have to improvise.

I picked up my phone, scrolled to Nick's number, and hit "call."

My heart knocked against my ribs. The phone was ringing. Except it was that international ringing tone. He was abroad already.

It didn't matter.

It rang a couple more times, then stopped.

"Hello?" I croaked.

No one answered. It had gone to voicemail. But it was one of those prerecorded messages, not Nick's usual one, in his own voice. Was this still his number? Had he changed it?

Okay, it was asking me to leave a message.

I drew a deep breath. Here goes…

"Hi, Nick, it's me. Zoë…Frixos. (Oh no, it was weird already.) *I'm ringing to wish you luck in your new job.* (No I'm bloody not!) *Sorry, scratch that, I'm ringing to say I'm sorry.* (Shit, now I've repeated myself.) *I've been an idiot. I'm like the base Indian in* Othello *who threw away the pearl.* (What. The. Actual. FUCK?? Shakespeare???? And RACIST!!!!) *Okay. I'm rambling.* (Accurate.) *My brother's getting married in an hour.* (Not relevant!) *And I wanted to tell you that I haven't forgotten what you said to me that night. You said you'd never met anyone like me, and well, I've never met anyone like you, either. I'm sorry I behaved so badly. You didn't deserve it. Thank you for taking me to karaoke. You were right; it was fun. And I was scared. So thank you for making me face that fear. I'll think of you whenever I hear Def Leppard. You're one of the best people I've ever met, and I'm going to miss you. A lot."*

Shit, his message box was full.

The phone beeped, then I rang off.

It was done. It wasn't pretty, but at least I'd said my piece.

A car horn honked outside. The taxi was here. No time to wee, or check my bag or makeup. But somehow, it didn't matter.

I picked up my bag, wrapped my shawl around my shoulders, and ran out of the house.

Thankfully, the rain had stopped. My parents chatted excitedly as we drove.

"You look lovely," said Mum, and Dad nodded.

"Alice won't be too happy," he said, winking.

"You both look great too," I said. They'd outdone themselves— Mum in an emerald-green shift dress that brought out the chestnut highlights in her hair and Dad in a navy suit complete with waistcoat.

"You need to undo the bottom button," I told him as I shifted uncomfortably in the middle seat.

"Why would he do that?" said Mum, horrified. "So people think he's too fat for his suit?"

Dad looked equally puzzled, although his concern was for the reputation of his tailor, who was also a second cousin. "Chris made this to measure. He'd be very upset if people thought he hadn't done his measuring right."

They both had a point, so I didn't bother explaining it was a tradition. I mean, it's not like the wedding would be written up in *Hello!* and everyone's appearances pored over by bored people in dentists' waiting rooms.

The Greek church—or rather, to give it its official name, the

Cathedral of St. Nicholas—was only a ten-minute drive from my house, so before long we were pulling up outside.

People were already milling on the pavement, avoiding the puddles and errant drops of rain from hanging branches.

I stepped out of the taxi and into the noisy embrace of my extended family.

"You'll be next, Zoë—God willing," said every single relative over thirty.

I nodded and smiled.

It was going to be a long day.

Alice looked radiant, Pete cried four times, and enough rice was thrown at the church door to send hundreds of pigeons swarming to our feet. They were shooed away by the church wardens, who pointed wordlessly to the signs prohibiting the throwing of perishables.

Then we were climbing into the vintage double-decker bus my brother had hired to ferry guests to the hotel in Russell Square.

I'd managed to not check my phone for two whole hours, but I glanced at it now. I had a message from Mike telling me that Rebel Alliance would be providing that evening's music.

I grinned. Pete and Alice loved that band.

I didn't have any other messages, but that was okay. It was their day, not mine.

It was eight o'clock and I was helping the band set up. They'd brought their own kit, but were using the hotel's microphones. There was a bit of a wobble when a lead didn't quite reach a socket, but an extension cord was produced by the hotel manager after lead singer Sienna offered him tickets for their next London show.

Sean, the drummer, was being an incorrigible flirt—telling my mum that she had to be my sister because there was no way she was a day over forty. She was chuffed, but I'm not sure I was.

Lucy, Gav, and Mike arrived after dinner. Pete had insisted they come once he knew the lengths they'd gone to find a band for him. My dad hassled the waiters for three extra meals, and like magic, another three *poulets à la provençale* appeared.

I was sitting by the side of the stage when the band struck up.

"How are you doin'?" yelled Sienna, like she was addressing a stadium of paying fans. "You ready to rock this fucking place?"

Oops. My parents hated swearing. But when I looked over at their smiling faces, they were obediently nodding their heads like everyone else.

The band played a couple of their own songs, then switched to a Rolling Stones medley that even had the oldies on the dance floor. They ended with "Wild Horses," which had everyone pairing off to slow dance, including my parents. Pete was in the middle, swaying to the music with Alice. When he caught me looking at Mum and Dad, he mouthed "Wow!"

As the chorus began, Lucy slumped into the seat next to me.

"You okay, Luce?"

She let out a long breath. "Yeah."

"Thanks for your help in finding a band."

"It was fun. People were surprisingly helpful. I must have left messages for twenty-five people, and they all got back to me within half an hour. Everyone except Nick Jones."

The mention of his name made me stiffen, but Lucy didn't seem to notice. "He didn't get back to me at all," she went on. "Bit rude."

"He's out of the country," I said, as casually as I could.

She turned to face me but didn't say anything.

We were into the second verse of "Wild Horses." It really was a pretty song.

Gavin was nursing a drink a couple of tables over. He was wearing jeans and trainers, but in his defense, they were his smartest jeans and his cleanest trainers. The white soles looked showroom clean.

When I turned back to Lucy, she was looking at him and frowning.

Poor Gav. Lucy really wasn't interested. I waited for her to comment on something he'd done that had annoyed her, but instead, she took the wineglass out of my hand, downed it, then strode over to Gavin.

I couldn't hear what she said to him, but I didn't need to. The look of amazement on Gav's face told me everything. She pulled him to his feet, walked him to the dance floor, and wrapped her arms around his neck. Gav's expression had meanwhile morphed from abject disbelief to pure joy. He gingerly placed his hands around her waist, and the two of them started swaying to the music.

If I hadn't witnessed the entire thing with my own eyes, I'd have never believed it. I felt ridiculously proud, like a mother hen watching her hatchlings find their feet.

When the song ended, and the band launched into their own material, Gav and Lucy stayed on the dance floor. They might not have been locked in an embrace any longer, but their shoulders and hips were angled toward each other even if their heads were turned toward the band.

After a quarter of an hour, as the set was coming to an end, I went to the corner of the room to ready the next playlist. But lead singer Sienna seemed to have other ideas.

"And now, we've got a very special treat for you," she shouted over the noise of the crowd. "Ladies and gentlemen, please put your hands together for Ms. Marcie Tyler."

I froze.

What did she just say?

A roar went up from the assembled guests as a tall figure in a long black dress climbed onto the stage from the opposite side.

Jesus. It was really her. Marcie Tyler was singing at my brother's wedding.

She beamed at the audience. "What a good-looking bunch you are." She pointed at Pete. "Especially you, young man, but I gather you're taken."

Pete went red, and everyone laughed.

"Thank you for inviting me," she went on. "Now, let's stop talking and crack on. I hear this one's a favorite of the bride."

Alice pumped one delicate fist in the air. I smiled—I'd make a rock chick of her yet.

The drummer counted four beats with his sticks, then the band launched into "It's Too Late for Love."

This was unreal.

Alice tore her attention from the stage and whipped her head toward me. "Thank you," she mouthed.

I started to nod, but stopped myself. I couldn't accept credit— Marcie's appearance had nothing to do with me. Had it been Lucy, Gav, or Mike?

That didn't feel right either. None of them would have been able to keep it secret long enough, especially with the amount of wine they'd necked.

I tried to concentrate on the music. Marcie's voice soared over the guitars; sweet and controlled, but always a hair's breadth from running wild and breaking free. It's why I always held my breath when I listened to her. And here she was, singing a few feet from me. Her shoeless feet planted on the makeshift stage, her raven hair shining like vinyl.

But the thought kept circling back, catching like a hangnail—who had pulled off the impossible and brought her here?

Every pair of eyes was on Marcie, but I suddenly had the eeriest feeling that someone was staring at me.

I turned away from the stage and scanned the edge of the room. A man in a tuxedo was walking toward me.

My heart almost stopped.

I knew that gait, that fluid movement. I would have known it anywhere.

It was Nick.

Hope fluttered in my chest.

He'd come.

The music receded, and all I could hear was my pulse beating in my ears.

I blinked twice, terrified he was a product of too much champagne. But he was still there when I opened my eyes again.

My heart knocked against my ribs, and I found myself walking toward him, as if drawn by a string.

"Oh my God," I breathed. "You're here. And you brought Marcie."

He nodded. "Yeah, I was staying with friends in Paris, but then I had a couple of interesting phone calls. One was from Lucy."

"And the other one?"

"The other one confused me."

"Will you let me explain?"

He nodded, and I closed my eyes. I had so much to tell him. So many feelings to express. But where to start?

I took a deep breath. "I know you're leaving the country and that you and Marcie have a sort of thing."

He grabbed my forearm. "Hang on a sec. What do you mean, 'a sort of thing'?"

His hand was warm and his skin unbearably soft; I had to lower my gaze to the parquet floor. "I saw you," I whispered.

He tipped my chin up and forced me to look at him. "Zoë, what are you talking about?"

I swallowed. "You care about her—Marcie, I mean."

"I do."

My heart sank, but I forced out a smile. "She's a hell of a woman, so who can blame you?"

He took hold of my hand, his long fingers slotting around mine like they belonged there. "You're right, I do care about Marcie. It wasn't always the case, but we've rebuilt our relationship over the last few years."

The last few years? "I don't understand."

He gripped both my hands tighter. "She's my mother."

"Wh-*what...*"

I must have blacked out for a moment or been sucked into a parallel universe.

Had I heard him right?

"Marcie is your *mother?*"

He nodded. "I'm sorry I didn't tell you before, but only a handful of people know. The pregnancy was kept secret. She spent those months in the foothills of the Alps in Italy, far from the cameras, and then she left me with my father."

"Was Benedict your father?"

He shook his head. "My father is Italian. He fell in love with

Marcie but had to marry someone else." He looked uncomfortable, and I didn't want to ask any more questions. Then very quietly he added, "He came from the sort of family who considered rock stars unsuitable wives."

A memory was stirring in my head. "Oh my God, your dad's the bald count!"

He half frowned, half smiled. "How on earth do you know about him?"

"When I went to Marcie's house she mentioned she'd been given this amazing Jacobean chest by an Italian count."

Now Nick looked alarmed. "*Really?*"

"Not in relation to you, of course." We were getting sidetracked. "How often did you see Marcie when you were growing up?"

"I only found out who my real mother was when I was sixteen."

"Oh my goodness."

"Yeah, that was my reaction too. With a bit more teenage angst and creative swearing. I didn't want to know her, but I'd always been drawn to the music industry. I promised myself I would make it without her help, so I changed my name to Jones so no one would link me to either of my parents. Once I'd established myself at Pinnacle, she got in touch and asked me to help her out in London. Guess it was the right decision. It led me to you."

He smiled and my knees buckled. "Oh God, I've been such an idiot."

"Like the Indian from *Othello*?"

I groaned. "Please say you deleted that message as soon as you heard it."

He smiled. "Not a chance."

"Okay, but let me have another try at telling you how I feel."

He pointed to the stage. "Don't you want to see Marcie's first performance in nine and a half years?"

"No, I don't," I said. "Because that's not the thing that's making me shake with joy right now."

His voice was low. "Then what is?"

I clenched and unclenched my hands. "You're the reason, Nick." I swallowed. "I want to cringe when I think of how I've treated you. I was rude, I snapped at you, I mocked you, but still you kept coming back. I was terrified of my feelings, so I buried them as deep as I could. I let the past rule my life, and I was too scared to question what I needed to make me happy."

A restless, nervous energy had taken hold, and I barely had enough breath to get the words out.

"But I know now, Nick. It's been in front of me all this time. From the moment you accosted me in that cloakroom. I'm sorry it's taken me this long—and God knows I don't deserve you—but if you still want me, here I am."

His eyes flicked away from me, and for a moment, I thought he was going to tell me that we'd got our wires crossed, that he didn't feel that way about me. I held my breath.

"That was quite a speech."

"I mean every word."

He nodded. "You've put me in a bit of a predicament."

Shit. I was right. He didn't feel the same way.

I swallowed. "I'm a big girl, just tell it to me straight."

He held my gaze, and the heat in his eyes made my heart stop. "You have no idea how much I want you right now."

Every nerve in my body crackled. My dress felt too tight and the three inches between our bodies felt like an ocean. *Sweet Jesus.* I was going to *die.*

"So my predicament is this," he continued. "There's a priest dressed in black with a long gray beard who's been staring at us this whole time."

Why was he talking about Father Michalis?

Nick wrapped his arm around my waist and pulled me tight against his body. "So, if you get excommunicated, I take full responsibility."

"For what?"

"For this," he said, bringing his lips to mine.

Everything went still, and all I could feel was his mouth against mine.

When he broke contact I shivered. "It'll take more than that to get me excommunicated."

He raised an eyebrow. "Is that a challenge?"

I nodded and his eyes darkened.

His arms circled my body, and he wrenched me closer. Then he bent his head to mine again, and the touch of his lips was like fire.

Uh-oh. My immortal soul was damned.

But it was going to be worth it.

34

I FEEL THE EARTH MOVE

TWO MONTHS LATER

"GOD, I CAN'T BELIEVE YOU'RE dating a publicist," said Lucy as she topped up both our glasses. About thirty of us were crammed in the *Re:Sound* office with wine and a portable karaoke machine—guess whose idea *that* was?—to celebrate record sales and our new secure future.

"What do you mean?" I asked, offended. Swap the word "publicist" for "politician" and you'd get an idea of her tone.

"You always said publicists were dull."

"I've had my horizons broadened."

She raised an eyebrow. "Oh aye, is that what the oldies call it?"

Jesus, since when did thirty-four count as old? "When you first saw Nick, you called him sexy AF."

"Yeah, but hotness isn't everything. Look at Gavin."

"I do look at Gavin. Every day. He sits opposite me."

They'd been seeing each other for a couple of months and somehow Lucy—ten years my junior and never one to miss an opportunity to remind me—had now turned into a relationship expert. I didn't really mind, though. My mood these days was pretty invincible, and not only because of a certain sexy AF publicist.

Our September issue had sold out in two days, and the Marcie interview had been syndicated around the world, producing some healthy bonus income. Even the Hands Down issue—which included the last interview with all five members—had become a collector's edition. It had featured on both the BBC and Sky News to illustrate the breakup of the band. And on top of everything else, we had the first performance of the band as a four-piece—thanks to some impressive phone footage that Gav had shot when they'd come to sing for Lucy's birthday.

Jonny's solo career was still trying to get off the ground, but Hands Down as a four-piece were going from strength to strength. They'd been asked to sing the next Bond theme—a proper rabbit-out-of-a-hat masterstroke from Nick, resulting in him being able to keep his job in London.

Everyone around me looked happy. Gavin's shoulders were permanently relaxed instead of looped around his ears, and I'd even caught him smiling to himself when he thought no one was looking. Mike had kicked his vaping habit and shed ten years. A two-week family holiday to the Algarve had also endowed him with a Jeff Goldblum tan and an expensive new golf habit.

I'd suggested we make tonight's party optional fancy dress—which meant only three people had bothered. Rob had brought along a pair of bongo drums and announced he was Matthew McConaughey, while Gavin had slapped on a pirate's hat and taped a clothes hanger to his cuff as a makeshift hook-hand. In comparison, my punk rocker's outfit looked like I'd spent days on it: ripped tights under denim shorts and Doc Martins, backcombed hair, and black lipstick.

Simon was here too. He'd come straight from work in his civvies and couldn't understand why Gavin had greeted him with, "Gareth Southgate, cool." I'd had to explain it was because he was wearing a waistcoat just like the one the England manager had worn during the World Cup. Simon had never really followed football.

"How's the training going?"

Simon nodded. "Really well. I'm going for a run after this."

I was impressed. "Your third this week—and it's only Thursday."

After his hospital scare, Simon had embraced a healthier lifestyle and was training for the London Marathon. I'd never seen him so much as run for a bus, but his new exercise regime seemed to make him happy. He certainly seemed calmer and more grounded than he'd been when he'd first arrived in London all those weeks ago.

He leaned over and kissed me on the cheek. "Right. I'm off, Frixie. Catch you at Pilates."

He'd joined Alice's studio, and the two of us went together once a week. There was a moment when I'd worried he'd go full *Eat Pray Love* on me and give up caffeine, carbs, and capitalism, but his love of Starbucks, steak sandwiches, and stock markets kept him on the right side of that particular line.

I watched him go and thanked my lucky stars that our friendship had weathered our weird summer. After I'd gotten together with Nick, I'd been concerned that Simon would fall back into a dysfunctional relationship with Jess, but he'd been surprisingly lucid about the importance of staying single.

I'd even had good news from Jess herself. A couple of weeks after my brother's wedding, she rang and asked me to set up a meeting with Marcie. They spoke on the phone a couple of times, then Marcie invited Jess to her Oxfordshire estate. The two women spent a weekend together, which culminated in Jessica agreeing to check into rehab, finally understanding that she needed treatment for her performance anxieties and reliance on drugs and alcohol. Marcie had insisted on picking up the tab and both of them seemed to find a sense of peace in the arrangement.

Peals of laughter erupted by the door. Someone new had arrived and I craned my neck to get a better view. Whoever he was, he was wearing a clingy electric-blue shirt and low-slung leather trousers held up by a rhinestone belt and witchcraft. From his height and gait, it had to be Nick, but I could only see the back of his head. He appeared to be wearing a long black wig, made of hair that you'd usually find blocking your drain. Good God, it was shiny. The fluorescent tube lighting bouncing off it made my eyes hurt.

Then he turned round, and it was like an orchestra had struck up.

The top three buttons of his shirt were undone, exposing a slash of golden skin and an oversized crucifix. Strands of hair were falling into eyes that were ringed with jet-black eyeliner. He should have looked ridiculous, but he didn't.

Sexy AF didn't come close to covering it.

I swallowed as he walked toward me. His eyes were spellbinding. The black kohl brought out all the different shades of green in them. I was almost too embarrassed to look.

This was crazy. I'd had sex with the man. *Multiple* times.

He had a question on his lips. Whatever he was about to ask me, the answer would be yes.

Join the Flat Earth movement? *Sure.*

Prove the moon landings were faked? *No problem.*

Form a Spice Girls cover band? *Fit me up for a headset mic.*

Before he could reach me, Lucy was standing between us.

"Are we going to start this karaoke or what?"

I refocused on her and tried to shake off my lust fog.

"Um, sure. Why don't you go first?"

Nick reached my side and snaked his arm around my waist. He nodded at Lucy, who stared at him, openmouthed. How had she only just noticed him?

"Are you okay, Lucy?" he asked.

She nodded, her mouth still not fully closed. "You look like a rock star."

Well, it was an improvement on her "dull publicist" assessment from earlier.

When neither of us answered, she continued, "Seriously, Nick. Do you have rock star DNA or something?"

I froze and felt Nick stiffen too. I hadn't told a soul who his mother was. The only other person who knew about Marcie was Justin, Patrick's partner. And that was enough, for now.

Nick recovered first. "I went through a glam rock phase growing up. But doesn't everyone?"

Lucy seemed satisfied with his response. Not that she would have believed him if he'd told her the truth.

"Why don't you pick the first song?" he told her. "I'll play backup bongo drums."

Lucy skipped to the karaoke machine, which was set up in the corner on top of the photocopier.

Nick leaned forward and whispered in my ear. "You look *sensational* in that outfit."

Then he kissed me and followed Lucy over to the karaoke machine. After a brief discussion, Lucy punched in a song and a few moments later the office was filled with the opening notes of the Doors' "Light My Fire."

I had no idea how Lucy sounded. My attention was glued to Nick.

Suddenly I couldn't breathe. He had the bongos set up on a desk and his drumming fingers were keeping perfect time. But everything was muffled.

This wasn't Nick in front of me, hips swaying hypnotically, head thrown back as he sang. In front of me was the rock star hero I'd created all those years ago.

The image knocked me out. It was so familiar, so precious, so part of the girl I'd been growing up.

This was the closest I would ever come to Zak Scaramouche made into flesh.

And as he played along, I wanted to burst out laughing.

After all these years, I'd finally got to meet him! Zak was in the building.

And maybe he wasn't exactly as I'd expected; maybe I'd changed my expectations of him. But I couldn't have been happier.

They say never meet your heroes, and I agree.

Go out there and invent your own.

LOVE SONGS FOR SKEPTICS
PLAYLIST

"The First Cut Is the Deepest" by Sheryl Crow

"Love's a Slap in the Face" by Kiss

"You're So Vain" by Carly Simon

"Heroes" by David Bowie

"Nothing Compares 2 U" by Sinead O'Connor

"Norwegian Wood" by the Beatles

"My Heart Will Go On" by Céline Dion

"Alive" by Pearl Jam

"Damn, I Wish I Was Your Lover" by Sophie B. Hawkins

"Only Happy When It Rains" by Garbage

"Both Sides Now" by Joni Mitchell

"You've Got a Friend" by Carole King

"Express Yourself" by Madonna

"500 Miles" by the Proclaimers

"Over the Rainbow" by Judy Garland

"I Just Can't Get Enough" by Depeche Mode

"Bring Me Sunshine" by Morecambe & Wise

"If I Were Your Woman" by Gladys Knight & the Pips

"MMMBop" by Hanson

"Under Pressure" by Queen

"Every Rose Has Its Thorn" by Poison

"I Just Called to Say I Love You" by Stevie Wonder

"Love Is a Battlefield" by Pat Benatar

"Back in Black" by AC/DC

"You Can't Hurry Love" by the Supremes

"Hit Me with Your Best Shot" by Pat Benatar

"That Don't Impress Me Much" by Shania Twain

"Angel" by Aerosmith

"Elegantly Wasted" by INXS

"Heart of Glass" by Blondie

"Material Girl" by Madonna

"I Hate Myself for Loving You" by Joan Jett & the Blackhearts

"If I Can't Have You" by Yvonne Elliman

"Smooth Operator" by Sade

"Temptation" by Heaven 17

"Nowhere to Run" by Martha and the Vandellas

"Everybody Hurts" by R.E.M.

"YMCA" by the Village People

"The Macarena" by Los del Río

"Achy Breaky Heart" by Billy Ray Cyrus

"Gangnam Style" by PSY

"The Loco-Motion" by Little Eva

"Oops Upside Your Head" by the Gap Band

"Torn" by Natalie Imbruglia

"Never Ever" by All Saints

"Smells Like Teen Spirit" by Nirvana

"Goodbye Yellow Brick Road" by Elton John

"I Can't Make You Love Me" by George Michael

"Don't Speak" by No Doubt

"Somethin' Stupid" by Frank Sinatra

"I Want You" by Marvin Gaye

"Come On Eileen" by Dexys Midnight Runners

"Pour Some Sugar on Me" by Def Leppard

"Love in an Elevator" by Aerosmith

"I've Got You under My Skin" by Frank Sinatra

"Zorba's Dance" by Mikis Theodorakis

"I Don't Want to Talk about It" by Everything But the Girl

"Happy Birthday"

"Total Eclipse of the Heart" by Bonnie Tyler

"Love Is for Suckers" by Twisted Sister

"I Can See Clearly Now" by Johnny Nash

"This Ain't a Love Song" by Bon Jovi

"Maria Me Ta Kitrina" by Nana Mouskouri

"Don't Know What You've Got (Till It's Gone)" by Cinderella

"I Guess That's Why They Call It the Blues" by Elton John

"I Close My Eyes and Count to Ten" by Dusty Springfield

"Wild Horses" by the Rolling Stones

"I Feel the Earth Move" by Carole King

"Light My Fire" by the Doors

"Kiss from a Rose" by Seal

"Bohemian Rhapsody" by Queen

READING GROUP GUIDE

1. What is it that makes your first love so different? Do you think Zoë's attachment to Simon is stronger than most? Who was your childhood crush or first love?

2. Zoë has a complicated relationship with her Greek heritage. How does her family shape the way she sees the world? What effect does your family heritage have on your attitude towards love?

3. Zoë relies on Patrick to guide her when she feels lost at work. How would you describe his mentorship? Do you have anyone you consider to be your mentor?

4. Simon admits that a big part of his failed marriage was avoiding problems until they spiraled past solutions. Do you think any other characters are hiding from their issues? Who? How do they resolve them?

5. Zoë has a flicker of doubt about using Jess to get through to Marcie. Did you think she was being manipulative? What consequences, intended and unintended, did she run into?

6. Nick calms Zoë down in the Eye by getting her to recite capitals. Have you ever used a strategy like that? What other advice would you give to Zoë if you saw her panicking?

7. Which of Zoë's suitors were you rooting for? Did your opinion change throughout the book?

8. Marcie highly values her privacy. Do you think the public demands too much of celebrities? Would you be comfortable in the spotlight?

9. The adage "never meet your heroes" might be the hardest advice to follow. How did you think Zoë's interactions went with Marcie? Would you have done anything else in her place? How would you feel if your idol acted like Marcie?

10. Zoë says she fell for the image of Simon rather than the person he became. Has that ever happened to you? Is it possible to see someone fully?

A CONVERSATION
WITH THE AUTHOR

You have a background in journalism. How does novel-writing compare? Did any of your own journalism experiences sneak into Zoë's work?

Writing a novel is really different to knocking out a 150-word news story or a 1000-word feature. I know that should have been obvious from the start, but as a journalist, you're so used to writing under tight deadlines and getting it right, more or less, the first time that it's a shock when you realise just how much re-writing and re-thinking a novel needs. Also, *Love Songs For Skeptics* ended up being over 100,000 words. Keeping all that in my head was a nightmare. I had to stick a ton of index cards to my wall—I still have the blue-tac stains!

Two things that happened to me as a journalist made their way into the book. First, I referred to someone as English when they were Scottish. One angry phone call later and I'd learned my lesson… I'm actually pleased that they called because if they hadn't, I would never have realised my mistake, and after that I was much more conscious of using "British," which covers Scottish and Welsh as well as English.

Another time, someone rang me to ask where they could get a life-sized cut-out of David Duchovny. (I wrote about TV production, so somehow this person thought this qualified me?) But instead of just saying no, I had a five-minute chat with him and gave him a couple of leads. I couldn't quite bring myself to say no and hang up! I have no idea if he found one, by the way, and now that I think about it, I'm worried that it was a friend winding me up because I was a huge *X-Files* fan…

Working as a journalist taught me to stop worrying about calling strangers with the oddest of requests because people did it all the time to me!

Do you listen to music while you write? What did your playlists look like for *Love Songs for Skeptics*? What's your favorite love song?

I love to listen to music while I write. At first it was to drown out other noise, but even silence can feel a bit daunting when you're staring at an empty page. Then I realized that the right song can make you feel exactly the emotion you're trying to describe, so now I always listen to Spotify when I'm writing. I made two playlists that I played constantly during the final push to finish the book. A couple of those songs are mentioned in the book: "Kiss from a Rose" and Marvin Gaye's "I Want You." It's the song Nick's playing in his car when Zoë realizes she might be developing feelings for him. Maybe Marvin was a clichéd choice, but unlike "Let's Get It On," I think "I Want You" is on the right side of cheesiness. It's about longing, and I love that in a song. And "I want you, but I want you to want me, too" is a great lesson in enthusiastic consent, kids.

My favourite love song? What a hard question! But, if I had to choose only one, it would be Elvis's "Can't Help Falling in Love."

Fun fact: I let my husband choose our first song at our wedding—how feminist am *I*?? He chose an instrumental piece which I never would have thought of, but it worked beautifully because some great love songs have fantastic melodies, but their lyrics sometimes let them down. I mean, what on earth is "Kiss from a Rose" actually about? I'm all ears, Seal!

Speaking of music, how did you pick the song titles for each chapter?

It was a bit tricky to be honest, because I needed to find songs that a lot of people knew but weren't too current as it would age the book. That's why so many songs are from classic artists rather than more recent ones. I also needed songs that had descriptive titles that told you exactly what the chapter was going to be about. So, for example, I knew upfront that I needed a song about unrequited love, and even though my favourite is Ray Charles's "You Don't Know Me," its title doesn't pack much of an emotional punch. However, "The First Cut Is the Deepest" is pure poetry, so it was an easy choice for chapter one. The songs that work the best in the book for me are: "Goodbye Yellow Brick Road," "Love Is for Suckers," and "Somethin' Stupid."

In the story, Zoë gets to meet her music idol—if you could interview any famous musician, living or dead, who would you choose?

I am terrible with famous people. I am far too easily starstruck. So, for example, a few years back, I left my paid lunch on the counter in a sandwich shop because Alan Rickman came to stand beside me. I later returned, red-faced, to pick it up, and the staff knew exactly what had happened.

Also, unlike Zoë, I've always loved boy bands, and I once ran across six lanes of traffic when I saw JC from NSYNC. I was fine, obviously, and more importantly I got his autograph.

The one famous person I would have loved to meet is George Michael. He always came across as very down to earth and fun.

You and Zoë share Greek Cypriot heritage. How does that shape your worldview and your writing?

I love my Greek Cypriot heritage, although like Zoë, I was a bit embarrassed by it when I was younger. My parents forced me and my sister to go to Greek school on Saturday morning for ten years, and although I hated it at the time (or least, until I was about thirteen and discovered boys), I'm so grateful I learned the language and made Greek friends that I still have to this day.

Did your own family inspire Zoë's?

In small ways. My parents always say "*The* Facebook," which makes me smile. They can also have long, detailed conversations about how good the most recent watermelon they bought was/wasn't. It's an art form. We also had a cat called Rambo growing up, and my cousins had one called Rocky. Don't ask me why we called the poor kitty Rambo as we didn't particularly like the film—actually, I'm not sure I've ever seen it. Still, it rolled off the tongue and worked in Greek. (Because obviously we all talked to him in Greek.) In later years it got quite embarrassing to admit we'd called our cat Rambo, but luckily the vet misheard my mum when she first told her, so his microchip identified him as Rumble, which is marginally better. I think.

What does your writing process look like?

Chaotic and inefficient, but I suspect that's the only way that works for me. It also involves a lot of index cards, late nights, and strong tea.

The Greek food is a sleeper star in this book. Do you have a favorite dish? Are you more of a Simon or Zoë in the kitchen?

I feel awful, but I'm not a natural cook, so sadly, I'm much more of a Zoë in the kitchen. Luckily, my husband is a great cook, so I don't just eat tinned beans at night.

My favourite dish is souvlaki—a pork or chicken kebab done over a charcoal barbecue, eaten with lemon, salad, and pita bread. Delicious!

What is your favorite part of a romance to write? The happy ending? The banter?

Oh yes, writing banter is a joy. Two characters disagreeing with each other is just inherently sexy, isn't it? It gets the blood flowing, feels physical, and keeps you up at night. (Or is that just me?) Of course, I also love writing a happy ending, and nothing gets me grumpier than having my expectations raised, then being sorely disappointed—I'm still angry about how they ended *Sanditon*. And don't get me started about *La La Land*. Angry face emoji.

What books are on your bedside table right now?

Mostly women's commercial fiction, so any one time will likely include: Marian Keyes, Mhairi McFarlane, Lucy Vine, Lindsey Kelk, Christina Lauren, Sarah Hogle, and Emily Henry.

ACKNOWLEDGMENTS

I'll try to keep this short, but the following people deserve special thanks:

My agent, Jemima Forrester, for believing in me so early on and being a kickass woman to have by my side.

Everyone at Simon & Schuster and Books and the City, especially Sara-Jade Virtue and Emma Capron, who saw something in my writing and took a chance on me. I wouldn't be here without you both.

My amazing editor, Rebecca Farrell. You *got* this book right from the start, and your brilliant suggestions made everything sparkle. Thanks for sorting out Simon and for all your encouragement and enthusiasm. You're a champion in every sense of the word, and I'm very lucky to have you.

The brilliant MJ Johnston, my American editor, who is now officially the third member of the Zak Scaramouche Fan Club, and all the other amazing folk at Sourcebooks.

Anna Davis, Chris Wakling, and everyone at Curtis Brown Creative. For cheerleading, goading, and downright bribing, I'd like to thank my spin-off writing group: Lisa Williamson, Maria Realf, James

Hall, Paul Golden, Sara-Mae Tuson (I owe you a cocktail for the title), and Fiona Perrin (cocktails also winging your way for coming up with *that* plot point).

For amazing input when I couldn't see the wood for the trees: Donna Hillyer, Gillian Holmes, Hannah Sheppard, Louise Buckley, Allie Spencer, Phoebe Morgan, and Eleanor Leese.

The Romantic Novelists' Association—an amazing bunch of people who tirelessly fight to ensure romantic fiction gets the recognition it deserves, and who have been so supportive of new writers. Special mention to Sophie Weston and Joanna Maitland for their incredible workshops.

To all the brilliant women out there writing romantic fiction who inspired me and gave so many hours of reading pleasure.

Denise, for all your support and for letting me write on your kitchen table. Sorry I inflicted the previous terrible version on you, and thank you for not mentioning it was terrible.

Mum and Dad, for giving me everything and asking for nothing (except for some help with your phones). I count my blessings every day.

Kat—you started me on this journey. For reading everything I've ever written and always laughing in all the right places. Your faith has kept me going over the years. Best sister ever.

Alex—you got me over the finishing line. For crossing your fingers before every submission, commiserating over every rejection, and celebrating every success. I wouldn't have wanted to take this journey with anyone but you. Thanks also for keeping our Wi-Fi password a secret so I could stay off the internet and do some actual writing. *Now* will you tell me what it is?

ABOUT THE AUTHOR

Christina Pishiris was born in London to Greek Cypriot parents. She studied English at the University of Sussex and went on to become a journalist. When not writing, her hobbies include compiling cheesy eighties playlists, coveting the neighbor's cat, and writing protest letters to Guerlain after they discontinued her favorite perfume. *Love Songs for Skeptics* is her first book.